FAST BREAK

DeMarcus's mind spun at Jaclyn's contrasts. Sweet and spicy. Bold and bashful. He wanted to taste her, all of her. He tightened his hold on her thigh and pressed his hips hard into hers.

Jaclyn broke their kiss. "Marc. Wait."

DeMarcus froze. His left hand pressed her breast; his right hand cupped her thigh. His body ached. "All right."

Jaclyn opened her eyes. She pressed her hand against his chest, creating more room between them. "I'd be lying if I said I didn't want you. What an understatement." Her chuckle was breathless and awkward. "But things are complicated enough for both of us without adding a sexual relationship."

DeMarcus made himself release her. He turned away from Jaclyn's scent and breathed deeply to clear his mind. "You're right. You're my boss. This isn't a good idea."

"I'm glad we can be sensible about this." She didn't sound glad. Small comfort.

DeMarcus collected his jacket from her kitchen chair before facing her again. His palm tingled from the feel of her. His body ached from the taste of her. "We can be sensible. But for how long?"

FAST BREAK

REGINA HART

Dafina
BOOKS

Kensington Publishing Corp.

http://www.kensingtonbooks.com

DAFINA BOOKS are published by

Kensington Publishing Corp.
119 West 40th Street
New York, NY 10018

All Kensington Titles, Imprints, and Distributed Lines are available at special quantity discounts for bulk purchases for sales promotions, premiums, fund-raising, and educational or institutional use. Special book excerpts or customized printings can also be created to fit specific needs. For details, write or phone the office of the Kensington special sales manager: Kensington Publishing Corp., 119 West 40th Street, New York, NY 10018, attn: Special Sales Department, Phone: 1-800-221-2647.

Dafina and the Dafina logo Reg. U.S. Pat. & TM Off.

ISBN-13: 978-0-7582-5881-6
ISBN-10: 0-7582-5881-X

First mass market printing: June 2011

10 9 8 7 6 5 4 3 2 1

Printed in the United States of America

To my dream team:

- My sister, Bernadette, for giving me the dream
- My husband, Michael, for supporting the dream
- My brother, Richard, for believing in the dream
- My brother, Gideon, for encouraging the dream
- My friend and critique partner, Marcia James, for sharing the dream

And to Mom and Dad, always with love

Acknowledgments

Sincere thanks to Artie Taylor, head coach of Ohio Dominican University's men's basketball team, and Nathan Bellman, head coach of Ohio Dominican University's women's basketball team, for allowing me to attend their teams' practices.

Prologue

"Clock's ticking, Guinn."

DeMarcus Guinn, shooting guard for the National Basketball Association's Miami Waves, looked at his head coach, then at the game clock. Thirteen seconds remained in game seven of the NBA finals. The Waves and Sacramento Kings were tied at 101. His coach had just called a time-out. DeMarcus stood on the sidelines surrounded by his teammates. He wiped the sweat from his forehead and drained his sports drink. It didn't help.

He looked into the stands and found his father standing in the bleachers. He saw the empty seat beside him. His mother's seat. DeMarcus rubbed his chest above his heart.

"Guinn! You need to step it up out there." His coach's tone was urgent.

Why? What did it matter now?

His coach grabbed his arm. "Do you have this, Guinn?"

The buzzer sounded to end the twenty-second time-out.

DeMarcus pulled his arm free of his coach's grasp. "I've got this."

He joined his teammates on the court, walking through a wall of tension thick enough to hammer. Waves' fans had been cheering, stomping and chanting nonstop throughout the fourth quarter. DeMarcus looked up again at the crowd and the empty seat.

"Are you with us, Marc?" Marlon Burress, his teammate for the past thirteen years, looked at him with concern.

"I'm good." *Was he?*

DeMarcus saw the intensity of the four other Waves on the court. He looked at his teammates and coaches on the sideline. He saw his father in the stands. He had to find a way to play past the pain, if not for his team or his father, then for his mother's memory.

DeMarcus took his position near midcourt. The Waves' Walter Millbank stood ready to inbound the ball. Marlon shifted closer to the basket.

The referee tossed Walter the ball. The Kings' Carl Landry defended him, waving his arms and leaping to distract him from the play. Marlon balanced on his toes and extended his arms for the ball. Thirteen seconds on the game clock. The referee blew his whistle to signal the play.

Ignoring the Kings' defender, Walter hurled the ball to Marlon. With the ball an arm's length from Marlon's fingers, the Kings' Samuel Dalembert leaped into the lane. Turnover. The crowd screamed its disappointment.

Eleven seconds on the game clock.

Dalembert spun and charged down court. Marlon and Walter gave chase.

Ten seconds on the game clock.

DeMarcus saw Dalembert racing toward him. The action on the court slowed to a ballroom dance. The crowd's chants of "Defense!" faded into the background.

DeMarcus's vision narrowed to Dalembert, the ball and the game clock. From midcourt, he stepped into Dalembert's path. His concentration remained on the ball. He smacked it from Dalembert, reclaiming possession. Waves fans roared. The arena shook.

Seven seconds on the game clock.

DeMarcus's vision widened to include his teammates and the Kings' defenders. With Marlon, Walter and the other Waves guarding the Kings, DeMarcus charged back up court. His goal—the net, two points and the win. He felt Dalembert closing in on him from behind.

Five seconds. Four seconds. Three seconds.

DeMarcus leaped for the basket, extending his body and his arm, stretching for the rim.

One second.

Slam!

Miami Waves, 103. Sacramento Kings, 101.

The crowd roared. Balloons and confetti rained from the rafters. The Waves' bench cleared. The team had survived the last-minute challenge from the Kings to claim the win and the NBA championship title.

DeMarcus looked into the stands and found his father. He was cheering and waving his fists with the other Waves fans. Beside him, the seat remained empty. His mother would never cheer from the stands again.

Less than an hour later, showered and changed from his Waves uniform into a black, Italian-cut suit,

DeMarcus entered the team's media room. Reporters waited for the post-finals press conference. They lobbed questions at him before he'd taken his seat.

"What does this championship mean to you?"

"Why did you seem dazed during the fourth quarter?"

"You made the winning basket. What are you going to do now?"

He latched on to the last question. "I'm retiring from the NBA."

DeMarcus stood and left the room.

I

Two years later

"Cut the crap, Guinn."

DeMarcus Guinn felt the sting of the honey-and-whiskey voice. It slapped him from the doorway of his newly acquired office in the Empire Arena. He looked up from his National Basketball Association paperwork and across the room's silver-carpeted expanse.

Standing in the polished oak threshold, Jaclyn Jones radiated anger. It vibrated along every curve of her well-toned figure. Contempt hardened her long cinnamon eyes. The media had nicknamed the former Women's National Basketball Association shooting guard the Lady Assassin. Her moniker was a tribute to her holding the fewest number of fouls yet one of the highest scoring records in the league.

As of today, DeMarcus called her boss.

DeMarcus pushed his heavy, black executive chair back from his massive oak desk and stood. He didn't understand Jaclyn's accusatory tone or her hostility, but confusion didn't justify poor manners. "Excuse me?"

"You took the Monarchs' head coach position." She threw the words at him.

DeMarcus's confusion multiplied. "Why wouldn't I? You offered it."

Jaclyn strode into his office. Her blood red skirt suit cut a wave of heat across the silver carpet, white walls and black furniture. Her fitted jacket highlighted the rose undertone of her golden brown skin. Slender hips swayed under the narrow, mid-calf skirt. Three-inch red stilettos boosted her six-foot-plus height.

She stopped behind one of the three black-cushioned guest chairs facing his desk and dropped her large gray purse onto its seat. Her red-tipped nails dug into the fat chair cushion. "That was my partners' decision. Gerry and Bert extended the offer. *I* was against it."

Her admission surprised him. DeMarcus shoved his hands into the soft pockets of his brown khaki pants. Why was she telling him this? Whatever the reason, it couldn't be good. "I didn't ask to interview for the Brooklyn Monarchs' head coach job. *You* came to *me.*"

Jaclyn shook her head. Her curly, dark brown hair swung around her shoulders. It drew his attention to the silver and black Brooklyn Monarchs lapel pin fastened to her collar. "Not me. Gerry and Bert." Her enunciation was crisp and clear.

So was her meaning. *You don't have what it takes. Stop wasting our time.*

Confusion made a blind pass to bitterness. DeMarcus swallowed it back. "Why don't you want me as your coach?"

"The Monarchs need a winning season. We need *this* season. You don't have the experience to make that happen."

"I don't have coaching experience, but I've been in the league for fifteen years—"

Jaclyn raised her right hand, palm out, cutting him off. "And in that time, you won two NBA championship rings, three MVP titles and an Olympic gold medal. I saw the games and read the sports reports."

"Then you know I know how to win."

She quirked a sleek, arched brow. "You can *play* to win, but can you *coach?*"

"Winning is important to me."

"It's important to me, too. That's why I want an *experienced* head coach."

DeMarcus clenched his teeth. Jaclyn Jones was a pleasure to look at and her voice turned him on. But it had been a long, draining day, and he didn't have time for this shit.

He circled his desk and took a position an arm's length from her. "If you didn't want to hire me, why am I here?"

She moved in closer to him. "Majority rule. Gerry and Bert wanted you. I'd hoped, after the interview, you'd realize you were out of your element."

DeMarcus's right temple throbbed each time he remembered the way she'd interrogated him a month ago. He should have realized she'd been driven by more than thoroughness. Gerald Bimm and Albert Tipton had tried to run interference, but the Lady Assassin had blocked their efforts.

DeMarcus shook his head. "I'm not out of my

element. I know the game. I know the league, and I know what it takes to win."

Jaclyn scowled up at him. A soft floral fragrance—lilac?—floated toward him. He could see the darker flecks in her cinnamon eyes. His gaze dipped to her full red lips

"But you don't know how to coach." Her expression dared him to disagree. "When you were with the Miami Waves, you led by example, picking up the pace when your teammates weren't producing. You were amazing. But I don't need another player. I need a coach."

DeMarcus crossed his arms. "We went over this during my interview. I wouldn't have taken this job if I couldn't perform."

Jaclyn blinked. Her gaze swept his white shirt, green tie and brown pants before she pivoted to pace his cavernous office. "We're talking about coaching."

"I know." DeMarcus tracked her movements from the black lacquered coffee service set against his far left wall and back to his desk. Her red outfit complimented the office's silver and black décor, the Monarchs's team colors.

The only things filling the void of his office were furniture—his oak desk, a conversation table, several chairs and a bookcase. The tall, showy plant in the corner was fake.

Jaclyn paced away from him again. Her voice carried over her shoulder. "The Monarchs finished last season with nineteen wins and sixty-three losses."

DeMarcus heard her frustration. "They finished at the bottom of the Eastern Conference."

"We were at the bottom of the *league*." Jaclyn turned to approach him. Her eyes were tired, her expression strained. "What are you going to do to turn the team around?"

He shrugged. "Win."

She was close enough to smell the soft lilac fragrance on her skin, feel the warmth of her body and hear the grinding of her teeth. "You sound so confident, so self-assured. It will take more than the strength of the Mighty Guinn's personality to pull the team out of its tailspin."

"I'm aware of that." He hated the nickname the media had given him.

"Then how are you planning to win? What's your strategy?"

As majority owner of the Brooklyn Monarchs, Jaclyn was his boss. DeMarcus had to remember that, even as her antagonism pressed him to respond in kind.

He took a deep breath, calling on the same techniques he'd used to center himself before making his free throws. "I'm going to work on increasing their speed and improving their defense. Your players can earn style points, but they do everything in slow motion." Jaclyn stared at him as though expecting something more. "I can give you more details after I've studied their game film."

He glanced at the tower of digital video discs waiting for him to carry them home. It was late September. Training camp had started under the interim head coach, and preseason was two weeks away. He didn't have a lot of time to turn the team around.

Jaclyn settled her long, slender hands on her slim hips and cocked her right knee. The angle of her stance signaled her intent to amp up their confrontation. DeMarcus narrowed his eyes, trying to read her next move.

"Maybe I should have been more specific." Her voice had cooled. "The players no longer think they're capable of winning. How are you going to change their attitudes?"

"By giving them the skills they need to win."

"These aren't a bunch of high school kids. They're NBA players. They already have the skills to win."

"Then why aren't they winning?"

Jaclyn dragged her hand through her thick, curly hair. "Winning builds confidence. Losing breeds doubt. I'm certain you've heard that before."

"Yes." But why was she bringing it up now?

"Even with the skills, they won't win unless they believe they *can* win. How do you plan to make them believe?"

DeMarcus snorted. "You don't want a coach. You want Dr. Phil."

Jaclyn sighed. "And you're neither. I'd like your resignation, please."

DeMarcus stared. He couldn't have heard her correctly. "What?"

"It would save both of us a great deal of embarrassment and disappointment."

His mind went blank. His skin grew cold. Jaclyn had landed a sucker punch without laying a finger on him. "You want my resignation? I've only been here one day."

"Think of your reputation. Everyone remembers you as a winner. You're jeopardizing your legacy by taking a position you're not qualified for."

Blood flooded his veins again, making his skin burn. "I disagree. I have what it takes to lead this team."

Jaclyn didn't appear to be listening. She dropped her hands from her hips and paced his spacious office. "You can keep the signing bonus."

"It's not about the money." The vein above his right temple had started to throb. He heard the anger in his voice but didn't care. He was through playing nice with his new boss. She was threatening his goal and maligning his character.

Jaclyn frowned at him. "Then what *is* it about?"

DeMarcus doubted she was interested in his motives for wanting to be the head coach of the Brooklyn Monarchs. "I'm not a quitter."

"You're not a coach."

DeMarcus studied the elegant features of her golden brown face—her high cheekbones, pointed chin and long-lidded eyes—searching for a clue to her thoughts. What was her game? "Do you have someone else in mind for my job?"

Her full, moist lips tightened. "We interviewed several candidates I consider much more qualified to lead this team."

"Gerry and Bert hired me. Your partners don't respect your opinion."

Jaclyn made an irritated sound. "I've realized my business partners don't have the team's best interests at heart."

"Careful, or you'll hurt my feelings."

Jaclyn's eyes narrowed. "Are you helping them destroy the team?"

"What are you talking about" Was Jaclyn Jones unbalanced?

"Why would you stay where you're not wanted?"

He gave her a wry smile. "But I *am* wanted. I have the letter offering me this job to prove it."

"I didn't sign that letter."

DeMarcus turned to reclaim his seat behind his desk. "Two out of three isn't bad."

Jaclyn followed him, stopping on the other side of his desk. "You should be more careful of the company you keep. Gerry and Bert don't care about the team. They don't care about you, either."

"I don't need your help picking my friends." DeMarcus pulled his seat under his desk before giving Jaclyn a cool stare. "Now, you'll have to excuse me. I have work to do."

Jaclyn straightened. "I want your resignation. Now."

DeMarcus dropped his mask and let her see all the anger he'd been hiding. "No."

"Then you're not getting my support."

"Lady, you don't scare me." He leaned back in his seat. "You're convinced I don't have what it takes to coach your team, but you haven't given me one damn reason why you've made that call."

"I've given you several."

DeMarcus held up one finger. "You want someone who'll get in touch with your players' emotions. Look, if they don't want to win, they don't belong on your team."

"You don't have the authority to fire players." There was apprehension in her eyes.

He raised a second finger. "You think your partners aren't looking out for the team. That's only because you didn't get your way."

"That's not true."

He lifted a third finger. "You don't think I can coach." DeMarcus stood. "How do you know that? Have you seen me coach?"

"Have *you* seen you coach?" Jaclyn clamped her hands onto her hips.

DeMarcus jerked his chin, indicating his office. "This is what I want, an opportunity to lead the Brooklyn Monarchs to a winning season. And, in a few years, bring home the championship. We have to be realistic. That won't happen this season. But it will happen. That's my goal. And I'll be damned if I'm going to let anyone deny me."

Jaclyn's gaze wavered. But then she raised her chin and squared her shoulders. "That's a very moving speech, Guinn. Can you back it up?"

"Watch me." DeMarcus settled back into his seat and nodded toward his doorway. "But do it from the other side of the door."

The heat of her anger battered his cold control. DeMarcus held her gaze and his silence. Finally, Jaclyn inclined her head. She grabbed her purse from the guest chair and left.

DeMarcus scrubbed his face with both hands, hoping to ease his temper. The Lady Assassin had charged him like a lead-footed defender at the post.

Why?

They shared the same goal—a winning season for the Monarchs. Then why was she determined to get rid of him?

Cold air cut into Jaclyn's skirt suit as she exited the Empire Arena. Leaving her coat at home during autumn in Brooklyn hadn't been a good idea. But at least the chilled breeze was cooling her temper.

She shivered as she hustled toward the curb. "Thanks

for waiting, Herb." Jaclyn gave the liveried limousine driver a grateful smile.

Yes, she was angry about the Mighty Guinn's galactic stubbornness and mammoth ego. But she wouldn't project her wrath onto Herbert Trasker. The quiet older gentleman from the limo service she retained had been driving her around the city for years.

Herbert straightened away from the silver Bentley sedan. The black suit and tie made his wiry frame seem taller. "You're welcome, Ms. Jones."

Herbert's emerald eyes twinkled at her. With a familiar gesture, the driver touched the brim of the black leather hat covering his iron gray hair. He opened the back passenger-side door and waited while Jaclyn thanked him before settling in. Their routine eased some of her tension.

Herbert slid behind the wheel. "The Bonner and Taylor office, Ms. Jones?"

"Yes, thank you, Herb." She'd stopped trying to get him to call her Jaclyn.

Herbert muscled the Bentley into the crowded, chaotic streets and set it on a course toward the downtown law firm. Bonner & Taylor represented the owners of the Empire Arena, which had been the home of the Brooklyn Monarchs since the franchise's birth in 1956.

Herbert maneuvered them past the neighborhoods of the borough in which she'd been born and raised—the congested city sidewalks, packed bodegas and busy storefronts. Framing these streets were trees, young and old, their brilliant autumn colors vying for attention.

The glass and metal corporate building that housed Bonner & Taylor rose into view. Jaclyn beat back her cresting nervousness. Could she convince the arena owners' lawyers to extend the franchise's opt-out clause?

Herbert double-parked beside a delivery van and activated the Bentley's hazard lights. He climbed from the driver's seat and circled the sedan to hand Jaclyn from the car. Stepping onto the street, Jaclyn felt as though she were moving in slow motion.

"I'll meet you right here, Ms. Jones."

She smiled with more confidence than she felt. "Thank you."

Jaclyn strode to the offices. Revolving doors swung her into the tall, thin building. Her stilettos clicked against the stone floor as she crossed the lobby. The business directory mounted to the marbled teal wall listed Bonner & Taylor's offices on the twenty-eighth floor of the thirty-floor structure.

Jaclyn wove through the hustling crowd toward the express elevators. The lobby reeked of wealth, prestige and self-importance. As she waited for the elevators, Jaclyn straightened the jacket of her power suit. Hopefully, it would prove more effective with Bonner & Taylor than it had with the Mighty Guinn.

Despite its claim to express service, the elevator ride gave her plenty of time to settle her nerves. It wasn't until its doors opened to the firm's offices that she realized she hadn't been successful.

A thin-faced, blond receptionist looked up as Jaclyn approached. "Good afternoon. May I help you?"

Jaclyn tried another confident smile. "Jaclyn Jones to see Misters Bonner and Taylor."

The receptionist's expression warmed to a polite welcome. "Yes, Ms. Jones. They're expecting you." She gestured toward a grouping of beige armchairs to the left of her desk. "Please make yourself comfortable. I'll let them know you're here."

She'd just settled into the chair, which was as comfortable as her sofa, when a tall, middle-aged gentleman in a double-breasted, navy pin-striped suit strode toward her. "Ms. Jones, I'm Greg Bonner. It's a pleasure to meet you."

Jaclyn stood and accepted Gregory's outstretched hand. "Thank you for meeting with me, Mr. Bonner."

"Greg, please." The firm's senior partner studied her with sharp, gray eyes. His salon-styled chestnut hair grew back from his forehead.

"And I'm Jackie."

"Denny's waiting for us in the conference room."

Jaclyn recognized the name of his law partner, Dennis Taylor. She fell into step beside Gregory. Her stilettos sank into the plush teal carpet that led to a wood-paneled conference room at the end of the wide hallway.

Another tall, stylish middle-aged man stepped around an impressive glass conference table to greet her.

He gave her right hand a firm shake. "I'm Denny Taylor, Ms. Jones. It's very nice to meet you."

"The pleasure's mine, Denny. And please call me Jackie."

Jaclyn sat, waiting for the law partners to join her before beginning. She assumed the inscrutable expression she wore when negotiating contracts for her firm's corporate clients. "Gentlemen, you know why I'm here."

Gregory shifted to face her across the glass table. "This season is the Monarchs' final opportunity to earn a profit. If it doesn't, our client can break your contract without either party incurring a penalty."

Jaclyn corrected the senior partner. "Earn a profit or break even."

"That's right." Dennis nodded, his dark blond hair catching the light.

The lawyers' blank expressions were unnerving. Jaclyn folded her shaking hands together. "We have several programs we're implementing this season to increase attendance and ticket sales. We're offering discounts on multiple ticket purchases, and hosting fan contests and theme games." The beat of silence lingered. Jaclyn resisted the urge to chatter nervously.

Gregory picked up his platinum Cross pen and rolled it between his thumb and forefinger. "You reduced ticket prices last season. Sales didn't increase."

Dennis's concerned frown was disheartening. "If you reduce the price again, you'll have to sell even more tickets just to break even."

Jaclyn hid her own misgivings. "We've planned a more aggressive marketing campaign to increase sales."

Gregory shifted again in his maroon, straight back chair. "The Monarchs' fan base has eroded."

Dennis looked doubtful. "You'll have to do more than lower ticket prices to lure your fans back. Because of low attendance during the past three seasons, the Monarchs' games were blacked out of television more often than not. Without being able to see the games, a lot of your fans switched their loyalty to the New York Knicks. And the Knicks are winning."

Gregory nodded. "You'll have to win."

Dennis's smile was wry. "But that might not be so far-fetched now that you've hired Marc Guinn. He's a winner. He'll help revive the Monarchs' winning tradition."

Gregory brushed his hair back from his forehead.

"And with his reputation, people will attend the games just to see him."

Jaclyn kept her own counsel. The Empire owners' lawyers didn't need to know she was hoping the media's NBA darling would pack his bags and leave. "That's a possibility." Her vague answer appeared to satisfy them.

Gregory rolled his pen again. "Even that bump in sales won't be enough to get the Monarchs out of the red. Have you considered asking the mayor to support a levy? The revenue from the tax increase could save your organization."

Jaclyn stiffened. "That's not an option. My grandfather started the Monarchs to give something back to his community. I'm not going to dishonor his legacy by going to the community with my hand out."

Dennis glanced at Gregory before returning his attention to Jaclyn. "What do Gerry and Bert think?"

"We've only briefly discussed the contract deadline, but I assume they agree with me." Jaclyn had no reason to believe otherwise. "Why are you asking?"

Gregory sat back in his chair. His sharp gaze scanned her features. "They called a couple of days ago to discuss options for getting out of the contract and moving the team."

Jaclyn blinked. "They never mentioned this to me."

Gregory and Dennis exchanged looks again before Dennis spoke. "We'd assumed this was the reason you wanted to meet. But without access to your accounting records, we don't know what kind of an offer you can expect from markets looking for NBA teams."

Jaclyn's heart stuttered. Gerald and Albert wanted to relocate the team? They knew she would never agree to move the Monarchs out of Brooklyn. Gregory had unknowingly confirmed her suspicions about her partners' intent toward the Monarchs. Some of their business decisions—such as hiring an inexperienced coach to save a struggling team—had struck her as irresponsible.

Why would Gerald and Albert discuss their plans with outsiders before talking with her? When she'd invited them to this meeting, they must have known the lawyers would mention their conversation. Had they intended she learn of their plans this way?

Jaclyn swallowed her dismay. "We're determined to turn the team around and generate more revenue." Or at least *she* was. "Is it possible to get another year on the opt-out clause in our arena contract?"

Gregory's tone was sympathetic. "I'm afraid not. Your grandfather agreed four years was a fair amount of time to allow the team to recover in the event of financial difficulties."

But when her grandfather had passed away almost two years ago, he probably had never dreamed his beloved Monarchs would fair so poorly.

Jaclyn straightened her shoulders and rose to her feet. There was nothing left to say. For now. The law partners stood with her. "Gentlemen, thank you for your time."

Dennis extended his hand to her. She winced at the pity in his pale blue eyes. "Good luck, Jackie. We hope you're able to rebuild the team."

Gregory escorted her back to the lobby. "The Monarchs have been good for the community. The franchise brought a lot of jobs in addition to excitement to Brooklyn. I hope you're able to keep it here."

She considered the senior partner. Her employer,

Jonas & Prather Legal Associates, had negotiated with Bonner & Taylor on behalf of their clients in the past. Bonner & Taylor had always been diligent in protecting their clients' interests but fair in their dealings. "Do you have any advice for me?"

"We care about what happens to the community. But our client's interests have to come first." Gregory gave her a sympathetic smile. "Make the play-offs."

"I'll do my best." But it wouldn't be easy with her partners working against her. The weight on her shoulders was steadily increasing.

2

"Jackie. I wasn't expecting you." Gerald Bimm looked as surprised as he sounded.

Jaclyn's franchise partner was old enough to be her father. Her grandparents had raised her to respect her elders. But that upbringing struggled to assert itself over her nearly overpowering urge to blacken Gerald's beady brown eyes.

"I don't know why not, Gerry. You knew I was meeting with Bonner and Taylor today." Her voice was cool, masking the anger that was eager to break free.

Gerald opened the door wider and let Jaclyn inside. He closed the door behind her. "So?"

Jaclyn hoped counting to ten would help her regain control. She held her ground in the center of the spacious ivory and blue entrance of Gerald's Park Slope home. "Didn't you think the lawyers would tell me you and Bert are planning to move the team out of Brooklyn?"

Gerald's eyes moved over each of her features as though trying to gauge her reaction to whatever lie he was concocting. Jaclyn in turn contemplated him, from his wavy, dark brown hair peppered with gray to his elegant mocha features. Tall and lean, Gerald was an attractive man. At fifty-seven, he appeared at least ten years younger. But his looks were marred by her growing awareness of just how treacherous he was. Gerald's betrayal would have broken her grandfather's heart.

Jaclyn gripped her purse strap and asked again. "Didn't you think Bonner and Taylor would tell me they'd spoken to you and Bert?"

"No, I didn't." His bare feet moved silently across the stone flooring, carrying him closer but still out of her reach. Smart man. Jaclyn couldn't guarantee she wouldn't punch his lights out.

Her brows knitted. Her eyes narrowed. "Where do you think you're taking the *Brooklyn* Monarchs?"

Gerald slipped his hands into the pockets of his black designer jeans. His white sweater shifted loosely around him as he shrugged his broad shoulders. "Let's sit down and talk about this. I'll fix you a drink."

He started to lead her farther into his home, but her voice stopped him.

"This isn't a social call. I want to know what your plans are for the Monarchs." Jaclyn struggled to keep her voice even. If only her father had survived. Then he'd have confronted Gerald as a peer. Jaclyn was at a disadvantage, confronting a man old enough to be her parent.

A lopsided smile curved Gerald's wide mouth. "We're looking at a couple of growing television markets."

"Where?"

"They're scattered around the country."

Jaclyn swallowed a scream. "You don't have a destination in mind? Give me a name, Gerry. Just one name."

He shrugged again. "Nevada."

Jaclyn's mind went blank. "Nevada? You want to move the *Brooklyn* Monarchs to Nevada?"

Gerald cocked his head. "Nevada Monarchs has a nice ring to it, wouldn't you agree?"

A red haze clouded her vision. "No. I would not. If you want to leave Brooklyn, Gerry, Godspeed. But you're not taking my team with you."

Gerald raised his brows. "*Your* team? I thought we were partners."

"So did I." Blood roared in her ears. "You and Bert must have been planning this for years."

"What do you mean?" Even now, he was trying to mislead her.

"Cut the crap, Gerry. You and Bert have been blocking me from getting capable coaches and drafting talented players. At first, I didn't understand what you were doing, but now I see your game."

Gerald's mask of urbane charm fell to reveal his irritation. "Can you blame us? You should be working with us to break the arena contract so we can get out of Brooklyn. Instead you're continuing on this Don Quixote mission to save an old man's dream."

Jaclyn fisted her hands. "That old man was my grandfather. And if you and Bert would get out of my way, I could restore the team to the winning legacy he created before the two of you destroyed everything."

"The Monarchs can't compete in the same market with the Knicks. We need a market of our own."

"This is New York." The volume of Jaclyn's voice rose to match Gerald's. "We have *two* football teams, *two* baseball teams and *two* hockey teams. Who said we can't support *two* basketball teams?"

"We've been losing revenue for the past three seasons."

"That's because of your spectacularly poor management decisions, which I now realize aren't criminally stupid but deliberately destructive." She tightened her grip on her purse strap, drilling her nails into her palm. "You're not moving the Monarchs out of Brooklyn."

Gerald gave her a pitying smile. "You can't save the team."

"I can, and I will." Jaclyn strode from his entranceway and slammed out of Gerald's house. She'd rather have punched his lights out.

Two quick raps on his open office door Tuesday morning interrupted DeMarcus. He turned away from his computer monitor to find Troy Marshall, the Monarchs' vice president of media and marketing, standing in his doorway.

From his close-cropped hair, goatee and moustache to his three-button Italian-style tan suit and brown Italian leather shoes, Troy looked more like a male model than a desk jockey. Well over six feet and physically fit, the business executive looked like he could have played professional ball. But he hadn't.

Troy crossed the threshold. "Do you have time to talk about the newspaper interview?"

DeMarcus's silver Movado watch read half past nine. The sports reporter was expected at ten o'clock. He saved the player information chart he was creating and spun his hulking executive chair to face the other man. "The *New York Sports* doesn't have much of a circulation. My father's the only one I know who reads it."

Troy sat in the black-cushioned guest armchair to DeMarcus's left and crossed his right leg over his left knee. He straightened the crease in his pant leg. "It's a free neighborhood newspaper. It's one of the few publications in the tri-state area that acknowledges New York has a professional basketball team besides the Knicks."

"It's hard to find." DeMarcus pulled an issue from a pile of papers on the corner of his desk. "My father got a copy from the grocery store yesterday. I also read the articles in the binder you gave me. Thanks for those."

Troy inclined his head. "Good. I want to make sure you don't underestimate Andy Benson. She makes Darth Vader look like Jar Jar Binks."

DeMarcus chuckled at the imagery of the very different *Star Wars* characters. Darth Vader was the archetypical unstoppable villain. Jar Jar Binks was the good-hearted buffoon. "Is this your way of making me comfortable for the interview?"

"I don't want you comfortable. I want you prepared. Andy will lull you into a false sense of security, then try to get you to say something you wouldn't confide to a blood relative."

DeMarcus considered Troy. "Are you speaking from experience?"

"I've had some close calls with her."

DeMarcus exhaled a deep breath. If the reporter caused the media-savvy executive to stumble, he'd better stay on his toes. "I don't like reporters. They're the ones who came up with 'The Mighty Guinn.'"

Troy grinned. "It's a great marketing tag."

"You try being a walking billboard twenty-four seven. It makes it hard to have a normal life."

"I imagine most future NBA Hall of Famers find it hard to have a normal life."

"The media make it harder."

A calculating gleam lit the vice president's dark eyes. "Does this mean you'd oppose Take-Your-Picture-With-The-Coach Day?"

DeMarcus wasn't amused. "Yes, I would." He tapped the cover of his *New York Sports,* which lay on top of his desk. "How many of these meet-the-coach interviews do we have scheduled?"

"Just this one."

DeMarcus's eyes widened. "You didn't contact any other media?"

"The outlets might run with the press release, but it's hard to get coverage for the Monarchs. They're more interested in the Knicks."

DeMarcus heard the wry humor in the marketing executive's voice. "But the team's getting a new head coach."

"The fourth one in three years. After a while, the franchise's coaching carousel loses appeal."

DeMarcus glanced at the paper again. "I would have thought my marketability would have been a bigger draw."

"There's some resentment that our native son earned his championship rings with the Miami Waves, our division rivals." Troy rubbed his bearded chin. "You might actually cost us ticket sales."

DeMarcus blew a heavy breath, dragging his hand

over his hair. "So the Lady Assassin isn't the only one I have to win over."

Troy frowned. "Excuse me?"

"Never mind. I'm surprised but I'm not disappointed that I don't have a lot of interviews scheduled. I don't enjoy them."

"What a shock." Troy's voice was dry enough for kindling.

The muscles in DeMarcus's shoulders bunched with tension. "I've seen a lot of good players—good people—ruined by reporters who've never run a mile in their lives. Still, they sit behind their laptops lecturing us on mental toughness and commitment. They think they know better than we do what it takes to win a championship."

Troy gave him a considering look, as though trying to read between the lines of DeMarcus's resentment. "It's a balance. On the one hand, we need the media to help promote our sport. On the other hand, fans give reporters' words a lot of weight. The power goes to their heads."

DeMarcus shrugged, trying to release his tension. "I wouldn't mind if it stayed in their heads. But instead it comes out of their mouths and causes people a lot of trouble."

"Your name hasn't been associated with any scandals."

"I was lucky. My parents were disciplinarians. They sacrificed a lot of time and money to get my career started. I made sure I repaid their sacrifice by making them proud. The media considered me boring."

Could he continue to make them proud? Or would this head coaching assignment irreparably damage the legacy he'd created?

A commanding knock on his office door interrupted his thoughts. Elia Gomez, his executive secretary, stood just inside his office. She nodded toward the young woman standing beside her. "Coach, Andrea Benson with the *New York Sports* is here for the interview."

DeMarcus got to his feet. From the corner of his eye he saw Troy stand. "Thank you, Elia."

DeMarcus rounded his desk to greet their guest, but Troy reached her first.

The media executive offered Andrea his hand. "Hi, Andy. It's good to see you."

Andrea Benson's smile was tight, her handshake brief. "Wish I could say the same, Slick."

DeMarcus's gaze bounced from the reporter to Troy. The other man looked amused.

The reporter's appearance was as straightforward as her writing style: tan blazer and black pants. Sensible black shoes boosted her five-foot-nine-inch height. Her dark brown hair fell in a straight shot just past her shoulders.

Troy made the introductions. "Andy Benson, DeMarcus Guinn, the Monarchs' new head coach."

"I prefer Andrea, but Slick here is hard of hearing." Her mocha cheekbones were dusted pink. She scowled in Troy's direction before taking the hand DeMarcus offered her. "It's a pleasure to meet you, Mr. Guinn."

"Marc." He smiled at the reporter before giving Troy a warning look. The vice president of media could cool his libido until after the newspaper ran the article. He didn't need the other man irritating the attractive sports reporter during his interview.

He gestured Andrea to precede him and Troy to the

conversation table. Andrea sat with her back to a window, casting her features in shadow. A deliberate move? She crossed her right leg over her left knee and opened her reporter's notebook on the oak table. De-Marcus chose a seat across from her. Troy sat beside her.

The reporter offered DeMarcus an apologetic smile. "Thank you for meeting with me this morning. I'm sure you're busy getting to know the organization and your new team."

DeMarcus relaxed into the black swivel chair and returned Andrea's direct gaze. Her brown eyes were friendly in her heart-shaped face. "I appreciate your interest in the Monarchs. I understand your paper's the only publication that regularly covers us."

Andrea settled back into her chair. She tucked her hair behind her ears. Silver sterling earrings, a match to her thin necklace, winked at him. "How does it feel to be back in New York?"

DeMarcus flashed a grin. "I've been home for about two years. It feels good."

The next twenty minutes passed with similar questions about his likes and dislikes. DeMarcus may have forgotten Troy's caution about the reporter except for the warning glares the other man kept sending him.

Andrea glanced up from her notepad. "It's not a secret the Monarchs have struggled for the past four seasons. What are your plans for turning the team around?"

They were moving into the meat of the interview. Her direct question relieved DeMarcus. Maybe Troy was worried for nothing. "We're going to get back to the basics—offense, defense, shooting and footwork."

Andrea entered his answer into her notepad as he

spoke, then paused as though waiting for him to say something else. DeMarcus didn't have anything to add.

The reporter glanced at her notes, then back to him. "The Monarchs have the oldest roster in the league. The average age of your players is thirty. Does that concern you?"

DeMarcus had been prepared for that question, too. "No, it doesn't. We have the talent and the experience to win."

"Then why aren't you winning?"

He couldn't ask for a more direct question than that one. Unfortunately, he didn't have an answer. Yet. He glanced at Troy. The media executive gave him an I-Warned-You look.

He turned his attention to Andrea's steady gaze. "It goes back to leadership. In addition to skills and experience, a team needs a stable structure to succeed."

Andrea recorded his response even as she kept her questions coming. "Then you're conceding this season?"

That pulled him up short. "What makes you ask that?"

She scribbled across the sheet of paper. "This is only your first season. You'll need more than one year to build a stable structure."

DeMarcus leaned forward, drawing her gaze to his. "We're going to have a winning season. I'm not conceding anything."

Troy shifted in his seat. "I'm sure you're aware of Marc's reputation. He's used to winning. Losing isn't part of his vocabulary."

"But it's very much a part of the Monarchs' vocabulary." Andrea shifted her attention from Troy back to DeMarcus. "They've struggled for the past four years. For the past two years, they've been at the bottom of the Atlantic Division. Do you really expect to turn them around in one season?"

Her follow-up questions had him against the ropes like a baby boxer facing a veteran pugilist. "Yes, I do."

Andrea arched a brow. "By getting back to basics?"

DeMarcus caught her faint sarcasm. "Yes."

Andrea recorded more notes. "What about the rumors that you were hired to lose?"

DeMarcus went cold. "What rumors?"

Troy turned toward her. "Where did you hear that?"

Andrea glanced at the media executive. "You know I can't reveal my sources." She returned to DeMarcus. "How do you respond to those rumors?"

DeMarcus ignored the seed of anger growing in him. "What are you talking about?"

Andrea paused. "You really don't know? There are rumors the owners hired you for your name, not your ability. They don't want you to win."

DeMarcus unclenched his jaw. "Why would I join an organization that didn't want to win?"

Andrea shook her head. Her straight brown locks shifted over her shoulders. "I don't know."

"I wouldn't. Not as a player or as a coach." DeMarcus no longer found her brown eyes friendly or her directness refreshing.

Troy leaned into the table, claiming Andrea's attention. "The Monarchs are committed to reclaiming the team's winning tradition. That's why we hired Marc Guinn as our head coach."

Andrea resettled her gaze on DeMarcus. There was speculation in her eyes. "But you don't have any coaching experience."

"I know the Monarchs' offensive and defensive playbooks." DeMarcus kept his voice level even as his mind spun. Where had these rumors come from? Who had started them?

Were they true?

Troy argued the point. "He was a leader on the court, and he has what it takes to win."

Andrea tilted her head. "What's that?"

Troy sat straighter. "A winning attitude. A winning philosophy."

DeMarcus interrupted Troy before the media spin cost him his breakfast. "The proof will show in the number of *W*'s at the end of our season." Confidence and conviction prompted him to predict more wins than losses this year.

Andrea rose from her chair. "Monarchs fans will be keeping count. Thank you again for the interview. It's been informative."

DeMarcus stood. "I take my job as seriously as you take yours, Andrea. To me, winning is everything. Otherwise, why play the game?"

"I wish you luck." She nodded toward Troy.

DeMarcus escorted Andrea to the door, then shook her hand. With his back to Troy, DeMarcus watched the reporter walk past the assistant coaches' offices before disappearing beyond Elia's desk.

He kept his attention on his executive secretary's desk. "What do you know of these rumors Andrea's talking about?

3

Silence stretched a little too long. The media executive's hesitation wasn't a good sign. DeMarcus half turned to look back into the room. "Was I hired to lose?"

Troy stood beside the conversation table and met DeMarcus's gaze across the cavernous office. "I don't know what Andy's talking about. I haven't heard any rumors about your being hired to lose."

Shit. The media executive was more cautious giving an answer than a rookie point guard was at taking a shot. "Let's try this again. Was I hired to lose?"

Troy shook his head. "I don't believe that. Jackie wouldn't do anything to hurt the team."

"But?"

Troy's sigh raised his shoulders. "But it's not all up to her." He paced back to DeMarcus's desk. "Combined, Gerry and Bert own fifty-one percent of the franchise. Gerry's also the interim general manager."

"Gerry and Bert hired me. Jackie didn't sign my contract." DeMarcus read his deduction in Troy's eyes. *Jaclyn* wouldn't do anything to hurt the team. But

Gerald and *Albert* had hired him. Did they want the team to lose? DeMarcus didn't like uncertainties. "Why would Gerry and Bert want the Monarchs to lose?"

Troy's expression was tight with frustration. "No idea. But most of Gerry's personnel decisions don't make sense. He trades promising young players for older players or problem ones. He forced out one of the best coaches the franchise has ever had for a coach with a losing record."

"And hires one with no experience."

"No offense."

"None taken." What had he gotten himself into? "How far has the rumor spread? Are the other coaches and players aware of it?" *Are people whispering behind my back?* He wasn't used to being a laughingstock.

Troy pushed his hands into his front pants pockets. "I haven't heard anyone talking about it."

"Someone must be talking about it. How else would a reporter have heard of it?"

Troy raised an eyebrow. "Don't look at me. I don't feed gossip about my team to the media."

DeMarcus needed to move. He dragged a hand through his hair as he crossed the room. "Would Jackie?"

"Not on your life." Troy's answer was quick and definite.

Some of DeMarcus's tension left him. At least his boss wasn't known to air her grievances in the media. Dammit. She'd tried to tell him yesterday, but he hadn't believed it. He still didn't want to believe it.

DeMarcus checked his watch. It was almost half past eleven. Gerald should be in his office. He pivoted on his heel and marched to his door. "I'm going to talk to Gerry."

"What will you say?"

DeMarcus pulled up short. "I'm going to ask him about the rumors."

"What good will that do?"

"If I'm going to turn this team around and start winning, I'll need the general manager's support."

"*Interim* general manager. And if you don't have his support?"

DeMarcus continued toward the door. "I'll quit."

"Tell me what's wrong." Jaclyn frowned at Violet Ebanks O'Neal.

Her friend and former WNBA teammate stood beside her, serving food to the hungry and homeless at Morning Glory Chapel's kitchen and homeless shelter. Jaclyn added a serving spoon of mixed vegetables to an older homeless woman's lunch plate.

Violet shrugged listlessly, then added a spoon of mashed potatoes to the plate. "I don't want to talk about it."

Jaclyn bit her lower lip. The situation was getting worse. Last week, Violet had claimed to be tired. Now her friend wasn't bothering with an excuse.

Violet had been her teammate for three years and a friend for what seemed a lifetime. But Jaclyn hardly recognized the woman these days. Their teammates had nicknamed Violet the Beauty Queen. But the woman standing beside her had scraped her auburn hair into a stubby, sloppy ponytail beneath the hairnet. Her violet blue eyes were dull, and her porcelain skin was devoid of makeup. The Violet she'd known for the past eleven years had worn cosmetics on the basketball court.

Jaclyn glanced at the clock mounted to the wall across the recreation area. It was almost noon. One day a week for the past five years, she took a longer break to help the lunch crew at the chapel. She'd talked Violet into joining her almost two months ago. The activity wasn't helping.

She served an older gentleman a spoonful of vegetables. "Is Dawnie OK?"

Violet had blamed her two-year-old daughter for her fatigue. The little girl had a truckload of energy. Violet's parents claimed Dawn was payback for Violet having run them ragged until she'd been drafted to the WNBA.

"Everyone's fine." Her friend served the older man mashed potatoes. "It's me. I'm bored out of my mind and driving everybody crazy, including myself."

Jaclyn glanced at a young mother comforting her sobbing toddler daughter before returning her attention to Violet. Her friend looked bored and frustrated. And a little scared. "What do you want to do?"

Violet shrugged again. "That's just it. I don't know. But I've got to do something."

Jaclyn's shoulders tensed as she took on her friend's frustration. "Something will come to you, Vi. You'll figure it out."

"When?"

She wished she had the answer. "Be patient. Maybe right now, you just need to get away from the house a couple of afternoons a week to just think. Dawnie can stay with your parents or Aidan's."

"I hope you're right." Violet shifted her troubled gaze to Jaclyn. "But, Jackie, what kind of mother wants to be away from her own child?"

Jaclyn shook her head adamantly. "Vi, just because

you want a few hours to yourself doesn't make you a bad mother."

"I love my daughter. I really do."

"I know."

"Then why do I want to be away from her?"

Jaclyn continued to add vegetables to the plates of stewed chicken as guests moved down the serving line. "You're not trying to get away from Dawnie. You just need a little time for yourself."

"I'm not being selfish?"

"Of course not. A couple of hours away from you won't hurt her. She'll be with your parents. And it will help you relax so you don't drive your family crazy."

Violet's chuckle wobbled. "Thanks. I'll take your advice. Maybe then Aidan will stop looking at me as though he thinks I need therapy."

Jaclyn smiled. "How is our favorite financial advisor?"

"Busy taking care of his accounts."

"That's good to hear." Jaclyn paused as the young mother with the sobbing toddler stopped in front of her. Jaclyn nodded toward the little girl. "Will she be all right?"

The mother nodded. "She lost her teddy bear."

Jaclyn looked at the little girl. Silent tears streamed down her flushed, rounded cheeks. "I'm sorry, honey." The little girl returned her gaze with wounded big green eyes. "I'm Jackie. What's your name?"

"Tiff." The watery whisper was barely audible.

"Tiffany." The mother extended their two lunch plates.

As she nudged vegetables onto each of the dishes, Jaclyn noted the two tote bags that dragged on each of the thin woman's shoulders. Heavy makeup didn't mask the bruises on her face, nor did the limp, honey-blond hair swinging loosely to hide her features. Tiffany's mother moved on to Violet, checking to make sure her daughter kept up with her.

Violet added mashed potatoes to both plates. "Enough about me. How was your meeting with the Empire owners' lawyers?"

Jaclyn looked away from Tiffany and her mother. She scowled. "The lawyers told me Gerry and Bert want to end the arena contract so they can move the team."

Violet gasped. "Are you kidding me?"

"No." Jaclyn served another guest.

"Where do they want to go?"

She shrugged, checking the clock. She'd have to return to her office soon. "Someplace where they won't be competing with another basketball team. Gerry likes the sound of the Nevada Monarchs."

"Nevada?" Violet sounded as baffled as Jaclyn felt. "Have they gotten any offers?"

"He wouldn't tell me."

"I can't believe them. Is Bert really on board with Gerry's plan?"

Jaclyn had been wondering the same thing. "I haven't spoken with him yet."

"Jackie." Her former teammate's tone demanded her attention. Violet's eyes were dark with concern. "I know you're upset. But, if you're going to save the team, you've got to keep your emotions on the side-lines and approach this problem as a business."

That pulled Jaclyn up short. "I *am* treating this as a business."

"Then why don't you know whether Gerry has an offer from another market?"

"He wouldn't tell me." Jaclyn pursed her lips. "And I was too upset to push."

"You've got to ask. Gerry's decision to move the team isn't an emotional choice. It's a business decision. You've got to treat it the same way."

"You're right."

Violet used her serving spoon to gesture toward Jaclyn. "You can start by reclaiming your position as general manager. Your grandfather made Gerry interim GM when he was sick and you were taking care of him. Gerry's been interim for almost two years now. You need to take your spot back before Gerry grows roots."

Jaclyn relaxed slightly. "I know. I wasn't ready before, but I am now. I gave the firm my two weeks' notice this morning."

"Good for you." Violet's eyes twinkled. Color warmed her cheeks. "You have to regain control. Gerry and Bert are on the verge of destroying everything your family helped build. You need to stop them."

Jaclyn nodded. "I've also got to figure out a way to increase the franchise's revenue."

Violet smiled as she added potatoes to another plate. Concentrating on Jaclyn's problems seemed to lift her spirits. "Pre-sales will shoot up with the Mighty Guinn taking over as head coach."

"Maybe for the first game. But to sustain sales, we've got to win."

"Don't worry. The Mighty Guinn knows how to win."

Jaclyn paused as their replacements showed up. The two women took over Violet and Jaclyn's stations.

Jaclyn walked beside Violet back to the kitchen area. She tossed her apron and hairnet into the laundry basket. "But does he know how to coach? You know as well as I do that it takes three things for a team to win—talent, coaching and chemistry. We have talent. But we need coaching and chemistry to bring it out."

"You don't think Marc Guinn has what it takes to bring out the chemistry in the Monarchs?"

"No, I don't. And, even worse, he doesn't want to." Jaclyn led the way out of the chapel. She stood at the top of the front steps and swept her gaze over the aging storefronts, pedestrian lunch traffic and persistent street vendors. "After three losing seasons, if we don't change the team's attitude, we won't have a prayer of winning."

Gerald Bimm was pretentious. His office was a showcase for his museum-quality art. DeMarcus considered the track lighting that lit the professionally framed modern paintings hanging on every wall. Abstract metal sculptures posed on shelves and tables all around him. There wasn't a single picture of the Monarchs or any team paraphernalia in the room. Not even a logo.

DeMarcus sat in one of the three green armchairs facing the franchise partner's desk. His office was smaller than Gerald's. Still, he felt lost in his room, whereas Gerald had wedged himself into this space. DeMarcus felt crowded by the other man's belongs.

"Is it true you hired me to lose?" DeMarcus didn't see the point in beating around the bush.

Gerald's body seemed to relax. His narrow form was impeccably dressed in a pin-striped brown suit. He was buttoned into his jacket even as he reclined behind his desk. "I'm glad that's out in the open. Who told you?"

He couldn't have heard correctly. "It's true?"

There was an edgy look in Gerald's small brown eyes. "It doesn't matter how you found out. All that matters now is that you know the plan."

DeMarcus narrowed his eyes. "You lied about the reason you were hiring me."

Gerald looked surprised. "I didn't tell you I wanted you to win."

DeMarcus gritted his teeth. "It was implied."

Gerald waved a hand. "It doesn't matter. You're in on the plan now."

"You want me to lose." Losing was a foreign concept to DeMarcus. He never allowed himself to imagine it. He always envisioned success.

"Yes, we do." Gerald's tone was definite.

"*We* who? You and Bert?" DeMarcus pictured the third Monarchs franchise partner, Albert Tipton. The smaller man hadn't spoken much during DeMarcus's job interview.

"And Jackie. All of us."

DeMarcus stilled. "The *three* of you discussed it?"

"Yes. We've had several in-depth discussions." Gerald's expression was earnest. The liar made a good actor.

"And what did Jackie say?"

Gerald shrugged his shoulders. "She agrees that we should go for a losing season."

DeMarcus's blood heated. Gerald's dishonesty didn't bode well for their working relationship. "Why?"

Gerald pulled his chair farther under his desk and leaned across it. "We want to break the arena contract and relocate the team."

DeMarcus hadn't considered that. "Have you had any offers?"

"Not yet. But I'm sure the offers will come once we put out the feelers."

"Where are you looking?"

Gerald shrugged again. "We'd prefer a state that doesn't have an NBA team. Like Nevada."

The situation couldn't get any worse if he tried. "What would my role be?"

"Of course, we want you with us." Gerald settled deeper into his green executive chair. "Once we're out of this arena and have an NBA market to ourselves, we want someone who can take us to a winning season. Someone who could rebuild the team for us and create a dynasty."

Gerald lied as easily as he breathed. Could DeMarcus trust anything out of the man's mouth? A deep breath eased the tightness in his shoulders. His eyes were cold and his voice flat as he began to unravel Gerald's tall tales. "Jackie Jones would never go along with this idea."

Gerald narrowed his eyes. "What makes you say that?"

"She told me when she asked for my resignation." DeMarcus took small satisfaction from Gerald's shock.

The other man's eyes stretched wide. His mouth opened, then closed. "Don't worry about Jackie. Bert and I can handle her. After all, she was against hiring you, but you're here, aren't you?"

"You and Bert offered me this job under false pretenses."

Gerald frowned. "What do you mean?"

"I thought you wanted me to coach. Instead you want me to bend over."

Gerald shook his head. "We're just asking you not to win. Not this season."

"When I accepted your offer, I wasn't handing over my integrity." DeMarcus stood. "I quit."

Gerald raised his chin to maintain eye contact with DeMarcus. "You can't quit. We have a contract."

"My lawyers will shred your contract."

Gerald popped out of his chair. "That contract is airtight."

"You misrepresented your intent." DeMarcus laughed without humor. "You don't want to go public with that when you're looking for a new market. You won't come across as trustworthy."

"How will you come across once the media reports that you couldn't keep the coaching job for even a week?"

DeMarcus remembered the reason he'd wanted to coach the Monarchs. "My integrity is more important than what the media thinks."

"Dammit. We just need one more losing season. You can win next year."

DeMarcus pinched the bridge of his nose. "You don't have any idea what it takes to be a champion. A champion doesn't take a season off. Ever."

"I thought you wanted to coach."

"You don't want a coach. You want a stooge. I'm not anyone's stooge." He ignored the partner's demands and turned to leave.

DeMarcus strode into the main office area. The two administrative assistants regarded him with open curiosity. Two doors to the right, Troy stepped from his office. DeMarcus exchanged a long look with him before marching down the hall.

"Marc."

DeMarcus couldn't hear Troy's footsteps on the plush, wall-to-wall silver carpet behind him, but the other man's voice sounded close. He didn't stop until he came to the elevators.

"The rumors are true?"

DeMarcus looked over his shoulder at Troy. "Yes."

The elevators arrived. Troy stepped on with him. "Are you really going to quit?"

"I already have." DeMarcus ignored the sudden silence surrounding him and watched the elevator's liquid crystal display count down the floors. He didn't know why the media executive was following him around the arena to his office. He didn't care.

DeMarcus strode to his desk and punched the keys to log back on to the system.

Troy finally spoke. "You should talk to Jackie."

"We talked yesterday." He should have listened to her. She'd told him Gerald and Albert weren't trustworthy.

DeMarcus selected the word-processing program and typed a short, curt resignation letter. Two more mouse clicks and he sent the document to the printer.

"It doesn't matter if you don't have Gerry or Bert's support as long as Jackie's on your side."

"She's not." DeMarcus went through the process of shutting down programs that were running on his computer.

"What makes you think that?"

"She asked for my resignation."

"What? When?" Troy seemed as baffled as DeMarcus was angry.

"Yesterday." DeMarcus switched to his Microsoft Outlook program. He checked his Calendar schedule and scanned his e-mails. He forwarded his messages to other coaches to handle and canceled meetings he'd scheduled for the day. He didn't bother with explanations. He didn't have the time or the patience to make them.

"You should call her. Tell her what Gerry told you."

"She already knows." DeMarcus stood. "I can't dig this team out of the league's basement without management's support, and I don't have that. Two of your three partners don't want me to win, and the third one doesn't think I can."

DeMarcus gathered the few belongings he'd brought to what used to be his office. He shoved his stopwatch into the front pocket of his dark gray warm-up pants. He placed the antique silver-framed photograph of his parents into his briefcase. But he'd carry the green and blue Miami Waves water bottle.

"What are you going to tell the media about your quitting?"

DeMarcus studied the other man. He had the sense Troy wouldn't let him leave the arena until he was satisfied with DeMarcus's response. "I'm not speaking to the media."

Troy gave a dry laugh. "You were our coach for one day. They'll want to speak with you."

DeMarcus expelled an impatient breath. "Fine. I'll feed them the usual leaving-for-personal-reasons crap. Tell them I want to spend more time with my father."

"That won't satisfy them."

"It'll have to." DeMarcus itched to walk out the door.

Troy shoved his hands into the front pockets of his tan suit pants. "All right. And I'll tell them we're sorry things didn't work out, but that we understand your reason for leaving."

The media executive's statement seemed personal. His words helped ease DeMarcus's temper. "I appreciate that."

Troy inclined his head, then left the office.

DeMarcus dropped back into his chair and scrubbed his palms over his face. What a rotten option: lose or quit. He couldn't stomach either choice. DeMarcus dropped his arms and clenched his fists. Being a quitter seemed the lesser of two evils, but it still didn't sit well.

He grabbed the executive binder human resources had given him yesterday—his first and only full day on the job—and turned to the contact information page. DeMarcus found Jaclyn's direct phone extension at the fancy law firm where she worked. He punched the number into his cell phone and waited for the call to connect. Her voice mail activated almost immediately.

Jaclyn's honey-and-whiskey voice took the edge off his temper. He remembered her pacing this office. The sway of her hips; the fire in her eyes. The discordant beep at the end of her message broke the spell.

DeMarcus straightened in his chair. "This is Marc Guinn. You were right. Gerry admitted he'd hired me to lose. I'll leave my resignation with his secretary." He hesitated, unsure how to end his message. "Good luck. With Gerry and Bert as partners, you'll need it."

He disconnected the call and stood. Removing his resignation letter from the printer, he folded it into an envelope he found in one of his desk drawers. He'd deliver the letter on his way out. Then he had to tell his father why he'd quit the team.

4

"You did the right thing." Julian Guinn's response came after a contemplative silence that had stretched forever. However, the clock above their fireplace mantel said it had only been minutes.

Some of DeMarcus's tension drained with his father's approval. Would his mother also have agreed with his decision?

The Park Slope neighborhood outside the den's bay window was quiet. It was after noon on a sunny and warm Tuesday. Most of their neighbors were working. The retirees were enjoying Brooklyn's waning summer. The long, dark winter wasn't far away.

DeMarcus paced away from the bay window toward the fireplace. His sneakers were silent against the rich mahogany floor. He stood with his back to his father. "I've never given up on a job without at least trying. I wasn't cut out to be a broadcast reporter, but I stayed with ESPN for a full NBA season. I wasn't comfortable in that management position with the sports apparel line, but I stayed there, too."

"Those situations were different. The Monarchs

organization doesn't want you to win." Julian paused. "As a Monarchs fan, I'm disappointed by that."

DeMarcus paced back to the window. "You and Mom didn't raise a quitter."

"If your mother were still alive, she'd support your decision, too."

The rest of DeMarcus's tension drained away. "I hope so."

"I know so." Julian settled deeper into the overstuffed, dark brown armchair. His stocking feet were flat against the scarlet-patterned Oriental rug. "Coaching the Monarchs now would be an exercise in futility. Jackie Jones doesn't trust you with her team, and the other two don't care about it—or the fans."

"Could I have helped the team win despite that? I'll never know because I didn't try." DeMarcus paced back to the fireplace.

"Marc, sit down, son. You're making me dizzy." His father gestured toward the matching armchair.

DeMarcus looked at the plump, brown chair before lowering himself into it. For years, he'd considered it his mother's chair. After her passing, it had taken him months to feel comfortable sitting in it. "Sorry, Pop."

His father's eyes were solemn. "Son, I understand you think there are only two ways of looking at this situation: losing or quitting. You've always seen things as either win or lose, right or wrong, early or late. No one was ever on time." He smiled to soften the observation.

"Eighty percent of a game is mental. That's why you can't arrive on time. You have to be early to prepare."

Julian raised his left hand, palm out. "I know, son. But what I'm saying is, sometimes there's a third perspective, another way of looking at the situation. And this is one of those times."

DeMarcus's brow knitted. "What do you mean?"

"I'm glad you quit."

His brows jumped. "Why?"

"Because Gerry and Bert were trying to buy your integrity." Julian's voice deepened with anger. "They were trying to buy the name and reputation you've worked so hard to build your entire life."

DeMarcus sat back in his mother's armchair and considered his father's observation. Julian had a point. Instead of beating himself up for quitting, he should consider whether his motivation for leaving was as valid as the reason he'd wanted to stay. "I'd wanted to win a championship for you."

Julian looked bewildered. "You've already won two."

DeMarcus shook his head. "I wanted to win this one with your team. You've been a Monarchs fan all of my life."

"Longer than that." Julian cleared his throat. "I appreciate that, son. But I'm glad you didn't stay. I hope they don't find anyone to help them with their scheme. The franchise founders are probably spinning in their graves."

"The four men who started the Monarchs in 1956?"

Julian nodded. "Four friends who loved basketball and loved their community, so they formed a team as a way to give something back. Their investment in the community brought excitement. More importantly, it brought jobs. And, until about four years ago, they were one of the elite NBA teams."

"It amazes me that black men owned a competitive basketball team back then." DeMarcus leaned forward, propping his forearms on his thighs. "That was during Jim Crow."

"And the start of the civil rights movement and the Harlem Renaissance," Julian pointed out. "But it helped that one of the friends, Gene Mannion, was white."

"What happened to Mannion's heirs?"

"He didn't have any. In his will, he left his franchise shares to Jackie Jones's grandfather, Franklin Jones. When her grandfather died two years ago, those shares went to Jackie."

DeMarcus straightened in surprise. "She's the majority shareholder?"

"She has forty-nine percent." Julian tipped his graying head back as though remembering that time and the way the news had traveled through the community. "Franklin Jones didn't think one partner should own half of the franchise, so he sold one share to Cedrick Tipton, Bert's father. Combined, Gerry and Bert have fifty-one percent of the franchise."

"That's how they're able to outvote Jackie on franchise decisions, like moving the team out of Brooklyn."

"And personnel decisions that have caused the team several losing seasons."

"Why didn't Gene Mannion split his shares with all of his partners? Why did he give them all to Franklin Jones?"

Julian shook his head. "After a couple of seasons, Quinton and Cedrick lost interest in the Monarchs. Gene and Franklin were the only ones who still cared what happened to the team."

DeMarcus frowned. "Why?"

Julian seemed to collect his memories. "Cedrick used his profits from the franchise to build a department store."

"Tipton's Fashionwear."

"Quinton's story was different. He seemed to be jealous of all the attention Gene and Franklin were getting for the Monarchs' success. He started drinking more. Alcoholism eventually ruined his marriage. It also killed him."

DeMarcus lifted his right ankle to his left knee. "I feel sorry for Jackie having to deal with Quinton and Cedrick's descendants when she's trying to save her team."

Julian angled his head. A light danced in his dark eyes. "Have you ever seen Jackie Jones play basketball?"

"A few times."

Julian winked. "My money's on her. She'll find a way to keep the team in Brooklyn."

"She'll be devastated if she doesn't."

Julian sobered. "She's not the only one. If the Monarchs leave Brooklyn, the whole community will be devastated."

Jaclyn sat forward in the backseat of the Bentley as Herbert Trasker stopped the automobile in front of the Guinns' residence. "This is the address. Thank you, Herb."

Herbert turned sideways in the driver's seat and ducked his head to study the four-story, single-family mansion through the front passenger window. "I'll park here and wait for you."

Jaclyn gave the driver a wry smile. "This will probably take a while."

He gave her an ironic look. "Or it may not."

Her cream midcalf skirt rose slightly as Jaclyn scooted

forward on the backseat. She laid her hand on Herbert's shoulder. "It's almost six o'clock. Go home to your family. I'll call you when I'm ready to leave."

Herbert climbed out of the car and opened the back passenger door for her. He watched her step onto the sidewalk. "Are you sure?"

Jaclyn let Herbert's concern help steady her nerves. He worried over her like a parent. "Positive. I'm not going to be tossed out of the game that easily."

"All right, Ms. Jones." Herbert touched the brim of his black leather cap. "I'll wait for your call. Good luck."

Jaclyn mounted the steps to the Guinns' house and pressed the bell. She looked over her shoulder to see Herbert leaning against the Bentley, waiting with her. Moments later, the locks turned and the door opened. She faced an older version of the Mighty Guinn.

Jaclyn waved to Herbert to let him know someone had answered. Then she turned back to the gentleman. "Good evening. I'm Jaclyn Jones from—"

The stranger opened the door farther. "I know who you are, Ms. Jones. I'm Julian Guinn, Marc's father. Please come in."

"It's a pleasure to meet you, Mr. Guinn." Jaclyn extended her hand as she entered the residence. "May I speak with Marc, please?"

"Of course." DeMarcus's father led her down the polished mahogany hallway. A staircase wound upward on her right. A cozy den beckoned her to the left. "He's cooking dinner."

Jaclyn stumbled over her feet. Julian reacted, his right arm shooting out to steady her. Jaclyn gave him a tentative smile. "Now I know where Marc got his catlike reflexes."

His startled expression replaced his concerned frown. The twinkle in Julian's coal black, almond-shaped eyes—so like his son's—invited her to smile with him. "The idea of the Mighty Guinn wearing an apron knocked you off your feet, didn't it?"

Jaclyn's face warmed. "No, I didn't—"

Julian laughed, a warm rumbling sound that swept away her unease and coaxed a chuckle from her. "You should see your face." He kept his hand cupped around her elbow. "He's a very good cook. You should stay for dinner."

The elder Guinn escorted her across a formal dining room to the kitchen doorway. The scene stopped Jaclyn's mushrooming embarrassment. DeMarcus stood in profile to them at a large, rectangular ash wood island. A salad bowl perched in front of him. A tomato, cucumber, celery and two types of peppers surrounded the chop block on which DeMarcus was slicing a fat red pepper.

Julian released her elbow. "You have company, son."

DeMarcus's contented expression tensed when he saw Jaclyn. "What are you doing here?"

Julian sighed. "We now know why they didn't nickname you the Charming Guinn. I've asked her to stay for dinner." With that pronouncement, his father left them alone.

Jaclyn surveyed the large, octagonal kitchen hoping to distract the nerves bouncing in her belly. Stainless steel appliances stood on white counters. The walls, cupboards and shelving also were white. The wide gold trim separating the walls from the ceiling was a warm hug in the cool room.

She shifted her weight from one leg to the other.

"I'm sorry to interrupt your dinner with your father. It's nice that the two of you get together to share a meal."

DeMarcus gave her a curious look. His black gaze bore into her. "It's not that hard. We live together."

"Oh. That's nice." The Mighty Guinn lived with his father. "That's lovely."

DeMarcus returned to slicing vegetables. His long, brown fingers braced the red pepper with a firm but delicate touch. "I moved in after I retired from basketball."

That was the season after his mother passed away. Jaclyn's nerves settled and her heart softened. Who'd been in more need of the other's company, father or son? Probably both, but it didn't matter. What mattered was that DeMarcus had cared enough to come home.

"There's more than enough room for the two of you." Jaclyn watched DeMarcus slide the red pepper slices from the chop block to the salad bowl. There was something intensely sexy about a man who knew what he was doing in the kitchen. "I moved back in with my grandfather after I finished law school."

DeMarcus glanced over his shoulder. "Franklin Jones was a remarkable man."

"Yes, he was." Like Julian's home, her grandfather's house was large enough to give each of them privacy, but they'd enjoyed each other's company. Now that he was gone, his mansion was too large. She felt lost in all of that space. But, somehow, she felt at home in the Empire.

DeMarcus sprayed fat-free oil into a pan and adjusted the heat to low. His muscles flowed across his back and shoulders as he sautéed the vegetables. His silence was disconcerting. Jaclyn laid her hands flat against her cream skirt to keep from wringing them.

Her gaze swept the room's perimeter with its multitude of white cabinets, shelves and counter space. The rainbow of Tupperware sitting on the shelves added whimsy to the otherwise staid room. "Your kitchen is spotless."

He didn't turn around. "It should be. We prepare food in here."

"What are you making?"

DeMarcus turned up the heat under a nearby pot. "Curried chicken, couscous, chickpeas and salad."

Jaclyn blinked. Her gaze moved over his lean, six-foot-seven-inch frame clothed in a long-sleeve, green and blue Miami Waves jersey and black warm-up pants. His large, dark feet were bare. The image of the Mighty Guinn heating a can of soup was odd. The idea of his cooking an exotic meal stretched the bounds of credulity. It also was a reminder never to judge a book by its cover—or an athlete by his image. "Sounds delicious."

DeMarcus moved to the range and lifted the lid from the skillet. Mouth-watering fragrances exploded into the kitchen—curry, cumin, paprika and more. "Did you get my message?" He checked the stewing chicken, adding the sautéed vegetables, before resetting the lid.

"Yes, I did. Thank you." Jaclyn wandered farther into the kitchen, her low-heeled, cream suede pumps tapped against the small, gold and white square tiles that patterned the floor.

DeMarcus glanced at her over a broad shoulder. His expression wasn't readable. "Are you here to gloat?"

Jaclyn's stomach was jumping. Her heart did a

pick-and-roll in her throat. Sheer willpower restrained her from twisting her fingers together. "I'm here to ask you to reconsider your resignation."

DeMarcus's eyes widened. His lips parted. "Yesterday you stormed my office demanding my resignation."

"And, today, I realized I made a mistake."

DeMarcus stirred the couscous, then turned up the heat under the chickpeas. "When I wanted to stay, you told me to leave. Now that I've left, you want me to stay. Lady, you need to get your head together."

Jaclyn appealed to his back. "I thought you were working with Gerry and Bert to ruin the team."

"You should have asked me. I would have told you you were wrong." DeMarcus checked the chicken again.

"You're right. I'm sorry. I jumped to conclusions. But the fact you chose to resign rather than go along with their plan means you're committed to winning. I need someone with that level of commitment."

DeMarcus covered the chicken, lowered the temperature and checked the time. "What level of commitment do you have?"

"I'm fully committed to winning."

DeMarcus leaned his firm glutes against the nearby counter, finally facing Jaclyn. "Your team didn't start losing yesterday. The Monarchs have been getting worse over the past four years. Where were you while this was happening?"

The question, though fair, stung. "Gerry and Bert blocked many of the operational and personnel decisions my grandfather thought would benefit the team. When my grandfather became ill three years ago, we weren't able to give the franchise the attention it needed."

"Your grandfather's illness gave Gerry and Bert free rein to destroy the franchise."

"It seems that way."

DeMarcus gentled his voice. "Your grandfather has been gone for almost two years. What have you done to help the team?"

Jaclyn clenched her fists. "We need a majority vote to approve major decisions. They've formed a solid block against me with the intent of driving the franchise out of the city."

"Troy kept referring to Gerry as the interim general manager. Who's the GM?"

Jaclyn closed her eyes briefly, realizing where DeMarcus was taking her. "I am. I've given notice at the law firm and I'm taking back the GM responsibilities tomorrow."

DeMarcus cocked his head. "It took you two years to make that decision?"

"I realize—"

"Do you see why I don't think you're committed to the team? I need management support to save the Monarchs."

Jaclyn dragged her fingers through her hair. The glint in DeMarcus's eyes made her wonder whether he was enjoying the frustration he was visiting on her. Was this his payback for her attacking him yesterday? If so, she'd pay it gladly. For her grandfather, she was prepared to beg. "Marc, I know this looks bad."

"It *is* bad."

Jaclyn wished he'd stop interrupting her. "I know I should have been more engaged sooner. I'm trying to fix my mistake. Will you help me?"

DeMarcus felt himself responding to her plea. He stared into Jaclyn's cinnamon eyes. She spoke so sweetly, but did she understand what she was asking him? He straightened away from the counter. "The team is on a losing slide and two of the three partners want to throw away the season."

"I know it won't be easy. Will you help me?"

DeMarcus's gaze dipped to the silver and black Monarchs lapel pin fastened to the collar of her cream suit jacket. Was it the same pin from yesterday or did she have one for each outfit?

He turned to check the chicken and chickpeas. He stirred the couscous. The pot spoon moved in time with his thoughts. There was too much to lose. "I'd have to make changes with the team and with the coaches. The team will resist it. The coaches will resent me. And Gerry and Bert will side with them."

"But *I'll* side with *you*. You have my word."

DeMarcus considered Jaclyn's earnest expression. She could make him a believer. Almost. "When? In another two years?"

She bit her plump lower lip. "Before my grandfather died, he warned me Gerry and Bert don't have the same commitment to the franchise that he and I have. He said I'd have to fight to save the team." Jaclyn shook her head. "I never imagined they'd try to take the Monarchs away from Brooklyn."

DeMarcus was hesitant to end the heavy silence. "I can't guarantee you a winning season."

"No one could make a promise like that." Jaclyn stepped closer to him. Her voice was urgent. "I know you have doubts about the team, about the coaches— about me. But I'm not giving up. I can't. There's too much at stake."

He sensed Jaclyn willing his gaze to meet hers. He raised his eyes. "I can't help you."

"Please, just think it over." She hesitated. "You don't have to answer tonight. You can call me tomorrow."

The extra time must have cost her. Preseason was twelve days away. She'd asked so sweetly, still she'd asked too much. DeMarcus didn't want to think it over. He wanted to walk away. The Monarchs were a disaster from the basketball court to the front office. It would take a miracle to realize a winning season.

He hated himself. Still he couldn't be the one to steal the hope from her bright eyes. "I'll think it over."

Jaclyn's face glowed with pleasure and relief. De-Marcus stared at her radiance and lost his train of thought. He felt like a hero, like he'd made the winning basket at the buzzer.

She reached out and wrapped her long, slender hand around his forearm. "Thank you."

"Don't thank me. I've only agreed to think about it." DeMarcus returned to the range, breaking the spell Jaclyn had cast over him. "Dinner's ready. You and my father can wait in the dining room. I'll bring the food out."

"Oh, but—"

He looked over his shoulder. "Aren't you staying for dinner?"

Jaclyn's eyes shifted between him and the pots on the range. Her consternation disappeared and she smiled again. "I'd love to. Thank you."

DeMarcus watched her walk out of the kitchen. His gaze slipped over the flow of her long, slender figure, the sway of her firm, rounded hips. Somehow he had to find a way to resist the Lady Assassin's lure or risk losing his focus on what mattered most.

5

DeMarcus hadn't heard his father laugh this much in almost three years. Not since his mother's sudden death. For this, he could thank the woman sitting across the table from him, on his father's right.

Jaclyn was still grinning at a comment Julian had made. Her riot of dark brown curls framed her face and cascaded around her shoulders. She looked like an angel in her cream two-piece outfit. Where was the avenger who'd stormed his office in a blood red business suit? Angel or avenger? Which was the real Jaclyn Jones? He needed to find out.

Jaclyn scooped coucous with her fork and smiled at him. "The meal's delicious. Where did you learn to cook like this?"

DeMarcus's shrug masked his pleasure at her words. "It's a hobby. Cooking relaxes me."

From his seat at the head of the table, Julian grunted. "If only he could bake."

DeMarcus arched a brow. "Pop, if you want pastries, *you* can make them."

Jaclyn drank more iced tea. "My cooking skills aren't in your league, but I would like to try baking."

Julian winked at her. "You can try your recipes on us."

DeMarcus sipped his iced tea. "Be careful. Pop has a sweet tooth."

Julian sobered. "Why did you leave the WNBA to practice law?"

Her smile had a trace of mystery. "Judges don't penalize you if you argue in court."

DeMarcus's laughter joined Julian's. There was more to the Lady Assassin's reason for retiring from the game she loved. He was sure of it.

Julian returned to his dinner. "The Monarchs have an impressive past."

DeMarcus selected a juicy chunk of curried chicken. "You've got Pop on a roll, talking about one of his favorite subjects."

"Your father and I have that in common. Basketball is one of my favorite topics, too, especially the Monarchs." Jaclyn filled her fork with couscous. "We have ten players and three coaches in the NBA Hall of Fame, but we've never won a championship."

DeMarcus shrugged. "A championship would be nice, but not everyone can achieve it."

"So speaks the three-time MVP who has two championship rings." Jaclyn's smile teased him.

DeMarcus winked at her. "There are thirty teams playing for one ring. Those are tough odds."

Jaclyn nodded. "Yet teams like the Chicago Bulls and the Los Angeles Lakers have multiple rings from back-to-back titles."

DeMarcus gestured toward her. "You have a

championship ring of your own from your years in the WNBA." And still she'd retired. Why?

Jaclyn sighed. "I want the Monarchs to bring home the ring."

Julian gestured toward her with a forkful of chickpeas. "Even without a championship, the Monarchs have a storied history of a team and a community. As the team grew, so did the community because of the money the franchise brought in."

DeMarcus swallowed a mouthful of couscous. "You can't live in the past. You have to build for the future."

Julian shook his head. "Young people don't understand that, if you don't know your past, you can't build a future."

Jaclyn looked to DeMarcus. "There's been a connection—a bond—between the Monarchs and this community for more than half a century."

Julian grinned. "Yes, indeed. A lot of the players—like Lenny Smith, Willie Jones and Bobby Miller—grew up in the neighborhood, went to school here, stayed to play here, raised families here. They were our neighbors. They made the community feel like the team was theirs."

DeMarcus stared at his dinner plate. The Waves had drafted him after college. Should he have tried to be traded to the Monarchs? He would have been closer to his parents. He looked up and saw the concern in Jaclyn's cinnamon eyes. He shifted his gaze away.

Jaclyn returned her attention to his father. "You've followed the Monarchs for a long time."

"Yes, indeed. Since I could turn on the radio." Julian pointed his fork toward Jaclyn. "The Monarchs will rebuild its glory days."

Jaclyn arched a brow at DeMarcus. "To do that, we'll need a coach who knows what it takes to be a champion." Her eyes twinkled as she switched her gaze to his father. "You must have been devastated when the Monarchs' conference rival drafted your only child."

Julian winked at her. "There were pros and cons. Of course you always want your child to succeed. But when the Miami Waves played the Brooklyn Monarchs, no matter who won, I went home happy."

Jaclyn laughed. "I like your style, Julian."

His father continued. "Marc's mother wanted him to play for the home team, though. But everything happens for a reason. Marc fit in well with the Waves. He had good chemistry with the other starters."

DeMarcus swallowed more iced tea. "Which resulted in the team earning those two championship rings you mentioned."

Jaclyn turned again to his father. "You must have been excited when Marc was offered the head coach position for the Monarchs."

Julian held DeMarcus's eyes. "I've lost track of the number of times my son has made me proud. Two championship rings, three MVP trophies, Olympic gold. The day he learned to ride a two-wheeler." He turned to Jaclyn. "Should I mention the day he was potty trained?"

DeMarcus closed his eyes and raised his voice to be heard above Jaclyn's surprised laughter. "Please don't, Pop."

Julian inclined his head. "We raised Marc to make his own decisions. He's shown good judgment so far."

DeMarcus dropped his gaze to the table. As always, he was humbled by his father's faith in him.

Jaclyn squeezed his father's forearm. "You and your wife did an excellent job with your son. You're right to be proud of him." She turned to address De-Marcus. "And you're lucky to have such good parents. As I said earlier, I was wrong to have asked for your resignation yesterday. I think you're the coach the Monarchs need."

DeMarcus returned her direct stare. "You could be wrong."

Her hand fell away from Julian's arm. "I know I'm not."

DeMarcus pressed for more. "And what about Gerry and Bert? Will you be able to prevent them from throwing away the season?"

Jaclyn didn't waver. "Yes, I will."

DeMarcus could almost believe her. "I'll think it over."

"Then I'll leave you to it." Jaclyn pushed away from the dining table and stood to collect her dishes. "Gentlemen, thank you for dinner and your wonderful company."

Julian took Jaclyn's dishes from her. "It was nice having a lady at the dinner table again."

DeMarcus again wondered about the effect Jaclyn's presence had over his father. He circled the dining table and took the serving tray from her. He set it back on the table. "You're our guest. We'll clear the table."

Jaclyn's arms dropped to her sides. "Then I'll get my cell phone so I can call my driver."

"I'll take you home."

She glanced at her watch. "I'd appreciate that, if you're sure it's not an imposition."

Behind her, Julian snorted. "An imposition? Taking you home gets him out of kitchen duty."

DeMarcus tried to look offended. "I cooked dinner."

Julian snorted again, then extended his right hand toward Jaclyn. "It was nice to meet you, Jackie. Good luck with the season."

Jaclyn took Julian's hand. "Thank you. Hopefully, we'll meet again."

DeMarcus took Jaclyn's elbow to escort her from the dining room. "I'll be right back, Pop."

DeMarcus put on his sneakers while Jaclyn called her driver. He then collected their coats from the front closet before leading her through the back of the house to his garage. DeMarcus breathed in the chilled air that carried the faint scent of autumn leaves.

He used a remote opener to raise the garage door. Another remote control deactivated the alarm and unlocked the doors to his black Audi sedan. DeMarcus held the front passenger door open, closing it after Jaclyn had settled into the seat. He rounded the car and slipped behind the wheel. "Where to?"

He recognized the street Jaclyn mentioned. It was only a few blocks away in their Park Slope neighborhood. DeMarcus fastened his seat belt and waited while Jaclyn did the same before he drove the car out of the garage and into the heavy nighttime traffic.

Jaclyn's soft, whiskey voice broke the pensive silence. "Your father is charming. I enjoyed the evening."

"So did we." The truth of his words surprised him. His first impression of the Monarchs co-owner during his job interview hadn't been positive; neither had his second encounter with her yesterday in his office. But she'd been a different person tonight. She'd listened to and laughed with his father. Julian had seemed happier than he'd been in a long time.

A comfortable silence settled into the car until DeMarcus's curiosity kicked in. "I've seen you play. You were good. Why did you leave basketball for law?"

"Thank you." Jaclyn didn't take praise from this gold-medal Olympian and future NBA Hall of Famer lightly. She shifted in her seat to look at him. She liked the clean, strong lines of his profile—high forehead, long nose, squared chin—almost as much as she enjoyed looking into his dangerous, dark eyes. "I didn't leave basketball. I just stopped playing professionally."

"Why?"

"I wanted experience in contract and employment law. I thought it would help me manage the franchise."

"But it's taken you two years to claim your position as general manager."

Jaclyn stared through the windshield, trying to shake off her guilt. "My grandfather had been sick for a long time. Still, losing him was hard. I thought I'd left the franchise in good hands with Gerry and Bert. I was wrong."

DeMarcus stopped at a red light. "Why are they trying to move the team?"

Jaclyn felt his gaze on her. They were discussing business. Why did his attention make her want to change the subject? "Gerry and Bert don't appreciate the historical relationship of the franchise and the community as much as my grandfather and I do."

"Why not?"

Jaclyn shrugged. "Gerry didn't grow up around the franchise. He inherited his shares from his uncle. Bert inherited his shares from his father. But he also has Tipton's Fashionwear. My grandparents raised me after my parents and older brother were killed in a car accident."

"You were very young when that happened, weren't you?"

Why had she introduced this topic? Jaclyn's stomach tensed. "I was three. After my grandmother died when I was eleven, my grandfather and the team were my only family."

The light changed. DeMarcus crossed the intersection. "I'm sorry for your loss."

"There's never an easy time to lose a loved one." Jaclyn glanced at him. "I'm sorry about your mother's passing."

"Thank you."

The atmosphere in the car weighed heavy with regrets. Silence stretched before Jaclyn changed the subject. "Thank you for reconsidering your resignation."

There was a smile in DeMarcus's voice. "If you could afford an experienced coach, would you have asked me to stay?"

Jaclyn suppressed a smile. The Mighty Guinn didn't miss a trick. "I thought you weren't in it for the money."

"I'm not. But I am curious." DeMarcus turned onto her street.

"Frankly, if the franchise weren't so dysfunctional, we wouldn't need a new head coach." Jaclyn dug her house keys from her purse.

"True." DeMarcus parked behind a dark blue Mercedes. He got out of the car, then came around to assist her.

"Thank you." Jaclyn took his hand. His palm was big, rough and warm. Had he noticed she'd held on a little too long? She climbed her front steps, enjoying the feel of his presence behind her a little too much. "You're right. It's more fiscally responsible to hire a promising new coach than to lure a more established one."

"A promising new coach." His tone was dry as he quoted her. "Yesterday, I was the man who'd destroy the team."

He stopped a step below her, but Jaclyn still had to look up to meet his eyes. His broad shoulders sheltered her from her surroundings. He was strong enough for her to lean on. But would he keep her from falling? Could he? Was he the franchise's savior or its destroyer? The evening was suddenly too quiet. "If the salary wasn't your motivation, why did you want to coach the Monarchs?" He stayed silent so long, she considered repeating her question.

But then he smiled. His tempting lips parted to reveal perfect white teeth. Deep grooves bracketed his mouth. "My father would get a kick out of it." DeMarcus nodded toward her door. "You should go in. It's getting late."

What didn't he want her to know? Should she press him or shelve her curiosity for another day?

Jaclyn unlocked her door. The lights she kept on in her entryway masked the house's emptiness. It was a noticeable contrast from DeMarcus's home. "Thank you again for dinner and for seeing me home. I hope to hear good news from you tomorrow."

His eyes creased at the corners. "Good night."

She entered her grandfather's house under DeMarcus's careful regard, locking the door behind her.

Unease shadowed Jaclyn as she climbed the stairs to her bedroom. Even if DeMarcus agreed to coach the Monarchs, would she be able to keep the team in Brooklyn? And would her growing attraction to the former NBA superstar and his dimples further complicate the situation?

DeMarcus found his father reading in the sitting room. "Are you waiting up for me?"

Julian gave his son a skeptical look. "Why? You're not sixteen anymore." His father closed the hardcover novel he'd been reading. "Are you going to coach the Monarchs?"

Trust his father to get right to the point.

DeMarcus settled into the matching armchair. His mother's chair. "Should I?"

"It's your decision."

DeMarcus pushed out of the soft armchair and wandered across the room. The days were getting shorter. Long, evening shadows protected the view of the neighborhood from the sitting room window. "I'm risking my reputation if the team continues to lose."

His father snorted. "No matter what happens, no one will take away your awards. You've earned them."

DeMarcus turned from the window, shoving his hands into the front pockets of his black warm-up pants. "Those are things. What about my image? I've built a name as a winner. What happens to that if I coach the team to another losing season?"

Julian shook his head. "It doesn't matter what other people think. At the end of the day, all that matters is what you think."

"But what do *you* think?"

"Listen to your gut. It hasn't failed you yet."

"Why won't you give me your opinion?"

"You aren't sixteen anymore."

DeMarcus scrubbed a hand over his face. In his mind, he held the image of Jaclyn's cinnamon eyes sparkling with the light of the street lamp outside her mansion. His shoulders tensed. "I can't guarantee her a winning season."

"Did Jackie ask for a guarantee?"

"No."

"If you take the job, do your best. That's all anyone can expect from you and all you can expect of yourself."

DeMarcus's chuckle was dry. He perched on the edge of the bay window's shelf. "I remember that lecture from my years at basketball summer camp. You and Mom gave me some version of that speech before every game."

Julian put the novel on the small table between the two armchairs and settled further into the overstuffed brown cushions. "The philosophy was right then, and it's right now."

"But Jack needs a winning season."

Julian cocked his head. "That responsibility wouldn't be just on you. It's on the entire coaching staff, the players and the front office."

"That's what I told her." DeMarcus straightened off the window shelf. He propped his hands on his hips and studied the gleaming hardwood floor. "I can coach her team, but she has to keep Gerry and Bert out of trouble."

"Can she?"

DeMarcus looked up. He couldn't read Julian's expression. He had a lot riding on this decision. Whatever he chose to do, he didn't want the outcome to reflect badly on his family's name. "I don't know. What should I do?"

Julian arched a brow. "If you decide to coach the Monarchs, you'll give the team your best effort. But no one could blame you if you decide not to. The front office is in disarray."

"Jack called it dysfunctional."

"That, too."

"I wish I knew whether we could win." DeMarcus sighed. "The Monarchs have taken all the losing they can stand. It's time to put up some *W*'s."

"Sometimes winning isn't determined on the scoreboard."

DeMarcus's brows knitted. His father was doing his *Star Wars* Obi-Wan Kenobe impersonation again. "What does that mean?"

"As far as the community is concerned, a winning season means the Monarchs stay in Brooklyn."

DeMarcus blew out a breath. "I can't guarantee that, either."

Jaclyn rubbed her eyes. That annoying noise was her cell phone ringing beside her. She checked the clock on her home laptop. It was almost ten o'clock at night. Who was that? She saved the client summary she was drafting and picked up the phone. She didn't recognize the number. Great. "Hello?"

"Jack, it's Marc Guinn. I hope I'm not calling too late."

Her mind spun, trying to anticipate the reason for his call. Had she left something in his car? At his home, perhaps? And why was he calling her Jack? "It's not too late. What can I do for you?"

A heavy sigh. "I'll coach the Monarchs, but on one condition."

Her grip tightened around the slim, black metal phone. "What's that?"

"I want a one-year contract. At the end of the year, we'll reevaluate the situation and decide whether we want to continue the agreement."

Jaclyn wanted to do back flips across her cramped and cluttered home office. Instead, she swallowed a primeval scream of victory and responded with admirable calm. "That's fair."

She closed the client summary—it could wait—and opened the electronic file of DeMarcus's employment contract. "I'll e-mail the new contract language to you in the morning. If you still agree to the terms, Gerry, Bert and I will sign it tomorrow."

"Fine. Then I'll be in the office Wednesday." His tone was resolute, determined. Sexy.

Jaclyn hesitated. "That's tomorrow. You don't want to wait until you get the revised contract?"

"I don't have time to wait. Preseason starts in twelve days, October fourth."

Jaclyn wanted to pump her fist. The team had a coach committed to winning. She had an ally to help her save the franchise. Her joy had nothing to do with DeMarcus's coal black eyes, chiseled chin or the dimples that creased his cheeks when he smiled. She wouldn't dwell on his lack of experience. That would come. For now, she'd focus on his drive and dedication.

"Thank you, Marc. I appreciate your giving us another chance." Jaclyn didn't care if DeMarcus heard her relief. He'd just given her the best news she'd had in years.

"I can't guarantee a winning season."

She recognized concern in his voice. "All I'm asking is that you try. The team can win. I know we can. We just need someone as committed to the season as we are."

"You've got that. I hate to lose. I really hate to lose, even more than I love to win." His chuckle was self-deprecating.

"We have that in common, then. I'll call you in the morning."

"Good night, Jack."

Jaclyn hesitated. "Jack?"

"It suits you, don't you think?"

"No. I don't."

He chucked a low, wicked sound that did things to her. "I do." He ended the call.

Jaclyn glanced down at her B-cups. "Not hardly."

She touched her cellular screen to disconnect the call. Jaclyn closed her eyes. She wasn't alone anymore. Someone else was willing to help keep her grandfather's dream alive. Now, she needed to keep her end of the bargain and make sure Gerald and Albert didn't stand in their way.

6

"I convinced Marc Guinn to stay on as head coach. His only requirement is that we alter his contract term to a one-year commitment." Jaclyn shifted forward in the guest chair opposite Gerald Bimm's desk— soon to be her desk—Wednesday morning. She gave him the revised contract. DeMarcus had already e-mailed his approval. They were both early risers.

Gerald's incredulous look passed from the contract lying on his desk to Jaclyn and back. "How did you change his mind?"

Jaclyn settled into the green-cushioned chair and crossed her legs. "A better question is, why didn't you contact me as soon as Marc resigned?"

Gerald scanned the first two pages of the five-page document. "I knew you hadn't wanted him in the first place."

Jaclyn gripped the arms of her chair but kept her voice cool. "The regular season starts in a month, Gerry. The team needs a head coach."

Gerald shrugged as he finished scanning the contract. "Oscar isn't doing a bad job as interim."

The careless words put Jaclyn's teeth on edge. "Oscar Clemente is a good offensive strategist for the Monarchs and has been for well over a decade. But he knows he doesn't have the strategic mind a head coach needs."

"Well, you've got Marc back." Gerald smirked. "It seems like the only thing that changed is the length of the contract."

"I'll stop by Tipton's Fashionwear to get Bert's signature this afternoon."

Gerald folded the document to the final page and signed his name with a flourish. "We're back in business." He handed the papers to Jaclyn.

Jaclyn checked to make sure Gerald had both signed and printed his name. "Almost."

He grinned, satisfied and confident. "What else can I do for you?"

Jaclyn smoothed the hot pink silk skirt over her knee. Her gaze roamed the office before coming back to him. Gerald had removed everything her grandfather had displayed when this office had belonged to him. Nothing remained of Franklin Jones—or the Monarchs. "I'm ready to assume my position as Monarchs general manager."

"That's wonderful, Jackie. How soon were you planning on starting?" Gerald's lips curved into a stiff smile. His eyes looked through her.

Jaclyn sensed his mind churning. What was he up to?

"Now. Althea Gentry, my executive assistant at Jonas and Prather, has already sent an e-mail to the organization announcing the management change."

Was that panic that flashed in Gerald's brown eyes? He spun his red leather throne toward his computer monitor. A few key strokes called up his e-mail system.

Jaclyn couldn't see his messages, but she could read his reaction. Gerald was unhappy.

The traitor wheeled his chair to face her again. His eyes were stormy. "This announcement is sudden, Jackie. I wish you'd given me the courtesy of an advance notice."

Was he kidding? "Like the advance notice you gave me before you contacted the Empire owners' lawyers to discuss breaking the contract?" Jaclyn smacked her right palm against her forehead. "Oh, that's right. You didn't notify me in advance. I found out from the lawyers."

Gerald narrowed his eyes. "Is that what this is about? Revenge? That's petty, Jackie."

"This has nothing to do with revenge. I'm trying to save the organization."

"By going behind my back and having your law firm assistant e-mail a message about the management change? Nessa could have sent the announcement. You didn't have to go outside of the organization."

"As your assistant, Nessa's loyalty is to you. That's one of the reasons Althea will work with me. I need someone whose loyalty won't be torn."

Gerald's eyes sparked with irritation. "What will happen to Nessa?"

Jaclyn suspected his concern was more for himself than for his secretary's livelihood. "She can continue to support you. If she has time, she also can help with other administrative duties."

Gerald's gaze iced over. "This is bullshit."

"No, Gerry. It's business." She enjoyed turning his words back to him.

"Are you doing this because Bert and I want to

move the team out of Brooklyn? What do you have against that plan?"

Jaclyn sat forward in her seat. "Why would you want to separate the franchise from its community?"

"Oh, I don't know. Maybe to make money?" His voice rose. Her business partner was losing his cool. "The Monarchs aren't a nonprofit organization. If we had a bigger market share, we'd make more money."

Jaclyn's pulse kicked into overdrive. "We were profitable before you and Bert started making colossally ignorant decisions that dropped our team into the league's basement and cost us revenue."

Gerald sneered. "Oh, that's right. You and Frank were the only ones who knew anything about basketball. How could I have forgotten that?"

Confusion blunted her anger. Where had Gerald's resentment come from? Why hadn't she seen it before? "We never said that. But your decision to relocate the Monarchs has to do with more than just money. What are you really after, Gerry?"

"Money is at the root of everything, Jackie."

"Have you received inquiries from other markets? Have you heard from anyone in Nevada?"

"No."

The hesitation was brief, but it was there. Jaclyn didn't know whether to believe him. Her heart sank. "Have you approached anyone in Nevada?"

Gerald sat back in his chair. He picked up his pen and rolled it between the fingers of both hands. "We're still compiling our wish list. These things take time. There's a lot to consider when you're selecting a new home for your franchise."

Every word was a blade punched into her heart. Despite her upbringing to respect her elders, Jaclyn didn't think she'd hated anyone as much as she hated Gerald in that moment. From the look in his eyes, the feeling was mutual. "Just remember, Gerry. A franchise decision this big, which impacts so many members of the Monarchs family, requires a unanimous vote, and there's no way on God's green earth you'll get mine."

"Bert and I are committed to this move, so unless you buy the franchise outright, you won't have a choice. And, at the end of the year, you'll lose the Empire."

"Your uncle must be turning in his grave. You have no regard for the legacy he helped build."

"I do appreciate his legacy. It will make me a very rich man."

Jaclyn rose from the chair. "I'm moving into this office after lunch today."

Gerald barely glanced at his gold Rolex. "That doesn't give me much time."

Jaclyn arched a brow. "Do you need help?"

Gerald studied her face for several silent moments. "An excellent idea. I'll get Nessa to help me."

Anger carried Jaclyn to the door. "As long as you're gone before I return."

DeMarcus took the seat opposite the Monarchs' assistant coach at the small oak conference table. Oscar Clemente either had somewhere else to be or he was timing their meeting. Since he'd entered DeMarcus's office, the former interim head coach had checked his black wristwatch three times.

DeMarcus laid the printout of the team's roster on the table's surface. "I want to meet with each assistant coach individually to discuss issues they may have with the team."

Oscar's intense dark stare stayed steady on his. "OK."

DeMarcus waited, expecting Oscar to say more. "Since you were the interim head coach, I want to hear your impressions first."

"Appreciate it."

With their gazes locked, it became a battle of wills. Who would look away first? Oscar shifted his ample bulk in the black-cushioned chair. His eyes never wavered. What was the assistant coach trying to read in DeMarcus's mind?

DeMarcus finally spoke. "What's wrong with the team?"

"It's losing."

DeMarcus tightened his jaw. The pissing contest had officially started. "Speak your mind."

Oscar didn't blink. "Heard you were hired to lose."

For a franchise that didn't have any leaks, a lot of people were asking about this rumor. He'd have to talk with the media executive about that. "Your source is wrong."

"Yeah?" Oscar didn't sound convinced. His Brooklyn accent and attitude were in full display. If DeMarcus was going to work with the other man, he'd have to show him that the fifteen years he'd spent in South Florida hadn't softened him.

DeMarcus leaned back in his chair. He gave his assistant coach a cool look. "Does being passed over bother you?"

The big man bristled. "I don't want that job."

"No?" He matched Oscar's insolence.

"Hell, no. You think I want this cluster—" Oscar bit

off the obscenity. The few gray hairs circling his round, pink pate stood on end. "Gerry doesn't know what he's doing. Bert can't wipe his ass without Gerry, and Jackie doesn't give a shit. I wouldn't take your job on a bet."

"Then why do you stay?" He really wanted to know.

"Because Frank Jones was one of the greatest men who ever breathed." Oscar's reply was just short of a roar.

How about that? DeMarcus considered the coach's glowering brown eyes. This hostile stranger and his genial father had in common an admiration for the Monarchs' cofounder. Sports really was the great equalizer.

DeMarcus raised his right ankle to his left knee. Now to diffuse the situation. "You're wrong, you know."

"About what?" Oscar flushed a deeper shade of pink. His rounded features quivered with rage.

"Jack cares a lot."

The coach strained forward in his seat, still on the attack. "Then why did she allow her grandfather's team to go to shit?"

DeMarcus flinched. Why should Oscar's assault on Jaclyn's work affect him? Hadn't he accused her of the same thing? Somehow that was different. "Her grandfather's death knocked her off balance, probably more than she'd even realized. And she trusted Gerry and Bert."

Oscar grunted. "That was her first mistake."

"She knows that now."

The assistant coach gave him a speculative look. "Yeah?"

"Yeah."

Oscar glowered a bit longer. "What's she going to do about it?"

"Win."

The coach barked a laugh. "With *you?*"

Not a ringing endorsement. "With *us.*"

"You were a hell of a player. What makes you think you can coach?"

"You'll see." DeMarcus was getting used to the insolence. "So, what's wrong with the team?"

Oscar grunted again. "The first thing you have to do is get them to act like a team instead of thirteen separate egos."

"*I* have to do?" It was a test. He knew it and Oscar knew it. The sooner Oscar accepted that this experiment would be a team from the top down, the better. DeMarcus kept his gaze steady.

"*We* have to do." The acceptance was grudging, but it came.

The office of the president and chief executive officer of Tipton's Fashionwear resembled a family sitting room. Jaclyn eased into one of the two overstuffed, yellow and blue armchairs bracketing a round mahogany coffee table. Albert Tipton Jr. sat in the other. The matching sofa crouched across the room. Family photos placed on the tops of file cabinets, bookcases and corner tables carried her back in time. She and her grandfather had attended those parties, graduations, weddings and baptisms.

Jaclyn tapped into those memories as she faced Albert. "How's Cheryl? She's a sophomore at Georgetown now, isn't she?" She sipped her coffee as she studied Albert's friendly, open features. Gray hairs scattered among the tight black curls along his temples. He was only a few years older than her father would have been if he'd lived.

Albert beamed as she'd known he would. His eyes moved to the photos on his desk. "Yes, she is. She's majoring in business with a minor in design. Going to take over her old man's company."

His voice sang with pride as he continued to boast the accomplishments of the youngest of his four children.

Jaclyn strained against the bittersweet feelings. "That's wonderful, Bert, that your daughter would want to continue your family business."

A flush highlighted Albert's cocoa cheekbones. "Yes, it is. I'm very proud of her."

"I'm sure that's what she wants. For you to be proud of her, the same way I want my grandfather to be proud of me."

Albert's smile wavered. He lowered his coffee cup from his mouth. "Frank *was* proud of you, Jackie."

Her breathing quickened as though she'd sprinted across the basketball court in hot pursuit of an opponent. "I don't think so, Bert. My grandfather entrusted me with his franchise, his dream. And, while I was wallowing in self-pity after his death, you and Gerry have been destroying it."

Albert's lips parted as though her attack surprised him. His reaction was understandable. In the past, she'd been deferential toward the elder partners. Today, the gloves were off.

Albert's eyes darkened with confusion. "We're not trying to destroy the Monarchs. We want to improve the franchise by finding a bigger market for it. We need to move the team to a state where we won't have to compete with another franchise for market shares."

"I've negotiated contracts for years with Jonas and Prather. Do you know what I've noticed over my career?"

"What?"

"When people parrot other people, they don't sound sure of themselves. That's because they're expressing someone else's decision."

A spark of anger straightened Albert's back. "I'm not parroting Gerry."

Jaclyn crossed her legs. "Do the math, Bert. There are more than eight million people in New York City. Almost two-and-a-half million of them live here in Brooklyn. The Empire Arena only seats twenty thousand ticket holders. How much of a market share do we need?"

Albert stared into his coffee. "We aren't filling the arena."

Jaclyn eased her grip on the fragile cup, afraid she'd crush it and stain her russet-heather sweater dress with Folgers's breakfast blend. "You're not going to automatically fill an arena once you move the team."

"We need to fill the arena."

Albert's tone told Jaclyn he was sticking to the script Gerald had given him. "Then help me rebuild the team." She pushed herself to the edge of her seat. "The best way to fill the arena is to win. The fans came when we were winning."

Albert shifted in his chair. "Gerry said you'd have an emotional reaction to our decision to move the team. But, Jackie, this is business. Our fathers would agree with us."

Jaclyn blinked. Did he really believe that? "Why?"

Albert frowned as though he didn't understand her question. "Because we'll bring in more money."

She could hear her pulse beating in her ears. "Our families didn't start the Monarchs to become rich. The franchise is for the community. Neighborhoods in this area were dying. Businesses were failing. When the Monarchs started playing, people came back. Jobs came back. Kids who grew up here returned to raise their own families in their neighborhood."

Albert gripped his coffee cup like a shield. "If the neighborhood starts to struggle again, someone else will help."

Shock stole her thoughts. "Someone else? What would your father think if he could hear you?"

What could she say to reach him? What could she do? He didn't have the connection to the community that his father or her grandfather had had. If he did, he wouldn't leave the neighborhood to others to help. He wouldn't move the Monarchs.

Albert flushed. "I'm sorry, Jackie."

Frustration threaded her words. "How much money do you need? How much is enough for you?"

Albert shifted in his seat. "It's not just the money. I'm tired of having to worry about the team as well."

Jaclyn gripped her coffee cup between her palms. "Then sell your shares to me."

Albert shook his head. "I promised Gerry I wouldn't."

That caught her off guard. "Why not?"

"He said having three partners keeps us honest. Otherwise, it would just be you and him butting heads all the time."

In other words, Gerald wanted to keep Albert as his puppet and force Jaclyn to divide her attention and energy between the two of them. Clever.

She settled back into the thickly padded chair. "If the solution to keeping the franchise in Brooklyn is to fill the arena, then I expect your support in bringing the fans back."

Albert returned his gaze to her. "What do you mean?"

"If we're going to increase attendance, we have to win. So I expect your support for the personnel and marketing decisions I make to help turn the team around."

Albert frowned. "I saw the e-mail message announcing you're the GM now. But the franchise doesn't have much money."

"I know. Gerry spent the franchise's money as though it was his own. I'll have to put us on a stricter budget and get creative."

"Is that why you replaced Gerry?"

"Gerry's interim term was over." Jaclyn stood, setting her half-empty cup on the small coffee table. "Can I expect your support?"

Albert's smile didn't mask the unease in his inky eyes. "Of course, Jackie."

Jaclyn turned to leave. "I'm glad to hear it." Even if she didn't believe it.

She knocked this time. DeMarcus looked around to see Jaclyn standing in his office threshold. Her fist was still raised and resting on his door. The bright orange dress followed her slender curves. Her smile and that dress lit up his office like a bolt of lightning.

She waved a stack of papers in her left hand as she strode into his office. "I have your revised contract. Gerry, Bert and I have signed it."

DeMarcus stood, reaching for the documents she

extended to him. He caught a whiff of lilacs and inhaled again. "That was fast."

Her lips parted in a teasing grin. "I didn't want to give you a chance to change your mind."

DeMarcus caught the sparkle in her cinnamon eyes. Disarming. Where was the woman who'd wanted to rip him a new one two days ago? He gestured toward the three black guest chairs between them. "Do you have time to wait while I sign these?"

"I believe I do. I'm just upstairs now." Jaclyn swayed around the chair to slip onto the seat.

DeMarcus sat. "How did Gerry take your e-mail reclaiming your GM position?"

Jaclyn crossed her long legs. She swung her shapely right calf to an idle beat only she could hear. "I've learned that Gerry doesn't believe in confrontations. I'm sure he's planning a sneak attack. You should watch for those, too."

DeMarcus shrugged his eyebrows. "Thanks for the warning. You're in the office starting today?"

Jaclyn nodded. "Close at hand to lend managerial support."

He dropped his gaze to the contract. Her response sent a dangerous shot of heat to his stomach. The words in the document finally pulled into focus. Jaclyn grew still as he reviewed the new contract. He couldn't block out her presence, though. He doubted any man could.

He signed his name to both copies and returned one to her. "Thanks for revising the contract."

Jaclyn relaxed into the armchair. "I'm glad we were able to find a suitable compromise. How are things going today?"

DeMarcus propped his right ankle onto his left knee. "I met with Oscar Clemente this morning."

Jaclyn's eyes sparkled with mirth. "How did that go?"

"Is it true he doesn't want the head coaching job?"

"Absolutely." She didn't hesitate.

"How do you know?"

"Gerry offered it to him twice. Oscar stopped taking Gerry's calls."

DeMarcus's eyes widened. "He stopped taking a franchise owner's calls?"

Jaclyn's lips twitched with a persistent smile. "Oscar doesn't like to repeat himself. Be sure to listen the first time."

DeMarcus absorbed that. It was a lot to take in. "Why do you keep him?"

Jaclyn freed her smile. "Some people find Oscar difficult to deal with. But he has a brilliant offensive mind and he's passionate about the team."

She was loyal to the assistant coach. It was in her words, in her voice, in her smile. DeMarcus couldn't look away from that smile. If it ever came down to a choice between him or Oscar, DeMarcus was sure the man who could make her smile like that would win.

He put that thought aside. "I met with all of the coaches and the trainers. They're good, but they're not excited about the new season. There's no energy or enthusiasm."

"That's what I was talking about Monday. We've assumed a culture of losing. They expect losses now. So what is there to get excited about?"

"They don't have to be happy about the season, but I expect them to be excited about their jobs."

Jaclyn shook her head. Her shiny brown curls bounced around her head and shoulders. "We need them to be enthusiastic about both. We need the whole organization to be excited. The Monarchs season isn't a job. It's a quest for the championship. And that quest starts with you."

DeMarcus lowered his right leg from his left knee. "Preseason starts in eleven days. The regular season starts in four weeks. I don't have time to do some pep squad routine while Oscar tightens up the defense."

Jaclyn propped an elbow on the chair's arm and shrugged. "Managing personalities—of the coaches as well as the players—is an important part of managing the game. And, by the way, Oscar's weak on defense."

"No one's ever managed my personality."

"There's a lot to manage."

Her tone was solemn, but DeMarcus caught the twinkle in her eye. Was she flirting with him? The idea piqued his interest. "We need to improve our speed and get back to basics."

"Just remember the goal, Marc." Jaclyn stood. "We have to get to the postseason. We need those ticket sales to stay in the Empire."

DeMarcus stood as well. He watched her smooth the sweater-like material of her dress and almost swallowed his tongue. "I'll get us to the postseason. You keep us in the arena."

Jaclyn smiled. "In other words, I should stick to the front office and leave the coaching to you. I know a thing or two about what it takes to win basketball games, too."

"I've got all the assistant coaches I need."

Jaclyn turned to leave. "We'll see how the season goes. If we're not winning, prepare to watch Dr. Phil's show."

7

The Monarchs roster no longer boasted marquee players. DeMarcus had known that stepping into his role. Thirteen men sprawled before him on the bleachers of the Monarchs' training facility Thursday morning. They were NBA veterans several seasons past their glory days. The notable exception was a young rookie whose headstrong attitude had kept him from being a high pick in the 2011 draft.

DeMarcus continued his preseason speech despite his certainty no one was listening. Still his words echoed off the court, coming back to him. "We're going back to fundamentals—footwork, shooting, rebounds. Every time we touch the ball, we need to score."

He was interrupted as footsteps squeaked against the hardwood. Barron Douglas sauntered toward him. The point guard's oversized black T-shirt hung past his hips. It bared tattoos extending like sleeves down his dark brown arms to his wrists. Baggy, black nylon shorts, a match to his teammates', skimmed his knees. His wraparound black sunglasses and silver chains weren't regulation. A rebel. Every team had at least one. How did this one become captain?

DeMarcus inhaled a calming breath as well as the faint scent of floor wax from the high-gloss court. "Barron. Nice to finally meet you."

The six-foot-five player stopped and jerked his chin upward in greeting. "Coach." Barron shoved his sunglasses to the top of his head, balancing them on his thick cornrows. "You can call me Bling."

Great. They were bonding. Jaclyn would be pleased. "What time is it, Barron?"

Barron lifted his left wrist to read his watch. De-Marcus caught the play of light off the wide silver band. Was the point guard going to practice with that Wonder Woman wristband on his arm? Basketball was a contact sport. His teammates wouldn't want to get anywhere near that silver cuff.

Barron stared at the watch as he read the time aloud. "It's almost eleven-thirty, Coach."

"Practice starts at eleven. The schedule's been the same for the four years you've been here." DeMarcus took note of Barron's bloodshot eyes. How late had the guard gone to bed and how inebriated had he been?

The Monarchs' captain relaxed into a cocky pose. "I had stuff to do."

"Like getting to practice on time."

"Whatever, man." Barron passed DeMarcus without another word or look.

DeMarcus tracked the captain's progress over the bleachers. "I'm docking your pay."

Barron turned to DeMarcus. "That's bullshit."

DeMarcus shrugged. "You don't want to be fined? Get to practice on time."

Barron stomped to a seat, grumbling under his breath.

DeMarcus addressed the other players. "That goes for all of you. Get to practice on time and be prepared to give me one hundred and ten percent. Every practice and every workout we do is for June."

"For June?" Anthony Chambers, the starting forward, grinned. His dark olive eyes twinkled in his fair skin. His rounded natural was a 1970s throwback. "You mean the championship?"

"Yes." DeMarcus's tone was meant to squelch any humor. Anthony didn't get the message.

The forward laughed. "Man, have you seen our record? We haven't had a winning season in three years. We don't have a prayer of even making the play-offs."

DeMarcus paced closer to the bleachers, where Anthony sat four rows up. "You're laughing at the *idea* of making the play-offs? That's funny to you?"

Anthony's grin faded to uncertainty. "No, Coach. It's not funny."

DeMarcus turned to Barron. "Wins don't just happen. You have to work for them. Are you telling me you're not going to work this season?"

Barron glanced arond. His movements were sluggish. "You know that's not what I'm saying."

Serge Gateau, the team's six-foot-ten-inch forward, raised his hand. The Frenchman from Lourdes wore his dark blond hair pulled straight back in a shoulder-length ponytail. His lean, square features were clean-shaven and earnest.

DeMarcus inclined his head. "Yes, Serge?"

"I would like for you to trade me." Even after ten

years in the league, his accent still heavily inflected his words.

DeMarcus studied the faces of the men he'd be spending the next seven months with—nine, if they made the championship. Long months of physical and emotional strain. He'd spoken to the team for almost twenty minutes about his goal for their season. In response, he'd received laughter, distain and a request to be traded.

DeMarcus returned his attention to Serge. "This isn't the time or the place for this conversation."

Serge's blue eyes widened. "*Merde.* That I want to be traded, this is not a secret."

DeMarcus was decades away from high school French, but he was fairly sure *merde* was not a polite word. "We're not going to trade you, Serge, and—"

Jamal Ward, the rookie with the attitude, sprang to his feet. He stroked his hand over his freshly shaven head. "If you're going to talk about players who stay or start, I'm going on record that Jam-On-It is not a sixth man. I'm not coming off the bench."

At nineteen years of age, the wiry, six-foot-five-inch shooting guard was well on his way to challenging Barron "Bling" Douglas for most body paint in the league.

Jamal hadn't taken even one pass in an NBA game but was declaring himself a starter. They'd have something to talk about if he'd been a top draft pick. The muscles in DeMarcus's shoulders bunched. He scanned the faces of the coaches, players and trainers observing the meeting. They regarded the brash shooting guard with either disbelief or disinterest.

"Sit down, rookie." DeMarcus watched the younger man hesitate before complying. "You don't *claim* a starting position. You *earn* it." He repositioned his gaze to the twelve other men who finally seemed to hear his words. "That's right. You may have started last season. But if you want to start this season, you'll have to earn it. And we're going to the finals, Monarchs. We're going to play for the championship. If you aren't willing to put in the work, you can ride the bench."

They all thought he'd lost his mind. DeMarcus could tell by the looks on their faces. Maybe he had. He'd do whatever it took to bring his father the trophy. This was about more than his competitive drive. It was about more than his ego. It was about finally repaying his parents for everything they'd sacrificed for him. Thanks to his parents, he'd proven himself a winner. He wasn't going to let this team make a loser out of him.

With his speech this morning, he'd set the course for them. But, to reach their destination, the coaches and players would have to row together. Right now, he couldn't see any of them picking up an oar.

If she could just ingest this cup of coffee, she'd make it through this Friday morning. She was sure of it. Jaclyn inhaled deeply as she filled her official Brooklyn Monarchs mug from the coffeepot in the franchise's kitchen.

The steam warmed her face. She took a long drink of the sweet, black beverage, then sighed. "Saved."

"Another late night?"

Jaclyn turned toward her assistant's voice. Althea Gentry looked neat and efficient in her chocolate coat dress. A gold, flower-shaped brooch pinned the red and brown checked scarf to her shoulder.

Jaclyn rested her hips against the kitchen counter and cradled her Cup o'Joe protectively in her palms. "I'm prepared for a series of them while I'm juggling my general manager responsibilities and wrapping up the client files for J and P."

Althea's sharp, black eyes darkened with worry. Her dark brown hair swung around her jawline as she shook her head. "I wish you'd waited the two weeks before taking your position with the Monarchs. It's too hard on you, doing two demanding jobs at once."

Truer words may never have been spoken. Jaclyn felt as though she'd been beaten like a rug and thrown into the street.

She straightened from the counter and wrapped her free arm around the much shorter woman's shoulders and led her from the kitchen. "Stop nagging. You know we talked about this. Gerry has done enough damage to the team already. More than enough. I couldn't wait two more weeks before stopping him."

"And how much good are you going to be either here or for Jonas and Prather with only two hours of sleep each night?" Althea's voice was heavy with concern.

"It's three hours. And this schedule won't last forever. All of my client files will be transferred by late next week. How are you managing the transition?"

"I'm fine. In fact, I can help you reassign your client files."

Jaclyn stopped, smiling at the twenty-something administrative assistant walking their way. "Hi, Nessa. How are you?"

Vanessa Klayer gave them a broad smile though her dark eyes remained wary. "Good morning, Ms. Jones."

Jaclyn dropped her arm from Althea's shoulders. "When did I become Ms. Jones? We've known each other since you started working here four years ago."

Vanessa's shoulders dropped and her smile relaxed. "I'm sorry, Jackie, I wasn't sure how you wanted us to address you."

Jaclyn swallowed more coffee. "The only thing that's changed is that I'm the general manager now, not my grandfather. And he asked everyone to call him Frank." She nodded toward her assistant. "Vanessa Klayer, I'd like you to meet Althea Gentry. Althea and I worked together at Jonas and Prather, my old law firm."

Vanessa's demeanor cooled as she extended her right hand. "Oh, you're my replacement."

"No, she isn't." Jaclyn kept her voice casual as she corrected Vanessa. "You're Gerry's assistant. Althea's mine."

Vanessa's gaze shifted between Jaclyn and Althea. "Oh, I see."

Jaclyn hoped the younger woman did in fact see. "By the way, Nessa, who do the Monarchs play for the first game of the preseason?"

Vanessa's eyes widened. "I don't know, but I can find out for you."

"That's OK. It's the Washington Wizards. I hope you watch the game." Jaclyn walked on.

Althea caught up with her. "What was that all about?"

"My grandfather made sure everyone knew the Monarchs' schedule. He's only been gone two seasons, but I bet Nessa's not the only one who couldn't name the team's first preseason opponent. She probably doesn't know which college our draft pick, Jamal Ward, attended, either."

Althea frowned. "I thought you didn't want that player."

"That's a different story." Jaclyn marched into her office and across the silver carpet. She settled into her ergonomically correct, black executive chair. She'd had Facilities remove Gerald's red throne. "I want the entire franchise to memorize the Monarchs' schedule. The games aren't just about the players. Everyone should support the team."

Althea smoothed her scarf. "Vanessa was interesting."

Jaclyn swung her attention to Althea's change of subject. She gave her friend a crooked smile. "You make understatement an art."

"Flattery got me to take this position. Now I want to know exactly what the situation is."

Jaclyn leaned into her desk, folding her hands together. She put into words her fears and dread. "I need someone with me whom I can trust."

Althea grew still. Her thin black brows knitted. "You're a franchise owner. You've known everyone here for years. Why do you think you can't trust them?"

Tension crept into Jaclyn's shoulders. She sipped more coffee. It was growing cold. "I don't know who I can or can't trust. I've removed the snake from the Empire. But I have a feeling Gerry's cultivated loyalties among the staff, people who would tell him what I'm doing."

Althea's jaw dropped. "I can't believe that. I'd never betray my employer's confidence."

"I know. That's why I asked you to come work with

me." Jaclyn sensed the other woman's continued unease. "Gerry and Bert caught me off guard with their plans to relocate the Monarchs. I don't want them to find out what I'm doing to prevent that."

"What are you doing?"

Jaclyn sat back in her chair, trying to relax. "The finance department ran the numbers for me yesterday. Merchandising sales have more than doubled, and preseason ticket sales are up almost fifty percent. I underestimated the welcome our fans would give their prodigal son returning as the Monarchs' head coach."

Althea wagged her finger. "I told you so. Marc Guinn may not have played in New York, but he's from New York. And he's going into the Hall of Fame. He's going to raise the team's profile."

Jaclyn waved a hand. "Whatever the reason, let's hope the revenue continues to increase. It will give a healthy boost to the Empire's profit share and persuade them to keep us as tenants."

"The owners get rent plus profit share?"

"For ticket sales only. The profit share allows us to keep our rent low. At first, the arrangement worked in the owners' favor. Now it doesn't, which is the reason they want us out."

Althea smoothed the skirt of her dress. "So, you're meeting with the Empire owners' lawyers again?"

Jaclyn checked her watch. Her stomach knotted as she thought of the upcoming presentation. "I'm meeting with Gerry and Bert this morning to discuss the numbers. But, yes, this afternoon I have a meeting with Bonner and Taylor."

"Have you considered bypassing the lawyers and going straight to the owners?"

Jaclyn frowned. "That's not the way negotiations are done."

Althea shrugged a shoulder. "So? You have too much to lose to follow the rules. Remember, nice guys—or girls—finish last."

"Dorothy Parker?" Jaclyn enjoyed guessing the source of the quotes Althea frequently used. She was usually wrong.

"Leo Durocher, former Brooklyn Dodgers manager."

Jaclyn watched her friend and assistant stride from her office. Althea had worked for the Monarchs less than a day, but already she was using sports references. Another Monarchs fan converted. Jaclyn smiled. Cool.

Gerald and Albert were waiting for Jaclyn in one of the Monarchs' smaller conference rooms. They grew quiet as her three-inch stilettos tapped across the threshold. What had they been talking about? Jaclyn clenched her teeth. She wouldn't give in to crippling paranoia.

She noted the blush in Albert's cheeks and the tightness around his mouth. Strain. He'd adjusted his red and blue patterned tie and unbuttoned his conservative navy blue suit jacket. What was bothering him?

"Good morning, gentlemen." Satisfaction warmed her when her steps didn't falter.

Gerald had taken the chair at the head of the small rectangular mahogany conference table. It was the position of power in any meeting. It was a good offensive strategy, making sure to keep her on the defensive.

Jaclyn's stilettos tapped across the silver-tiled floor as she circled the table, handing both men copies of the report the finance department had generated. She then sank into the seat opposite Gerald.

Gerald smirked. His ruby knit crewneck sweater warmed his mocha skin and made his beady eyes and wavy hair look even darker. "I hope you're not going to make a habit of calling these last-minute meetings, Jackie. You have to get organized."

Jaclyn returned Gerald's gaze without reaction. How could her father have formed a friendship with anyone from Gerald's family?

"Thanks for the tip, Gerry." She folded her arms on the table in front of her. "The report I just shared with you shows the income from franchise merchandising and ticket sales. As of yesterday—September twenty-fourth—our profits are almost double last September's revenue."

Albert's mouth relaxed into a smile. He flipped through the report, stopping at the summary sheet. "This is great news. What do you think caused it?"

"Our decision to hire Marc Guinn as the Monarchs' head coach, of course." Gerald's tone was as dry as an emery board.

"That does appear to be the main influence on the increased sales." Jaclyn always gave credit where it was due, just as her grandfather had taught her.

Albert nodded at Gerald, chuckling. "Then I'm glad we pushed for him."

"So am I," Jaclyn agreed. They had no idea how much.

Gerald's penetrating stare attempted to read her

mind. "You didn't want to hire him at first. What made you change your mind?"

Jaclyn returned Gerald's gaze. "The numbers speak for themselves. Hopefully, the increased sales will continue."

Gerald skimmed his right index finger down the report. "Ticket sales are still lagging. The Empire still won't be full."

Jaclyn turned to the report summary. "We'll be close. It's a beginning. If this sales rate continues, we'll be up more than sixty-five percent once the regular season starts."

"That's incredible." Albert's demeanor was much more upbeat than it had been in months.

Jaclyn smiled at him. "I'm hoping these numbers will convince the Empire owners to give us a grace period, at least one more season, to stay here."

Gerald laid the report in front of him on the small conference table. "Bert and I aren't going to stay here another year."

Jaclyn turned to Albert. "What do you say, Bert? Do you want a grace period to stay in the Empire another season?"

Albert's puzzled gaze bounced from Gerald to Jaclyn, then down the report. "I—"

Gerald cut off his partner's answer. "We've already been over this, Jackie. The Monarchs deserve their own market."

Jaclyn leaned into the conference table and enunciated. "Bert, what do you want to do?"

Albert's gaze wavered away from Gerald, dropping back to the report. "I want to do what's best for the team."

Jaclyn stayed on him. "What do you think is best for the team?"

Gerald spoke for him. "Moving to another market where it could have the limelight."

Jaclyn gritted her teeth. "This isn't about the Monarchs, Gerry. It's about you."

Gerald glared at her. "Are you calling me a liar?"

Jaclyn matched his tone. "If *you* want to move, move. But Brooklyn is the Monarchs' home."

"Says who?"

"Says me." Jaclyn dropped her hands to her lap and clenched her fists. She was allowing Gerald to shred her temper. She had to regain control.

Gerald sneered at her. "You're president and general manager of the Monarchs by virtue of carrying majority shares, *not* by virtue of your brains, obviously."

Her temper flew out the window. "Excuse me?"

"Stop it." Albert's low-voiced request barely registered to her.

"You're holding the Monarchs back." Gerald pointed his finger across the table toward her. "They'll never be a world-class organization as long as they're in the Knicks' shadow."

"How dare you." Jaclyn's voice trembled with the rage she'd just promised herself she'd hold on to. "Under your management, we lost top draft picks and quality coaches. Yet you have the audacity to blame me for the Monarchs' problems?"

"Jackie, please calm down." Albert spoke louder.

"Yes." Gerald sprang to his feet, continuing his condemnation. "You have the chance to make it better and you're not taking it."

Jaclyn rose for equal footing. "You think moving the team to Nevada would increase our revenue?"

"Yes." Gerald leaned toward her from his end of the table.

"How? The *state* of Nevada has less than three million people. The *city* of New York has almost four times that."

"But New York already has a basketball team." Gerald's voice raised another decibel.

Jaclyn stared at the angry partner as though she'd never seen him before. "What are you really trying to accomplish by moving the Monarchs?"

Albert surged out of his chair. "Stop it." His voice was loud, his tone angry. He glared from Jaclyn to Gerald and back again. "We all want the same thing— what's best for our families and the franchise. Why does every meeting turn into an argument?"

Jaclyn faced Gerald. "Do we want the same thing, Gerry?"

Gerald gave her a look of cold contempt. "No, we don't."

Albert pushed away from the table. "I have a business to run. In the future, Jackie, if you want to update us on our revenue and expenses, just e-mail the report to me. I can think of much better ways to spend my mornings." Vibrating with anger, he stormed from the office.

Gerald moved away from the table. At the doorway, he stopped, half turning to face Jaclyn. "Maybe Bert and I should just stand back and let you ruin your grandfather's legacy."

Jaclyn pushed her chair under the conference table and gripped its back. "We both know I'm not the one trying to destroy the Monarchs."

Gerald turned to leave. He hadn't even bothered to deny her accusation. What would be the point? She was right and he knew it. Jaclyn's knuckles burned from gripping her chair's back. Now what should she do?

8

The rhythmic *thump-thump-thum*p—the sweet cadence of a basketball kissing a court—led DeMarcus to Jaclyn's driveway. A waist-high, teak wood fence barred him from her backyard. DeMarcus didn't hesitate. He braced his arms on the fence and vaulted over. His sneakered feet landed on a paved walkway between the Jones's residence and a well-manicured lawn as lush as a deep green carpet.

Past the house, the walkway opened to a space half the size of a basketball court. The lawn bracketed the court's thick, shock-absorbing tile. Two strong maple trees stood guard on either side. And in the center of the setting was the source of the steady thumping.

Jaclyn dribbled an NBA-regulation basketball. The Lady Assassin charged the post. She was part modern dancer and part ruthless predator. Her slender arms worked the ball hard to the basket. She spun, dodged and weaved around imaginary opponents foolish enough to challenge her. A foot from her goal, she leaped into the air, arched her lithe body and slammed the ball through the net. She landed on her feet as graceful as a cat.

"Two points." DeMarcus applauded her game.

Jaclyn whipped around, eyes wide in the evening shadows. Her hand flew to her chest. "Good grief. You scared the life out of me."

DeMarcus took in Jaclyn's skimpy gray T-shirt darkened by sweat and the tiny black shorts baring never-ending legs. She'd gathered her riot of thick, inky curls to the top of her head and restrained them with one of those clip things. Without makeup, she looked like a co-ed, not the confident businesswoman who'd persuaded him to risk what he valued most.

He stepped forward. "I'm sorry. I didn't mean to startle you."

"How did you get back here?"

DeMarcus jerked a thumb over his shoulder. "I hopped the fence."

Jaclyn's gaze shifted to the walkway behind him, then back. "I need a taller fence. What are you doing here?"

"Elia said you'd wanted to talk to me." His executive secretary had implied Jaclyn had been upset when she'd asked to speak with him earlier.

Jaclyn retrieved the basketball. It had rolled to a stop a few feet from the post. "It could have waited for the morning. I didn't mean for you to go out of your way to see me."

Her voice was tense. He heard a hint of loneliness. Why was she out here tearing up the court?

DeMarcus tipped his head toward her regulation basketball hoop. "Who are you scoring on?"

"Gerry." She'd spat her partner's name.

This couldn't be good. "What has he done now?"

Jaclyn wiped the sweat from her eyes with the tips of her right fingers. "He's not interested in finding a larger market or raising more revenue for the Monarchs. He just wants to destroy us."

That was dramatic phrasing. "He said that?"

"He didn't deny it. That's why I came to see you earlier." Her shrug was self-conscious. "I wanted someone to talk to."

There was the source of the loneliness he'd heard earlier. DeMarcus glanced at her large house. With her grandfather gone, to whom did she turn? How lost would he feel if his father weren't there to confide in? DeMarcus wished he'd been there for her sooner. "Why would Gerry want to destroy the franchise?"

Jaclyn settled the ball on her hip. "Before my grandfather died, he warned me that I'd have to fight Gerry and Bert to save the Monarchs."

DeMarcus remembered her saying that before. "I don't understand."

"Neither did I, at first. But they don't have an emotional connection to the organization."

"Why is that important?" He didn't get the touchy-feely stuff Jaclyn was hung up on.

Confusion and fatigue dimmed her eyes. "If they cared about the franchise, they'd never dream of moving it. Bert's more interested in Tipton's Fashionwear. I understand that. *That's* his family's legacy. Not the team."

"What about Gerry?"

"He inherited his shares from his uncle. Apparently, he also inherited his uncle's resentment toward my family."

"Why?"

Jaclyn shrugged a shoulder, causing her T-shirt to

expose another inch of midriff. "I'm trying to figure that out. Basketball helps me think." She passed the ball to him. "Show me what you've got."

DeMarcus caught her sudden pass by reflex. He looked from his gray warm-up suit and white sneakers to her skimpy T-shirt and barely there shorts. Somehow a game of one-on-one with his sexy boss didn't seem like a good idea. "Sorry, I'm not up for a game."

She cocked a brow at him. "What are you afraid of, Guinn? Losing?"

Jaclyn caught her breath. The competitive spark that lit DeMarcus's coal black eyes at her challenge sent a charge through her blood. It heated her skin.

"You're on." DeMarcus sent the ball back to her. He crossed to her deck, shrugging out of his jacket. His white Reebok jersey was revealed underneath.

Jaclyn's attention dropped to his glutes. Retirement hadn't softened the former shooting guard. DeMarcus tossed his jacket onto her deck's railing. He turned back to her. Jaclyn jerked her gaze upward. His long legs brought him closer.

Her fingers pressed into the basketball. Its skin was rough beneath the pads of her fingers. Her heart pounded against her chest. She'd never dreamed she'd compete against the Mighty Guinn. During her three years in the WNBA, she'd matched up against numerous future Hall of Famers. But DeMarcus Guinn was different. In so many ways.

Jaclyn bounced the ball once. It snapped against the tiled court before returning to her. She spun it back to DeMarcus. "Show me what you've got." She balanced on her toes, ready to defend the basket.

DeMarcus stepped back as he dribbled the ball. "What are we going for?"

"Ten points with two-point baskets?"

He took her measure. What did he see? A woman? An athlete? His boss? What did she want him to see?

DeMarcus arched a brow. "Ten points? Is that the best you can do?"

Jaclyn grinned at his taunt. "It won't take me long to school you."

DeMarcus threw back his head and laughed. The sound was full, deep and just a little cocky. It strummed a chord—or two—in her lower abdomen. Jaclyn could listen to the sound forever.

Still grinning, DeMarcus drove to her right. Jaclyn favored her left side, forcing him back. She could smell him, spice and musk. The warmth of his body tempted her to relax into him. It wasn't easy to resist his appeal.

Jaclyn widened her stance, bent her knees and spread her arms to her sides. She danced with him as she guarded the perimeter. It was like confronting Mount Kilimanjaro.

DeMarcus stepped back, set his stance and leaped. The ball flew over her head. Nothing but net. "You thought you could school me? I just made honor roll."

Jaclyn hustled for the ball, keeping DeMarcus on her left. His movements were tentative as he tried to block her. She snatched the ball in mid bounce, spun and pitched it into the hoop. Two points. DeMarcus got the ball. Crowding him on her left side, Jaclyn forced his turnover. DeMarcus tried to circle her. With her elbows, Jaclyn kept him back. She bounced the ball twice, spun and stuffed the basket, doubling her lead. "I just sent you to detention."

DeMarcus caught the ball from under the basket. He dribbled it with him as he moved farther down the court. "I won't give up the valedictorian title that easily."

Jaclyn maintained the pressure, trying to steal the ball out from under him. She placed her hand on the small of his back. Through his white jersey, she felt his damp, hot skin. His muscles flexed under her palm as he moved, sending a current up her arm and into her breasts. Jaclyn stumbled back, losing focus.

DeMarcus spun, lifted the ball and aimed for the basket. He jumped—and Jaclyn's competitive motor restarted. She moved in and stretched with him. Her arm lifted to block his shot.

Their bodies brushed together, her breasts grazing his chest. Their gazes held for the longest second. The moment ended painfully as the basketball dropped onto her shoulder and bounced to the ground.

"Dammit." White light exploded before her eyes. Jaclyn landed on her feet.

DeMarcus reached for her, his expression stricken. "Are you all right?"

Returning to her senses, Jaclyn took advantage of DeMarcus's concern. She sprinted after the ball and drove to the basket. A hook shot lengthened her lead to 6 to 2. "I'm fine."

Laughing and shaking his head, DeMarcus grabbed the rebound. He dunked on her, bringing the competition to 6 to 4. He chased after the ball, but Jaclyn wasn't giving up her lead. She cut off his route to the basket. Planting her feet, she forced him to either give ground or go around her. DeMarcus tried to circle her strong right side. Jaclyn maneuvered him to her left. DeMarcus drew back. Quick as a wink, Jaclyn stole the ball. She sent a rainbow shot sailing through the net. She led, 8 to 4.

DeMarcus chased down the ball. Jaclyn followed, closer than his shadow. He claimed the ball a fingertip from her reach. Jaclyn guarded him as he tried to get free of the post. He feinted to his right, but Jaclyn anticipated his ploy and blocked him. He danced backward. Jaclyn waltzed with him. Her hand hovered just above his muscled back. No sense courting distraction again.

DeMarcus chuckled. "Your opponents must have cheered when you announced your retirement. You earned your nickname."

Jaclyn's heart floated. "That's high praise from the Mighty Guinn."

"I'm serious."

"I know." Jaclyn faked left, drawing DeMarcus to her right. She snatched the ball from him—and let it fly to the winning basket.

"Whoa!" DeMarcus shouted his approval. He turned toward her, applauding. "Good game."

"Thank you." Jaclyn took her eyes off the dimple in his left cheek and accepted his proffered hand. His grip was warm and firm. "Can I buy you a drink?"

The dimple deepened. "Yes, you can."

Jaclyn mounted the four steps of her cherrywood deck. DeMarcus grabbed his jacket from the railing and followed her. He tried not to notice the sway of her rounded hips beneath her short shorts.

A burst of pleasing spices drew his attention. DeMarcus moved to the deck's side railing and discovered rows of leafy plants set into a side garden. He smelled thyme, oregano and rosemary. "You grow your own herbs. Do you cook?"

Jaclyn's response came from behind him. "Yes, but not as well as you. Maybe we can work something out in your next contract."

DeMarcus tossed her a smile from over his shoulder. "You're barely paying me to coach. You definitely couldn't afford my cooking."

Jaclyn tried to look sad, but the laughter in her eyes betrayed her. "It was worth a try." She opened the back door, which led to a solarium. DeMarcus paused before the flat-screen television. He studied the entertainment center and scanned several titles on the bookcases.

Jaclyn crossed into the kitchen and gestured toward the ash wood table and four matching chairs in the center of the room. "Have a seat."

DeMarcus hung his jacket over one chair and sat in another. He scanned the stainless-steel appliances and gray and black marble counters. The décor was a sharp contrast of bright walls and dark accents, but he thought the patterns had more to do with the Monarchs team colors.

Jaclyn took two tall glasses from an ash wood cabinet. She filled them with ice from the refrigerator's ice maker and water from the filtered tap.

She offered him one of the glasses, then took the seat to his right at the head of the rectangular table. "Would you like to know how I beat you?"

DeMarcus gulped a mouthful of the cold water. It soothed his dry throat and cooled his heated body. "I think it was the shoes."

Jaclyn looked from his white sneakers to her silver and black cross-trainers. She swallowed more water. "Maybe. But you have half a foot and almost one hundred pounds on me. How did I beat you?"

DeMarcus recognized the line from the science fiction movie *The Matrix*. Had she quoted it on purpose? "I don't know, Morpheus. Tell me."

Jaclyn smiled at his reference to Laurence Fishburne's character in the movie. "I've studied you."

"What did you learn?"

"You're a gentleman."

He arched a brow. "That's bad?"

"Not at all. I find the quality very attractive."

The buzz in his blood settled a little lower in DeMarcus's stomach. A slow, easy breath helped him think. "But?"

"No buts. I was able to use that quality to my advantage during the game. For example, you didn't want to play on my left because you assumed it's not my strong side."

DeMarcus smiled. "I was wrong."

"And you said you'd watched me play in the WNBA." Jaclyn tutted. "You also didn't want to charge me because you didn't want to risk hurting me."

"I noticed you didn't worry about me."

"Sorry." Jaclyn finished her glass of water.

DeMarcus kept his eyes glued to hers, ignoring the damp T-shirt that clung to her curves. "Is there a lesson in your game?"

Jaclyn's grin revealed even, white teeth. "Of course. I love a well-educated man." She stood and moved to the sink to wash her glass. "I used what I know about you to beat you. By getting to know our players, you can make the best match of their personal ticks against our opponents."

DeMarcus followed her to the sink. Beneath the earthy scent of sweat was a hint of lilacs. Intoxicating.

"I don't have to psychoanalyze the players to develop the team's game plans."

Jaclyn's shoulder brushed his chest as she turned to him. She stepped back. "I used more than my physical abilities to beat you." She took his glass, washed it, then set it beside hers on the gray plastic drain board.

DeMarcus moved closer, drawn by her warmth, her scent, her magic. "What would I learn by bonding with the players?"

"Their temperament." Jaclyn shifted sideways, opening more room between them. "You don't want a hothead guarding someone who could taunt him into committing a foul."

Why did she keep moving away? DeMarcus closed the gap. "The team needs discipline more than anything else."

Jaclyn stepped back. "Exactly. But to bring discipline to our team, you need to know what's happening to them off the court as well. Players listen to coaches who listen to them."

DeMarcus stepped forward. "I'm a coach, not a priest."

Jaclyn's back bumped the fridge. "Did you know Bling has a drinking problem? I'm sure you've noticed Jamal is a ball hog. That's going to be an issue. And Rick second-guesses himself. That's going to be a problem, too."

"I can't be their coach and their friend. It's one or the other. You want me to get them to the play-offs. Let me do my job."

Jaclyn sighed. "All right. Preseason starts in nine days. We'll see whether your strategy works."

"It will."

She pressed her right hand against the center of his chest. "In the meantime, when did you become a close talker? Back up."

DeMarcus shuddered. Jaclyn's touch scorched his skin through his jersey. He was edgy, anxious. Like a sixteen-year-old with his first crush. DeMarcus flattened his palms against the refrigerator behind her, caging her in. "You said you can read me. What am I thinking now?"

Her voice was as husky as his. "I can read you loud and clear. But I don't know if this is wise. I'm your boss."

His gaze dropped to her lips, full and moist. "Harass me." DeMarcus waited, willing her to toss caution to the wind with him.

Jaclyn's hand slid up his chest and curved around the back of his neck. She brought his face closer to hers and raised up on her toes to meet his mouth. DeMarcus groaned. His body warmed as he rubbed his lips across the warm, soft plumpness of hers. He nibbled at them, sipping their sweetness. Her body shivered against him. DeMarcus dropped his hands from the refrigerator to hold her closer against him. Her soft breasts pressed against his chest. He caressed her lithe waist before moving his hands lower to cup her full, firm derriere.

Jaclyn shivered again. She dug her fingernails deeper into his back. DeMarcus felt his heart beat slow and heavy in his chest. His blood heated in his veins, boiling until it whistled in his ears. He pressed into her.

He stroked his tongue against her mouth, coaxing her to open for him, wanting a deeper taste. Jaclyn parted her lips to accept him. DeMarcus was swept away. He slipped between her lips and explored her wet warmth. He tasted her inner walls then stroked her tongue. Jaclyn's tongue reached out to touch his, sliding along its length, wrapping around its width, then taking it into her mouth.

DeMarcus groaned at her acceptance. His body heated. A low, deep throbbing started inside him. He slid his hand over her hip to the cool, bare skin of her thigh. Hooking his hand behind her knee, he lifted her leg, pressing her thigh against his hip. They fit together perfectly. At well over six feet tall, DeMarcus often had to fold himself over to embrace his date or lift her from the ground to kiss her. But not with Jaclyn. She fit with him as though she were made for his arms.

DeMarcus caressed Jaclyn's small waist. His fingers slipped beneath the hem of her scanty T-shirt. Her skin was hot, just a little damp. He skimmed his fingertips down her abdomen to her waist. Her stomach muscles quivered. DeMarcus groaned. His hand lifted farther up her torso to cup her breast. Jaclyn moaned, pressing into him. She opened her mouth wider, deepening their kiss. DeMarcus responded, his blood on fire.

His mind spun at her contrasts. Sweet and spicy. Bold and bashful. He wanted to taste her, all of her. Her breast was warm and soft, its weight a temptation in his palm. He tightened his hold on her thigh and pressed his hips hard into hers.

Jaclyn broke their kiss. "Marc. Wait."

DeMarcus froze. His left hand pressed her breast; his right hand cupped her thigh. His body ached. "All right."

Jaclyn opened her eyes. She pressed her hand against his chest, creating more room between them.

"I'd be lying if I said I didn't want you. What an understatement." Her chuckle was breathless and awkward. "But things are complicated enough for both of us without adding a sexual relationship."

DeMarcus made himself release her. He turned away from Jaclyn's scent and breathed deeply to clear his mind. "You're right. You're my boss. This isn't a good idea."

"I'm glad we can be sensible about this." She didn't sound glad. Small comfort.

DeMarcus collected his jacket from her kitchen chair before facing her again. His palm tingled from the feel of her. His body ached from the taste of her. "We can be sensible. But for how long?"

9

"A losing preseason is a good sign." Julian sat beside DeMarcus on the thick-cushioned brown sofa.

Sometimes DeMarcus didn't understand his father. "Why?"

"It betters the odds of a team winning in the regular season."

"Then the Monarchs should go undefeated." DeMarcus turned off the digital video disc recorder and the sixty-eight-inch high-definition television. He couldn't stomach any more footage of the Monarchs' preseason games.

Julian shrugged. "So the team lost all of its preseason games. Take whatever you can learn from this experience and throw the rest out."

DeMarcus set the universal remote control on the mahogany coffee table and stood to prowl the family room's dark green carpet. "The losses left me with more questions than answers."

Julian shifted sideways on the sofa. "Like what?"

DeMarcus dragged both hands over his hair. He

paced toward the mahogany shelves of DVDs and compact discs. "Do those guys even want to win?"

"Of course they do."

DeMarcus gestured toward the DVD machine. "You can't tell that by the way they played."

"That's not fair, Marc. Most of your players have been in the league ten years or more. You know as well as anyone—and better than most—how much sacrifice and commitment that takes."

DeMarcus settled his hands on his hips and stared out the picture window. This view gave him a different angle of the neighborhood from the den's bay window. "There's no passion. They're going through the motions and collecting a paycheck."

"You're wrong, Marc."

DeMarcus heard the disappointment in his father's voice and regretted being the one to cause it. "I don't mean to be hard on your team, Pop. But over the past four seasons, the Monarchs have lost their competitive drive."

"What they've lost is hope. Help them regain it."

DeMarcus faced his father. "How? We open the regular season with the Miami Heat Wednesday. That gives me six days to figure out the magic combination of players."

"You will." In the dark depths of Julian's gaze was a steadfast assurance.

DeMarcus's stomach muscles knotted. He turned away from his father's expectations. "I've never been on a team with a losing record. For three of the last four seasons, that's all the Monarchs have known. We weren't competitive in any of our preseason games."

"Dick Vermeil said the real test comes when you lose."

It was a struggle to keep his back straight, his voice

steady. "Despite what legendary NFL coaches say, the media's saying I've made a mistake. They think I'm ruining my legacy."

"What do you think?"

DeMarcus flexed his shoulders. The tension remained. Outside, the shadows fell faster now as the autumn evening arrived. "We've already lost seven games. I think we've been tested enough."

"Be patient. You'll figure it out. It didn't take one season for the Monarchs to fall to the Eastern Conference basement. You can't expect to turn them around overnight."

DeMarcus looked again at Julian. "You have more faith in me than I have in myself."

Julian smiled with an understanding and wisdom DeMarcus hoped to have one day. "Who knows you better than your parents?"

DeMarcus checked his silver Rolex. It was almost half past seven. "I'm going back to the office to look at more game film and prepare for the Heat.

"That's what a champion would do."

DeMarcus sent his father a smile before leaving the family room. "Don't wait up."

DeMarcus tossed the *New York Sports* onto Troy Marshall's desk. The Friday morning headline read, MONARCHS' INFIGHTING THREATENS SEASON. He relaxed his jaw. "Have you read the paper?"

Troy spun his black leather executive chair away from his computer table and pulled it under his desk. He tipped his head back to meet DeMarcus's glower. "First thing this morning."

DeMarcus jabbed a finger toward the newspaper. "Aren't you supposed to prevent articles like this?"

"I'm the VP of media and marketing, not a magician."

DeMarcus narrowed his eyes. "Was that a joke?"

"Andy Benson doesn't ask my approval before she submits her stories."

DeMarcus picked up the paper. "She writes that Serge has wanted to be traded for years."

"That's not a secret." It was only eight in the morning, but Troy's jacket was off, his tie loosened and his sleeves rolled to his elbows. "The problem is no other team will buy Serge's contract."

DeMarcus scanned the article again. "She quotes Jamal complaining that he wants more ball time."

"Jam-On-It is a ball hog. He won't be satisfied until he's handled the ball for the whole forty-eight minutes."

DeMarcus's gaze bounced around the media executive's office. The black-lacquered furniture and silver carpeting reminded him of Jaclyn's office. Framed reprints of newspaper articles memorializing the Monarchs' past glory hung from his walls. Business marketing and communications awards paraded across his bookcases.

DeMarcus jerked the folded newspaper in his hand. "The team doesn't need this distraction. What are you going to do about it?"

Confusion darkened Troy's eyes. "What do you mean?"

"Are you going to ask for a retraction?"

"Based on what? We don't like the article, but it's not inaccurate. It's a true picture of how the players feel and what they've already told us."

"But the paper doesn't have to print it."

Troy sighed. "Look, I know the story hurts the Monarchs' image. But, if I called Andy to complain, we'd make the situation worse."

DeMarcus dragged his right hand over his hair. "The Waves didn't have articles like this."

"I'm not surprised." Troy's tone was dry. "The Waves have been winning for years. They don't have any reason to complain."

"You're saying it's the players' fault?"

Troy shrugged. "They're the ones quoted in the article."

DeMarcus scanned the article again before tossing it back onto Troy's desk. It felt as though someone had hidden a microphone in the Monarchs' locker room and played the tape for the salacious satisfaction of their readership. "What do we do?"

Troy leaned back in his chair. "Tell the players not to take their grievances to the media. Keep their concerns about their contract or playing time or whatever in the family. I know you want an immediate solution, but complaining to Andy or any member of the press gives the situation greater emphasis."

"I'll talk to the players before today's practice." DeMarcus glanced at his watch. Practice was still almost three hours away. Could he wait that long? At least everyone would be on time. The late fine was working.

"I'm glad you've solved that problem." Jaclyn's voice came from behind DeMarcus. She shut Troy's office door before continuing. "But why did Andy Benson decide to write this story?"

Troy shrugged. "Player dissatisfaction on a losing team isn't uncommon."

Jaclyn crossed into Troy's office. Her dark blue

dress hugged her small waist. The hem ended at mid-calf. Beside her, DeMarcus felt her tension.

She stared down at the article. "But this isn't our first or even second losing season. Why did she choose to publish this story now?"

Troy inclined his head toward DeMarcus. "Maybe because our new head coach is one of Brooklyn's favorite sons."

Jaclyn shook her head. "She works the player dissatisfaction angle. She barely mentions Marc."

DeMarcus folded his arms. "Do you think someone asked her to do this story?"

Jaclyn shrugged one slender shoulder. "It's possible."

DeMarcus grunted. His annoyance multiplied. "I'll institute a hefty fine for any player who takes negative stories to the press."

Jaclyn's troubled gaze lifted to his. "Suppose it wasn't the players?"

"Who else would it be?" Troy straightened in his chair. "Do you suspect Gerry or Bert?"

Jaclyn seemed to hesitate. "I . . ."

An expression of disgust crossed Troy's features. "My loyalty is to the team. I won't break your confidence."

Jaclyn sat in one of Troy's guest chairs. "I trust you. Unfortunately, I can't say that about everyone in our organization. This conversation can't leave this room."

Troy nodded. "Of course."

"Agreed." DeMarcus took the other vacant chair. Curiosity and concern made him want to touch her. It had been weeks since they'd been even this close to each other. Absence hadn't lessoned the hunger.

Jaclyn took a deep breath. "Bert wouldn't go to the

media. But I could see Gerry planting a story like this to build on the team dissension we already have."

Troy drummed his fingers against his teakwood desktop. "Knowing the negative publicity would damage the team."

DeMarcus glanced from Troy back to Jaclyn. "Which is what he wants."

Troy made a note on his memo paper. "I'll find a way to subtly ask Andy for her story's source."

DeMarcus cocked a brow. "While you're at it, use your charm to convince her not to do any more negative stories on us."

Jaclyn rubbed her forehead. "I'll pretend I didn't hear that."

Troy chuckled. "You may have noticed that Andy Benson is immune to my charms. In fact, I don't think she likes me."

DeMarcus snorted. "You'd better work on that. We can't have the press hating our media executive."

Troy spread his arms. "Image is everything."

DeMarcus locked gazes with Jaclyn. "That's not what I've heard."

Jaclyn gave him a wry look before returning her attention to Troy. "Andy's too smart to give up her source, but ask her anyway."

Troy nodded. "Are you going to talk to Gerry?"

Jaclyn rose from her chair. "Yes, although he'll deny any involvement in this story. We need to stop this negative publicity. It'll turn the fans against us when we're trying to increase ticket sales."

DeMarcus wanted to fight these battles for her. She already was trying to prevent Gerald and Albert from moving the team. And she was trying to keep the Monarchs in the Empire. Now she had to add combating negative press to her plate. That was too much for one person to shoulder alone.

DeMarcus stood. "What can I do to help?"

Jaclyn gave him a grateful look. "Talk to the team. Tell them we can't afford negative publicity. But, more than anything else, we really need a winning season so we can pack those seats."

DeMarcus winked at her before walking toward the door. "That's why you hired me."

"And the Monarchs lose their home opener to the Miami Heat one sixteen to eighty-six." The announcer's voice bounced around the arena.

DeMarcus crossed the court to shake Erik Spoelstra's hand. "Good game, Coach." He forced the words past the lump of shame burning his throat. This was the most embarrassing loss of his basketball career—and it happened on his home court in his home city.

DeMarcus followed his assistant coaches and the security guards off the court, maneuvering past television crews, sports reporters and arena staff. He ignored the crowd of scantily clad groupies cooing to him from beside Vom One, the tunnel that led to the Monarchs' locker room.

What would he say to the team? He needed something more constructive than "What the hell happened out there?" That was the question he'd hear from fans—and Jaclyn. And the media. DeMarcus's stomach soured. The postgame interview. He had to give one. Great.

The locker room stank of sweat and defeat. Dark gray metal lockers for the thirteen players—starters and bench—outlined the square room. Clothes, shoes and personal items were strewn chaotically in and around the lockers. Players were getting ready for the showers. The quiet was crushing. Their movements were trancelike. Their posture was broken.

Why weren't they angry? Where were the accusations? Instead, their silence spoke of acceptance, and that he wouldn't allow. They couldn't accept any loss, especially such a humiliating one.

DeMarcus marched to Jamal "Jam-On-It" Ward and ripped the iPod headphones from his ears. Players glanced at him but otherwise didn't react. Their lack of concern pushed him almost to the edge.

He hooked his hands on his hips and asked the first question on his mind. "What the hell happened out there?"

"We lost." Team captain Barron "Bling" Douglas didn't bother to turn from his locker to respond. The tattoos across his brown back flexed with his muscles as he shrugged off his shirt.

DeMarcus glared at Barron. "Is that OK with you?"

Jamal scowled up at him from his seat in front of his locker. The number twenty-three was tattooed on his pale brown skin right above his heart. "We wouldn't have lost if I'd gotten more playing time. I told you before, I'm not a sixth man. I can't come off the bench."

DeMarcus gritted his teeth. He was fed up with the broken-record complaints from the overeager rookie. "And I've told you, you have to earn the start."

Anthony Chambers pulled a wide-tooth comb through his throwback natural. "Have mercy, Coach. We just want to get out of here."

DeMarcus's eyes widened. Had he heard the power forward correctly? "You want to go home? Is it past your bedtime? This isn't summer camp. It's the NBA."

Warrick Evans sat at the bench in front of his locker. His forearms rested on his thighs. "We know where we are, Coach. We also know we were outplayed." The shooting guard dragged a hand over his cleanshaven, brown head. "The Heat was faster and didn't make any mistakes."

Jamal turned on Warrick. "Gramps, you're the one who should be coming off the bench. I could keep up with the Heat."

Warrick gave the brash shooting guard a tight smile. "You heard Coach. If you want my spot, earn it."

Jamal jabbed a finger toward the veteran player. "Keep playing like you're playing and you'll lose it. At least you'll have the best seat in the house when I take us to the championship."

DeMarcus watched Warrick's eyes ice over at the rookie's challenge. The veteran stood. DeMarcus braced himself to stop a locker room brawl. Instead Warrick striped off his sweat-laden jersey. DeMarcus relaxed tense muscles.

"Maybe we were outcoached." Serge Gateau's theory was delivered with a heavy French accent and plenty of spite.

DeMarcus faced him. "How could I have better prepared you?"

Serge's gaze wavered. The Frenchman scanned the room. Not finding the assistance he searched for, he returned his attention to DeMarcus. "I want to be traded."

Another broken record.

DeMarcus scanned the faces in the room. The bench players looked bored. Barron was sullen. Jamal acted offended. Serge seemed irritated. Anthony appeared to have put the game behind him. Warrick seemed depressed, and Vincent Jardine, the center, appeared distracted.

DeMarcus pushed to the front of the room, commanding their attention. "We're done with losing. I don't care what it takes. This season, we're making it to the play-offs."

Barron snorted. "You think just because you said it, it's going to happen?"

DeMarcus shot the team captain a hard glare. Barron looked away. "Friday, we're going to Atlanta to play the Hawks. We have two days to prepare. They're going to play us as hard as the Heat did tonight. They won't let up. And, tomorrow at practice, neither will I."

DeMarcus stormed from the locker room. He was still angry, embarrassed and disgusted. And he had a press conference to get through.

A hand grabbed his arm, stopping him mid-stride. DeMarcus looked around to find Gerald Bimm invading his personal space.

The owner gave him a smug look. "Can we talk privately?"

DeMarcus wanted to say no. He didn't have the stomach for the other man's subterfuge. But Gerald was one of the franchise owners. DeMarcus stepped out of the heavy pedestrian traffic and followed his boss a short distance from the Monarchs' locker room.

Gerald stopped to face him. "It seems odd to say good job after a losing effort, but there you have it. Good job."

Anger took supremacy over embarrassment. "Good job? We lost by thirty points on our home court."

Gerald chuckled. "That's the goal, Marc. We need a losing seasoning. Or have you forgotten our conversation?"

DeMarcus blinked to clear the red haze from his vision. It didn't work. "I haven't forgotten, but you must have. I told you I'm not a stooge."

"Then tonight was a happy accident."

"Don't expect a repeat of it."

"On the contrary, Marc. I suggest that you repeat yourself often. I want to see empty seats. A lot of empty seats. The arena was too full tonight."

DeMarcus narrowed his eyes. "Why do you want to destroy the team? What's in it for you?"

Gerald's smile dimmed. "I'm not trying to destroy it. I'm trying to make it more profitable."

DeMarcus's jaw tightened. He hated when people lied to him. "Try again, Gerry. You don't make a team profitable by chucking it into the league's basement."

"I'm willing to accept short-term loses for long-term gains."

"And I've got a bridge in Brooklyn to sell you." De-Marcus turned away.

Gerald caught his arm again. "If you want to keep your job, remember our conversation. Jackie didn't want to hire you in the first place. If you don't cooperate, it would be easy to convince her to fire you."

DeMarcus stared at his boss's thin, light-skinned hand on the arm of his black suit jacket until the other man released him. "I quit once before, and it was Jack who convinced me to come back."

"I could get her to change her mind about you."

Under other circumstances, DeMarcus would laugh in Gerald's face. Tonight, the older man annoyed him. "You couldn't convince her to come in out of the rain."

Gerald's lip curled. "If you aren't worried about job security, maybe you'll care about your reputation."

"Meaning?"

"What would the public think about your drug addiction?"

DeMarcus frowned. "I've never used drugs."

"And you can explain that to the media once the story breaks."

The image of what such a story circulating their community would do to his father threatened to drop DeMarcus to his knees. "If the Monarchs don't have a losing season, you'll lie to the public, claiming I'm addicted to drugs. That's how you intend to get me to cooperate?"

Gerald slipped his hands into the pockets of his navy suit pants. "The press will jump all over the story, don't you think? I can see the angles now. The Mighty Guinn a drug abuser. Is that why he retired early? Did his coaches and trainers know? How will it effect his Hall of Fame induction?"

Blood rushed through DeMarcus's veins, burning his skin. "No one would believe you."

The franchise partner's smile shone with malice. "Are you sure?"

DeMarcus spun from Gerald before he gave in to the desire to remove his boss's smile, taking several teeth with it.

No one would believe Gerald's lies that DeMarcus had a drug addiction. He may have lived in Miami the past fifteen years, but he'd grown up in Brooklyn. People in the community knew him. They knew his character. They'd never believe Gerald.

Would they?

Could he risk it?

10

"How's your back?" Jaclyn was a little breathless as she ran beside Warrick Evans on the boardwalk behind the Empire, which tracked the marina. She'd picked up her pace to keep up with him, but she was fairly certain the six-foot-seven-inch shooting guard had slowed to accommodate her.

"The spasms come and go. Some days are better than others." The shooting guard sounded distracted. He'd been that way for a while.

"Was yesterday a good day or a bad day?" The home game against the Utah Jazz Monday night had been the team's eighth straight loss.

"I was off my game yesterday. I know that and so does everyone else." Warrick's terse tone was out of character.

It was eight o'clock Tuesday morning. The November sun had risen late, and the lamps crowning the slender black posts along the marina fence had long since gone out. The fall air blew crisp off the water. She was comfortable this morning, but soon it would be too cool to run here.

"Why were you off your game? Was it because of your back?" Jaclyn's gaze dropped to Warrick's legs. Had he sped up? Probably. He usually ran faster when he was agitated, as though he was running away from something. What was it?

"Are you asking as a franchise owner or as a friend?"

That hurt. Jaclyn lengthened her stride to match his pace. "After twelve years, you should know the answer to that."

"You've never been my boss before."

Jaclyn stared hard at him until Warrick's eyes met hers. "I'm the granddaughter of one of the founding owners. I've always been your boss."

Warrick looked away. "Point taken."

She heard his contrition. "For the record, if I'd wanted to have a conversation with you as your boss, I'd have had it in my office wearing a business suit. I wouldn't race after you in a T-shirt and shorts, sweating like a pig."

His surprised chuckle drew the tension from their run. Jaclyn breathed easier as Warrick slowed his speed. She brushed the sweat from her brow.

"I'm sorry." Warrick was subdued.

"You should be." Jaclyn glimpsed Warrick's smile in her peripheral vision.

"Thanks for running with me this morning. I wanted to try a couple of miles out here to test my knees and back."

Jaclyn gazed around the marina. Winter blue waves bounced the scattering of yachts still on the waters. Chatty seagulls danced on the chilly breeze. "Don't worry about it. I'm glad to be on hand in case your back locks up and you have to be carried back to the Empire."

"You're a pal."

Jaclyn tossed him a look. He still seemed preoccupied. "So, what's bothering you? You've been sullen and distracted for weeks. And now we can add paranoid."

"Paranoid? How's that?"

"You said everyone knew you were off your game yesterday. That sounds paranoid to me."

"I'm not paranoid." Masculine irritation tightened his voice.

"By everyone you mean Jamal, don't you?"

Warrick was silent for several strides. They were following the path of an incline about halfway through their workout. Jaclyn felt the strain in her hamstrings. She shortened her strides and leaned into the hill. They finally crested the incline, then circled back to the Empire.

Warrick swiped the sweat from his brows. "Jamal wants my spot."

"Why do you allow him to get to you?" Jaclyn's blood started a slow boil. Right now, Jamal Ward wasn't one of her favorite people.

"Maybe he has a point."

Jaclyn tucked a stray strand of hair behind her ear. "You're one of the most consistent players in the league."

"Then why don't I have a ring?"

Strain. That's what she heard in her friend's voice. It made her worry about him even more. "A lot of NBA players don't have rings. Some of them are even in the Hall of Fame."

Warrick looked at her. "I don't have many more opportunities to get to the Finals."

With his chronic injuries both to his back and his knees, Jaclyn could understand Warrick's concern. "I want to make it to the postseason, too. But it takes a team to win a championship."

His voice was reflective. "We don't play like a team. And each season, it gets worse."

The Empire came into sight. Jaclyn glanced toward the practice facility on the left. Was DeMarcus in his office? She'd noticed the head coach usually started his day early.

She glanced at Warrick. "Why didn't you take more shots last night? You had several sweet looks, but instead of shooting, you passed the ball. Why?"

He picked up the pace. "I thought someone else had a better shot."

"Why have you started second-guessing yourself? Sometimes, Rick, you can't pass the ball. You have to take the shot. You know that."

"And if I miss?"

"When did you lose your nerve?"

Warrick was silent for a distance. "Your grandfather tried to build the team around me. Twelve years later, we still don't have a ring. The front office brought in Bling for energy and Jamal for excitement. I'm no longer team captain and a rookie's after my spot. I have good reason to wonder whether I have what it takes to contribute to the team."

"I disagree." Jaclyn wiped the sweat from her stinging eyes. "If you don't even try, you have no one but yourself to blame if you fail."

The truth of her words applied to her just as well as they applied to Warrick. But had she waited too long to save the Monarchs? Gerald and Albert had devastated the team and divided the loyalty of the front office. They'd crippled sales and rendered the

Monarchs virtually invisible in their own community. Was there anything left to save?

DeMarcus strode into Oscar Clemente's office and dropped a sheaf of papers on the assistant coach's cluttered desk. "Why did you change the game plan for Atlanta?"

Oscar sprawled back in his chair. Either he hadn't noticed or didn't care about DeMarcus's anger. "Your plan didn't give Rick enough touches."

Warrick Evans. DeMarcus's nostrils flared at the thought of the other man. "According to whom?"

"According to everyone who's ever watched his game footage." Oscar swung his black leather chair side to side. The motion was easy and unconcerned. "It takes him a little longer to warm up. But once he's warm, he's our best weapon on the court."

DeMarcus stepped back from the paper-strewn desk, drawing his gaze across the disheveled office. News clippings of every play-off win, conference final and community commendation the team earned during the almost twenty years since Oscar had been with the team lined his office walls.

A Monarchs mug and stress ball sat on Oscar's desk. A Monarchs mouse pad lay beside his keyboard, and the franchise logo decorated his computer desktop.

DeMarcus noticed the Monarchs pin on Oscar's jersey, similar to the one Jaclyn always wore. How many of those did the man own? Should he be reassured by or concerned about the assistant coach's obsession with the team?

DeMarcus rubbed his eyes with his right fingers. "And while he's warming up, Atlanta will build a huge lead over us. Rick needs to be warm as soon as he steps onto the court."

"Rick is a great ballplayer and an important member of our team. His game gives us another dimension."

DeMarcus removed stacks of papers from one of the guest chairs before settling into it. The resentment boiling inside him had nothing to do with his seeing Warrick and Jaclyn jogging together this morning. "Rick hesitates to take the shot, even when he has the look. I need a bold player to fire up the team."

Displeasure pinched Oscar's face. He sat forward, leaning into his desk. "You mean Jamal."

"He's not afraid to shoot."

"Even when he shouldn't."

"He's an aggressive competitor."

"Who gets into foul trouble five minutes into the game."

"That's an exaggeration."

Oscar returned his gaze with a silent, steady stare.

How much aggravation was he going to have to deal with to make it through the season? He'd challenged a franchise owner who wanted to move the team from Brooklyn. He was fighting players who'd accepted the idea of not making it to the play-offs before the season had even started. Now he was butting heads with one of his assistants who still acted like the interim head coach.

DeMarcus propped his right ankle on his left knee. "If you didn't agree with my plan, why didn't you talk to me instead of substituting your own?"

Oscar folded his hands on top of the stack of papers on his desk. "You wouldn't listen."

A weak excuse. "I'm listening now."

"Then change the plan."

"No."

"Why not?"

"I don't agree with you."

Oscar sat back again. "We're oh-and-eight. Your plans don't work."

The muscles in his shoulders knotted even as De-Marcus tried not to react to the criticism. "Is it the plan or the players?"

Oscar shook his head. "You don't know these players like I do."

"If you know them and what they're capable of, why didn't you apply for the head coach position?"

Oscar glared at him. "Didn't want it."

He'd hit a nerve. "Didn't want or weren't offered?"

Oscar clenched his fist. "That butt wipe, Gerry, offered me the position. And I knew why. I'm a good assistant. A damn good one. But I'm not head coach material. I know that and he knows it, too. That's why he wanted me for the position. Like you, he wanted me so the team would lose."

DeMarcus took a deep breath. Oscar had hit back. Hard. "The team won't lose because of me. But it will if we don't work together."

"Rick needs more touches."

DeMarcus shook his head at the other man's stubbornness. "You've routinely given Rick's thirty percent of the touches. But for the past four seasons, you've been losing."

"He didn't have the right players around him."

"He's lost his nerve."

"He needs new players."

"The franchise doesn't have the money for quality

trades." DeMarcus sighed. "We have to build the team around another player."

Oscar's expression tightened. "I've been with Rick his whole career. He's the leader of this team."

DeMarcus pushed himself to his feet. "He *was* the leader of this team."

Oscar lifted his head to maintain DeMarcus's eye contact. "We can win with Rick on the court."

"The definition of insanity is doing the same thing over and over again and expecting a different result. The team needs a change." DeMarcus took the copy of Oscar's game plan from the assistant coach's desk and tore it in half. "If you disagree with me in the future, talk to me. Don't go behind my back."

DeMarcus gripped the pieces of the plan in his fist and strode from Oscar's office.

Jaclyn stood with her back to the kitchen door of the Morning Glory Chapel. She pinned her curls up and tucked them under a hairnet. The sound of the door opening preceded the brisk clicking of stiletto heels.

She glanced over her shoulder and froze. A grin stretched her lips. "Welcome back, Violet Ebanks O'Neal."

Violet strutted across the room clothed in skinny navy jeans and a tight lavender cashmere sweater. Her makeup emphasized her violet eyes and high cheekbones. She drew her fingers through her salon-styled, auburn hair and grinned back. "I feel like my old self. You were right."

"Of course I was. What about?"

Violet secured her hair under a net. "That I needed

some time on my own to figure out what I was missing in my life. That's what I've been doing these past two weeks."

Jaclyn hefted a pot of mixed vegetables and waited while Violet lifted a pan of ground turkey. "Did you figure it out?"

Jaclyn nudged the kitchen door open with her right hip and held it while Violet walked through. The dining area buzzed with the energy and chatter of other volunteers preparing dinner for the food bank's customers, the community's homeless and working poor.

"I want to go back to work." Violet's voice preceded Jaclyn to the staging area where the volunteers and food bank employees arranged pots and pans of food as well as disposable plates and utensils.

Jaclyn set down her pot of vegetables and glanced over at Violet. "What do you want to do?"

Violet arranged her station next to Jaclyn's. "I don't know yet. Maybe coaching, either in a high school or a college. I have a business degree. I could do something with that. All I know is that I want to work with other adults."

Jaclyn thought of Gerald and Albert, and the divided loyalties of her administrative staff. "That can be challenging."

"Mish Jones." The high-pitched voice came from the other side of the serving tables.

Jaclyn smiled in anticipation of seeing the little girl who'd called her name. She approached the table and looked down at the honey-blond head. "Tiffany. How are you, sweetheart?"

The three-year-old girl tugged on her mother's hand and dropped her green gaze. "Fine." The word emerged on a shallow breath. Tiffany was still a little shy, but over the past two weeks, she'd started talking more.

Jaclyn circled the long line of serving tables to join mother and daughter in the dining area. She switched her welcome to the blond woman who was never far from Tiffany's side. "How are you, Connie?"

Constance's green gaze, identical to her daughter's, still wavered whenever someone addressed her directly. "Fine, thank you." Her Midwestern accent identified her as a recent transplant to the Big Apple. How long had she been in Brooklyn?

Jaclyn kept the easy smile on her lips although the large bruises just beginning to fade from the young mother's fragile features made her want to cry. "Are you still comfortable at the shelter?"

Jaclyn had a vested interest in Constance's answer. The Monarchs' staff, players and administration donated time, money and materials to the Morning Glory Chapel's homeless shelter.

Constance's eyes widened. "Oh, yes. Tiff and I are very comfortable there."

"Good." Jaclyn turned to Tiffany, whose curious gaze shifted between Jaclyn and her mother. "I have something for you."

She went to Violet, who was handling her station as well as Jaclyn's for the moment. Her friend found the shopping bag waiting under her station. Jaclyn returned to present the bag to Tiffany. The little girl looked to her mother.

Constance stroked her daughter's neat, blond locks. "Say thank you, honey."

"Thank you." Tiffany accepted the bag. Her eyes widened as she pulled out the chubby, brown teddy bear. "Wow. Thank you." Her face glowed with joy.

Jaclyn laughed. "You're very welcome. I heard you were lonely. I thought he could keep you company for now."

Tiffany showed the bear to her mother. "Mama, look."

Constance blinked. Her voice shook. "I see, honey. What will you name him?"

Tiffany hugged the stuffed toy. "Bear."

Constance chuckled. "That's fitting." She turned to Jaclyn. "Thank you so much. She has been lonely. And scared, I think. How did you know?"

Jaclyn extended her hand and touched the other woman's thin forearm. "Father Leonard told me. I'd better get back to the line. We're serving ground turkey and vegetables tonight." She gave Constance an encouraging smile before leaving.

Violet handed Jaclyn her apron. "You should be a mother."

"Hopefully, one day." Jaclyn heard the wistful note in her voice. She shook off the feeling and tied the apron around her waist. "But we're talking about you. It sounds as though you've made a major breakthrough."

"I did. I don't feel like I'm being a bad mother because I want to go back to work."

"You're not." Jaclyn moved to her station and picked up her serving spoon. "Dawnie won't be neglected just because you're working."

Violet spoke with confidence. "I'll make sure of that. If it comes to a choice between my daughter and my work, Dawnie will always come first."

"That's the way it should be. My grandfather made me his priority, even missing away games if I had a school event that he thought he should attend."

Violet checked her silver wristwatch. "Speaking of

away games, aren't you flying to Atlanta with the team tonight?"

Experience helped Jaclyn keep up with her friend's frequent conversation bounces. She checked her own watch and her pulse leaped. The Monarchs were leaving for Atlanta in just over two hours. Would they finally win a game tomorrow night or extend their losses to zero and nine two weeks into the six-month season? "I'm already packed. I'll meet them at the airport once we're finished."

Violet nodded. "I'm lucky that my parents and Aidan's parents are available to babysit when I go back to work. Although I'd like to put Dawnie in nursery school when she's older."

Jaclyn stared across the room at the crowd making their way into the dining area. Men and women, young and old. Mothers with their children. "My grandfather had wanted to open a daycare center in the arena and offer it to the community. He said parents should never have to choose between their family and their job. I'd like to fulfill his wish."

"How are the negotiations going with the Empire's owners?"

Jaclyn's grip flexed around the serving spoon. "It all comes down to what they'll make from our rent. We've got to increase our event revenue. Failing that, I'll have to figure out another way to raise the money."

"Like what?"

Jaclyn's gaze took in the people seated at the shelter's dining table. Her neighbors. "I don't know. But saving the Monarchs is about more than protecting my grandfather's legacy. It's about serving the community. I'll do whatever it takes to keep it going. I just wish I knew what it would take."

* * *

Jaclyn hesitated in front of DeMarcus's hotel room. They hadn't had an opportunity to talk on the plane. She wanted to know what he thought of the team's chances of beating the Hawks, especially since they were playing in Philips Arena, the Hawks' home court. Jaclyn rapped three times on the door. She looked around the pale gold walls and burgundy carpets. The hotel was clean, quiet and nice. The players should get a good night's sleep here. She hadn't been able to sleep all week. Her team needed a win.

She stared at the door. What was taking DeMarcus so long to answer? He wasn't at dinner. They'd eaten with the players earlier. He couldn't be asleep. It was just after nine P.M. She raised her fist to knock again. Before she could, the door swung open. DeMarcus stood in the threshold. He wore tan sweatpants and a blue Miami Waves jersey.

Jaclyn's inspection slid to his bare feet. "I'd rather my head coach didn't wear our division rival's logo."

"Sorry." DeMarcus's expression was as cold as it had been hot the night he'd held her against him and explored her mouth with his tongue.

Jaclyn glanced into his hotel room. For the first time it occurred to her DeMarcus might not be alone. "Am I . . . interrupting . . . anything?"

DeMarcus leaned a thickly muscled shoulder against the threshold. "What are you doing here?"

"I need to talk to you. Is this a good time?"

He hesitated. Finally, he stepped back, pulling the door wider. "Sure."

Jaclyn moved past him. His warm, musky scent brushed her like a physical touch, stirring memories of the night they'd played basketball. She gave herself a mental shake. She needed to focus on the reason she was here and not get caught in desires that would only tangle an already-complicated situation.

Jaclyn followed the plush, royal blue carpet past the entryway, through the living space into the study area. "Ticket sales have slowed, which I'm sure we can attribute to our oh-and-eight start." She turned to face DeMarcus. "This isn't going to bring in the crowds we need."

DeMarcus propped his shoulder against the wall separating the entryway from the rest of the room. "You should have given the team's postgame speech after we lost to the Jazz Monday night."

Jaclyn's eyes narrowed at the bite in his voice. "I'm sure you handled it well." She noticed again the distance in his eyes and the tension in his stance. "How are the players? Are they tight, loose?"

"They're fine."

"And you?"

"Fine." DeMarcus straightened from the wall and paced past her to the French doors on the other side of the small, mahogany writing desk. He drew the curtains back to study Atlanta at night.

Jaclyn circled to keep him in sight. His movements were stiff, his expression strained. "No, you're not. What's wrong?"

DeMarcus turned to meet her eyes. "Is Rick your spy?"

She wanted to laugh. "What makes you think that?"

"I saw you running with him this morning." He looked so serious.

Jaclyn swallowed a chuckle. In his current mood, DeMarcus wouldn't appreciate her humor. "When I wanted you to resign, you threw me out of your office." She crossed her arms over her chest. "When Gerry wanted you to coach a losing season, you quit. If you have something to say, Marc, you'll say it. Why would I need Rick to spy on you?"

DeMarcus leaned his hips against the writing table. "He's a married man."

Jaclyn blinked at the sudden topic shift. "I know. I went to his wedding."

"He's a married man and an employee, but you're still having a personal relationship with him."

Jaclyn was speechless for several heartbeats. "You think I'm having an affair with Rick?" DeMarcus didn't answer. Jaclyn felt her temper stir. "Rick and I have been friends for twelve years. He's like a brother to me."

"That's not the way it looked to me."

She arched a brow. "Your office is on the other side of the arena. How could you possibly have seen us?"

"I'd gone back to the parking lot before you'd started your run. I'd left something in my car." DeMarcus stood up from the writing desk and stepped closer to Jaclyn. "I saw you put your arms around him like this." He lifted her arms and wrapped them around his taut waist. "And Evans put his arms around you like this." The muscles of his forearms pressed into her sides. "And then he pressed his cheek against yours like this." DeMarcus husked the words into her ear as he pressed his cheek against hers.

Jaclyn shivered from head to toe. The light stubble on his unshaven cheek rasped against her skin. She took a deep breath to steady her trembling muscles, drawing in his soap-and-sandalwood scent. The strings of desire were reaching out to her. With an effort, she pulled back, lowering her arms from his body. "Marc." She cleared her throat. "Rick loves Mary. He and I are just friends."

DeMarcus drew his hand down her back, bringing her close again. "Good. Because I want to be much more." He covered her mouth with his.

11

Sensation, sharp and sweet, shot through Jaclyn, top to bottom. His touch, his taste made her scalp tingle and her toes curl. Everywhere he touched her— back, waist, hips—burned. His taste made her blood sing. She wanted to get closer to him. She needed to have more of him. She yearned to give him more of her. The strings of desire had captured her. In truth, she'd wanted to be ensnared. She threw caution— and freedom—to the winds.

His scent clouded her mind. She moaned, anxious to feel more of him. Jaclyn rose onto her toes and arched her torso into his. She sighed when DeMarcus held her closer. She slipped her palms beneath his jersey, reveling in his smooth, warm flesh. His hard muscles flexed beneath her fingertips.

DeMarcus released her but didn't move away. "You know where this is going."

Jaclyn opened her eyes. Cool air brushed over her heated face. She blinked. "What?"

A shadow of a smile eased DeMarcus's strained features. "I want you. But are you sure you want this?"

Jaclyn reached up, cupping the side of his squared jaw. "Very sure."

"You're still my boss."

Her lips curved teasingly. "Don't worry. I won't ask you to do anything kinky."

DeMarcus remained serious. "I don't want you to regret tonight."

"Then tell me you have condoms."

He finally smiled, bringing out the dimples she loved. "Condoms? More than one?"

"Am I scaring you?"

DeMarcus wrapped his arms around Jaclyn and pulled her closer. Their lips touched. His caress was demanding, encompassing, consuming. He lifted his head. "I can handle it."

Jaclyn smiled slowly. "I thought you could."

She slid her hands over the smooth, cool material of his jersey, across his well-developed pecs and six-pack abs. His body was a fine-tuned machine, ripped and ready for action. She wanted to savor every flexing muscle. Her fingers trembled and her body warmed. DeMarcus's chest rose and fell faster as he watched her watching him. Jaclyn slipped her hands under the hem of his jersey, raising it as she slid her palms back up his torso. All that power beneath her fingertips. He'd been a champion, performing at the highest level of his sport. But he'd walked away from the game when his father had needed him. Courage and heart, an arousing combination.

DeMarcus pulled the sport shirt over his head. Jaclyn moved back and swallowed. She'd been turned on by the feel of him. She was overwhelmed at the sight of him. His dark brown skin was stretched taut over well-developed muscles—sculpted shoulders, sinewy arms, deep pecs and tight abs. The fine hair covering his chest narrowed to a tempting trail down his torso. It disappeared beneath the low waistband of his tan sweatpants. Jaclyn came forward to trace its course. She lifted her eyes to his. "You're amazing."

DeMarcus closed the distance even further, till his warmth wrapped around her and his scent spun her thoughts. "Your turn." He reached behind Jaclyn's back and drew down her zipper.

Jaclyn raised her arms as DeMarcus lifted the dress over her head, leaving her in only her demi-cup royal blue bra, matching thong, panty hose and stilettos. She was singed by the heat in his eyes.

"You're the amazing one." DeMarcus slipped his arms around her.

Jaclyn felt a tug and her bra fell away. DeMarcus let the garment drop. Feather-light caresses made her nipples tremble and her breath catch. He wrapped his arms around her, pulling her in close. His hard muscles braced her back. His body heat scorched her skin. The deep muscles of his chest pressed against her breasts, causing the fine hairs on his chest to tickle her skin. Jaclyn's head tipped back as she struggled with sensory overload.

DeMarcus kissed her neck. "You're so beautiful. And you smell so good."

"So do you. Like sandalwood and soap." Jaclyn pressed her fingertips into the corded muscles of De-Marcus's shoulders. "You make me weak."

It took too long to take their clothes off. DeMarcus snatched his wallet from the pocket of his sweatpants. He was torn between speed and finesse. He'd never felt that way before. DeMarcus left the garments scat-

tered in and around the study area and lifted Jaclyn
into his arms.

She gave him a startled look. "The last man who carried me to bed was my grandfather. I think I was six."

He arched a brow. "That knowledge doesn't de-
press me."

Jaclyn chuckled low in her throat. The sound was
as sexy as her honey-and-whiskey voice. She could
probably read a cereal box and make him hard.

DeMarcus stopped beside the hotel room's king-
sized bed. He tossed his wallet onto the mattress. He
lowered his right arm, freeing Jaclyn's long legs. Her
right thigh brushed his arousal as she stood. He took
Jaclyn into his arms again and kissed her. His tongue
caressed the seam of her lips and she opened for
him. DeMarcus slid his tongue into her mouth, tast-
ing all of her flavors again—sweet and sexy, bold and
bashful. He explored her as he'd done before, as he
wanted to do again and for a very long time.

Jaclyn wrapped her arms around his shoulders.
Her fingers stroked the back of his neck. Her hands
smoothed over his close-cropped hair. Her movements were soothing and seductive. DeMarcus drew
a hand down her back. Her body arched into his, and
he swallowed her sigh. He grasped her hips, pulling
her even closer to him. She rubbed herself against
him, and DeMarcus's legs began to shake.

He reached up to cup her breast. Her nipples pebbled in his palm. DeMarcus lifted Jaclyn to her toes
as he lowered his mouth to her breast. He licked the
trembling tip and heard her gasp. The sound shot
straight to his gut. He licked her again and Jaclyn
held his head steady against her. DeMarcus drew her

breast into his mouth, suckling her and grazing her nipple with his tongue.

Jaclyn moaned. The sound heated his blood. She released his head and trailed her fingernails down his back. His knees shook. Jaclyn shifted her right hand to his front and took hold of his arousal. She caressed the length of him with soft, slow strokes. DeMarcus felt his hips pumping into her palm.

He lifted his knee onto the mattress, settling Jaclyn beneath him. He straddled her thighs, giving her access to him while he kissed and caressed her other breast. His senses had narrowed to know only her— her touch, her taste, her scent, her moans and the beauty of her passion as she writhed beneath him.

A shudder worked through DeMarcus when Jaclyn released him. She pressed her palms against his chest. "Let me up."

"Why?" DeMarcus rolled over—and found himself pinned below Jaclyn. Her knees pressed into his hips. Her hands were on either side of his head.

Jaclyn buried her face in his neck. "It's my turn to taste you." She kissed his mouth, quick and hard.

Jaclyn covered his chest with soft kisses, quick bites and long licks. Her hair tickled his chest as she traveled down his body. If she continued this all over his body, he'd never survive.

Her hands were everywhere. She stroked his rib cage, caressed his thigh and traced his chest. Jaclyn nibbled her way to his navel. He'd never considered the spot an erogenous zone, but when her hot, wet tongue laved across it, his hips rose from the mattress.

"I'm on the edge." He gritted the words through his teeth.

"Where's your condom?"

"Under my right thigh."

Jaclyn looked up at him, her eyebrows knitted. De-Marcus shifted to his left. She found his wallet and handed it to him. He retrieved the condom and tossed his wallet behind him in the general vicinity of the nightstand. The thump beside his bed told him he'd missed.

Jaclyn extended her hand. "Let me."

DeMarcus hesitated. "I won't last much longer."

Jaclyn smiled. "You can handle it."

She tore open the packet, withdrew the condom, then tossed the empty wrapper behind him to join his wallet. She positioned the protection on his tip and smoothed it down his length. DeMarcus swallowed.

Jaclyn felt hot and damp with arousal. DeMarcus had said he wouldn't last much longer. Well, neither would she. Jaclyn moved farther up DeMarcus's thighs and positioned herself above his rock-hard erection. Her nipples puckered at the feel of him at her entrance. She held her breath as she lowered onto his length. Her breasts tightened. Her pulse quickened. DeMarcus lifted to meet her. She gasped, tipping back her head and closing her eyes. They moved in a slow and easy rhythm. Pleasure was a hot, summer breeze rolling over her skin.

DeMarcus's large palms moved with a consuming fire up her thighs, past her hips, along her waist and over her torso to cup her breasts. His fingers pulled and plucked at her nipples, intensifying her hunger. Jaclyn increased her rhythm, bringing him with her. She bent her body backward, gripping DeMarcus's thighs behind her. Her muscles were drawn tight enough to snap.

DeMarcus lowered his hands to her hips, pulling

her tighter against him. He surged up, gathering her to him and flipped them over so he was on top.

Jaclyn's eyes popped open. DeMarcus covered her mouth with his, kissing her deeply. Jaclyn closed her eyes and held on tight. DeMarcus drove deeper inside her, harder against her. Jaclyn felt her muscles straining toward him. The pressure built within her. DeMarcus slipped his hands between them and touched her. She dug her nails into his back and screamed into his mouth. Her body shuddered through her climax, wave after wave of explosive pleasure. DeMarcus held her tighter.

As their bodies stilled, she kissed his shoulder. "I told you, you could handle it."

Jaclyn felt his smile against her hair. She was happy and relaxed, replete with satisfaction. This step in their relationship had been worth the risk. But as she drifted into sleep, Jaclyn hoped they'd both still be smiling in the morning.

DeMarcus hunkered down. With his left hand, he collected the complimentary copy of the *Atlanta Constitution* newspaper the hotel had laid in front of his room. His right hand balanced his day's first cup of coffee. Straightening, he turned back into his room, pushing the door closed with his elbow.

The state legislature's budget battle was the day's headline news. DeMarcus wandered back to the sitting area, skimming the other front-page stories. He laid the newspaper on the table and pulled out the sports section. He sipped his coffee. What was Atlanta saying about tonight's matchup between its Hawks and his Monarchs?

Coffee spewed from his mouth as he stared at the front page photo of Jaclyn in his arms as he gave her a final kiss good night from his hotel room doorway. The article's headline read, A ROYAL INTERLUDE.

His skin iced over. His muscles went numb.

Who had taken this photo? Why had they taken it? And what gave them the right to invade his privacy?

DeMarcus spun toward the door, bringing forward a mental image of last night—this morning. He couldn't recall seeing anyone in the hallway. He'd checked because he hadn't wanted players or other coaches, who also were staying on this floor, to see Jaclyn leave his room.

Anger exploded through him, heating the blood now rushing through his system.

"Jack."

What would she think? How would she feel when she saw their picture in this morning's paper? He started back to his door, then stopped. He wasn't thinking clearly yet. He was just too angry. Talking to her now, he'd probably make the situation worse, and Jaclyn had enough to worry about. He needed advice.

DeMarcus unclenched his fist and snatched his cell phone from the front pocket of his black warm-up pants. He knew who to call.

His father answered on the second ring. "Yes, the papers here ran the photo as well."

DeMarcus gritted his teeth. "I'm going to sue these papers for invasion of privacy."

"You'll lose. You're a public figure. This story isn't false. Is it?"

He rubbed his eyes with his forefinger and thumb. "No, Pop. It isn't."

"Then you can't claim malicious intent." Julian

didn't sound disapproving. He didn't sound disappointed, either.

"What gives them the right to spy on me? This article isn't news. It's personal."

"Well, as you can see, your personal life makes other people a lot of money." His father's voice was dry.

"They're making money off of the sacrifices you and Mom made, and the effort I put into building a name for myself." DeMarcus turned his back to the newspaper. He glared across the room.

"I know it's not fair, Marc. I'm sorry this has happened."

DeMarcus barely heard his father above the pulse pounding in his ears. "This is bullshit."

"I know, son."

DeMarcus turned back to the table and gripped the sports section in his fist. He wanted to grab the reporter's throat the same way. "I'm going to call the publisher and tell him he needs to focus on what's important—education, crime and health care—and stay the hell out of my privacy."

"I wouldn't recommend doing that."

"Why not?"

Julian sighed. "I know this is new to you. You led a relatively quiet life as an NBA player. For the most part, reporters left you alone. But you'll only make the situation worse if you call them."

"So what should I do?" DeMarcus prowled his room.

"Focus on the team and tonight's game. The story will blow over. If you call the papers, you'll only give them something else to gossip about."

DeMarcus's temper cooled. His father was right. Still . . . "What am I supposed to say to Jack? She has

bigger problems to deal with. She shouldn't have to
worry about this crap as well."

"Remember, the only one at fault is the press. You
and Jackie didn't do anything wrong."

DeMarcus sighed. "So we should act like nothing
happened."

"Yes. Put this behind you and get ready for the
game."

DeMarcus checked his watch. It was seven o'clock.
He was sure Jaclyn was already up. She was a morning person, just like him. "OK, Pop. But, first, I'll
check on Jack. Make sure she's OK."

"Then you'd better calm her down before she calls
the paper."

DeMarcus stood away from the table. "Thanks, Pop."

"You're welcome. And, Marc . . ."

"Yes?"

"Invite Jackie to dinner." His father disconnected
before DeMarcus could respond.

DeMarcus knocked on Jaclyn's door, which was
just down the hall from his own. He waited only moments before she answered. She grabbed a fistful of
his silver Monarchs jersey and jerked DeMarcus into
her room. The door automatically shut behind him.

Jaclyn released him to stomp across the hotel's
thick blue carpet from the dining area, across the
living room and into the work space. She was dressed
in a cool green coat dress, a marked contrast from
the fury coming from her in waves. Had he looked as
incensed as she did now? Even her riot of rich, dark
brown curls were vibrating.

"Have you seen the paper?" Her voice shook with rage.

Had he sounded as infuriated?

DeMarcus watched her march back and forth across the room. "That's why I'm here."

"The papers in New York ran the story, too." Her eyes glowed with temper.

"I know. I just spoke with my father." DeMarcus walked farther into the room. Sections of the *Atlanta Constitution* were spread across the dining table. The front page of the sports section featuring their photo topped the pile.

"How did they even know that I would be in your room?"

"I'd wondered the same thing."

"I'm going to call the newspaper." Jaclyn reached for the papers, presumably to search for the publisher's phone number.

DeMarcus stepped forward and pressed his hand on the newspaper. Jaclyn's hand settled on top of his. "To say what?"

She looked at him with wide surprised eyes. "That I don't want the paper's staff skulking around my employees' hotel rooms. They have a right to feel safe and to be left alone during away games."

DeMarcus hesitated. He turned his hand over to hold hers. "That sounds reasonable."

Jaclyn waved the cell phone clenched in her left fist. "Then I'm going to tell the scum-sucking rodents that the next time I see them and their morally deficient minions, I'm going to tear their throats out."

DeMarcus froze. "That's not a good idea."

"Why not?" Jaclyn slipped her right hand from his grasp. Storm clouds settled over her features.

DeMarcus held her sizzling cinnamon gaze. She'd moved seamlessly between cool entrepreneur and hot-headed warrior. She was a confident, beautiful woman and a talented, driven athlete. "I know you're upset. So am I. Neither of us has ever had our personal lives on display before. But we can't give the media the satisfaction of a reaction."

His father's advice seemed even more sound as he spoke it to Jaclyn. But it seemed to irritate her.

She threw her hands up. "Why not?"

"Giving them a reaction will keep the story in the news. If we ignore it, it'll go away."

Jaclyn lifted the sports section, waving its crumpled front page in her hand. "I want to meet this photographer."

"What good will that do?"

"First, I want to make sure he's not included in our media events or press release distribution."

Again she sounded reasonable. But this time, DeMarcus was suspicious. "And then what?"

"And then, when I see whoever took the picture, I'm going to shove his pencil up his nose."

DeMarcus took her hand between both of his. It was cool and delicate, in contrast to her fierce mood. "You've got to let this go. Focus on the franchise, the players and the season. They're what's important." He nodded toward the newspaper. "That isn't."

Jaclyn returned the sports section to the dining table, her gaze fixed on their photo. "The people who expose these private moments don't realize or care about the damage they could be doing. How am I supposed to face Gerry and Bert? Or the other members of our franchise?"

Still holding her hands in one of his, DeMarcus

rubbed the area of his chest above his heart with his other palm. "We didn't do anything wrong."

Jaclyn's eyes met his. "I know that. I don't regret last night. Not one bit." She frowned. Her attention shifting back to the paper. "But I'm really not pleased about this morning. How are you supposed to coach the team?"

Her words stopped the tearing in his heart. "I'll be fine. So will you. But in the meantime, if the team continues to lose, people will think you're keeping me as the coach because we're sleeping together."

Jaclyn shrugged. "We know you're my head coach because you have what it takes to turn the Monarchs around."

"Thank you." His throat dried at her words.

"But to win, you have to get to know the people behind your game plans. What motivates them? What keeps them from winning?"

DeMarcus crossed his arms. "I can't be the Monarchs' counselor."

"Try, you stubborn man. If you'd like, I'll even order your subscription to Oprah Winfrey's magazine."

DeMarcus arched a brow. "You're barely paying me enough to be their coach."

"You're going to need the players behind you, and the only way to ensure that is to get to know them."

He frowned. "I don't believe in that touchy-feely stuff."

Jaclyn moved closer. She ran the fingertips of her right hand over his forehead. "I believe in you, and I believe in the team. The team won't keep losing. And I don't care what other people think. So don't worry about that."

DeMarcus dragged his fingers over his close-cropped hair and paced away. "There's something you should know."

"What's that?"

DeMarcus claimed her gaze. "I don't do one-night stands."

Jaclyn arched a brow. "Never?"

"Never."

She cocked her head. "Ever?"

DeMarcus smiled at her teasing. "Ever."

"That's good because neither do I." Jaclyn crossed her arms. "So what was last night?"

Despite her banter, DeMarcus sensed Jaclyn's unease. He read the caution in her eyes and the tension in her posture. He approached her. "I work for you."

"And I'm your boss everywhere but in the bedroom." Jaclyn let her arms drop.

DeMarcus reclaimed her hands. His thumbs massaged her palms. He felt a fine tremor in her fingers. That was the effect he had on her. And she took his breath away. "And if I want to get to know you outside of the bedroom?"

Jaclyn smiled. "I'd like that, too. We'll just have to keep our personal and professional lives separate. Can you manage that?"

DeMarcus brought her hands to his lips. He touched the tip of his tongue to the back of her fingers and watched her eyes darken. "I can handle it."

"Good." Jaclyn moved closer to him. "And we won't worry about what other people think." She raised on her toes and pressed her lips to his.

DeMarcus's stomach muscles tightened. In that moment, he wanted to coach the Monarchs to a winning season, not for his reputation or for his family's name. He wanted to win for Jaclyn.

DeMarcus prowled the basketball court's sidelines in his black Italian suit and best poker face. His muscles strained as he willed the Monarchs to hold on to their 97 to 90 lead over the Atlanta Hawks. His eyes darted to the game clock. Two minutes remained in the fourth quarter. Too much time. They'd been here before, battling to a fourth-quarter lead that he couldn't keep from evaporating with seconds to go.

Too much time.

Mike Bibby, Atlanta's seasoned guard, blew past the Monarchs' porous defense. Bibby caught an easy shot from behind the arc. Three points. Monarchs, 97; Hawks, 93.

Hawks fans, sensing their team's resurgence, rose to cheer them on. Chants of "Defense!" filled the arena. DeMarcus clenched his teeth.

Barron Douglas took possession of the ball and jogged back down the court.

One minute twenty-four seconds to go. They were losing their lead. He had to stop the bleeding. "Time-out!"

The Monarchs dragged their feet to the sidelines. DeMarcus marched up to them. He clenched his fists to keep from shaking his starters. "The game's not over yet. Why have you stopped playing?"

Anthony drained the bottle of water a teammate passed to him. "We haven't stopped."

DeMarcus glared at him. "Then what's happened to our lead?" He turned to the other players. "Shore up the defense. Talk to each other. The game's not over."

He quickly gave each player individual instructions before the buzzer rang. The players walked back onto the court. Where was their energy?

"Pick up the pace." DeMarcus shouted to be heard above the primal screams of the Hawks' faithful.

Atlanta's Jason Collins covered Vincent, the Monarchs' center, at the left perimeter. Collins's teammate, Al Horford, defended Serge at the right perimeter. The Hawks' Marvin Williams and Josh Smith double-teamed Anthony in the paint. Jamal stood wide open at the post for an easy layup. Barron ignored the rookie and took the shot over Bibby's extended arm. Bibby barely touched it, but that was enough. Barron missed. Hawks' fans went wild.

DeMarcus ground his teeth, resisting the urge to loosen his silver silk tie. He watched, incredulous, as Jamal raced across the court without even trying to defend the ball. The Hawks' Collins took it instead.

"Jamal, defend the ball." DeMarcus fought the urge to run across the court to get it himself. He was tired of repeating those words. Why wouldn't Jamal listen?

The rookie's reputation as a ball hog had spread across the league. Opponents didn't worry about covering him because they knew Jamal's teammates wouldn't give him the ball. DeMarcus added that to the list of transgressions he'd address in the locker room.

Collins passed to Williams. The Atlanta guard lobbed the ball to Bibby, who advanced it to half court. Bibby waited while his teammates took positions around the basket. Vincent covered Collins. Serge took Horford. Anthony guarded Williams, and Jamal stood with Smith. Barron defended Bibby, watching for an opportunity to force a turnover.

The Monarchs were too quiet. Two months into

the season, they still played like five individuals instead of a team.

"Talk to each other." DeMarcus clapped his hands until they stung.

Bibby sent the ball down the open lane opposite Anthony. His teammate Williams snatched it. Unable to shake Anthony, Williams passed to Collins. Collins handed off to Smith. Smith side stepped Jamal. He backed out of the perimeter and arched the ball over the rookie. Three points. The Hawks cut the lead to 97, 96. Fifty-two seconds remained in the fourth quarter.

DeMarcus thought his eyes would bleed. "Move. Set up. Move. Move."

Jamal ignored the order to sprint across the court.

Warrick ran from the bench to pace Jamal along the sideline. "Be aggressive, Jamal. Pressure your man."

Jamal scowled at the veteran as he ran past. "Sit down, Grandpa."

DeMarcus frowned at Warrick. Why was he coaching the rookie who was after his job? He'd benched the veteran in the middle of the third quarter. Warrick wouldn't take shots and Jamal wouldn't pass the ball. DeMarcus scrubbed his hands over his face. If he could combine the two players, maybe the team would get a win.

Vincent plucked the ball from the Hawks' post and dribbled three steps before tossing it to Barron. Barron took the ball to the perimeter, slowing the Hawks' frantic pace.

The game clock read forty-five seconds and counting. The shot clock flashed seventeen seconds. The arena's chant of "Defense!" build to a crescendo.

The Monarchs set up their positions, drawing their

defenders with them. Vincent took the post as the Hawks' Collins guarded him. Anthony was ready in the paint. The Hawks' Williams defended him. Jamal and Serge had opposite perimeters with the Hawks' Smith and Horford, respectively. Barron charged the post, braving the triangle defense. Bibby moved in for the block. Two seconds on the shot clock. Barron carried the lay up over Bibby's head. Williams slapped the shot away—but not before it touched the rim. Loose ball. Serge and Anthony moved in for the rebound. Thirty-one seconds on the game clock. The shot clock started fresh.

The Hawks' Horford snatched the ball away. DeMarcus tensed. The Atlanta forward prepared to sprint the length of the court. He seemed focused on the Hawks' net and the two-point shot that would give his team the win with less than thirty seconds to the game.

DeMarcus cupped his mouth and shouted over the crowd's deafening screams. "Get after him. Quick! Quick!"

But Vincent was already giving chase. The Monarchs' center extended his left arm. With a twist of his wrist, he stole the ball from the Hawks' veteran. Vincent pivoted, dribbling twice. The game clock drained to six. Five. Four. At half court, he made a no-look pass to Jamal. The wide-open rookie stepped into the lane.

12

Jamal palmed Vincent's no-look pass. He hopped to the edge of the perimeter. Four seconds and counting. Defenders converged toward him. Jamal bent his knees. He launched himself into the air. Nine bodies leaped with him. Two seconds and counting. Jamal drew a rainbow to the basket.

Three points. Nothing but net.

One second remained on the clock. Serge grabbed the ball and let the time run out. Final score: Monarchs 100, Hawks 96.

DeMarcus dropped his stoic mask. His features flashed into a broad grin. Their first win of the season. They'd proven it was possible.

He lifted his gaze to the visiting owner's box. Through the glass, he caught sight of Jaclyn. Her fists were raised and a wide grin spread across her glowing face. He saluted her, and she blew him a kiss.

Behind him, the Hawks faithful roared their disappointment. But they couldn't drown out the Monarchs' cheers. Euphoria lifted them from the bench. Warrick Evans reached him first, wrapping him in a bear hug before joining his teammates on the court. Other players followed Warrick's lead, hugging DeMarcus and patting his back on their way off the court. The win had brought them closer together than they'd been all season. This is what they had needed—a connection, a sense of unity to carry them through. Maybe Jaclyn had a point. Maybe he needed more than X's and O's.

DeMarcus pushed his way across the court, past devastated Hawks players to their head coach, Mike Woodson. He extended his right hand. "Good game, Coach."

Woodson congratulated him, shaking his hand before turning away. DeMarcus didn't blame the other man for the brevity of their exchange. No team wanted to break an opponent's losing streak. But, then, no team wanted to lose forever.

"Yeah, Pop. We still have a lot of work to do on speed, defense and Jamal's ball hogging." DeMarcus checked his watch. It was more than an hour after the game, but he'd wanted to check in with his father before getting on the plane back to New York.

"At least now we know the Monarchs can play all four quarters." Julian's words tumbled over each other in his excitement. "That's great progress."

"It is. The locker room had a lot more energy tonight than it had on Wednesday after our road loss to the Golden State Warriors in California."

"I know you were reluctant to take this job, but you're starting to turn the team around."

"We still have a long season ahead of us. We're only

halfway through November with seventy-three games to go."

"Still, I'm proud of you, son."

DeMarcus closed his eyes, absorbing the words that never lost their value. "Thanks, Pop." He hefted his bag from his hotel bed. "I'd better check out of the hotel and get the shuttle to the airport."

"OK. I'll meet you at JFK. Safe trip."

DeMarcus confirmed his flight information, then disconnected the call.

His parents had always insisted on picking him up from the airport. DeMarcus treasured the bittersweet memory of them waiting together for him. Now, his father insisted on continuing the tradition alone.

DeMarcus had started across the suite to the door when his cell phone rang again. Was his father calling back? He took the phone from the front pocket of his suit.

He recognized the number. "Hello, Gerry."

"I thought we had an agreement." The franchise partner was doing his best mafia impersonation.

DeMarcus folded into the living area's sofa, settling his travel bag beside his feet. This could take a while. "I told you I wouldn't deliberately lose."

"A couple of wins at home are understandable. If you win on the road, you run the risk of rebuilding the team's momentum. I can't allow that."

"I'm not worrying about you. The Monarchs are my responsibility." In the silence that followed his response, DeMarcus checked his watch. He could give Gerald a couple of minutes before ending the call. The team and the airport shuttle were waiting.

"Do you really want me to leak a story to the

media about your drug addiction? Is that what you want?" Gerald's tone was taunting.

DeMarcus clenched his teeth. *I'm proud of you, son.* His father's love and respect were all he needed. What would he do if he lost that?

DeMarcus breathed deeply, easing the pressure in his chest. "If you took that lie to the press, do you think I wouldn't tell them you're smearing my reputation because you want to move Brooklyn's team to Las Vegas?"

Gerald's chuckle mocked him. "Who do you think they'll believe? A respectable businessman or yet another drug-dependent athlete?"

DeMarcus shot off the sofa. "Try it." With that dare, he disconnected the call and exited the room.

He wasn't going to hand Gerald his self-respect on a silver platter. He put the other man's threat out of his mind. If Gerald tried to destroy DeMarcus's family's name, he knew his father would support him. He could only hope the community would do the same.

Jaclyn practically floated up to the shuttle she'd arranged to transport her and the team to the Harts-field-Jackson Atlanta International Airport. DeMarcus stood beside her. She clasped her hands together to keep from touching him—part excitement from the win and part reaction to the way he looked in that sexy Italian suit. As the team arrived, Jaclyn stepped forward to congratulate each sharp-dressed player and coach as they boarded the vehicle.

"Great pass," she praised Vincent Jardine, the quiet center who'd made the winning play.

"Nice shot," she said to Jamal Ward, the hot-dogging rookie who'd scored the winning basket.

"Good game," she cheered Barron Douglas. The team captain had shown strong leadership on the court.

"I'm not trading you," she told Serge Gateau, who'd protected the ball—and their win—in the final second of the game.

"Great defense," she complimented Warrick Evans. The shooting guard had spent most of the final two quarters on the bench. But his defense in the first half of the game had positioned the team to win.

Jaclyn made a mental note to talk with DeMarcus about benching Warrick, but not while they were surrounded by players and coaches. She slid a sideways glance toward the head coach, who stood by her side, watching the exchanges. She'd wait until they were alone.

"Good game," she told Anthony Chambers. The forward had managed incredible acrobatics at the net despite being double-teamed for most of the game.

Jaclyn preceded DeMarcus onto the shuttle and waited for the players and coaches to settle into their seats. "As I said at the beginning of the season, we've had a couple of tough years. But I believe in this team." She met the eyes of each player, starters and bench, and every coach. "I believe in you. And tonight, you proved me right. You played like champions. You played with heart and snapped the twenty-three-game losing streak that we'd carried over from last season. I have faith that, at the end of this season, you're going to bring the trophy to Brooklyn."

The shuttle swayed a bit as the team accompanied its thunderous cheers with foot stomping and hand clapping. She felt DeMarcus's hand at her waist to steady her. Still, Jaclyn sat before she lost her footing.

"No wonder the team loves you." There was humor in DeMarcus's voice that belied the clouds in his coal black eyes. What was on his mind?

"And I love the team." She shifted in her seat to better study him. He was sexy in the warm-up suits he favored. But he was incredible in the black Italian suit, white shirt and silver tie he'd worn tonight. He'd been a distraction to her during the game.

Jaclyn lowered her voice. "Did the players give you a hard time because of the newspaper article?"

He shrugged. "Practice was awkward at first, but it blew over."

What did that mean?

The players and coaches hadn't looked at her any differently, so they must have put the article behind them. So would she.

"Good." She stopped feeling awkward about sitting beside him on the shuttle. After all, she'd sat beside him when they'd first arrived at the hotel.

The vehicle pulled away from the curb. Jaclyn paused to enjoy the view of the Atlanta Hawks' home, the Philips Arena, at night. "We've won other games, but this one will always be special to me."

"Me too. My first win as a head coach." DeMarcus spoke softly.

Jaclyn touched the back of his hand as it lay on his lap. DeMarcus turned to look at her.

She gave him a smile. "Your father must be very proud."

"Yes, he is. I called him before I left the hotel."

"Then what's wrong? You won an important game

tonight. You should be excited. Instead you seem almost moody."

DeMarcus turned his attention to the scene outside. "I don't want anything to ever ruin this memory."

Jaclyn gave a startled laugh. "What could possibly ruin it? It's perfect."

"Sooner or later, all good things come to an end."

Jaclyn frowned. Why would they have to end? Until this moment, she hadn't realized how much she'd come to depend on his staying with the team for the entire season. Was he still thinking of leaving? Why? He couldn't have lost faith in the team. They'd just won.

Jaclyn stilled. A cold hand fisted in her gut. Had he lost faith in her?

"Thank you for giving up your Saturday on such short notice." Gerald addressed Jaclyn, DeMarcus and Albert the day after the Hawks' game. He pontificated from the head of the mahogany table in the Monarchs' largest conference room. Albert was silent on his right. Jaclyn observed Gerald from her seat at the foot of the table. DeMarcus was to her left.

Jaclyn leaned back in the well-cushioned, black swivel chair. She adjusted the skirt of her burnt-orange wool dress. "This is the NBA, Gerry. We don't work Monday through Friday, nine to five, especially during the season. Just because we played Atlanta last night doesn't mean we have today off."

Perhaps her comment was unnecessary. She'd concede it was mean. But she'd had enough of Gerald's pompous attitude. Why hadn't she noticed it before? Maybe she hadn't been around him as much.

Gerald's lips tightened. A red flush a few shades lighter than his crewneck sweater dusted his high mocha cheekbones. "Your comment brings us nicely to our reason for being here."

Jaclyn glanced at the other men in the room. De-Marcus's shoulders under his silver Monarchs jersey seemed taut. Albert looked uncomfortable in his conservative brown sweater. Was she the only one who had no idea what Gerald was talking about?

Jaclyn touched her silver and black Monarchs lapel pin. She made herself appear relaxed. She'd had plenty of experience doing that when she'd practiced corporate law with Jonas & Prather. "Why are we here, Gerry?"

"This is why we're here." Gerald slid a newspaper down the table. The journal stopped about midway across the high-gloss surface.

Jaclyn didn't need to pick it up. She knew what it was. It was Friday's sports section from the *New York Post*. Yesterday's section opened with the photo of her kissing DeMarcus.

In her peripheral vision, Jaclyn saw DeMarcus straighten in his chair. She felt the anger building within him. Jaclyn spoke, hoping to distract DeMarcus from saying something they'd both regret. "I'm still unclear, Gerry. Why are we here?" She kept her tone cool, her voice steady despite her own rising temper.

Gerald pointed toward the newspaper no one else had touched. "What were you doing outside Marc's hotel room?"

Jaclyn's gaze shifted to Albert. The third franchise

owner looked like he wanted to be anywhere else. Anywhere. She turned back to Gerald. "I was leaving."

Gerald's mouth curved upward. "And what were you doing *in* his hotel room?"

Jaclyn struggled to keep her breathing even. "I'm not here to satisfy your prurient interests, Gerry. I don't owe you an explanation."

DeMarcus waved toward the newspaper. "This is your way of trying to get me to throw away the season. I'm not going to allow you to insult Jack to try to get to me."

Jaclyn stared at DeMarcus. He was angry and determined, a warrior ready for battle. He tugged at her heart. Was she falling a little in love with him?

Gerald offered a cold smile. "I don't want your co-operation. I want your resignation."

Jaclyn's eyes flared wide. "What?" Her attention shifted again to Albert. He remained still. Why was he here if he wasn't going to say anything?

From his briefcase of tricks, Gerald produced a stack of white sheets, stapled together in a corner. "Marc is in violation of his contract's morality clause."

Jaclyn would have to rein in her temper if she were going to get through this. "How?"

Gerald stood, carrying a copy of DeMarcus's contract with him. He found the page he was looking for and set the document on the table in front of her before returning to his seat. "Under paragraph eleven, section D, the contract states, in essence, that franchise employees will not engage in romantic liaisons while both parties are employed by the franchise."

Jaclyn skimmed the familiar passage, blocking out the escalating tension she sensed in DeMarcus. "My grandfather wanted that language added to the employee contracts. He wanted to raise awareness of sexual harassment and make sure everyone knew such conduct wouldn't be tolerated in his organization."

Gerald nodded. "So, since your grandfather realized the importance of the clause, I'm sure you'll do the right thing and enforce the language."

Jaclyn met her partner's eyes. "I'm happy to, especially since I drafted the language."

Gerald's lips parted in shock. He rallied quickly. "In that case, fire him. Or don't you believe what you wrote?"

Jaclyn smiled. "I do believe what I wrote, Gerry. But it doesn't apply to Marc." She felt DeMarcus's surprise. Her smile broadened.

Gerald frowned. "Yes, it does. Your sweet good night photo appears on the pages of several newspapers."

Jaclyn tapped the stack of papers in front of her. "The language prohibits employees from fraternizing. DeMarcus is an employee. I'm not."

"She's right, Gerry." Albert finally spoke, looking over his shoulder to address Gerald. "They may not have shown the best judgment in the when and the where of their . . . activities. But neither one of them violated the contract." He turned his attention to Jaclyn and DeMarcus. "Just, both of you, please exercise better judgment in the future. The franchise doesn't need this type of publicity."

Jaclyn faced Albert. "You're right, Bert. I apologize."

DeMarcus inclined his head. "So do I."

Albert nodded. "Good. Now that we've cleared that up, Marc, please don't let us hold you any longer. Thank you for coming."

"But—" Gerald raised his hand to stop the activities.

Albert grabbed Gerald's arm and returned it to the conference table. "We're done, Gerry."

Jaclyn stood with DeMarcus to leave, but Albert stopped her. "Jackie, just a few more moments of your time, please."

Jaclyn hesitated. She felt DeMarcus's touch on her forearm. She smiled and shook her head at the concerned look in his dark eyes. Jaclyn returned to her seat. "Sure, Bert. What is it?"

Albert waited for DeMarcus to leave before he began. "I've had enough."

"Enough of what?" Gerald shifted to face Albert. His voice was pitch-perfect irritation.

Albert glared at Gerald. "Enough of the fighting between you and Jackie. Marc was right, Gerry. It was distasteful of you to exploit Jackie's personal life to get your way."

Gerald stabbed a finger toward the newspaper laying ignored in the center of the table. "Are you happy to have the franchise in the paper's gossip section?"

Albert flung his arms in the air. "Give me a break, Gerry. Where were you when the *New York Sports* printed the article airing the players' complaints about the team?"

Gerald shifted a look at Jaclyn. His temper seemed to evaporate. "I was busy."

Jaclyn's heart beat faster. Her gaze dropped to the newspaper before narrowing on Gerald. "Busy doing what? Planting more negative stories about us in the press?"

Albert followed her gaze from the paper to Gerald. "That's too far-fetched, Jackie. How would Gerry know you'd spend the night with Marc?"

Gerald rolled up the sleeves of his apple red

13

Jaclyn stopped breathing. Albert had refused to sell his shares to her earlier. Gerald had asked him not to. So what was he planning to do now?

She swung her attention to Gerald. She sensed her adversary's shock even from the other end of the conference table. Albert had caught him off guard as well.

Gerald leaned into the table, closing in on Albert. "To whom are you going to sell your shares?"

Albert didn't appear intimidated by the muted anger in Gerald's voice. "Don't worry, Gerry. I'm going to sell my shares to both of you." He waved his right hand from Jaclyn to Gerald. "One share to Jackie and twenty-five shares to you, making you both equal partners."

The knots in Jaclyn's stomach unraveled, allowing her to breathe again. At least Albert wasn't going to sell all of his shares to Gerald, which would have made Gerald the majority owner with fifty-one percent of the franchise.

Still, she was disappointed—and a little sad. Four friends had started the franchise fifty-five years ago.

Soon, only two descending families would remain. She folded her hands on the table's smooth, cool surface. "I'm sorry that you no longer want to be a part of the Monarchs family, Bert. But I appreciate your dividing your shares evenly. That's very fair."

"No, it's not." Gerald sounded indignant. "I have to buy a lot more shares than you do."

"Calm down, Gerry." Albert stood to leave, shoving his chair under the table. "You don't have to write the check now. We can work something out."

Jaclyn caught the bite in Albert's voice. How anxious was he to get away from the strained atmosphere? "Or I can buy all of your shares, Bert."

She'd have to sell some of her investments. Her portfolio would take a big hit, but it would be worth it. Albert held her gaze. Was he considering her offer?

He glanced at Gerald, then back to Jaclyn. "I'll let the two of you figure that out." Albert strode from the conference room without another word or a second glance.

Jaclyn turned away from the door as Albert disappeared through the threshold. She faced Gerald. "How about it, Gerry? Do you want to make a deal?"

Gerald pushed away from the table. "It will be a cold day in hell before I let you have majority ownership of this franchise." He followed Albert from the room.

A cold day in hell? One way or another, she'd see to it that Gerald needed a lot of sweaters.

* * *

DeMarcus blew the heavy black whistle he carried around his neck, commanding his players' attention from their Monday morning practice. "Bring it in."

He waited for the thirteen Monarchs to gather with him and the other coaches near the polished wood bleachers. Their sneakers squeaked as they crossed the practice court. Their bodies dripped sweat from their ninety minutes of warm up and fundamentals—dribbling, shooting, passing and footwork, core skills that would carry the team at least into the play-offs. Hopefully.

DeMarcus settled his hands on his hips, letting his gaze take in the varied expressions looking back at him. "We're coming off of a hard-earned victory. But it was one win out of nine games. We have another seventy-three on the calendar. Another five months to the season."

Point guard Barron Douglas folded his long, damp frame onto one of the bleachers. He ran both hands over his thick cornrows. "Why can't we just enjoy the win? Why do you always have to look at the negatives?"

The team captain was frustrated. So was DeMarcus. He dropped his arms to his sides. "We're still last in the Eastern Conference. Do you like being there?"

Barron dragged his tattooed forearm across his damp upper lip. "Of course I don't."

DeMarcus lifted his gaze to the other Monarchs. "We need to build on the single success we have."

"What do you mean?" Jamal set the basketball on the tip of his left index finger and started it spinning with a slap of his right hand.

DeMarcus stepped forward and took the ball from

the younger man's fingertip. "As a team, against Atlanta, we were stronger on defense in the first half and committed fewer fouls. We're improving in those areas. But we couldn't match them for speed or shooting accuracy."

Jamal barked a laugh. "Maybe these old men were slow and nearsighted. But I ran with them, and I got the looks, too."

"What looks?" Anthony Chambers glanced at his teammates in confusion before turning back to Jamal. "You were shooting bricks, son."

Barron Douglas chuckled. "You need glasses if you thought those were good looks."

"We could have used your help on defense." Warrick's tone forced the young shooting guard to hear the truth.

Jamal bristled. "Coach said I was good on defense."

DeMarcus shook his head. "I said as a team we were strong on defense and played a clean game. Individually, you carried the most fouls playing the fewest minutes. You have to do better."

Anthony tapped his shoulder. "And God knows you were missing in action on the defense."

Warrick shrugged. "What good are all those fancy shots if you don't get the ball back?"

Jamal's expression darkened. "At least I got game, old man. Your best playing days are behind you."

Warrick crossed his arms. "If you want my spot, earn it, rookie."

"That's enough." DeMarcus passed Oscar the basketball he'd taken from Jamal. The assistant coach caught it with one hand, then tossed it into the large metal cart with the other balls.

DeMarcus returned his attention to his team.

"Thursday, we're playing the Pacers in Indianapolis. The week before Thanksgiving. They're a faster, more accurate team as well. We need to stick with what worked for us, a strong defense and a clean game."

"And a late-night booty call." A salacious grin spread across Jamal's face.

DeMarcus's body iced over. He turned to face the rookie. "Excuse me?"

The shooting guard chuckled knowingly. "You heard me. Ms. Jones fine-tuned your coaching."

Icy anger melted to red-hot rage. DeMarcus clenched and unclenched his fists, straining against the urge to knock the lascivious smile from the younger man's face. "Jaclyn Jones is your employer. She owns this team. You'd better use a respectful tone and language when you talk to or about her."

A rebellious flame sparked in Jamal's black eyes. "Were you using a respectful tone when she was using her skills to relax you?"

Caution exploded as DeMarcus lunged for the smaller man. Jamal jumped back.

Someone grabbed DeMarcus from behind. Heavily muscled arms wrapped around his chest. Oscar's urgent voice came from behind his ear. "Don't do it. He's not worth the hassle."

Jamal bounced on his toes. His words tumbled over each other in an adrenaline rush. "Yeah. You know what they'd do to you if you hit me, man? You know what they'd do? They'd suspend your ass. Yeah. And they'd probably fine your ass, too. Yeah. Come on, then. Hit me. You want to hit me? Come on, then."

DeMarcus saw red. He forced himself to remain still within Oscar's hold. He couldn't pummel his players, no matter how much they deserved it. Not only was it against NBA rules, but it also was not the way to maintain discipline and control of the team.

DeMarcus's chest rose and fell with a deep breath, loosening Oscar's bond across his chest. "I'm all right."

As Oscar stepped back, a movement from the corner of his right eye distracted DeMarcus.

Two strides carried Warrick to Jamal's side. He drew back his right arm and planted a punch to the rookie's jaw that knocked the younger man on his butt and silenced the court.

Rubbing his fist, Warrick turned to DeMarcus. "Go ahead and suspend me. And I'll pay the fine gladly."

DeMarcus glanced up from Jamal's shocked and pained expression to Warrick's strained and tight features. "Suspend you for what?"

The two men exchanged a long look. Warrick relaxed. DeMarcus inclined his head, giving his veteran guard a small smile of gratitude.

Anthony scratched his head. "I didn't see anything."

Barron stood, putting distance between himself and Jamal. "Me neither."

Vincent Jardine, the quiet center, slapped Warrick on the back. "Not a thing."

Serge Gateau spread his arms wide. "Que s'est produit?"

Oscar scowled at Jamal. "What are you doing on the floor, rookie?"

DeMarcus listened to the chorus of disclaimers all avowing that they hadn't seen Warrick knock Jamal to the ground. He turned to his assistant coach. "Hundreds of hours of practice, travel and games couldn't bring them together. But seeing Jamal knocked on his ass has helped them bond."

Oscar grunted. "It's united them against Ward. That won't help us in the long run."

DeMarcus watched Jamal limp toward the bleachers. His lip was busted. It would bloom like a red rose before the end of the day. "He brought it on himself."

"The kid's got a bad attitude, that's for sure. And the older players all like and respect Jackie. So do I." Oscar shifted to look DeMarcus in the eyes. "Treat her right."

DeMarcus watched his assistant coach walk away. This practice had gone more like a daytime drama. He didn't know what to expect after the commercial break.

"You're very persistent, Jaclyn." Mortimer Gandy's thin, wrinkled lips curved with unwilling amusement.

The Empire Arena's majority owner helped her out of her silver cashmere coat. There was more than a week until Thanksgiving, but already it felt like winter.

Mortimer cupped her forearm as he and Jaclyn crossed the two-story entrance of his Saddle River, New Jersey, home. Mortimer was approaching ninety years of age, if he wasn't already there. Jaclyn cupped her hand over his frail one. Who was leading whom?

Jaclyn's scarlet stilettos—a perfect match to her power skirt suit—tapped against the green and brown stone flooring. She was careful to match his much slower pace. "I appreciate your time, Mr. Gandy."

His brother's voice reached her just as she accompanied Mortimer into his sitting room. "Come now,

Jackie. Your grandfather never called either of us Mr. Gandy. I'm Sandy and he's Morty. Otherwise how will we know to whom you're speaking?"

Jaclyn smiled at Mortimer's younger brother. Sanford Gandy's scarlet Rutgers University sweatshirt and baggy black jeans stood in striking contrast to Mortimer's beige and cocoa, diamond-patterned sweater and cocoa corduroy pants.

"You know that I don't like to be called Morty, Sanford. Franklin Jones never called me that." Mortimer spoke with long-suffering patience. They must have had this conversation numerous times before.

Hiding her amusement at the brothers' exchange, Jaclyn allowed Mortimer to escort her to an armchair beside the fireplace. Assured Jaclyn was comfortable, Mortimer ambled to the matching chair on the other side of the tan sofa.

"And I don't like to be called Sanford, Mort." Sanford filled a gold-rimmed china cup from the tea service on the coffee table in front of him. He rose from the sofa to offer the cup to Jaclyn. "It's Earl Grey. Would you like a cookie?"

Jaclyn took the cup and used the napkin Sanford offered to select a lemon cream cookie. "Thank you, Sandy."

Mortimer lifted his teacup and saucer from the corner table on his right. "If my brother is done with his petulance, perhaps you can tell us how we can help you, my dear. Our attorneys assured us they have explained that we're not inclined to change the terms of the Empire contract."

"Yes, they have." Jaclyn shifted forward on the

fluffy chair and crossed her ankles. "But I wanted to present my proposal to you personally."

Sanford settled back in the sofa. "Great. We're listening."

Pushing past her nerves, Jaclyn noted Sanford's excited energy and Mortimer's respectful silence. She called upon her cool negotiator's personae from her days with Jonas & Prather. But this negotiation was too personal. The outcome meant too much.

Jaclyn lowered her shoulders and straightened her back. "Our event revenue is up more than seventy-five percent over last season from ticket, refreshment and product sales. This season, we should double our income compared to last year."

Mortimer crossed his right leg over his left and balanced the cup and saucer on his knee. "You said you *should* double your income. What would prevent you from accomplishing that goal?"

Jaclyn didn't blink. "We'll need to make it to the play-offs."

"Play-offs?" Sanford looked from Jaclyn to Mortimer and back. "You're one and nine. It's last season all over again. How are you going to make it to the play-offs this time when you couldn't last season?"

Jaclyn felt the muscles in her neck and back tightening. "The season's still young, Sandy. We have seventy-three more chances." Her heart beat loudly in her ears, almost drowning her words. Jaclyn switched her attention to Mortimer's gaze. She took a moment to slow her breathing. "The Brooklyn Monarchs and the Empire Arena have been partners since both organizations started."

"That's fifty-five years." Sanford's nod lent emphasis to his observation.

"That's right." Jaclyn gripped the dainty teacup with sweaty fingers. "The Monarchs played their first game in the Empire the day the arena opened."

"I remember that night as though it were yesterday." Mortimer's sigh seemed to transport him and his younger brother to their opening night.

Sanford's laughter cracked the silence. He pointed a thin finger toward Jaclyn. "Your grandfather was so nervous. In the third quarter, I thought he'd put on a uniform and run some plays himself."

Mortimer nodded. "He willed the Monarchs to win."

Jaclyn leaned forward. "The Monarchs had a Cinderella run their first season. They didn't win the championship, but they made it into the play-offs. I know we'll have another Cinderella run this season. It's still early. I'm confident we'll make it to the play-offs. We have veteran players and a Hall of Fame coach."

Mortimer scratched his chin. "Marc Guinn doesn't have any coaching experience."

Jaclyn waved her hand in a dismissive gesture. "He has championship experience." Adrenalin flowed through Jaclyn's system, replacing her nerves with energy. She spoke with more confidence than she'd felt in months. "The Monarchs and the Empire are more than companies. They're part of each other, and part of the community. I don't want to see that partnership end. Do you?"

Jaclyn waited for the Empire owners' response. She glanced between the two brothers. Was it her imagination or did they appear uncomfortable?

Mortimer exchanged a look with Sanford. His

younger brother looked away. Mortimer met Jaclyn's eyes. "No, we don't want to see it end. But we don't have a choice."

Jaclyn shifted her gaze to Sanford. The minority arena owner wouldn't meet her eyes. She looked again at Mortimer. "What do you mean?"

Mortimer sighed, staring into his teacup. "The day-to-day management has become too much for us. Our heirs have their own interests, which don't include the Empire."

Shards of ice piled into Jaclyn's chest. "You're selling the Empire." She made the statement with numbed lips.

Sanford spoke plaintively. "We don't want to, but we don't have any other choice."

Mortimer sighed. "And, frankly, our books look more attractive without the Monarchs. Other events bring in a greater profit."

"We're sorry, Jackie." Sanford tucked his chin into his chest.

A weighted silence fell into the sitting room. Jaclyn's gaze dropped to her cup of tea. The deep brown liquid shimmered in front of her, like her hopes. She took a drink to compose herself. Right now, she would have preferred coffee, really strong coffee. "How much are you asking for it?"

Mortimer's asking price stole her breath.

Jaclyn sipped more Earl Grey tea. The uneaten lemon cream cookie was heavy in her left palm. "Will you still end our partnership when we make it to the play-offs?"

Mortimer hesitated. "Yes. The Monarchs have three losing seasons. For two of those seasons, we've been losing money."

Jaclyn nodded at the older man's response. She sipped more tea to remove the lump in her throat.

Sanford slumped farther into the sofa. "We're sorry, Jackie. We don't have a choice."

Jaclyn lowered her teacup. "I understand your decision. But I have to believe that there's always a choice."

What were her choices? Finding another arena for the team or moving the Monarchs out of Brooklyn. Her heart squeezed in her chest. Were those really her only options?

"How did your meeting with the Empire Arena owners go?"

Althea's question pulled Jaclyn's attention away from her computer. She swallowed a spoonful of the chicken noodle soup she'd microwaved for her late lunch before answering. "Not well. How was your morning?"

Althea walked farther into her office. She fiddled with the silver decorative pin on her plum crewneck sweater. "I hate to pile more bad news on you, but you need to know the office gossip is at a fever pitch."

Jaclyn placed her plastic soup bowl on her desk and spun her chair to face her executive assistant. "What are they gossiping about?"

Althea smoothed her midcalf, smoke gray skirt. "You and Marc Guinn."

Jaclyn groaned and covered her face with her hands. "I can't believe I'd forgotten about that stupid picture." Especially since that stupid picture had already caused problems for her and DeMarcus.

"You've had a lot on your mind."

Jaclyn dropped her fists onto her desk. "I just wish

I knew how that scum-sucking photographer knew to wait outside of Marc's hotel room."

Althea clasped her hands together. "I think you were right. There's a leak in the franchise."

Jaclyn leaned back in her chair, disgusted. "First our players were complaining about management to the newspapers. Now our front office is calling the media to give us negative coverage. Why would anyone on our staff do that?"

Althea shook her head. "I don't think the leak is contacting the media directly. I think the person she's talking to called the media."

Jaclyn arched an eyebrow. "Do you know who the leak is?"

Althea shrugged. "My money's on Vanessa. Her tongue's been wagging the hardest about you and Marc."

Jaclyn closed her eyes. She didn't want to believe it. "Nessa's been with us for four years. Why would she want to hurt our image in the community?"

"She was Gerry's executive assistant. I think she feels a stronger commitment to Gerry than to the franchise. And she's still upset about what she sees as a demotion."

Jaclyn's mind was spinning. "But how would she know that I would be in Marc's room that night?"

Althea gave her a sarcastic look. "You and Marc are single and attractive, and you can scoop the sexual tension between you with a spoon."

Jaclyn fought against a blush. She wasn't successful. "Why would Nessa betray the organization?"

"Maybe she doesn't consider it being disloyal to the team. Maybe she considers it being loyal to Gerry."

Jaclyn pondered Althea's words. They made sense.

Still, she wanted to hear the explanation from Vanessa. "I hate to think of anyone in our franchise family making us vulnerable to negative media coverage."

"I'll keep an eye on her."

Jaclyn's mind remained on Vanessa and Gerald. "Let me know what you find out. We can't have someone we can't trust on our staff."

Jaclyn shoved aside the remains of her chicken noodle soup, spilling broth on a manila file folder.

She'd been right. Gerald had a spy. Why was he so determined to destroy their franchise? And what other schemes was he planning against them?

14

"Working late again, player?"

DeMarcus watched Jaclyn close his office door and walk toward him. She wore her power suit again. With whom had she met today? Her franchise partners or the Empire owners' lawyers?

The deep red jacket cinched her small waist. The matching skirt traced her slim hips and slender thighs. Her red stilettos made her legs seem even longer. He remembered the way those long, athletic limbs had felt wrapped around him.

DeMarcus stood, not caring whether Jaclyn noticed the effect she had on him. "You too."

"As Anthony Chambers would quote, 'There's no rest for the wicked, but the righteous don't need any.'" Jaclyn circled his desk, then cleared a spot on it to sit. She raised herself onto its corner and crossed her legs. "How was your day?"

DeMarcus sat again. He took a deep breath of her soft, lilac scent. "Uneventful."

Jaclyn leaned forward. Her fragrance wrapped around him. Her cinnamon eyes hypnotized him.

She brushed the fingertips of her right hand over his forehead, and the last of his tension drained away. "Are you sure? Because Oscar told me he had to restrain you this morning to keep you from knocking Jamal's teeth out of his head."

His tension returned. "Oscar didn't have the right to tell you about that."

"*You* should have told me." Jaclyn maintained her soft, slightly amused tone. Her fingertips stroked over his forehead again. If she was angry, she was doing a damn fine job of hiding it.

"I had it under control."

Her lush red lips curved. "You should have told me that, too."

"You have enough, dealing with Gerry and Bert."

Her expression sobered. Her hands dropped to his shoulders. "I need to know everything that involves this team, whether it's the condition of the training facilities or tension between players and coaches. As head coach, I expect you to tell me. Immediately. I don't want to hear about it from the media."

DeMarcus searched her eyes. She wasn't flexing her authority or exuding her charm. It was a matter-of-fact statement that nevertheless didn't leave room for negotiation. "You're right. I'm sorry."

Her hands linked behind his neck and she pulled him closer. She closed her eyes as she leaned in, covering his lips with hers. Her mouth nibbled at his, teasing him. He stroked his tongue across her lips, coaxing them to part. He'd been too long without her taste. Jaclyn moaned and opened for him. DeMarcus slipped his tongue inside her mouth to play and explore. He gripped her waist and plucked her from his desk, settling her onto his lap and into his arms. His body stirred.

Jaclyn shifted even closer to him. Her breasts pressed against his chest. Her bottom wiggled in his lap. DeMarcus groaned and pulled her tighter. She caressed his tongue with her own. DeMarcus's body heated. He caught his breath. He squeezed her thigh through the wool material of her skirt before moving over her hip and up her waist to cup her breast. The warm, soft weight against his palm brought images of their night together. Jaclyn trembled within his embrace. She pressed her hands against his chest.

DeMarcus leaned away. "What is it?"

Jaclyn kept her hand on his chest. "Could you take me home? I gave Herb the rest of the night off."

"I—"

A low grumbling interrupted him. The sound quickly grew to an angry roar. DeMarcus's gaze bounced to Jaclyn's flat stomach, then back to her face. Her eyes had stretched wide. Her golden brown skin burned bright red.

An incredulous grin lifted DeMarcus's cheeks. "Have you eaten at all today?"

"Apparently not enough." She bit her bottom lip.

Laughter grew from deep inside DeMarcus and burst free. His shoulders shook with it. He gathered Jaclyn into his arms and rocked her. Could he even remember the last time he'd laughed this hard?

Jaclyn punched his shoulder. "That's enough. It's not even funny." The humor in her voice showed she was lying.

It wasn't easy, but DeMarcus controlled his amusement. "You shouldn't skip meals." He cupped Jaclyn's shoulders and held her from him. "Before I take you home, we'll stop by my house and I'll make dinner. My father's been asking to see you again, anyway."

Jaclyn's stomach murmured its approval. DeMarcus chuckled.

She pressed the heel of her left hand against her abdomen. "If you're sure it's not an imposition."

He couldn't squelch another grin. He didn't even try. The situation was too comical.

DeMarcus inclined his head toward her stomach. "Listening to that all the way home would be an imposition." He lifted her from his lap and rose from his chair. "We'll stop at the vending machine on our way out and get you a carton of milk."

DeMarcus straightened from the dishwasher. He turned to reach for another dish and was hip bumped from the counter. He looked around.

Jaclyn gave him a winning smile as she placed more dishes into the machine. "Dinner was delicious. Thank you, Marc."

He shook his head. "I told you my father and I would clear the table. You're our guest."

She bent over the dishwasher, organizing the silverware into its holders. "I was a guest the first time. This time, I'd feel like a freeloader if I didn't help clean up."

DeMarcus's gaze wandered to her well-shaped hips. He remembered the feel of her derriere in his hands—soft skin, firm muscles. His palms itched to caress her again. He raised his gaze and met Jaclyn's eyes. She'd caught him staring at her. The knowing twinkle in her eyes meant she'd guessed his thoughts. Her smile said she shared them.

His lips twitched. "Kitchen duty isn't my favorite chore."

Jaclyn wiggled her bottom. "Think of it as foreplay."

A slow smile stretched his lips. He could learn to like kitchen duty.

"This is the last of the dishes." Julian's pronouncement preceded him into the kitchen.

DeMarcus met his father halfway and took the empty serving bowls and platter from him. "Thanks, Pop." He turned and found Jaclyn standing between him and the sink.

She extended her hands for the serving dishes. "Your dishwasher's full. I'll wash these by hand."

DeMarcus hesitated. "Thank you."

Julian sat at the kitchen table. He stretched his legs and crossed them at the ankles. "Thanks, Jackie. I hate kitchen duty."

Jaclyn carried the dishes to the sink. "It's a family aversion." She let the water run over the dishes before scrubbing them with the soapy sponge. "Marc, your mother did a great job teaching you to cook."

DeMarcus settled into the chair across from his father. He extended his legs, crossing them at the ankles. "She was a great cook."

Julian's tone was nostalgic. "Brenda should have been a chef, but she loved teaching children."

"So did you, Pop." DeMarcus reached for the saltshaker in the center of the table, spinning it on the walnut wood surface.

Jaclyn pitched her voice over the sound of the running water. "I'd forgotten both of your parents were teachers. That must have been a lot of pressure on you in school."

DeMarcus stilled his hand on the saltshaker. "Not really." It was odd that someone with whom he was having a relationship knew so much of his personal life from media interviews. What had *he* read about *her*?

"Marc always did his best," Julian said. "He always gave two hundred percent. He graduated with honors from high school and magna cum laude from college. I'm very proud of him, and so was his mother."

DeMarcus swallowed twice before speaking. "Thanks, Pop."

The words weren't enough. He could never repay his father for everything Julian had helped him achieve. And he'd run out of time to thank his mother.

DeMarcus followed Jaclyn into her turn-of-the-century red brick mansion. The pentagonal entryway was tiled in the black and silver Monarchs colors. He slowed as he past the large, black and white framed photographs of historic Brooklyn landmarks adorning the white walls—the bridge, the museum, Prospect Park, Grand Army Plaza.

Jaclyn's stilettos tapped against the flooring as he followed her down a wide hallway to the kitchen. "Would you like something to drink? Ice water? Juice?"

He propped his shoulder against the archway separating the kitchen from the hall. "Water, please."

Jaclyn took two beveled glasses from a cabinet. She filled each with water and ice, then crossed the kitchen to give him the drink. "You once told me it wasn't the salary that interested you in the Monarchs' head coaching position."

DeMarcus winked. "I'm pretty sure my hourly pay is below minimum wage."

Her eyes danced with amusement. "You have an odd sense of humor."

"I think the same about you every time I look at my pay stub." He drank the ice water. It cooled him from the inside out but couldn't douse the fire her smile had sparked within him.

The muscles in Jaclyn's throat flexed as she swallowed her water. "I think I've figured it out."

DeMarcus dragged his gaze from her neck to eyes. He'd lost track of their conversation. "What?"

"You took the job with the team because of your mother. She'd always wanted you to come home and play for the Monarchs, but you were drafted to Miami and never left."

DeMarcus gripped the cool glass in his fist. She had his full attention now. "What?"

Jaclyn's gaze bore into him. "Why else would a multimillionaire ex-NBA player without coaching experience take a head coaching position with a franchise he claims doesn't pay well?"

"You don't pay well."

"I initially thought you wanted to coach the Monarchs because of your father. I thought you wanted to help improve the team because he's a fan."

DeMarcus drained his glass of water. It bought him time and eased the sandpaper dryness of his throat. "So what?"

He surged away from the archway. He wanted to pace. He needed to move, but he didn't want Jaclyn to know she was making him uncomfortable. He thought she'd asked him to take her home for a very different reason, one that didn't involve clothing or psychoanalyzing him.

Jaclyn studied him like a lab experiment. "But your

father knows you love him, and you know he's proud of you. I've seen that each time I've had dinner with the two of you."

"What's your point?"

"You're not as certain your mother knew how much you loved and appreciated her."

DeMarcus marched across the kitchen. He slammed the thick glass into the sink. With his back to her, he clenched and unclenched his fists. "Why do you care why I took the head coaching job?"

"Because I care about you." Jaclyn's words eased the tension threatening to snap him in half. "And because I want to know you in and out of bed."

He looked at her over his shoulder. She waited patiently in the corner of her silver and white kitchen wearing the same suit she'd worn the day she demanded his resignation. Their relationship definitely had taken a one-eighty.

DeMarcus leaned his hips against her sink and crossed his arms. "I thought I'd have time to show them how much I appreciated the sacrifices they'd made so that I could play in the NBA." He stared at the marbled tile. "I bought them that house in Park Slope, convinced them to retire early so they could travel. I bought them vacation packages to Europe, Africa and the Caribbean."

"I'm sure they appreciated that."

"But I should have spent more time with them." He faced her despite his shame. "When they were exploring Europe, I was playing in the All-Star game. When they were touring Africa, I was training for the Olympics. When they were sailing the Caribbean, I was working on my sports apparel deal."

"Didn't they want to see those games?"

"They were at the games. But I was too busy before and after to join them on their trips."

"I'm sure your parents understood."

"Mom was disappointed." He went back to contemplating the tiles. "I'd always intended to come back to Brooklyn after I retired. Twelve, fifteen years tops. Then I'd spend more time with them. Start a family of my own. But I ran out of time. Mom had a heart attack. I was in Miami when she died."

Jaclyn went to him and took his hand. "I'm so sorry."

DeMarcus felt her fingers, long and slender, in his grip. "At the funeral, her friends and family were whispering about how much money and time she and Pop had spent on my basketball training. They'd tried to discourage them, but my parents wouldn't listen. They believed in me."

"And they were right." Jaclyn's tone was fierce. She sounded like she wanted punch the people who'd spoken those hurtful words.

DeMarcus lifted his hand to massage away her frown the way she'd soothed his forehead earlier. "I spent money on my parents instead of spending time with them."

Jaclyn shook her head. "You weren't with them every day, but you came home often. There were Mighty Guinn sightings in the paper every time you came back to Brooklyn."

DeMarcus couldn't return her smile. Criticism from family and friends during his mother's funeral still plagued him. "Did she know how much I appreciated their faith in me?"

Jaclyn stepped into him and rested her head on his shoulder. "Yes."

He frowned, wrapping his arms around her. He let her warmth take the edge off his fear. "How do you know?"

"Your father knows how much you appreciate them. Your mother must have known also." Jaclyn raised her head and met his eyes. "But, if you're still unsure, ask him."

"I will."

Jaclyn wasn't feeding him platitudes. He saw the concern in her eyes. DeMarcus wasn't used to women who wanted to get into his head as well as his pants. His former lovers had used his body like a well-muscled sex toy. They'd performed sex instead of making love. Having someone care about what he thought and how he felt was a turn-on—once he got past the initial discomfort.

He buried his hands in the vibrant curls tumbling around Jaclyn's shoulders. "I've never shared that with anyone." His words were a whisper.

Moved that such a strong man could be so vulnerable, Jaclyn kissed his cheek and whispered in his ear. "You should have."

Sliding her hands under his jersey, Jaclyn felt the warmth of DeMarcus's skin against her palms. The muscles in her arms trembled as she lifted the garment over his head.

DeMarcus pulled her into his arms and lowered his head to nuzzle her throat. "You're the one who wants to get inside a person's head. I prefer to act."

Jaclyn caught her breath at the feel of his tongue against her skin. She leaned her head back to give him better access to her neck. "There's a time and a place for everything."

He chuckled low, the sound strumming the muscles in her abdomen. "What time is it now?"

Jaclyn stepped out of his arms. Her muscles wept in protest. "It's time I showed you to my room."

She turned to lead him back down her hallway to the staircase. Suddenly, her feet were swept out from under her and her body cradled against DeMarcus's torso.

Jaclyn gasped as DeMarcus mounted the stairs. "What are you—? Put me down before you drop me."

"Trust me."

Jaclyn realized she did. Still, she was a tall woman and there were a lot of stairs. "Who do you think you are? Superman?"

His dark gaze touched her heart. "You make me feel that way."

Jaclyn melted against him. "Keep talking like that, and I'll start without you." She inclined her head toward the upstairs hallway. "My room is to the right at the end of the hall."

DeMarcus crested the staircase, then turned toward her room. His steps never faltered. He crossed the threshold and lowered her beside the bed. He bent his head toward her, and Jaclyn rose on her toes to claim his lips. She shivered as DeMarcus traced his hand down her back, molding her body to every hard, hot inch of his. His arousal pressed against her. Jaclyn moaned into his mouth.

He traced his tongue over her parted lips before sliding deeper into her mouth. Jaclyn dug her fingers into the deep muscles of his shoulders, straining against him. She was restless. She was aching. She was impatient for him.

DeMarcus pulled back and stripped her bare of

her suit. Her undergarments and hose disappeared. His nimble athlete's fingers stroked her bare skin. His breath teased her as he whispered against her ear. "I need to feel you naked against me."

The image in his words made her pulse for him. His touch set her body on fire.

Jaclyn slipped her hands beneath the waistband of DeMarcus's athletic pants and drew down both the pants and his underwear. She lowered to her knees in front of his erection. Her fingers traced the hot, smooth flesh over the rigid length of him. In the silence surrounding them, she heard his ragged breathing, felt his tense anticipation and realized she'd cast her own spell over him. It was a heady sensation, having his strength and power react to her slightest touch. Jaclyn dampened with arousal.

She braced her hands against his muscled thighs. Slowly, teasingly, she took him into her mouth. A tremor shook DeMarcus's body. Jaclyn smiled. With just one lick, she could fall an MVP.

She felt his fingers wrap around her shoulders. Jaclyn caressed his arousal with her tongue, taking him in and out of her mouth. His breathing grew deeper, faster, rougher. His hips pumped in time with her movements. Jaclyn raked her nails lightly down his thighs and felt DeMarcus's hands tighten on her shoulders.

He pulled her up, hooking her under her arms and tossed her onto her bed. He kicked away from his pants, removed his shoes and socks and loomed over her.

Jaclyn smiled, reveling in her power, drinking in his. She had driven him to this. He was desperate for her. "Had enough?"

"I'm just getting started."

The heat in DeMarcus's eyes set fire to her blood. Her nipples tightened in anticipation. DeMarcus lowered onto her. His body heated hers. The fine hairs covering his chest grazed her sensitive nipples. His right leg settled between her thighs.

He took her mouth. His kiss was hard and rough. Urgent. Demanding. His tongue surged deep inside before pulling back, then pressing into her again. His movements were full and forceful, foreshadowing what was to come.

Jaclyn's body lifted against him, silently begging for his possession. DeMarcus's right hand stroked over her bare breast, cupping its fullness, teasing its nipple. Jaclyn's belly ached. Sexual hunger clawed inside of her, desperate to be fed. His hand traveled lower. The rough pads of his fingers feathered her waist. Lower still, his hands molded her hips before settling between her thighs.

Jaclyn writhed beneath him. "I want you now."

"Not yet." DeMarcus slid one finger inside her, seeking her core beyond her damp folds.

Jaclyn's body shook. She moaned at the intensity of her desire. Her head pressed back into the mattress. Her back arched, lifting her breasts. DeMarcus caught one breast into his mouth and palmed the other. Her body was battered by sensations. The feel of DeMarcus's tongue laving her pebbled nipple. The rhythm of his hand stroking her core. The movement of his nimble fingers molding her breast. He made her lose her mind.

Jaclyn gasped. "Now, Marc."

"Not yet." He slid down her body, touching, kissing and licking every inch of her on the way.

He spread her thighs and kissed her intimately. Jaclyn screamed. Her body levitated off the bed. Blood rushed like rapids through her veins. The sound drowned out her pleas. DeMarcus grasped her hips and pulled her closer. Wave after wave of pleasure crashed over her. She panted. Her heart raced. Her body soared and rocked, trembled and twisted before she collapsed back onto the mattress.

DeMarcus's hand shook as he reached for the condom in the pocket of his discarded athletic pants. He ripped open the packet, covered himself and turned back toward the bed.

He had never been so hard. The sight of Jaclyn naked on her knees loving him with her lips had driven him mad. It had taken everything within him not to plunge himself inside of her to ease his painful desire. He'd focused on her pleasure instead—and made his arousal even stronger.

Jaclyn's body was languid. A sultry smile curved her lips. She lifted an arm toward him. "I want you so badly."

Her words shot straight to his erection. DeMarcus climbed onto the mattress and lowered himself to her. Jaclyn parted her legs and wrapped her arms around his shoulders. He sighed, kissing her neck, her cheek, nibbling on her ear.

He found her entrance hot and moist. His heart beat hard against his chest. DeMarcus clenched his teeth at the painful pleasure of joining with her. He pressed farther. Jaclyn wrapped her legs around his hips and urged him deeper. He slid all the way in. Jaclyn closed her eyes and moaned.

"You feel so good." DeMarcus's muscles trembled.

"So do you."

DeMarcus moved his hips, seeking Jaclyn's spot. When she gasped, he knew he'd found it. He moved against her, loving the feel of her heat wrapped around him, her soft smooth skin beneath his hands. He tucked his face beside her neck and breathed in the scent of lilacs and sex.

He loved the way she felt. He loved the way she smelled. He loved her.

DeMarcus stiffened. He looked at Jaclyn. He did love her. She was strong, beautiful, brilliant and sexy as hell. She made him feel invincible—and not just in bed.

Her eyes were closed. Perspiration dampened her skin. He felt the tension in her as her body strained toward completion. DeMarcus slid his hand between them and touched her there. Jaclyn gasped. Her hips pressed against his hand as her body bucked beneath him.

DeMarcus lowered his head and flicked her hardened nipple with his tongue. He moved his hand faster and harder against her. Jaclyn's inner pulse drew him deeper, forcing him to a faster rhythm. Beneath him, Jaclyn arched, then shattered, pulling him with her over the edge. He gathered her close as his body shook.

Jaclyn's arms came around him. With slender strength, she squeezed him tight, kissed his ear, then rubbed his back. He was drained. He was sated. He was in love. With his boss.

Here was yet another complication to pile onto their season. And he thought all he'd have to worry about was making it to the play-offs.

15

"You look happier than I've seen you in a long time." Jaclyn studied Albert.

It was the end of January, almost three months since she'd last seen him, when she'd paid him for his Monarchs share. He was seated across from her in the matching armchair in his office at Tipton's Fashionwear. Her former partner had complemented his pinstriped espresso suit with a thin, emerald green tie. He looked the role of a corporate executive of an exclusive apparel store.

"So do you, Jackie. You have a glow about you. Things are going well with you and Marc?"

"Very well. Thank you." Was she blushing? Hopefully not. "But you obviously made the right decision in leaving the organization."

"My daughter said the same thing." Her former partner gave her a rueful smile. "I hadn't realized how tense I'd been about the franchise."

Albert was only a year or two older than her father would have been had he lived. Would the pressure of owning a struggling NBA team have affected her parent the same way? She couldn't answer that. But her grandfather would have fought for the team just as hard if not harder than she was fighting.

"Why didn't you say something sooner?" Jaclyn sipped coffee from the dainty eggshell china cup Albert had served her. She winced at its bitter taste. Jaclyn leaned forward for the pitcher of skim milk on the serving platter. She poured some into her cup until the coffee rose to its rim.

Albert's eyes were distant as he frowned across the room. "No one wants to admit that they can't manage their family's business. My father helped form the Monarchs. I should have been able to maintain it."

Jaclyn flinched. Albert had expressed her own fears. "Things have changed since your father and my grandfather founded the organization."

"I've noticed." He paused, staring into his cup of black coffee. "Still, I was reluctant to dissolve our partnership. I have a feeling my father would have been disappointed."

Jaclyn's attention was drawn to the family photos crowding the top of Albert's file cabinets, bookcases and desk. Her shoulders slumped. She understood his concern over disappointing a parental figure.

She hadn't realized they had so much in common. Albert had surrendered, but she was still in the game. Who'd made the right choice?

"I understand your decision, Bert. Your children don't want to manage the franchise, and you're more interested in the other family business your father started."

Albert followed her gaze. "I'm proud of my children and glad they're excited about running Tipton's

Fashionwear." He gave Jaclyn a considering look. "Frankly, I thought you were going to stay in law."

"I thought the experience of practicing business law would help me better manage the franchise. So far, it isn't turning out that way." Albert's intense scrutiny made Jaclyn feel like a culture in a petri dish.

The retail executive sipped his coffee. "You've given me excellent legal advice in the past."

"Thank you."

"Be patient, Jackie. Everything will work out in the end." He sounded like a fortune-teller who had seen their future.

"How can you be so sure?"

Albert crossed his legs and balanced his coffee cup on its saucer. "You're a lot like your father, who was just like your grandfather. Stubborn and determined. The Monarchs are a successful franchise because of the force of your grandfather's personality. They didn't start losing until he became ill. Once you get your feet under you, you'll be the same way and the Monarchs will thrive again."

She wanted him to be right. She needed him to be right. The alternative was that she would fail to protect the legacy her grandfather had entrusted to her. The legacy she wished her father had lived to guide her through. She was the only thread left to hold the franchise intact. She felt like she was fraying.

Jaclyn sipped more coffee. It could use more sweetener. "So, would I be able to will you into selling all of your shares to me?"

Albert's expression was apologetic. "No."

"I didn't think so, which makes me wonder why you agreed to meet with me."

"I wanted you to understand why your owning the majority shares won't get you what you want."

"What do you mean?"

Albert lifted the matching eggshell china pot. "More coffee?"

Jaclyn quelled her impatience. "No, thank you."

Albert refreshed his cup. "You want to keep the team in Brooklyn."

Jaclyn leaned back in the floral-patterned armchair. "That's right." Where was Albert going with this?

"Then it doesn't matter whether you have five percent of the team or ninety-five percent. If you can't renew the arena contract, you're going to have to move the Monarchs."

Jaclyn battled back a feeling of hopelessness. "The Gandy brothers are selling the Empire. They want to drop the Monarchs because they don't think our account will attract potential buyers."

"I know that. And so does Gerry."

Jaclyn gripped the teacup. Why did their betrayals continue to surprise her? "Thanks for letting me know." Her sarcasm wasn't lost on Albert.

"I'm sorry. I should have told you."

"But Gerry told you not to." When Albert nodded, she continued. "Why is he so determined to destroy the Monarchs?"

"It's personal."

"I can tell."

"He's holding onto old resentments."

"Is he still angry that Gene Mannion left his shares of the franchise to my grandfather?" Jaclyn pressed the china cup into its saucer.

"Gerry has a long memory. But it's more than Mannion's shares. It also has to do with your mother."

Jaclyn's brows knitted. "What about my mother?"

Albert hesitated. Jaclyn bit her lip. If he offered her another cup of his diesel-fueled coffee, she'd scream.

"Haven't you ever wondered why Gerry's never married?"

Jaclyn shook her head. "If it doesn't have to do with the Monarchs, it's none of my business."

"It does have to do with the Monarchs. Gerry was in love with your mother. Your father, Gerry and I attended New York University together. Gerry met your mother first. But when she met your father, it was love at first sight."

Jaclyn's eyes stung. She blinked to hold back tears. "My grandparents never told me that." She'd missed her parents' love-at-first-sight story because she had lost them at such an early age. What other family stories had she missed? There was no one left to ask.

"Frank wouldn't have told his parents about Gerry's jealousy. I don't think he gave it much thought." Albert placed his empty cup and saucer on the low, walnut table between them. "But Gerry had always been envious of your father. Your father was smart, handsome and popular. Everything Gerry wanted to be."

Jaclyn ran her right index finger back and forth over the china cup. Her mind tumbled with thoughts of Gerry's envy, his unrequited love and her parents' romance. "That explains Gerry's mission to ruin the Monarchs. He wants to destroy what matters most to my family."

"I've told him that he needs to let go of his resentment for your family. You have nothing to do with what happened in the past. But he doesn't care. He's had these bad feelings for so long, I don't think he'd know what to do without them."

Jaclyn studied Albert. "Why are you telling me this now, especially after the role you played in helping Gerry destroy the franchise?"

Albert was silent, staring into his coffee cup. After several long seconds, he raised his gaze to hers. "I'm so very sorry for what I did."

Jaclyn read the regret in Albert's eyes. She heard it in his voice. It didn't relieve her anger. "Then why did you do it?"

"I believed Gerry when he said the franchise would make more money in its own market. But then you reminded me that the franchise isn't just about money. It's about community."

Jaclyn set her cup and saucer on the low table and stood. "I wish you had remembered sooner, Bert."

"I'm sorry, Jackie. Your grandfather was a great man. He really cared about this community, and so do I."

"Then help me figure out a way out of this mess."

"The key is the arena."

"I need more than that. I need a way to keep the team in the Empire. But you and Gerry have taken that possibility out of my reach."

Hours later, Jaclyn was still fretting over her meeting with Albert and his less-than-helpful advice. She stood beside Violet at the Morning Glory Church, serving dinner to the homeless and trying to make sense of Albert's words.

"Bert said I should focus on keeping the team in the Empire and not worry about getting the majority shares." Jaclyn added mixed vegetables to the shelter guest's plate of stewed chicken. She smiled at the older man. "Enjoy."

Violet added rice to his plate and wished him a good evening before turning back to Jaclyn. "What is he going to do to help you?"

"Nothing. He and his family don't have any interest in the franchise." Jaclyn served a young father and his son. She frowned at the thin material of their coats. February in Brooklyn demanded thick winter coats. She made a mental note to hold another winter clothing drive with the Monarchs and their corporate partners before the All-Star game.

Violet added a spoon of rice each to the father and son's plates. "You can handle the day-to-day. Bert can be a silent partner."

"Bert doesn't want any part of it, Vi. He told me the Empire is the key and now his involvement with the Monarchs is over."

"That sounds like a line from *The Matrix*. Just remember, Jackie, there is no spoon."

Jaclyn grinned at her friend's use of the movie line. It reminded her of the night she beat DeMarcus at one-on-one basketball. "The difference is, Laurence Fishburne's character didn't help create the world Keanu Reeves's character needed to save."

"And neither did Keanu Reeves's character."

The hesitancy in Violet's tone brought Jaclyn up short. "What are you trying to say?"

Violet served a spoonful of rice to another guest, then looked at the long line of people still waiting to be served. She lowered her voice. "What Gerry and Bert did was unfair and misguided."

"In Gerry's case, it was spite."

"True. But, sweetie, you enabled them."

The accusation stung. Jaclyn gave her a sharp look. "What do you mean?"

"You didn't think you could take your grandfather's place, even though he'd groomed you to do just that. So while he was sick and for almost two years after his death, you left everything to Gerry and Bert."

Jaclyn stiffened. "I'd just lost the last member of my family. I was grieving."

"I understand. But, sweetie, your grandfather had counted on you."

Her heart squeezed. "I know."

"Even when you were suspicious of the decisions Gerry and Bert made, you didn't follow your instincts."

Jaclyn breathed deeply to ease the constriction in her chest. "I should have."

She served the shelter's diners in silence for several heavy heartbeats. Violet's words rang true. She had to accept responsibility for at least part of the mess the Monarchs were in.

"You OK?" Violet's tentative question broke her concentration.

Jaclyn spooned vegetables onto a diner's plate before smiling at her former teammate. "You're a good friend."

Violet gave her a curious look. "Oh, yeah?"

"Only a good friend would risk ticking someone off by forcing them to face the truth."

Violet giggled. "You've done it for me often enough.

You're the one who told me to figure out what I needed to do to get out of my bad mood."

"What are friends for?" Jaclyn grinned. "Speaking of which, how's your search for a coaching position going?"

Violet sighed. "Not well. School boards are cutting their budgets, so a lot of schools are getting rid of their extracurricular programs, including sports."

"I hate to hear that."

"So do I."

Jaclyn smiled at the middle-aged woman who'd come to the church for a meal. Her hands were wind-chapped. Jaclyn put a full serving spoon of mixed vegetables on the woman's plate and reminded herself to start the clothing drive tonight.

Violet added rice to the woman's plate. "I'm meeting with some community organizations. But I'm beginning to wonder if I should do something that uses my business degree."

"Like what?"

"I don't know. It's not as though I need the money. Aidan has a good salary and we've always had safe investments that are still doing well. But I wonder if I need a different challenge."

"Maybe you need to try a couple of things." They were finally coming to the end of the long line of diners. Jaclyn took heart. In a moment, she'd need a break. Her shoulder was beginning to hurt from the repetitive motion.

"You left basketball for the corporate world. It gave you an entirely different experience. Maybe I should try something different, too."

"You should decide what you want to do and not

worry about what I did. Thanks to your husband, my
investments are doing well, too. I'll need that money
if I lose the Monarchs."

Violet shook her head. "We won't let that happen.
We'll figure out a way to keep the team in Brooklyn."

"I'm all ears."

DeMarcus sensed Jaclyn's presence seconds before
she joined him in her family room. It was after mid-
night Monday, but he was still studying game film on
her sixty-eight-inch plasma screen, high-definition
television. The audio was off.

"Serge is playing with a lot more conviction these
days. What did you say to him?" Jaclyn curled up
beside him on the black polyester sofa.

DeMarcus spoke without looking up from his
notepad. "I told him if he wanted to be traded, he'd
have to improve his stats, otherwise no other team
would take over his contract."

"Brilliant. I wish I'd thought of that." Her sleepy
voice was warm with amusement. "Sounds like you're
getting to know our players."

A thick, ankle-length emerald cotton robe protected Jaclyn from the chill of the early February
morning. It covered her at her neck, but he enjoyed
the way it exposed her left leg when she walked.

Scouting reports detailing facts, figures and statis-
tics for each Washington Wizards player sat in a pile
on DeMarcus's lap. He stacked the reports on the
coffee table in front of them and paused the game
film. "It's late. Why aren't you in bed?"

"I woke up and missed you."

He reached for her ankles, settling her feet in his lap. Her toenails were polished a rich purple, matching her fingernails. "I miss you, too. But I want to beat the Wizards Wednesday for my boss."

"I do enjoy winning at home."

DeMarcus wrapped his hands around her left foot. "Good grief. Your feet are like ice."

Jaclyn closed her eyes and sighed, sliding deeper into the couch. "Your hands are so warm."

"Where are your socks?"

"Probably in my sock drawer." She shifted her right foot closer to DeMarcus's arms and sighed again when he wrapped one hand around that foot.

"It's too cold for you to walk around on bare feet."

Jaclyn gave him a noncommittal hum. "I noticed you're starting Jamal now instead of Rick." With her eyes closed, Jaclyn appeared ready to go back to sleep.

"Not a very subtle change of topic." DeMarcus pressed his palm into her high arches. Her skin was soft and smooth to his touch.

"Did you still want to talk about my feet?"

"No."

"Well, then." She opened her cinnamon eyes and claimed his gaze. "Why is Rick sitting on the bench?"

DeMarcus froze. He was the one massaging her feet. Why was she asking him about Warrick Evans? He flexed his shoulders beneath his thick blue sweatshirt to ease the grip of jealousy. "Rick's playing too tight. He's hesitating when he has good shots."

"Have you talked with him?"

"About what?"

"To find out why he's playing so tentatively."

DeMarcus stroked the sole of her right foot with the pads of his thumbs. "I'm his coach, not his pastor.

Rick knows his numbers are down, and he knew he was competing with Jamal for the starting spot. Jamal is one of our leading scorers."

"He also leads the league in fouls. For every four points he gets for us, he gives the other team two free throws."

His shoulders were tightening again. "We're working on that."

Jaclyn wiggled her right foot free of DeMarcus's hold and slipped her left foot into his hands. "But does Rick have to sit on the bench while you work with Jamal?"

DeMarcus's jaw tightened. "Did Rick complain to you?"

Her eyes twinkled at him. "Does Rick strike you as the kind of person who would complain to the team's owner about the way his coach was treating him?"

"No, but Oscar runs to you whenever the team takes a—"

"No, he doesn't. No one came to me. I'm the one asking the questions."

DeMarcus wrapped his fingers around her slender foot. Why was she questioning him? He thought she believed in him. "Are you telling me how to coach the team?"

Jaclyn's foot stiffened beneath his touch. "I tried that before. Remember? When I suggested you get to know the players on a more personal level. It worked with Serge. Why won't you give Rick a chance?"

"I don't want you to second-guess me."

"I can see that." Jaclyn sat forward and rubbed her right hand across his furrowed brow. DeMarcus fought against the soothing effect. "Relax, Guinn. I'm not second-guessing you. I'm making sure we're on the same page."

"We are. We're going to the play-offs. Trust me."

"I do. But I also want you to trust Rick."

"Rick lost his nerve. We need players with heart to take us to the postseason." DeMarcus felt her tense under his touch when he criticized her favorite player.

"Rick is a leader of this team. Not just by his character, but by his numbers. Something has been bothering him. What is it?"

"Whatever it is, he can work it out on the bench."

"But—"

DeMarcus stilled his hands. "Jack, we'll make it to the play-offs. I promise." He winked at her. "I'm planning for the Finals."

Jaclyn's expression eased into a smile. "Big talker."

"Talk is cheap. Actions speak louder." DeMarcus pulled Jaclyn into his arms.

He gave his promise he'd take them to the play-offs. But he needed the team's help to keep his word on the court. Would they come through for him? For Jaclyn? For themselves?

16

Gerald Bimm sat in smug silence on the other side of Jaclyn's desk Tuesday morning. If he'd won her mother's love, he could have been her father. The thought was unsettling. Jaclyn took a deep drink of coffee from her Monarchs mug. It didn't remove the unpleasant taste from her mouth.

The gleam in Gerald's brown eyes and the air of triumph circling his wavy dark hair knotted the muscles in Jaclyn's stomach. "Let me guess. You've bought Bert's shares."

Gerald bared his perfect white teeth in a victorious grin. "Right the first time. Finally, we're equal partners."

The bitterness in him stirred the anger in her. It was a struggle not to respond in kind. She gave Gerald's designer bronze silk pants and champagne cashmere sweater a cursory skim. "I'm surprised you were able to afford it. Saving money was never your priority."

Anger flashed in his eyes. "My finances aren't your concern."

"They are when they affect my team."

Gerald arched a heavy brow. "*Your* team?"

"*My* team, whose finances you've nearly drained."
She crossed her legs, smoothing the purple skirt of
her sweater dress over her lap.

His eyes circled her office with subtle contempt.
"We'll recoup those losses once we relocate the team."

What could she say to convince him to let go of his
bitterness against her family? How could she reach
him? "This franchise is a Jones family legacy."

"It's a Bimm family legacy, too. But your family is
always trying to rewrite history. In your version, the
Bimm family doesn't exist."

Stay on topic. Don't let Gerry distract you. "My mother
was a Jones."

Gerald scowled. "So?"

"If you truly loved her, you wouldn't deliberately
destroy something that belonged to her."

"What are you talking about?" Gerald's voice was
thin.

"You loved my mother, but she married my father.
That's one of the reasons you hated him. But the
Monarchs aren't only my father's and grandfather's
legacy. They're part of my mother and brother as
well."

Gerald's eyes narrowed meanly. "You've been talking to Bert. Well, this has nothing to do with Lynda."

"Yes, it does. It probably has everything to do with
my mother." Jaclyn pushed away from her desk and
strode to one of the office's large windows. The late-
morning sun danced on the Gateway Marina waters
in the distance. "My mother loved this community."

Her grandfather had told her everything she knew
about her parents, which didn't include how Lynda

Trainer-Jones felt about Brooklyn. It didn't include a lot of things. But how could her mother not have loved this place and these people? They got into your blood and overwhelmed your senses. Everything was needed yesterday; today wasn't fast enough. You took pride in your culture, and everyone else wanted a piece of it.

"You Joneses are so sentimental. Sentimentality doesn't belong in business." There was a bite in Gerald's words.

"So you're a cold-hearted businessman." Jaclyn turned from the window. "Destroying the franchise has nothing to do with the way you feel about my family."

Gerald leaned back in the thick visitor's chair. He'd buried his impatience and agitation and put his mask of superiority back in place. "I'm concerned with the bottom line. If that makes me a cold-hearted businessman, then that's what I am."

Jaclyn counted to ten. She kept her tone flat. "And you think the franchise's bottom line will improve if we move the team to Nevada?"

"I already have an offer."

He was lying. He had to be.

Jaclyn paced back to her chair. She needed to sit before she fell. "From whom?"

"A corporation in Las Vegas has offered to build the Monarchs an arena. All we'd have to do is move in." His words were muffled beneath the buzzing in her ears.

"What's the name of this corporation?"

"Abbottson Investments Inc. Carville Abbottson is the CEO."

Jaclyn's fingers itched to do an Internet search on

the corporation and its chief executive. Did they exist? She couldn't trust anything Gerald said. "Will the arena be ready by next season?"

Gerald shrugged. His eyes never wavered. "They haven't broken ground yet. They're working on financing now."

They didn't have financing? Astonishment wiped the frown from Jaclyn's brow. Could Gerald possibly be serious? "What are the contract terms?"

He crossed his legs. "Abbottson's coming in next week to discuss those."

Jaclyn blinked. "You scheduled a meeting with him without first consulting me?"

"I'm consulting you now."

Jaclyn lifted her right fingers, counting their unanswered questions. "Abbottson doesn't know how he's going to finance the arena. He doesn't know when the arena will open, and you don't know the contract terms. That's a lot of unknowns. Are you ad-libbing this or are you seriously considering this offer?"

Gerald's grin was mean around the edges. "You can ask him yourself."

"Wake up, Gerry. Abbottson didn't give you an *offer*. He expressed an *interest*."

Gerald straightened the crease on his silk pants. "Which is more than you have now, isn't it? Or didn't the Gandy brothers tell you that they're selling the arena?"

Jaclyn leaned back in her executive chair. Althea was right. They had a spy in the front office. That was the only way Gerald would have known she'd spoken with the arena owners. "I'm aware of that."

Gerald inclined his head. "Then you'd better hope Abbottson's interest becomes an offer and soon. Even if the revenues increase by the end of the season, it would be too little, too late, and the Monarchs will be homeless next year."

"This situation couldn't have worked out better for you if you'd planned it yourself." She tipped her head. "Or did you?"

"You give me too much credit." Gerald pushed himself to his feet and stared down at her. "You can either sell your shares to me or move with the team to Las Vegas. Either way, I don't care."

Her features stiffened. Gerald knew she'd never leave Brooklyn. "Sell my shares to you? Can your clothing budget afford another hit?"

Gerald's glare was pure hate. "You Joneses think you're better than everyone else. Enjoy it while you can."

"When is Abbottson coming?"

Gerald shrugged again. "We have to finalize that. The Monarchs have a couple of games next week, don't they?"

Was he baiting her or did he seriously not know the team's schedule? "We play the Sacramento Kings Tuesday, February ninth, then we break for the All-Star Game and weekend. Why don't you ask Nessa to send you a schedule so you can keep up?"

The right corner of Gerald's lips curved upward in a wry smile. He looked around her office again. "We should change the team's colors. Silver and black are too drab for Las Vegas. Of course, you'll have to redo your interior decorating."

"Don't get ahead of yourself, Gerry."

He turned to leave. "You can't fight progress, Jackie."

"If this were progress, I'd be worried. But it's just

your spite." She watched Gerald disappear from her doorway.

Albert was right. The Empire was the key. How could she use that knowledge to keep the Monarchs in Brooklyn?

DeMarcus stared at Jaclyn's bedroom ceiling. Shadows danced across its textured white surface as the traffic flowed sluggishly outside.

He flexed his left arm, drawing Jaclyn's slender nude body closer to his side. He inhaled her soft lilac fragrance. DeMarcus wanted to hold on to her warmth and this moment for a just a while longer. Then he'd leave her bed to work on the Monarchs' game plan for Tuesday's home game against the Sacramento Kings. Jaclyn's head rested on his shoulder. Her soft breaths stroked the side of his neck. Her smooth leg nestled between his. The bedsheets were still tangled around them. DeMarcus used his free arm to pull the comforter over Jaclyn's shoulder to protect her from the February evening's chill.

Jaclyn tangled her fingers in the hair on his chest. "I'm taking out a mortgage on my grandfather's house."

DeMarcus jerked his head toward her. "Why?"

"The Gandy brothers are selling the Empire. That's one of the reasons they're unwilling to extend our contract."

"You're mortgaging your home to buy the arena? Isn't that drastic?"

Jaclyn rolled over to lie on her back. "The team is more important to me than this house."

DeMarcus turned onto his side and propped

himself on his left elbow. He looked down at her, missing her warmth, her touch. "Let me help you buy the arena."

Jaclyn smiled up at him. "Thank you for the offer. But I think that would only complicate things. Besides, this is something I need to do for myself."

DeMarcus knitted his brow. "It's a big financial commitment. Have you thought this through?"

"Yes, I have."

He stilled beside her. Cold air cut into the space between them. "When did you talk to the Gandy brothers?"

"Three months ago—before Thanksgiving. They said the Empire looked more attractive to prospective buyers without the Monarchs on their books."

DeMarcus's brows flew upward. "You found out about this months ago, but you're only telling me now?"

Jaclyn frowned. "What's wrong?"

"Why did you wait so long to share with me something this important to you?"

Jaclyn still looked confused. "I didn't want you to worry about the Empire. You have enough on your mind trying to take the team to the play-offs."

DeMarcus rolled out of bed and paced the room. With his spiking temper, he was barely aware of the chill wrapping around his naked body or the plush carpet beneath his bare feet. "So I'm good enough to coach your team and good enough to take to your bed, but I'm not good enough to discuss what's important to you."

"That's not what I meant at all." Jaclyn sat up, shielding her breasts with the black and silver abstract comforter. Her lips parted in shock. "You matter to me. A lot. I guess our relationship is more complicated than I'd thought."

"I guess it is." The stricken expression in her eyes hurt him. DeMarcus looked away.

"I'm sorry, Marc. I never meant to hurt you."

"I know. Just, please, don't shut me out of your life again. Any part of it."

"I promise."

He heard the smile in her voice and faced her again. "Will mortgaging your home give you enough money to buy the Empire?"

Jaclyn sobered. "No. I'll have to sell some of my stock portfolio."

DeMarcus studied Jaclyn's expression. Her thoughts had transported her out of the room. Where was she? She looked determined, like a champion preparing for the finals. "Is it worth it? Is this what your grandfather would have wanted?"

Jaclyn started. "I don't know. But it's what *I* want. Once I own the Empire, Gerry won't have the money to break the arena contract and move the team."

"But is it worth mortgaging your home?"

This time, Jaclyn's smile was tinged with sorrow. "This isn't my home. It's my grandfather's house. It takes a family to make a home, and I don't remember mine."

DeMarcus returned to the bed and sat beside her. "I'm sorry."

"I try not to be. My grandparents loved me and I loved them. But there were times when I would have sold my soul to know the people whose pictures are in our family photo album—my mother, father and brother."

DeMarcus took her hands. He was grateful when

Jaclyn entwined their fingers. "You were three when your parents and older brother died in that car accident."

Jaclyn nodded. "It took my grandparents years to come to terms with their loss.

"And then your grandmother got ill."

"She died of cancer when I was eleven. She'd suffered a long time."

"I'm sorry."

Jaclyn squeezed his hands. "So am I. My happiest memories are of the Empire. Watching the Monarchs play—win or lose—and hanging around the practice court. I think that's why I've always thought of the Monarchs as my family, and the Empire as my home. I'll do whatever I can to save the team and keep them in Brooklyn."

"I'll do everything I can to help you."

The stakes just got a lot higher. He wasn't coaching just to safeguard his legacy anymore or to protect a franchise. He was coaching to save her family, the only family she'd ever known.

Losing had never been an option, and winning had never mattered more.

DeMarcus stopped in front of Jaclyn's executive assistant's desk and waited until she'd finished whatever she was typing. "Althea Gentry, I'd like you to meet my father, Julian Guinn."

Althea's smile was uncharacteristically bashful. "This is your father? The apple doesn't fall far from the tree, does it?" She turned to extend a hand toward Julian. "It's a pleasure to meet you, Mr. Guinn."

Julian took Althea's hand. "Please call me Julian. It's a pleasure to meet you, too."

Althea's smile broadened into a grin. A blush dusted her rounded brown cheeks.

DeMarcus looked from Althea to his father and back. "Is Jack in her office?"

"No, she's right behind you," Jaclyn answered.

DeMarcus turned as Jaclyn laid a folder on Althea's desk. She was wearing her red power suit adorned with the ever-present Monarchs lapel pin. "Pop and I came to see if we could take you to lunch."

Jaclyn stepped forward to embrace Julian. Her red stiletto boots brought her almost equal in height to his father. She stepped back, keeping one hand on Julian's shoulder as she addressed DeMarcus. "I'd love to, but the meeting I'd mentioned to you yesterday was moved up. I don't think I'd be very good company today. But thanks for the invitation."

Disappointment merged with DeMarcus's concern. "Why did they move up the meeting?"

Jaclyn let her hand drop from Julian's shoulder. "Apparently, Mr. Abbottson has a connecting flight to Miami for the All-Star weekend. He doesn't want to miss it."

Julian shifted to face Jaclyn. "The Monarchs will get some players chosen to the All-Stars next season."

A shadow crossed Jaclyn's face. "This is the second year in a row we were overlooked."

DeMarcus wanted to wrap his arms around her and give her comfort. But he didn't think such a display of affection was appropriate for the office. "Pop and I will give you a rain check on lunch."

She gave him her special smile, the one that softened her features and warmed her eyes. "I'd like that.

Thanks." She surprised him by kissing both his and Julian's cheeks before returning to her office.

DeMarcus and Julian walked the few blocks to a small, popular café. It was only eleven-thirty, and already the neighborhood establishment was packed. But the pair didn't have to wait long before being seated at a booth near a window.

Julian opened his menu. "I didn't mean to upset Jackie when I mentioned the All-Star weekend."

DeMarcus glanced up before returning his attention to the list of lunch items. "Don't worry, Pop. Jack will be fine."

"What meeting does she have today? You both looked like doom and gloom when she talked about it."

DeMarcus lowered his menu when the server arrived to take their drink order. He and his father requested unsweetened iced tea. The young man nodded without writing anything down, then walked away.

DeMarcus spread his cloth napkin on his lap. "Gerry arranged a meeting with a Nevada investor who's considering building an arena in Las Vegas for the Monarchs."

Julian's menu dropped from his fingers. "The Monarchs' founders must be spinning in their graves."

"Jack won't let anyone take the team out of Brooklyn." DeMarcus hesitated. "She's taken a mortgage on her grandfather's house. She's going to buy the arena."

Julian's brows almost disappeared into his graying hairline. "That's a little drastic, isn't it?"

"I said the same thing." DeMarcus scanned the entrée items without taking in a single word. "And there's nothing I can do to help her. She won't let me loan her the money for the arena."

"It isn't personal. I'm sure she'd have to clear that with the NBA. Besides, Jackie Jones is too independent to borrow money from her boyfriend. She's the kind of woman who pays her own bills."

Julian's description distracted DeMarcus. He was Jaclyn Jones's boyfriend. What had started as a casual relationship had grown to mean much more to him. What did it mean to her?

The server returned with their drinks, then took their orders. DeMarcus asked for a Philly cheesesteak sandwich. Julian wanted a meatball sub. They both ordered side salads.

DeMarcus waited for the young man to leave before continuing. "I have my self-respect, too. This relationship can't be one-sided. Even if I coached the team to the Finals and we won, she could still lose the arena. So what am I contributing?"

"A winning season and ticket sales." Julian's tone was dry. "You're the coach, Marc. That's all you're required to contribute. The franchise needs to increase its revenue base, otherwise Jackie will continue to struggle to keep the Empire." His father offered a smile. "She still needs a hero, Marc."

DeMarcus snorted. "I'm no one's hero."

Julian's snort was identical to his son's. "I've seen the way she looks at you. You're her knight in shining armor."

A part of him wished Julian was serious. But De-Marcus knew his father was trying to lighten the mood. "Somehow, I don't think a knight would put his lady in the position of having to mortgage her home."

"That has nothing to do with you." Julian was adamant. "The franchise began to deteriorate long before you came on the scene."

"What can I do to help her?"

"You're doing it. For the first time in three seasons, the Monarchs have a winning record. You have twenty-nine *W*'s to twenty-two *L*'s."

At the start of the season, there were days DeMarcus had wondered whether a winning season was possible. "We have to add to the wins column. But winning a ball game doesn't seem like enough."

He'd won games for his mother. Had it been enough? Had she known how grateful he'd been to her?

Jaclyn had urged him to ask his father months ago. But he couldn't. He feared what the answer might be.

For now, DeMarcus pushed the questions to the back of his mind. "You impressed Althea."

"She must be easily impressed."

DeMarcus's chuckle was real. "You don't know Althea. That lady isn't easily impressed by anyone or anything. Ever."

Julian shrugged. "You're just flattered by her comment about the apple and the tree."

"You're the one who should be flattered." DeMarcus enjoyed his father's laughter. It came a lot more frequently these days. Since Jaclyn had entered their lives.

They were quiet for a while, each enjoying the other's company and the view outside of Brooklyn in

February. The silence was interrupted when the young server returned with their sandwiches and salads.

DeMarcus kept his voice low. "Mom's been gone for almost three years, Pop. I don't think she would have wanted you to spend the rest of your life in mourning."

"I know." Julian stuck his fork into his salad and poked around. "But your mother and I were together for a very long time. It's not easy to let go of someone who'd been so right for me."

DeMarcus thought of Jaclyn. He understood what his father said. When you meet the right woman, it wasn't easy to let her go, under any circumstances.

17

"We're sorry to have kept you waiting, Jackie." Gerald didn't sound sorry. He sounded amused.

Jaclyn looked up from her marketing project folder and rose from her seat at the head of the small mahogany table. Gerald always kept her waiting. Why would today be any different? That's why she'd brought work with her into the conference room.

She fixed a smile on her face and offered it to Gerald and his guest. "I had plenty to keep me busy."

Gerald made the introductions. "Jaclyn Jones, Carville Abbottson. Jackie, Carville. I think we can all be on a first-name basis, don't you?"

"I don't know why not." Carville offered Jaclyn a firm handshake.

Jaclyn enjoyed his energy and enthusiasm. "It's a pleasure to meet you, Carville."

The real estate investor had a hearty Southern accent to go with his golden-age-of-Hollywood good looks. His silver hair and grass green eyes would have been startling in black and white film. Just over six feet tall, he was a commanding figure in his dark green pin-striped suit.

The two men chose chairs around the conference table. Gerald frowned at Jaclyn's location. If he'd wanted to sit at the head of the table, he should have arrived earlier.

Carville had claimed the seat to her right. "I appreciate your taking the time to meet with me, Jackie."

At sixty-three, the chief executive seemed as fit as someone half his age. His conditioning was a testament to the discipline that had driven him from a community college in a tiny Kentucky town to the corner office of his Las Vegas real estate investment firm. Yes, Jaclyn had done her research. She'd never stepped onto the basketball court without committing the scouting reports to memory, either.

Jaclyn closed her project folder and recapped her pen. "I don't know how fruitful this meeting will be."

Carville folded his hands on the table and leaned forward. "Las Vegas would welcome the Monarchs into our market.

Jaclyn noted the spark in Carville's eyes, the leashed energy in his posture. The self-made multimillionaire was an adrenaline junky. That probably contributed to his success. "How do you know the Las Vegas market could support the Monarchs?"

Carville gave her an engaging smile. "Well, first of all, your team would be the only NBA team in the market."

Had Gerald fed him that line or had Carville used it first? "The Monarchs have done very well sharing the New York City metropolitan market with the Knicks for fifty-five years. But will the NBA allow Las Vegas to establish a team? I thought the commissioner wanted casinos to take NBA games off their books before Las Vegas would be considered a viable location for a team."

Carville spread his hands. "We're going to petition the commissioner to consider Las Vegas as a host expansion city. I feel confident we have a good shot at it." He shrugged. "And being an inaugural team in Las Vegas would be a great draw for your Monarchs. I know you've struggled to make book, and your profits aren't what they used to be."

Jaclyn gave Gerald a brief glance. How much of their finances had he shared with the investor? "That has more to do with mismanagement on our part than the market. During my grandfather's illness and after his death, I didn't pay attention to the team as I should have. I'm correcting my oversight now."

Carville's eyes darkened with sympathy. "I understand."

Gerald interrupted. "But in Vegas, there wouldn't be another team to lure our fans away."

Carville's laughter was deep and full. "Gerry's right. Vegas is the entertainment capital of the world. In addition to the almost two million people in our metro area, you're going to be pulling Vegas vacationers into the games."

Carville Abbottson was smart, charming and exciting. Jaclyn liked him—and wanted him to leave. She wasn't going to change her mind about keeping the team in Brooklyn. Still, she wouldn't direct her impatience at Carville. Her target was Gerald. She glanced at her partner again. With very little prompting, she'd gladly poke him in the eyes.

She leaned back in her chair, crossing her legs.

She adjusted the material of her teal skirt over her knee. "Where would the team play?"

Carville inclined his head. "You're asking about the arena."

Jaclyn was gratified that the investor didn't pretend not to understand her question. He really was a likeable person. "How are you going to finance it?"

Carville folded his hands again. "We're hoping to put a measure on the May ballot for a levy."

Jaclyn blinked. "You're asking for taxpayer funding?"

Carville nodded. "Bringing a pro team to Las Vegas will improve the city's standing. The arena will bring jobs to the area. We're going to ask residents to help us make this possible."

Jaclyn frowned at Gerald. "Did you know about this?"

Gerald shrugged. "Carville mentioned it to me."

"But *you* didn't mention it to *me*." She turned back to the investor. "How do you think voters will respond to the levy?"

Carville's gaze sharpened. His tone was more cautious. "Our initial telephone poll results are mixed. But we've got some strong direct marketing and media campaigns that will help educate voters on why the levy is a good idea for the city."

Jaclyn lifted her pen, rolling it between her index finger and thumb. Her grandfather hadn't liked the idea of asking a tax-burdened community to pay for his franchise and neither did she. "What will you do if the voters reject the levy?"

Carville shook his head. "I don't think they will."

Jaclyn noted Carville's squared jaw and stubborn chin. The founder of Abbottson Investments had gotten his success through determination, hard work and positive thinking. In this case, Jaclyn didn't like his thinking.

She continued to roll her pen. "Even if they pass the tax levy in May, it will take at least a year after you break ground to build the arena. Unless we're able to get an extension on the Empire contract, the Monarchs will be without a home next season."

Carville looked from Gerald to Jaclyn. "If we're able to meet agreeable terms, I'm sure we'd work something out for next season. Maybe the Knicks would let us play some games at Madison Square Garden. Or we could play at a couple of nearby arenas."

Jaclyn would bounce her team between arenas when pigs flew. "That would be too disruptive to the team and our fans.

Carville looked concerned. "It wouldn't be for more than one season."

Jaclyn sighed. "Carville, I don't want to move the Monarchs out of Brooklyn, and I haven't heard anything in this meeting that would change my mind. Even if we have to move out of the Empire Arena, I want to keep the franchise in Brooklyn."

Carville shifted his surprised expression to Gerald. "I thought you both wanted to move to Vegas."

Jaclyn arched a brow at Gerald. "You were misled."

Carville leaned back in the thick, black-cushioned chair. "I want to bring an NBA team to Las Vegas. Is there a possibility that you'd change your mind about moving the Monarchs?"

Gerald answered. "Anything is possible."

Jaclyn ignored her partner. "Not even the slightest possibility."

Carville got to his feet. "Then I'm sorry I wasted your time, Jackie."

Jaclyn stood with him, extending her hand. "It wasn't a waste of time. It was a pleasure meeting you, Carville."

The executive gave her a silver screen idol smile. "The pleasure was mine. Good luck finding a new home for your team."

"Thank you." Jaclyn watched Gerald escort the real estate investor from the conference room.

How was her traitorous partner spinning this setback?

Once they'd disappeared across the threshold, she retrieved her cell phone from her skirt pocket and punched in the speed-dial code for Violet. Her friend and former teammate picked up on the third ring.

Jaclyn sat down again. "Vi, are you still looking for a business challenge?"

"Yes. Why?"

"I may have one for you. When can we get together to talk about it?"

"What's wrong with them?" DeMarcus studied the way Jamal defended Warrick. The Monarchs were more than an hour into their worst practice of the season.

Oscar Clemente shrugged. "Too tight."

"Because of Tuesday's loss in Boston?" Last night's flight back to Brooklyn after the Celtics game had been tense.

"No."

After five months—September to February—

DeMarcus should have known better than to ask his assistant coach a yes or no question.

He followed the action on the court. The Monarchs ran through the defensive strategy he and his coaching staff had planned for Friday's match against the Wizards in D.C. There were only two games left in February before they turned the calendar to March. Every one was critical. The starters—Jamal, Barron, Anthony, Serge and Vincent—wore silver T-shirts and black shorts. Warrick wore the black running shorts and matching T-shirt that identified him with the bench players on offense. Warrick did a better-than-credible impersonation of Gilbert Arenas, the Wizards' veteran guard. Jamal wasn't able to defend him.

DeMarcus crossed his arms over his chest. "They can't be worried about the Wizards. We beat them on their home court last month."

Oscar grunted. "The Wizards aren't better than us."

DeMarcus ignored Oscar's division rivalry smack talk and gestured toward the court. "Then what's the problem?"

"The rookie. He draws more fouls than flies are drawn to—"

DeMarcus raised his voice to be heard above the squeaking sneakers and thumping ball. "Jamal, check Rick. Don't hug him." He looked toward Oscar. "As often as I've had to repeat that, I should have a T-shirt made."

Warrick circled to Jamal's left, keeping the ball out of the rookie's reach. He was toying with the younger player.

Instead of moving back, Jamal pressed closer. "The

old man can't handle my pressure." The younger man's voice was short of breath and edged with anger.

"I can take the pressure." Warrick's tone was cool and controlled. "The team doesn't need you to foul." He stepped back behind the three-point perimeter and sank a basket.

DeMarcus narrowed his eyes. Was the benched veteran finally getting his game back? He glanced at Oscar. "Jamal's a pain in the ass, but he can score."

"He disrupts the team."

"He's brought the team together."

"Together against him. That's unhealthy."

"We have a winning record. It can't be unhealthy." DeMarcus brought his attention back to the court in time to see Warrick steal the ball from Serge and heave it to the member of his practice squad closest to the paint. That player, a back-up center, turned and slammed the ball into the net.

DeMarcus shook his head. "Our bench players are up eight points against our starters."

"They're not tight."

After a series of plays, the starters took a small and tenuous lead. Warrick remained cool and in control. But Jamal's game reflected his increasing agitation.

Warrick was dribbling the ball well outside of the three-point perimeter, biding his time until a teammate came open. Jamal's arm came across the veteran player from behind in a move guaranteed to earn the rookie a foul and send Warrick to the free-throw line during a real game. DeMarcus brought the whistle to his mouth, preparing to stop the game. He hesitated as Warrick dodged free, bringing the ball with him. Smooth move.

DeMarcus ran a hand over his close-cropped hair.

His tone snapped. "Jamal, play the *ball*, not your *man*."

Jamal's anger was palpable as he crowded Warrick again. "I'm sending Grandpa back to the bench."

DeMarcus clenched his teeth. "I said play the ball."

Warrick kept the ball out of Jamal's reach. "All of your fancy moves won't mean anything if you can't stay out of foul trouble. Work on your defense—and your temper."

Jamal sneered. "You're washed up, old man."

DeMarcus blew his whistle. "All right. Bring it in." His voice was sharp as the players gathered around him and Oscar. "Jamal, you're a good shooter."

Jamal swiped sweat from his brow. "Damn right, I am."

DeMarcus narrowed his eyes on Jamal. "But because you keep sending our opponents to the foul line, your teammates have to work harder and shoot more to stay in the game. You can't make those mistakes and expect to get to the play-offs."

"I can handle it." Insecurity lay beneath Jamal's cocky smile.

Anthony Chambers gave Jamal a hard look. "You'd better pray on that, brother. The truth will set you free."

Jamal glowered at Anthony. "What truth is that, St. Anthony?"

Anthony put his hand on the other man's shoulder. "That, if you don't heed Coach's wisdom, I'm going to knock your teeth out."

Barron Douglas settled his hands on his hips. "And I'll put you in traction."

Great. A brawl on the court was just what he

needed to catapult this practice right into the crapper.

"That's it. Practice is over. Hit the showers." De-Marcus watched the players walk toward the locker room. Jamal lagged behind.

"Thirty minutes left." Oscar's observation was less than helpful.

DeMarcus rubbed the back of his neck. "They wouldn't have gone any better than the first ninety minutes."

The older man moved to stand beside him. "Jamal's got flash."

DeMarcus stared toward the locker room. How would he take this team to the play-offs? "But?"

"He's immature."

DeMarcus couldn't argue with that. "I was hoping he'd grow up. But we're eighteen weeks and fifty-six games into the season, and I'm not seeing any improvement."

"Bench Jamal, start Rick." Oscar was persistent.

DeMarcus faced the assistant coach. The knots in his neck and shoulders remained. "Rick plays well in practice. But during a real game, he hesitates to take the shot. Why?"

Oscar shrugged. "Ask him."

"I'm asking you. Why are you so sure Rick gives us a better chance of getting into the play-offs?"

Oscar's tall, bulky body tensed. "I see what you can't."

"Which is?"

"Rick puts the team above himself. Whether he's sitting or starting, he'll do whatever it takes to help the team win. We were winning before you benched him." Oscar jerked a thumb toward the lockers. "But when that Air Jordan wannabe gets the ball, it becomes the Jamal Ward show. He'll make himself look good, even if it jeopardizes the team."

"I don't know what Rick is afraid of, but his fear is causing him to hesitate in real-game situations. I can't risk him freezing up and costing us the win."

Oscar gave him a scornful look. "Sometimes you have to risk losing if you want to win."

DeMarcus watched Oscar leave the court. The assistant coach was angry. Well, so was he. Oscar was convinced he was right. DeMarcus was just as certain he was wrong. Oscar was passionate about his position, though. DeMarcus could tell because never before had the assistant coach strung together so many words when speaking to him.

The knock on his office door Wednesday afternoon interrupted DeMarcus's review of the Washington Wizards' scouting report. Andrea Benson of the *New York Sports* waited in his doorway.

He stood and checked his watch. It was almost four o'clock. "Andrea, did we have a meeting?"

The reporter strode toward his desk. The wide-legged pants of her dark green suit billowed like a skirt around her legs. "No, Coach Guinn, we didn't."

His frown cleared as he took the hand she offered. "Call me Marc. I'm sorry. I don't have time for an interview right now. I have to prepare for Friday's game in D.C."

"I know. But this is very important. I have three questions that will take only a few minutes of your time."

DeMarcus released her hand and swallowed a

sigh. Andrea's dark eyes were troubled. His gaze dipped to her choke hold on the brown strap of her huge purse. What was on the reporter's mind? "How can I help you?"

"Thank you." Andrea lowered herself to the guest chair in front of DeMarcus's desk and waited for him to reclaim his seat. "Coach Guinn—Marc—are you addicted to cocaine?"

18

"What?" DeMarcus barely heard himself above the blood rushing through his ears.

Andrea settled back into the black cushioned visitor's chair. Her tension seemed to have transferred to him. "I didn't think so."

Anger replaced shock. "What are you talking about?"

Andrea opened her reporter's notepad. "I got a call from someone claiming to be your—and I quote—personal drug supplier."

"What?" DeMarcus was repeating himself, but he couldn't seem to think.

"He offered me an exclusive interview about your addiction to coke and heroine. He claimed he's been your supplier since high school."

DeMarcus fisted his hands on his desk. Living in the public spotlight, he knew people would try to tarnish his image. Competitors attempted to pull him into public feuds. Women claimed to be in a relationship with him. And so-called friends tried to sell his life story or get him to invest in their up-and-coming-can't-miss business deals, complete with shady front men. He'd avoided the worst of that by remembering the life lessons his parents had taught him and reminding himself that basketball was his job. But now he was being pulled into the nightmare. Who was targeting him and why?

Gerald.

Memory crashed into him like an ice-cold Atlantic Ocean wave.

DeMarcus reminded himself to breathe. "What did you say?"

Andrea searched his features. "I told him I'd get back to him. He said if I kept him waiting too long, he'd go to another paper."

Thoughts, questions and obscenities circled DeMarcus's mind with near warp speed. In self-defense, he grabbed one. "Why didn't you interview him?"

The intensity in Andrea's stare made him uneasy. What was she looking for and what did she find? He knew she'd found something. Andrea Benson was a very smart person.

"I don't believe him."

DeMarcus's shoulders relaxed. It was a ridiculous reaction. He knew he wasn't addicted to drugs. He'd never even tried them. Why was it important what other people thought of him? He didn't know why he cared; he just did.

He sat back and considered the reporter, who didn't seem as much like the enemy anymore. "Why don't you believe him?"

"I know what addiction looks and acts like. It doesn't look or act like you. And I don't think you would have made it into the NBA, much less have been so successful, if you'd been addicted to hard drugs."

"Especially since the NBA has strict drug-testing policies."

"There is that."

Silence extended while they took each other's measure. DeMarcus checked his watch, but was too distracted to register the time. "Have I answered your question?"

"The first one. I still have two more."

DeMarcus had never enjoyed media interviews, and this one was turning out to be the worst. "What are they?"

"Who's behind this fake story and why is he trying to ruin your image?"

DeMarcus was afraid Andrea would realize everything if he breathed.

Gerald had threatened to destroy DeMarcus's reputation if the Monarchs continued to win. He hadn't believed the franchise partner would go through with it. However, now that the team had a winning record, rumors were linking him to drugs. A coincidence? He didn't think so.

DeMarcus held the reporter's gaze. "I don't know."

Andrea gave him another intense scrutiny. "I don't believe you."

He'd have to brazen it out. "Why not?"

"A better question is, why are you protecting someone who's trying to hurt you?"

"I'm not protecting anyone."

"Then why won't you give me a name?"

"Because I don't have one." He wasn't lying. DeMarcus was pretty sure Gerald was behind the bogus story, but didn't have proof. Without proof, he wouldn't make allegations against the franchise partner—his boss—in the media. He'd deal with Gerald himself.

Andrea shifted in her chair, crossing her legs. "I'm curious—"

"I'm sure you are."

She continued as though DeMarcus hadn't tried to interrupt her. "Is the person behind this fake story trying to hurt you, your team, your family or all of the above?"

DeMarcus felt his tension building. The intrepid reporter was too close to the truth. "When you find the person, ask."

"I will. I respect that you don't want to get into an exchange of angry words or bad feelings in the press. That never helps anyone." Andrea stood. "But whoever planted this story doesn't care about you, your family or the Monarchs."

DeMarcus stood with her. "Apparently not."

"So what does he care about?"

"That's another good question."

"But one you won't answer?"

"I can't." That, too, was true. Whatever happened in the team had to stay in the team.

Andrea arched a brow. "I'm going to break this story. Not the one alleging your drug use. The one about the person attacking your reputation. And, when I do, I'll let you know what I find out."

"I'd appreciate that."

"Unless there's something you want to tell me first?"

DeMarcus spread his arms. "I don't have anything to say."

Andrea extended her hand. "I'm sorry for barging in uninvited, Marc. Thanks for your time, and good luck against the Wizards Friday night."

DeMarcus held Andrea's hand. "Thank you for believing me."

She grinned. "I've been a Marc Guinn fan longer than I've been a Monarchs fan."

DeMarcus relaxed enough to return her smile. "Thank you."

The reporter left his office. Her strides were brisk and confident. She would be disappointed when she learned he'd kept information from her. But as she'd said, he wasn't going to engage in a war of words in the media. He'd handle the situation quietly.

First, though, he wanted to talk with his father. DeMarcus hated that negative publicity against him would reflect on his parents. He'd warn his father tonight, prepare him for the fallout.

Then, he'd confront Gerald.

DeMarcus stabbed Gerald's doorbell. His anger had built by the minute since he'd realized the spineless franchise co-owner must have gone forward with his threat. The timing was too much of a coincidence. Who else would have started this story? He jabbed the bell again, giving serious consideration to kicking down the heavy oak barrier.

The door swung open. Gerald stood in the threshold, his bronze leather overcoat hanging open over a teal crewneck sweater and navy pants.

DeMarcus didn't wait for him to speak. He stepped forward, forcing the other man back into his white stone entryway. "What the hell are you doing?"

Gerald walked backward. "I'm meeting friends for a drink. Is there something I can do for you?"

The smug smile on the franchise partner's face

threatened to cut the last of DeMarcus's control. He slammed the front door closed behind him. "Grow a pair."

Gerald's eyes narrowed. His smile dimmed. "Excuse me?"

"There's no excuse for you. You're a coward and a liar."

Anger was edging out Gerald's self-satisfied expression. "Those are serious allegations against your *boss*."

"You can't deny them. You lied about why you wanted me to coach the Monarchs. You lied when you said Jack wanted to move the team. Now you're feeding the press a story about my being a drug addict."

Gerald held DeMarcus's gaze. "I don't know what you're talking about."

DeMarcus wanted to grab Gerald by his sweater and slam him against the wall. He stepped back before he could give in to the urge that would have landed him in jail. That was probably what Gerald wanted. "You mean it's just a coincidence that you threatened to plant a story about my being addicted to drugs if the Monarchs kept winning, and now people are asking me about these rumors?"

Gerald shrugged. "It seems that way."

DeMarcus narrowed his eyes. "I don't believe in coincidences."

"Then I don't know what to say. I don't think I can help you."

"I don't need your help." DeMarcus shoved his fists into the front pockets of his black suede jacket. "Do you think I won't tell the press that you've planted these lies?"

Gerald's smug expression returned. "They won't believe you."

"Is that a chance you want to take? I'll even tell them why you decided to sell lies about me. A large mansion for an aging bachelor. Priceless artwork hanging from your walls. Expensive clothes, while the Monarchs' revenue has been shrinking the past four years. You're living way above your means, Gerry."

Gerald's features hardened. He opened and closed his fists. "That's a lie."

"So is the crap you're peddling about me to the papers."

"No one will believe you." Gerald's voice was rough with anger.

It gave DeMarcus a fierce satisfaction to feed Gerald his own medicine. It didn't appear to be going down well. Hopefully, the other man would choke on it. "There's as much of a chance of the public believing what I say as there is of them believing your lies."

Gerald shook his head. "No, there isn't. Sex, drugs and violence. Those are a baller's vices. That's why the rumors of your drug activities will be infinitely more believable than lies about any corrupt dealings you allege against me. After all, I'm an upstanding team owner. We don't do things like that."

DeMarcus closed the distance between him and Gerald to add weight to his words. "I don't care if there are dueling lies about us in the media. If you try to destroy my family, I'll drag your name through the same mud."

Gerald arched a brow. "I don't know what you're talking about."

DeMarcus turned toward the front door. "You've been warned, Gerry."

"And I'm warning you. Lose or leave, Marc. Those are your choices."

Whether he stayed with the Monarchs and played Gerald's game or broke his commitment to the team, the result would be the same. The reputation he'd worked so hard to build to honor his parents' sacrifices for him would be ruined. Worse, he'd lose Jaclyn's respect. He'd lose Jaclyn. DeMarcus didn't have a choice. He had to stay and play this out. There was more than a season at stake. He was playing for his future.

"Why didn't you tell that reporter Gerry planted the story?" Julian stood in the kitchen behind De-Marcus. His voice was tight with anger.

DeMarcus dropped the last dinner fork into the dishwasher and shook in the detergent. It had been hard to tell his father what Gerald was doing. It would be even harder telling Jaclyn. "When you take arguments outside of the team, you can tear the team apart. That's why whatever happens in the locker room, stays in the locker room. You don't take it to the media."

"That's an admirable sentiment, son. What makes you think Gerry shares it?"

"I don't think he does, but I'm hoping he can learn." DeMarcus started the dishwasher.

"You're deluding yourself."

DeMarcus heard Julian pacing the kitchen. He kept his back to his father. He took a sponge from the corner of the sink and started wiping down the counter. "Maybe. But I'm not going to let Gerry change who I am. If I do, he wins."

"And if you let Gerry drag your name through the mud, he wins. So it's a win-win situation for him." Sarcasm, the second stage of his father's temper.

DeMarcus forced himself to face his father. Julian stood across the kitchen at the foot of the table. His hands were hooked on the hips of his blue Dockers. He'd rolled up the sleeves of his cream crewneck sweater. The older man looked ready to knock someone on his butt.

Even though his father didn't blame him for what was happening, DeMarcus blamed himself. He should have realized there was more to Gerald's interest in him than his playing days. He was embarrassed and angry—with himself. "Gerry's not going to push this story. He knows that, if he does, I'll tell the media he planted it and why."

"Because he wants to move the Monarchs to Nevada?"

"Right."

Julian rubbed his face with both hands. "That's fine, Marc. But by that time it will be too late. Once a lie is in print, people think it's true. You'll always have that shadow on your name."

Julian was right. DeMarcus continued wiping down the counter. He needed to think. There had to be another way. "If I respond to the press's questions, they'll have a story. If I don't, all they have are allegations from a drug dealer."

"Which some people would think is enough."

"Andrea Benson isn't going to cover the story."

"Good for her. But she isn't the only sports reporter

in the city." Julian's words were clipped with exasperation. "Call Jackie. Now."

DeMarcus rinsed the sponge and cleaned the stove top. "She's having dinner with a girlfriend. They're discussing the Empire." He turned away from the stove. His muscles tensed. "Besides, I can handle this."

"I know you can. That's not the point." Julian crossed to the kitchen table and lowered onto a seat. "Jackie needs to know about Gerry's threats. They affect her and her team just as much as they affect you."

"I know. And I'll tell her but not tonight."

"Why not?"

DeMarcus rinsed the sponge again and set it on the board beside the sink. "Jack's dealing with enough, trying to keep the team in the Empire and finding a way to prevent Gerry from moving the franchise to Nevada."

"Nevada," Julian muttered. "I still can't believe that."

"Yeah. Well, Gerry has his own agenda."

Julian sat back in his chair. "What's your agenda?"

DeMarcus's back stiffened. "What do you mean?"

"Why don't you want to tell Jackie what's going on?"

DeMarcus leaned his hips against the kitchen counter and crossed his legs at his ankles. He should have known his father would see through him. No one knew him better. "I don't want to lose Jack's faith in me. I don't want to lose her trust."

Julian looked startled. "Jackie would never believe you were addicted to drugs."

DeMarcus pushed away from the counter to wander the kitchen. "I know that."

"Then what is it?"

DeMarcus paused. He took a deep breath, a preamble to stating his fears. "I don't want her to ever have a reason to look at me differently."

"What are you talking about?"

"The next time I lose a game, will she wonder if I've lost on purpose because of Gerry's threats?" DeMarcus met his father's gaze, hoping he had the answer.

Julian's frown cleared. "Jackie knows what kind of man Gerry is and what kind of man you are. The last time Gerry tried to pull you into his scheme, you quit."

DeMarcus turned to cross the kitchen again. He needed a stronger guarantee. "I don't want her to ever doubt me. Not even for a minute. And I don't want to ever wonder if she does."

"Why are you worried? If you tell her the truth, she won't have a reason to doubt you."

But Jaclyn knew how important his image and family name were to him. The truth was, knowing that, she had every reason to doubt him.

How could he convince her he was willing to risk everything he was to give her all that she wanted and more?

"We need to talk."

Jaclyn looked up as Troy Marshall strode into her office Thursday morning, followed by Andrea Benson. They looked as serious as though they were going to announce the NBA was disbanding in the middle of the season.

She set down her pen and gave them her full attention. "What's wrong?"

Troy stepped aside to allow Andrea to precede him. He pulled Jaclyn's office door shut and approached her desk. The media executive was coatless. His pale gold shirt was tucked into navy blue pants, but the sleeves were rolled to his elbows. His copper-colored tie was loosened. Troy didn't usually achieve this level of disarray until late in the afternoon.

He pressed his fists into the top of one of Jaclyn's black visitor's chairs. "Andy got a call from a drug dealer claiming to be Marc's supplier."

Jaclyn wasn't following. "Marc who?"

Troy held her gaze. "DeMarcus Guinn. Our head coach."

Jaclyn's eyes widened. Her thoughts scattered and everything flashed white. "What?"

Troy shoved his hands into the front pockets of his slacks. "I take it you haven't spoken to him yet."

Jaclyn's gaze bounced from Troy to Andrea before dropping to her Rolex. It was just after eight o'clock in the morning. She and DeMarcus hadn't seen each other after work last night, but she knew he'd been in his office for at least an hour. He always arrived between six-thirty and seven o'clock in the morning.

Get it together, Jones. This isn't the time or the place to freak out.

Jaclyn looked up at Andrea, then Troy. "No, he hasn't stopped by." She gestured toward the chairs. "Please sit down, both of you, and tell me exactly what happened."

Troy waited for Andrea to sit before taking the chair to her left. "Tell Jackie what you told me."

Andrea crossed her legs and laid her hands on the beige material of her pantsuit. "I got a call yesterday from someone claiming to be Marc Guinn's cocaine supplier and offering me an exclusive interview. I didn't believe the guy. It's obvious someone put him up to posing as a drug dealer to the stars. But when I asked Marc about it, he said he didn't know who would have planted the story."

Jaclyn stared at Andrea. In the reporter's entire recount, Jaclyn was stuck on one point. "You spoke to Marc yesterday?"

Andrea nodded. "Around four o'clock. I told him the supposed dealer said if he didn't hear back from me by the end of the day, he was going to call around to other papers. Well, he must have started calling because there was a message on my machine from a reporter at another paper asking what I knew about Guinn and drugs."

Jaclyn bit back a stream of vocabulary words more suited to an assassin than a lady. She sat forward and looked the reporter in the eye. "Thank you, Andrea. You've always been very fair to the Monarchs organization, and we've really appreciated it. But what you've done now is tremendous. I don't know of another reporter who would have taken the steps you've taken to ensure a fair and accurate story. I'm glad you're where you are today."

Andrea blushed. "I didn't do this for the Monarchs, Ms. Jones. I did it for myself. I don't deal in rumors and innuendos. Not anymore. I deal in facts. I'm not going to cover the drug story. I know it's based on a lie. I'd rather do a story on the reason someone wants to destroy the Mighty Guinn's reputation."

Jaclyn smiled. "I think I can accommodate you, if I can ask for one more favor."

Troy looked at Jaclyn. "You know who's behind this?"

Jaclyn folded her hands on her desk. She looked from Troy to Andrea, then back to her media executive. "I'm ninety-nine percent certain."

Andrea shook her head. "Marc said he didn't know who was responsible for this story. How could *you* know if *he* doesn't?"

Jaclyn arched a brow. "Marc lied." She leaned back in her chair and held up her hands, palms out. "Maybe 'lied' is too strong of a term. He believes conflicts shouldn't be aired outside of the team. I agree with him—to an extent. But when someone is threatening my team, the code goes out the window."

Andrea leaned forward. "So who is it? Who's behind the story?"

"Let me talk to Marc first. Then I'll give you the exclusive you were hoping for." Jaclyn checked her watch. It was edging toward eight-twenty. She wouldn't have much time to talk with DeMarcus. Practice started at eleven o'clock. She turned to her media executive. "Troy, set up a press conference for ten A.M. Tell them I want to discuss rumors of the Monarchs' head coach's drug addiction. We need to get in front of this story before our alleged drug dealer lets his fingers do the walking to every news media in Kings County. For once, I'm not going to play catch up."

Andrea sat back. "What about the favor you mentioned?"

Jaclyn contemplated the reporter. "I think this could be a nice addition to your exclusive."

Andrea tilted her head. "What could?"

Jaclyn pursed her lips. She had to think this through. "A meeting between your drug dealer source and a couple of New York's finest."

Troy's eyebrows shot up. "The police? You can arrange that?"

Jaclyn nodded toward Andrea. "With a little help. I know a prosecutor in the Brooklyn District Attorney's office who might be able to interest a couple of police officers in having lunch with an alleged drug dealer."

Troy grinned. "You're going to have him arrested?"

Jaclyn shook her head. "Think of it as more of a friendly, nonthreatening version of *Scared Straight*." She turned to Andrea. "Do you think you could get him to meet you at that sandwich shop a couple of blocks from here?"

Andrea smiled. "What time?"

Jaclyn picked up the phone. "Let me make a call."

Then she'd ask her head coach why she was the last to find out that someone was trying to destroy him and her team.

19

Jaclyn knocked twice on DeMarcus's open door before crossing the threshold into his office. She closed the door quietly behind her. DeMarcus stood from his chair. The chivalrous gesture didn't evoke the pleasure it had in the past. She was too angry.

Measured steps brought her to the opposite side of his desk. He had plenty of time to break the silence. His expression was more curious than concerned, but he never uttered a word.

She kept her voice low and slow. "When were you going to tell me Gerry is spreading lies in the media about you being a drug addict?"

Shock cleared his features. "Who told you?"

His words sucked the breath right out of her. She'd been right. Gerald Bimm was behind this latest assault on her team. And DeMarcus hadn't warned her.

Why not?

She was looking at a stranger. "That's your response? Didn't it occur to you that I might find out from someone else if you didn't tell me first?"

At this moment, it was a toss-up as to whom she was angriest with, Gerald for his petty vindictiveness or DeMarcus for his damning silence. She hated being caught off guard this way. DeMarcus knew that. Yet he'd put her in the position of having to cross examine him like a criminal defendant at court to get the information she needed to protect herself and her team. She hated that, too.

"I was going to tell you, Jack." His coal black eyes apologized.

Jaclyn wasn't ready to see it. "I know you're not that crazy. That's why I asked *when* you were going to tell me as opposed to *were* you going to tell me."

"I was going to tell you today."

She clenched her fists. "When, Marc? I need to know when. Practice starts in two hours. Were you going to tell me on the hour-long flight to D.C. tonight? Were you planning on texting me during the game tomorrow? When?"

DeMarcus's gaze slid away from hers. Not a good sign. He was scaring her.

He ran his hand over his close-cropped hair. "I can't give you an exact time. But I promise I was going to tell you today."

Her knees gave out. Jaclyn dropped into the visitor's chair behind her. "Why didn't you tell me yesterday after Andrea met with you?"

DeMarcus circled his table and took the chair on Jaclyn's right. "I went to see Gerry after Andrea left. I told him, if he kept pushing the story, I would tell the media he planned to move the team."

He seemed confident that his warning had convinced Gerald not to pursue the libelous piece. Based on Andrea's update this morning, he was wrong.

Jaclyn gave him a flat look. "Your tactics didn't work, Marc. The drug dealer called at least one other paper this morning."

DeMarcus stood and paced the room. "Then I'll have to make good on my own threat."

Jaclyn tunneled her fingers into her hair. Her head was spinning. Andrea had told DeMarcus a drug dealer claimed to be his supplier. DeMarcus had exchanged threats with Gerald. All of this had happened yesterday without DeMarcus saying a peep to her.

She heard the blood rushing through her veins. "Why didn't you tell me this last night?"

"You were having dinner with Violet, discussing the Empire. I didn't want to interrupt you."

Her temper snapped. Jaclyn shot out of the chair and stormed after him. "That's absurd. Gerry's shopping a story—a lie!—that will not only ruin your reputation but also damage my team. Trust me, dinner and Vi would have waited."

DeMarcus turned to face her. "I was handling the situation."

Jaclyn froze. "*You* were handling it?"

His expression grew cautious. "Yes."

"What's *my* role, Marc?"

DeMarcus frowned. "What do you mean?"

Jaclyn struggled to rein in her emotions. This was business. *Then why did it feel so personal?* "If you're here to handle crises for the franchise, what's my role?"

"You're already dealing with Gerry's other schemes."

Could he hear himself? He couldn't possibly. "You're going to pick and choose which problems I work on?"

"I'm not trying to tell you how to do your job."

"It certainly appears that way."

"I'm trying to help you."

She was able to control her tone despite her growing agitation. "You thought I was too busy to be told about the libelous article concerning my head coach, which Gerry was shopping to the papers?"

DeMarcus shoved his hands into the front pockets of his black warm-up pants. "I thought I could handle it."

Jaclyn had heard enough. "Do you want to know what I think? I think you don't like having me for a boss."

"What?" He sounded stunned.

"Do you resent reporting to me specifically or women in general?"

DeMarcus pulled his hands from his pockets and hooked them onto his hips. "Now you're the one being absurd."

Jaclyn shook her head. "I don't think so. What am I supposed to believe when you withhold critical information from me regarding my team?"

DeMarcus paced his office. "It was a judgment call to talk to Gerry before I spoke to you."

"You exhibited very poor judgment." Jaclyn tracked DeMarcus's movements around his office. "And this isn't the first time."

DeMarcus frowned at her over his shoulder. "What do you mean?"

Jaclyn raised her right arm toward his desk. "We've had this conversation before, right here in your office. You were sitting in your chair. I was sitting on the corner of your desk. I told you I needed to know everything that affected the team from tensions between the players and coaches to problems with the equipment. Do you remember that?"

"I thought I had autonomy." DeMarcus faced Jaclyn. He seemed to vibrate with anger.

Jaclyn narrowed her eyes. What did he have to be angry about? "Don't try to paint me as some sort of control freak. I'm not a figurehead sitting at a desk approving expense reports all day. If you can't handle my being your boss, you should have said so that night in Atlanta."

Silence slammed into the room. Jaclyn stared at DeMarcus. His tall, lean, well-muscled body she loved to explore. His shared passion for the NBA. His quick wit and great sense of humor. She'd thought he was perfect for her. Deep down, were they really so incompatible? Realization was a crushing blow to her heart.

"What are you saying?" DeMarcus's words came on a faint breath.

She wouldn't cry. "I told you we needed to keep our personal and professional lives separate if this relationship was going to work."

DeMarcus went cold. His heart clenched. He was losing her. Dammit. What could he say? What should he do to turn this around? "How did my talking to Gerry cross the line from professional to personal?"

Jaclyn's eyes were sad. She was already saying goodbye. "If I were Donnie Walsh, president of the Knicks, would you have waited a day before telling me what Gerry was doing?"

DeMarcus didn't want to answer. "No."

"Why not?"

The answer was obvious. "Because it wouldn't matter as much to me whether Walsh believed Gerry."

Her jaw dropped. "I know you're not taking drugs."

DeMarcus closed his eyes. He didn't know what hurt more, losing her or having to explain why he'd been such a coward. He opened his eyes and met her gaze. "I know that. That's not the part that worried me."

Jaclyn prompted him when he fell silent. "Then what was it?"

DeMarcus swallowed. "I didn't want you to doubt me. I didn't want you to wonder whether I was losing on purpose because of what Gerry said. I need your faith in me."

Jaclyn rubbed the fingers of her right hand over her eyes, pinched the bridge of her nose. When she opened her eyes, they were damp. DeMarcus's heart clenched again.

Jaclyn took a breath. Her slender shoulders trembled. "You wouldn't have lost my faith in you if you'd talked to me. But you're keeping secrets, Marc. Maybe you're trying to protect me, but I can't do my job with your brand of protection. I can't wonder what else you're not telling me."

DeMarcus wanted to go to her. Take her into his arms and beg her for another chance. Instead, he braced his feet to the floor and shoved his hands into his pockets. "I'm used to protecting the people I care about."

"You don't need my protection, but the team does. As much as I care about you, if I have to choose between you and the team, I have to choose the team. It's all I have left of my family."

"I know." She could have both, if she'd just give him another chance.

Jaclyn checked her watch. "I have to go. I asked

Troy to pull together a press conference. I want to address Gerry's lies before they end up in print."

DeMarcus's eyes widened. "You're holding a press conference? Do you want me there?"

She finally looked at him again. Her cinnamon eyes were red and wet. "No. The press would try to corner you. I want to go on the offensive. Then I'm giving Andrea an exclusive on what Gerry's been up to. It's time we exposed him for the traitorous worm he is." She moved toward his office door.

"Jack." DeMarcus called after her. "I didn't mean to let you down. You have to believe that. I was trying to help."

She gave him a half smile. "We should have known we couldn't mix business with pleasure. We're not the first couple to fail at an office romance." She opened the door and walked out of his office.

DeMarcus stared at the open door. Jaclyn was wrong. They hadn't failed. There was still time left on the clock, and DeMarcus hated to lose.

The Monarchs' large conference room was crammed with reporters, cameras, tape recorders and microphones. Jaclyn was overwhelmed. Playing in the shadows of the New York Knicks, the Monarchs didn't hold many press conferences.

Jaclyn covered her eyes to avoid the blinding camera flashes as she walked with Troy toward the podium. "What a circus. We didn't have this kind of response when we announced Marc was joining the organization."

Troy used his bigger body to shield Jaclyn from the crush of people and equipment. He'd put his suit jacket back on and straightened his tie. "There's nothing like a scandal to bring out the media."

Jaclyn glanced up at the former newspaper reporter. "You used to be the media."

Troy smiled down at her. "That's how I know."

The former reporter turned media executive reached the podium and took the microphone first. "Ladies and gentlemen, thank you for coming. Let's get settled so we can start the press conference. We don't want to keep you too long."

Jaclyn looked at the wall clock mounted across the room. They still had a couple of minutes before the event was supposed to begin. She and Troy had a long day ahead of them. The sooner the conference started, the sooner they could prepare to leave for the Wizards game in Washington, D.C.

The crush of bodies, lights, cameras and other audio-visual equipment made the room almost unbearably hot. Someone was wearing a lot of cheap cologne. The chatter of personal conversations was making it difficult for Jaclyn to mentally review her speech.

Troy once again thanked the members of the press for coming to the event. "As I explained in the announcement, rumors are circulating about our head coach and drug abuse. Brooklyn Monarchs owner Jaclyn Jones wants to address those rumors. Ms. Jones, if you'll take the podium, please."

Jaclyn switched places with Troy on the makeshift platform. She exchanged smiles with Andrea Benson, who sat in the front row. Today, they were pals and co-conspirators in a strategy to stop the slander against DeMarcus and her team. Tomorrow, they could very well be on opposite sides of some other issue. That was the nature of their professional relationship.

As Jaclyn adjusted the microphone, she realized this was her very first press conference. And she was using it to tell the world her lover wasn't a drug addict. "Thank you for taking the time to attend this press conference. When we learned of the lies circulating about our head coach, DeMarcus Guinn, we wanted to address the allegations immediately to put a stop to these outrageous and completely false accusations. The Brooklyn Monarchs takes drug abuse very seriously. We support and strictly adhere to the NBA's drug-testing policy. We want all of our employees to be good citizens and role models in the community. They can't do that if they're crippled by drug addiction. That's why I can stand here with complete confidence and assure you that DeMarcus Guinn is *not* addicted to drugs. That's all that I wanted to say. Do you have any questions?"

An older gentleman with a receding hairline stood toward the front of the room. "Are you standing by The Mighty Guinn because the rumors aren't true or because you're lovers?"

Jaclyn would have been stupid if she hadn't seen that question coming. And Jaclyn wasn't stupid. "I don't sleep with drug addicts. It's a personal preference." She surveyed the rest of the room. "Anything else?"

A petite young woman toward the back of the room shouted to be heard. "Where's DeMarcus Guinn now?"

Jaclyn smiled. The question made it seem as though DeMarcus was a fugitive from the law. "He's practicing with the team. They're getting ready for tomorrow night's Wizards game."

A lanky young man in the front left corner of the room stood. "How did this rumor get started?"

Jaclyn shrugged. "How does any rumor get started? That's something we're looking into now."

An older man with a ruddy complexion used the back of Andrea's chair to push himself to his feet. "Ms. Jones, how will this rumor affect your season?"

Jaclyn didn't see a link between the Monarchs' season and DeMarcus not being addicted to drugs, but this sports reporter apparently did. "As you know, Coach Guinn has given us our first winning record in three seasons, and we have realistic hopes of making it to the play-offs."

An older woman in the center of the room waved her hands frantically. "How will this rumor affect your relationship?"

Jaclyn chose to misunderstand the reporter's angle. "Coach Guinn and I have a strong working relationship. The rumor won't have any affect on it."

The older woman persisted. "How will it affect your *personal* relationship?"

Jaclyn gave the reporter a steely stare. "My personal relationships aren't open for public discussion." She again scanned the room. "We have time for one last question."

Andrea stood in response to the invitation. Jaclyn blinked. Considering she'd promised the reporter an exclusive interview later that afternoon, she hadn't thought Andrea would have any questions for the press conference.

She faced the other woman. "Yes, Andrea?"

Andrea held her pen poised above her reporter's

notebook. "Ms. Jones, what do you think Franklin Jones's reaction would be to this situation?"

Jaclyn's eyes stung at the thought of her grandfather and the shambles she'd made of his legacy. Troy stepped closer, putting his hand on the back of Jaclyn's shoulder.

She blinked several times and cleared her throat before leaning closer to the mic. "My grandfather would be devastated that someone was spreading lies against a member of his team, especially a lie involving drugs. He helped found this franchise to be a positive presence in the community. That's what we've been for the past fifty-five years, and that's what we'll continue to be for many decades to come."

"Why would you not tell Jackie that Gerry was blackmailing you?" Troy stood in DeMarcus's doorway, one shoulder propped against the threshold. The media executive looked like he'd just finished a hard *Gentlemen's Quarterly* photo session. His tie was askew and he'd rolled the sleeves of his dress shirt up to his elbows.

DeMarcus dropped the Washington Wizards scouting reports he'd been trying to study onto his desk and sat back in his chair. "Because I'm an idiot."

Troy crossed into his office. "You won't get an argument from me. But what were you thinking, really?"

DeMarcus rubbed his eyes with the fingers of his right hand. How many times was he going to have to explain just how big of a fool he'd been? "Jack has enough problems to deal with. I thought I could handle this one on my own."

Troy lowered himself into one of the guest chairs in front of DeMarcus's desk. "But you were wrong."

DeMarcus didn't have much patience left. Troy's line of questioning was working the last of it. "Spectacularly wrong. What's your point?"

"My point is, you tried to play the Lone Ranger and face the bad guys by yourself. If Andy hadn't contacted me this morning, the situation would have gotten worse."

DeMarcus had never seen Troy so serious. He acted as though DeMarcus had personally wronged him. "Jack already gave me this lecture." *And so had my father.*

"And now you're hearing it from me." Troy balanced his elbows on the arms of the chair. "The team is depending on Jackie to keep us in the Empire. If Gerry succeeds in moving the Monarchs out of Brooklyn, a lot of us will be out of a job."

It was hard to hear the negative impact his actions—or inactions—had on other people. "I'm sorry."

Troy sighed, a mixture of exasperation and irritation. "Just don't go off on your own again. The front office needs at least the same level of communication you use on the court."

DeMarcus stared at the surface of his desk. Instead of the clutter of papers, he saw again Jaclyn's face as she told him good-bye. "Trust me, Troy. I've learned my lesson."

Troy settled back into the chair. "This is more than a job. This place is like a family."

"I can tell. It shows in the way people care about each other and talk to each other." DeMarcus shook off his melancholy. "How did the press conference go?"

"It was pretty rough." Troy gave him a pointed look. "They asked a lot of questions about her relationship with you."

DeMarcus's shoulders and back tensed. "I knew I should have been there with her."

"Jackie was right to keep you away. The media would have torn you apart."

He understood the professional reasons for excluding him from the press conference. But, personally, he'd wanted to support Jaclyn as well as shoulder his share of the blame. And crossing the line between the personal and professional is what started this problem in the first place. "What did they want to know about Jack and me?"

"They wanted to know whether the rumors would affect your relationship." Troy rested his right ankle on his left knee. "Jackie told them the rumors wouldn't have any impact on your professional relationship. She refused to answer personal questions."

"I see." DeMarcus stood to pace his office. He felt Troy's eyes boring into his back.

"She broke up with you."

DeMarcus felt the pain in his heart. He'd known it would hurt, but not this much. "She did."

"You should have seen that coming."

"I know, Troy. But this is worse." DeMarcus flexed his shoulders, trying to ease the tension in his back. "She doesn't think I can separate our personal and professional lives."

"She's right. You didn't tell her what Gerry was doing because you wanted to protect her. You wouldn't have wanted to protect Donnie Walsh."

He shouldn't have been surprised that Jaclyn and Troy had used the same example of the Knicks owner, but he was. "She also doesn't trust me anymore."

"Why not?" Troy sounded confused.

Outside his window, DeMarcus could see the marina. "Because she thinks I'm keeping secrets from her."

"You are. You should have told her right away that Gerry was blackmailing you."

DeMarcus turned to face Troy. "I was afraid to tell her about Gerry's threats because I was afraid to lose her. She found out from someone else and I lost her."

"Classic."

"Oscar was right." DeMarcus walked back to his desk.

"About what?"

"Sometimes you have to risk losing if you want to win."

Troy shook his head with a grin. "Who would have thought that grouchy old guy would be so wise in matters of the heart?"

"We were talking about the season. But I should have listened to him." DeMarcus sat, propping his right ankle on his left knee."

"What are you going to do?"

"I'm going to prove that I can keep our personal and professional relationships separate."

"How?

DeMarcus considered the media executive's question for several moments. "I don't know."

20

"Well played, Jackie." Gerald's voice came over her office phone line less than an hour after the ten o'clock press conference ended. His tone made the words sound more like an insult than a compliment.

"What is it, Gerry? I'm kind of busy getting ready for the trip to D.C." Jaclyn worked her computer's mouse. She selected commands that sent to the printer the documents she wanted to review during the trip.

"Why are you going to Washington?" Gerald's confusion seemed genuine.

Jaclyn almost dropped the phone. "The Monarchs are playing the Wizards tomorrow night." Was she more surprised or angry that Gerald wasn't aware of the team's schedule? "It wouldn't hurt you to post a copy of the Monarchs' season schedule on your refrigerator."

"I heard you held a press conference to dispel the rumors that our Golden Boy is a drug addict."

"Did your office spy tell you all about it?" Jaclyn reached for the printer beside her computer monitor.

She retrieved the first set of documents and stapled the pages together.

"I'm an equal partner in the franchise. You should have told me you were calling a press conference. I had a right to be there."

Jaclyn almost choked. He was the reason she had to call a press conference, and he wanted to know why he hadn't been invited? "First of all, Gerry, Marc Guinn isn't a boy. He's a man. Second, whoever started this rumor is a petty, vindictive little worm. Do you have any idea who it might be?"

"Haven't you heard, Jackie? Where there's smoke, there's always fire. Maybe Marc *is* addicted to drugs." Gerald sounded as though he relished the accusation.

"You and I both know Marc has never done drugs. We did a thorough background check and testing before we hired him." Jaclyn took another document from the printer and stapled it.

"And you don't sleep with drug addicts." Gerald's tone was dry.

Jaclyn froze at the familiar words. "Your spy gave you the play-by-play from the press conference."

"I should have been there."

"What would your presence have accomplished?"

"As an equal partner, I would have welcomed the opportunity to show my support for the Monarchs' head coach."

What a liar. "The only interest you have in the team is to ruin it. We both know that, so cut the crap, Gerry."

"That hurts, Jackie." He didn't sound as wounded as he wanted her to believe. "By any chance is your lack of faith in my intentions the reason you told Andrea Benson to call me?"

Jaclyn smiled. "Has Andrea contacted you already? That was quick."

"She seems to think I started the rumors of Marc's drug addiction. Do you have any idea why she would believe that?" An edge entered Gerald's tone. He wasn't happy or smug anymore. Good. It was past time he felt even a little of the anger he'd caused her.

"Because it's true. Marc told us you'd threatened to smear his character in the press if he didn't throw the season for you. Did you think he wouldn't tell us?" Jaclyn closed her eyes and took a deep breath. He almost hadn't.

"Maybe we should drug test Marc again. He sounds delusional. And, while we're at it, we should screen you, too." Gerald's pleasantries seemed to be over. He sounded ready to chew nails.

"Why would that be, Gerry?" Her documents printed, Jaclyn settled into her chair.

"Why did you tell Andrea about my intent to move the team to Nevada?"

Jaclyn pursed her lips to squelch a smile. She wanted to wine and dine the reporter for moving so quickly on the story. "Was that supposed to be a secret?"

"As a former contracts lawyer, I'd think you'd be aware that such delicate negotiations shouldn't be leaked to the media."

"I have a better question for you, Gerry." Jaclyn's temper had started to stir. "Why are you negotiating a deal when you know your partner is opposed to it?"

Gerald continued as though she hadn't spoken. "None of those plans are finalized. I'm still in the exploratory phase. It was very precipitous of you to leak the information to the media. You could have damaged my negotiations."

"Good." His accusation brought a sharp surge of satisfaction. "The Monarchs aren't leaving Brooklyn, Gerry. Get over it."

"And you had no right to give a reporter Carville Abbottson's contact information."

Jaclyn arched a brow at Gerald's raised tone. Her business partner was fraying around the edges. Good. She hoped the stress was getting to him. "I didn't trust you not to lie about your attempts to move the team to Nevada. Carville Abbottson corroborated your plans. You should be happy. Now all of your machinations are out in the open."

The silence on the other end of the line was long and tense before Gerald spoke again. "I don't know what you thought you'd accomplish by discussing my plans with the media, but you haven't won."

"But then again, Gerry, neither have you." Jaclyn recradled her phone, disconnecting the call.

Gerald was right. She hadn't won. The Monarchs had their first winning record in three seasons, but they faced a long and challenging road to the play-offs.

And despite the press conference disputing Gerald's claim that the Monarchs' coach was a drug addict, her business partner's threat to smear DeMarcus in the media still hung over them. Gerald had proven how easily he could destroy the image DeMarcus had worked so long and hard to build. What other lies would he spread to try to capture the media's attention? How long would it take before the public started believing him?

Faced with that realization, would DeMarcus still do all he could to lead the Monarchs to the play-offs? Jaclyn would have to wait and see.

* * *

DeMarcus knocked on Jaclyn's hotel room door just down the hall from his own. His pulse was racing and his palms were sweating. He hadn't even been this nervous during his NBA draft fifteen years ago.

During the team dinner, Jaclyn had kept herself surrounded by players who'd seemed to sense she wanted to be shielded from their head coach. He'd been frustrated, but he'd understood the team's desire to protect her. Despite Jaclyn's independent image, the Lady Assassin was the kind of woman who brought out the chivalrous knight in men.

The room door opened. Jaclyn braced one hand on the threshold. The other gripped the doorknob. "I'm not really surprised to see you. Pigheadedness is characteristic of a champion."

DeMarcus leaned against the outer wall, crowding her. He gazed down into her cool cinnamon eyes. "You have the trophies to prove it."

"It's not politic to call your boss pigheaded." She didn't give him the smile he'd been hoping for. "I don't know what you think you'll accomplish by coming to my room. We don't have anything to discuss, and I'm not interested in anything you have to say."

Her words rocked DeMarcus back on his feet, but he remained standing. "You're wrong. We have a team to discuss."

Jaclyn gave him a dubious look. "Why do I suspect you only want to discuss the team now because I'm angry with you?"

"Because you have a suspicious nature." He

lowered his voice and shifted closer. "If we're going to disagree, could we do it in your room?"

Her cheeks heated. Her gasp was audible. "No, we can't. Go away." Jaclyn stepped back to close the door, but DeMarcus pressed his hand against it.

"Please, Jack. I really do want to talk about the team."

Jaclyn glared at him. DeMarcus saw hurt was well as anger in her expression. How could he show her how very sorry he was?

Finally, she stepped back, letting him in. "Keep it brief."

He'd welcome even the little victories. "Thank you, Jack."

DeMarcus strode past the small dining section and into the living area. He lowered himself to the puffy green and gold sofa and waited for Jaclyn to join him. She came as close as the armchair that bordered the living area.

At one time, they couldn't get close enough to each other. Now, she couldn't get far enough away. This is what his fear had cost him. A priceless, irreplaceable treasure. How could he get her back?

Jaclyn gripped the chair's back. "What do you want, Marc?"

She looked beautiful in a long-sleeved orange dress, like a sunrise bursting over a gold horizon.

When had he become a poet?

DeMarcus collected his thoughts. "I heard the press conference this morning was rough. I'm sorry."

She shrugged. Somehow the movement created an even greater distance between them. "It wasn't as bad as it could have been."

"You mean if I'd been there."

"I'm certain, if you'd attended the press conference, the questions would have gotten out of hand."

DeMarcus inclined his head. "Probably. But my absence didn't stop them from asking about our relationship."

Jaclyn arched a brow. "It seems that everyone else has sources in the franchise. I'm the only one who doesn't have a connection to insider information."

He wasn't sure what she was talking about. "I'm sorry you had to go through that, but I appreciate your public support."

Her wave was dismissive. "Of course. If I thought you'd had a drug problem, I wouldn't ask you to lead my team."

DeMarcus met her troubled gaze. "If you believe in me, why won't you give me another chance?"

Her smile didn't lift the clouds from her eyes. "Because I also believe you can't separate your lover from your boss."

"Give me another chance, Jack."

Jaclyn's lips tightened. "I've already given you two. The first was after you and Jamal had an altercation during practice. Oscar told me about that. And, today, with the drug rumors that Andrea told me about. You know what they say? Fool me once, shame on you. Fool me twice, shame on me. I can't let you fool me a third time, Marc."

DeMarcus stood. "I never meant to hurt or disrespect you. When I get the ball, I tend to run with it. That's my failing. I can fix that."

Jaclyn shook her head. "You were never a ball hog, Marc. You just didn't trust me with the ball. You thought you could carry it better. Well, maybe you can. But, as the franchise owner, I'd like a chance to at least discuss it."

"OK. I can do that."

"You've said that before. I want to believe you, but I'm afraid that I'll keep being misled."

DeMarcus ran an impatient hand over his hair. His fingers were shaking. "Is it really that easy for you to throw away our relationship? Tell me how you've made it so easy so I can do it, too."

Jaclyn exploded. "You think this is easy for me? I'm in love with you. But I can't walk away from the Monarchs. It would be like walking away from my family."

DeMarcus saw stars. His blood buzzed in his ears. "You're in love with me? Since when?"

She made an irritated sound. "How does that even matter?"

"Then why are you keeping us apart?"

"I'm not the one keeping us apart." She swung her arm to point at him. "You are."

"No, I'm not. How can I when I'm in love with you, too, Jack."

Jaclyn blinked. She stared at him blankly as though trying to translate his words. She swayed forward, then stepped back. "You love a part of me. The part outside of the office. I deserve someone who loves all of me. Inside and outside of the arena."

DeMarcus spread his arms. "I was trying to help you. You're already stressed about the arena. I wanted to take care of the media problem for you."

"I don't need you to be my knight in shining armor in the office. I need you to be my head coach." Jaclyn spun away from him to pace into the dining area. "Between Gerry and Nessa, I have enough people to keep track of. I don't want to worry about what you're not telling me as well."

DeMarcus turned to keep Jaclyn in sight. If he remembered correctly, Vanessa was Gerald's administrative assistant. "What's Nessa doing?"

Jaclyn sighed, pushing her hair back from her face. "Don't worry about Nessa. I'll deal with her when we get back to Brooklyn."

"I can't believe you've put me in the same category as Gerry. He's trying to hurt the team."

Jaclyn froze him with her eyes. "And what were you doing when you didn't tell me about Gerry's blackmail?"

DeMarcus studied Jaclyn, her body language, her tone, the look in her eyes. "I'm not the only one who has trouble separating the personal and the professional."

"What are you talking about?"

DeMarcus paced toward her. "You don't trust me. But it's not professional. It's personal."

Jaclyn narrowed her eyes. "What do you mean?"

He stopped less than an arm's length from her. He felt her warmth, sensed her confusion. "You're not upset because you think I don't respect you professionally. You know that I do. You're upset because you think I'll choose my family over yours, and you'll be left alone again."

Jaclyn stepped back. A look of incredulity settled over her features. "Where did you get that idea?"

DeMarcus inclined his head. "From you." He followed her, refusing to let her put any more distance between them. "You lost your parents and your brother when you were three. You lost your grandmother when you were eleven. I figure that's about the same time you lost your grandfather."

Jaclyn shook her head. "My grandfather died two years ago."

"But he shut you out more like twenty years ago. He'd lost his son, daughter-in-law, grandson and wife. I don't know why, but he closed himself off from you and made you feel second best to a basketball team."

"Stop it." Jaclyn hissed the command between her teeth. "That's not true. I never felt that way. This franchise is his legacy."

"No, you're his legacy." DeMarcus cornered her against the sofa. "He may not have known that, but I do and you should."

"He left his team for me."

"He should have left you with memories of who your parents were. What your father was like as a little boy. After your grandmother died, the franchise became your family. Your words. You said yourself the house you grew up in was never a home. Instead, your grandfather left you with a cold building and a grown man's game."

Jaclyn blinked back the tears pooling in her eyes. She planted her hands on his chest and shoved at him. "My grandfather was a good man. You don't know what you're talking about."

DeMarcus stepped back, giving her a breath of room. "Deep down, because of Gerry's threats, you think I'm going to choose to protect my family and help him destroy what's left of yours. Just like Bert and just like Nessa."

Jaclyn's lips tightened. "Why else wouldn't you tell me he was blackmailing you?"

DeMarcus nodded. "I know you won't believe me if I *tell* you you're wrong. I'll *show* you instead."

Anthony Chambers snatched the ball and charged back up the court. The Monarchs trailed the Washington Wizards by one point. DeMarcus checked the shot clock. Sixteen seconds left. He read the game clock: 29.3 seconds. Anthony was driving to the basket.

DeMarcus clapped his hands. "Barron, guard the post. Jamal watch your defender. Stay aggressive. Keep moving. No fouls."

Anthony pulled up at the three-point line, passing the ball to Barron. The Wizards' Rashard Lewis and Andray Blatche swarmed the point guard, forcing him to bounce the ball to Serge. The Frenchman pump faked the ball before returning it to Anthony. Eight seconds remained on the shot clock. Jamal fought free of the Wizards' John Wall, signaling for the ball. Four seconds on the shot clock. Barron sent the ball to the rookie shooting guard.

DeMarcus watched in disbelief as Jamal stepped behind the three-point line. The shooting guard bent his knees and launched himself into the air. He propelled the ball over Wall and Lewis, a straight shot to the basket.

Silence dropped into the arena.

His shoulders tight, his neck tense, DeMarcus followed the trajectory of the ball from the tips of Jamal's fingers over the straining arms of Lewis and Wall, across the paint—short of the basket.

Wizards faithful chanted, "Air ball! Air ball! Air ball!" The buzzer sounded and the fans erupted into shouts and roars of approval.

The announcer screamed into the microphone. "Ward shot an air ball! The Wizards win! The Wizards win! Ninety-two to ninety-one."

DeMarcus turned to make the long walk across the court to congratulate the Washington Wizards' head coach, Flip Saunders. "Good game, Coach." The words felt heavy passing his numb lips.

He released Flip Saunders's hand and maneuvered his way to Vom Two, the tunnel to the visitors' locker room. DeMarcus passed reporters, television crews, rowdy fans and flirty groupies. He wasn't aware of any of them. He'd been so certain the Monarchs would win this game. He'd promised Jaclyn he'd give her a win. How had things fallen apart in the fourth quarter? It wasn't a rhetorical question. He needed an answer or he'd sit out the postseason—by himself.

DeMarcus stood as Jaclyn marched across his office. She circled his desk to confront him. Her stilettos brought her almost to eye level. Her lilac scent wrapped around him. "Start Rick. Jamal isn't ready."

He crossed his arms to keep from reaching for her and tried not to burn in the cinnamon fires of her eyes. He missed her. Did she miss him? At all? "We have a better chance of winning with Jamal."

"We've dropped four straight games—the Celtics, the Wizards, the Grizzlies and the Cavs. How many do we have to lose before you make a change?"

He didn't flinch. "We were winning with Jamal. We weren't winning with Rick."

Jaclyn planted her hands on her slim hips. The dark blue dress nipped her tiny waist and ended just below her knees. "Jamal's a grandstander. Who goes for a three-point shot when you only need two points to win?"

DeMarcus pinched the bridge of his nose. She was still bringing up the Wizards game. That was almost a week ago. "He made a mistake."

"One of many."

"He's aggressive."

She arched a brow. "He fouls our opponents' best free throw hitters. That's not a good strategy."

"He adds energy."

"The other players have to clean up his mistakes." Jaclyn turned to pace his office.

DeMarcus tracked her progress away from his oak desk, past his conversation table and fake plant to the bookcase against his far left wall. His office didn't seem as cavernous as it used to. He was growing into it.

He uncrossed his arms. "We have twenty-three games left. He'll turn around before them. We just need to channel his skills."

Jaclyn tossed him a look over her shoulder. "You mean rein them in." She stopped pacing to face him. "Why won't you bench him? What do you see in him?"

DeMarcus hesitated. "I see myself. I know that sounds ridiculous, but he reminds me of me when I played."

Jaclyn's lips parted. Her brows lifted. "You think Jamal is like you?"

"Yes."

She shook her head. "He's nothing like you, Marc. But there is one player on the team who is similar to you, at least in personality."

He brought a mental image of the Monarchs' roster. "Who?"

Jaclyn crossed her arms. "Get to know your players, Marc. Find out what makes them tick. Find out why they've started losing again."

"Why won't you just tell me who it is?"

"Because you need to hear it for yourself." She turned to leave.

DeMarcus watched the sway of her hips beneath the straight, tight skirt. He dragged both hands over his hair. What was behind the sudden marked slump in the Monarchs' game? He was out of ideas, running short of solutions. He might as well try Jaclyn's touchy-feely approach. What did he have to lose? Besides, he was curious to find out which player on their team reminded her of him. How would he feel about the comparison?

21

DeMarcus rapped on Oscar Clemente's door.

The assistant coach set his Monarchs coffee mug on a pile of printouts. "You need something?"

After six months, DeMarcus was accustomed to the older man's grumpiness. He wandered into the cluttered office. "I'm going to schedule one-on-one meetings with the team."

Oscar shrugged. He picked up his mug and continued reading whatever team report absorbed his attention. Since it was Tuesday morning, the assistant coach was probably preparing for the Monarchs' Wednesday evening home game against the Detroit Pistons.

DeMarcus moved the pile of papers from one of Oscar's guest chairs to the floor. "This is early March. We have twenty-three games left. Our record is thirty-two and twenty-seven."

"I watch ESPN, too." Oscar kept his eyes on the report, sipped his coffee.

DeMarcus shook his head. He'd actually grown to

like the mean old man. "Mathematically, we're still in the running for a play-off berth."

Oscar glanced at him before returning his eyes to the report in his hands. "What's your point?"

DeMarcus's gaze passed over the framed action photos that hung on the walls of Oscar's office. They were from the Monarchs' glory days. "Why do you think we've lost our last four games?"

Oscar took another sip from his mug. "We're playing like crap."

DeMarcus hadn't mastered the art of having a productive conversation with the other man. He was working on it, though, and making progress. "Why do you think we're playing like crap?"

"Ask the players."

"I want to know what you're seeing."

Oscar dropped the report and lowered his mug. "Why?"

DeMarcus found some satisfaction in having the assistant coach's complete attention. It hadn't taken him as long this time. "For starters, you've been with the team for almost twenty years. You know the players better than I do."

"I know."

DeMarcus frowned his surprise. "You're also my assistant coach. We're supposed to work together."

"I know."

"Then why are you giving me a hard time? Just tell me what you're seeing and why you think the team's losing again."

"Why waste my breath?" Oscar set his mug on another pile of reports. He laid his hands flat on the papers strewn across his desk.

"Why would sharing your insights be a waste of breath?"

Oscar shrugged. "You never listen. You think you have all the answers."

DeMarcus stood. He shoved his hands into the pockets of yet another pair of black warm-up pants. The assistant coach was right. Oscar had often volunteered his thoughts, but DeMarcus hadn't listened. "That was in the past. Look, I'm out of ideas. I'm asking for yours."

Oscar heaved a deep sigh. He settled back into his chair. "I'll tell you what I've told you before. The only person who likes Jamal is his mother."

DeMarcus was pretty certain that wasn't true. Although, in addition to Oscar, Jaclyn and his father also thought Jamal should be benched. "You don't have to like your teammates to win."

"It doesn't hurt." Oscar was back to pinching his words.

DeMarcus scanned Oscar's office. How did the assistant coach find anything in the chaos on his desk? With the reports and boxes lined up across the floor, there wasn't any room to pace. "I've had teammates I haven't liked. That didn't matter when we were on the court."

"That's one of your problems, Marc." Oscar rocked back in his chair. "You think everyone should be like you."

DeMarcus knitted his brows. "No, I don't."

"Teammates should be able to play to win whether they like each other or not."

"That's right."

Oscar shook his head. "That's you. Everyone's not like you."

"What are you suggesting? That I use Match.com to put the team together?"

The hint of a smile touched Oscar's lips. "Not everyone's a basketball machine. Those one-on-one meetings with the players aren't going to mean a damn if you don't remember that."

DeMarcus nodded. "Thanks for the tip. Anything else?"

Oscar leaned back in his seat. "Peacocks are very pretty birds, but they don't fly for long."

DeMarcus cocked a brow. "Meaning?"

"Just because a player draws attention to himself and has exciting moves doesn't mean he'll carry you to the play-offs. Take a look at a couple of pigeons. You find those birds everywhere, including—with the right coaching—the play-offs."

DeMarcus hooked his hands on his hips. "Are you going to point these peacocks and pigeons out to me?"

Oscar shook his head. "You'll recognize them."

DeMarcus turned to leave the office. Everyone was speaking in code this morning. He had no idea there was so much mysticism in NBA coaching.

"Are you going to fire me?" Vanessa lowered herself with a noticeable degree of caution onto one of the three black guest chairs in front of Jaclyn's desk.

Jaclyn folded her hands on the manila folder in front of her. She studied the younger woman. Vanessa's confrontational attitude was much subdued. Her almond-shaped, dark brown eyes were wide and wary. "Do you think I should?"

Vanessa angled her chin. There was the aggression to which she'd grown accustomed. "No."

Jaclyn hadn't expected any other answer. "Why not?"

Vanessa's gaze wavered. She bit her lip. "I haven't done anything wrong."

Jaclyn arched a brow. "You weren't gossiping with Gerry about Marc and me? You weren't giving him information about the players so that he could pass it on to the media?"

"Even if I were, you can't prove it."

Jaclyn opened the folder and lifted the first document, a two-page e-mail printout stapled together. "And I quote, 'The cow really has it bad for him. It's embarrassing the way she chases him around the office. I almost feel sorry for her. She may be rich, but Marc Guinn wants a lady, and she's too mannish.'"

Jaclyn returned the printout to the folder and raised her gaze to Vanessa. "I take it I'm the 'cow.'"

The administrative assistant didn't appear to be breathing. She'd gone as pale as a ghost. Her jaw had dropped open and she was shaking in her seat.

Jaclyn gestured toward the folder. "These are printouts of the e-mails you sent to Gerry letting him know when I was meeting with the arena owners' lawyers, the arena owners and my financial advisor. Would you like copies?"

"No." Vanessa's teeth were chattering.

"Needless to say, I've retracted your access to my calendar."

"Are you going to fire me?" Her voice was unsteady.

Jaclyn tilted her head. "Did you do something wrong?"

"Gerry's the team's owner."

"Part owner."

"He had a right to know what you were doing with his team."

Jaclyn's patience was shredding to its end point. "*Our* team. If Gerry wants to know what I'm doing, he should ask me instead of having you spy for him. When I want to know what he's doing, I ask him. I would never have Althea spy on him. It's not ethical."

Vanessa wrung her hands. "I've been trying to help Gerry save the team. If you move the Monarchs out of Brooklyn, I'll be out of a job. I've had this job since I graduated from high school. It's helping pay my way through college. What would I do if the team moved? I can't afford to start over in Nevada."

Jaclyn's eyes widened. There was a buzzing in her ears. "Gerry told you *I* wanted to move the team to Nevada?" At Vanessa's nod, Jaclyn's temper snapped. Who hadn't her business partner lied to? "*Gerry's* the one who wants to move the team. He's working on a deal with Abbottson Investors to build the Monarchs an arena in Nevada."

Vanessa's dark eyes were clouded with confusion. "But he told me it was you."

Jaclyn was baffled as well. "Didn't you see the *New York Sports* article quoting Carville Abbottson that Gerry was the one who approached him about building an arena for the team?"

Vanessa's gaze drifted away from Jaclyn. "But I believed him."

"Gerry lied. I'm fighting to keep the team right here in the Empire Arena." Jaclyn jabbed her right forefinger against her desktop. "How many other people did Gerry lie to?"

"He told me not to tell anyone." Vanessa dropped her head into her hands. "How could I have been so stupid?"

Jaclyn's tension evaporated at the devastated expression on the younger woman's face. "Don't feel too bad, Nessa. Gerry's lied to a lot of people, including me and my grandfather. We've all believed him."

Tears swam in Vanessa's eyes. "Are you going to fire me?"

"No, I'm not going to fire you. It will take a while before I can trust you again, though."

Vanessa wiped the tears from her cheeks. "I understand."

"And you won't have access to my calendar again for a very long time."

Vanessa swallowed. "I shouldn't have believed him."

"He's your boss. You wouldn't have expected him to lie to you."

"I'm really sorry. What can I do to make it up to you?"

Jaclyn gave the administrative assistant a warm smile. "The next time your boss asks you to spy for him, tell him that's not in your job description. It's not even part of your 'ten percent other duties as needed.'"

Vanessa seemed too upset to smile. "How am I going to continue working for him?"

"I've thought about that. I'll tell Gerry I've confronted you. Once he knows that I've realized you're his spy, he won't ask you to snoop around anymore."

Vanessa's sigh of relief was audible. Her eyes were wet with new tears. "Thank you, Jackie. I'm so grateful to you. I don't know what I'd do if I lost this job. I'm so close to completing my finance degree." She stood to leave. "I hope you're able to find a way to stop Gerry from moving the team."

"Thanks, Nessa. Good luck with your classes." Jaclyn blinked back her own tears. To think her initial reaction had been to fire Vanessa. She hadn't realized she was dealing with another one of Gerald's victims and not a coconspirator.

Jaclyn stared out her door. She heard the phones ringing, murmurs of conversation, footsteps coming closer then walking away from her office.

Gerald had warned Vanessa not to tell people about the plans to move the team to Nevada, but had he told anyone else his lie? How many other people working for her believed she was trying to move the Monarchs out of Brooklyn? Were they committed to helping Gerald as well?

"Is it true you're snorting coke?" Barron Douglas slouched his six-foot-five-inch frame onto the silver-cushioned chair on the other side of the small conversation table in DeMarcus's office.

This is the reason DeMarcus hadn't done these get-to-know-you chats with the players sooner. The team's captain didn't want to be here any more than DeMarcus wanted to bond with him. But Jaclyn wanted him to better understand his players and DeMarcus wanted to prove he didn't have a problem having her as his boss. Besides, he was out of ideas to turn the team around.

DeMarcus drew a deep breath and counted to ten. "No, it's not. I don't do drugs. Didn't you see the

New York Sports article? Gerry planted that story because he's trying to throw the season."

Barron's eyebrows hopped up his forehead. "That was true?"

"Didn't you believe it?"

"You can't believe everything you read in the papers."

"You believed I was taking drugs." DeMarcus couldn't ignore a twinge of anger.

Barron raised his hands, palms out. "No. I *asked* if you were taking drugs."

"Is this rumor the reason the team's been losing?"

Anger flashed in the point guard's dark eyes. He obviously wasn't keen on discussing his failures. "The team's been wondering whether drugs were the reason for some of the coaching decisions you've made."

Were they going to parry insults all morning? "Such as?"

"Jamal. He's a jack—"

"The Monarchs didn't pay all that money for Jamal's contract to sit him on the bench." DeMarcus was tired of having all of the team's problems dumped on Jamal. Didn't anyone have anything constructive—and realistic—to say?

"Get the money back."

Apparently not.

DeMarcus rubbed his forehead. "Besides his personality, what other issues do you have with Jamal?"

"Isn't that enough?"

"No, it's not. Disliking a teammate isn't a good enough reason to lose." Regardless of what Oscar thought. "Why do you think the team has dropped five straight games?"

Barron scowled. "I told you. It's Jamal."

Why was he putting himself through this? The Monarchs had lost to the Detroit Pistons last night. He should be preparing for their trip to Canada to play the Toronto Raptors Friday. Instead, on his off day between games, he was holding a pop psychology session with the team's captain, something neither of them was interested in doing.

"We've won thirty-two games with Jamal, so he can't be the reason we're losing again."

Barron leaned into the table. "I'm tired of having to play twice as hard to cover up for his mistakes. I can't get into my game with him throwing me off my rhythm."

DeMarcus spread his hands. "You're the team captain. Step up and help your teammates. Find a way to calm Jamal down."

"He doesn't listen." Barron made a fist with his left hand. "When Rick was on the court, he handled his business. He knew where he had to be and what he had to do. I didn't have to worry about him. I just had to worry about making sure that I shined."

DeMarcus glanced at the series of tattoos climbing up the point guard's bare arms. Maybe Jaclyn had a point. DeMarcus now understood the team captain's self-absorbed attitude during practice and on the court. "Basketball is a team sport."

"So?"

"There are times when, for whatever reason, a teammate is going to be off his rhythm and you're going to have to pick up his slack. I'm sure there have been times when someone's had to pick up your slack."

"Yeah. Rick. We're in sync on the court." Barron scratched his scalp where it was exposed between his thick, black cornrows. "We don't hang out much outside of basketball since he's married and I enjoy the single life. But we're brothers on the court."

DeMarcus shook his head. "I benched Rick because he's not aggressive enough."

Barron looked disgruntled. "You gave Jamal the ball and put him on the court, but he doesn't know the plays. That's another reason he's an—"

"I've given him extra practice time. The assistant coaches have worked with him, too. We need another strategy." DeMarcus hesitated, then mentally shrugged. "Do you have any ideas?"

Barron shook his head. "Why are you giving him so many chances? Bench him. Give Rick his spot back with the starters."

"Jamal has a lot of promise."

Barron's eyes stretched in amazement. "How can you tell? He doesn't even give fifty percent in practice."

"That's not true, Barron. If he were that lazy in practice, I'd have fined him."

"Maybe you should fine him for not knowing the plays."

DeMarcus paused. That was a good idea. "I will. Nothing else seems to be working."

Some of the aggression drained from Barron's eyes. DeMarcus thought he detected a spark of cautious optimism.

Barron nodded and made to rise from the table. "Good. Are we done here?"

DeMarcus tried to channel his more sensitive side. "No. I have one final question."

"What?"

DeMarcus tried not to wince. "What do you need to be more successful on the court?"

Barron gave him an odd look. "What do you mean?"

DeMarcus wasn't sure. "What can I or the coaching staff do to help you be more productive on the court?"

"I need to shine. I need to be a superstar. I can't do that if there's a circus act playing on the court with me. Bench. Jamal. Now."

DeMarcus sighed. This wasn't working. "In basketball, we play as a team. A team doesn't succeed with only one superstar. We need five or six or seven. If you can't get that concept, then you need to take up tennis. Are we clear?"

Seconds ticked by as the point guard glowered at him in silence. Finally, Barron gave in. "Yeah. We're clear."

DeMarcus nodded. "And get some of your teammates together to help Jamal learn to execute the plays. The coaching staff isn't getting through to him."

Impatience stirred again in Barron's expression. "Haven't you heard Rick out there on the sidelines feeding Jamal the plays?"

"Yes, I have." DeMarcus hadn't given much thought to it, though. But now that Barron had brought it up, why was the veteran helping the rookie who'd taken his starting spot? What kind of competitor did that? He should be trying to get his spot back.

Barron shook his head. "The rookie won't listen. That's why he's an—"

"The rookie won't listen to the player whose spot he took. Maybe he'll listen to you."

Barron leaned into the chair again. "Then do what you said you'll do and fine him if he doesn't learn the plays. And, if he still won't learn them, bench him."

"Deal. Get your teammates together to help Jamal."

Barron scowled. "Why do I have to pull people together?"

DeMarcus arched a brow. "You're the team captain."

The point guard pushed away from the table and turned to leave the room. "That's some crap, man."

DeMarcus smiled. "It's been a pleasure chatting with you, too, Barron."

"Yeah. Whatever."

DeMarcus scrubbed both hands over his face. One down, twelve to go. Would he be so lucky as to find the worst meeting was over and the other twelve would be easier? He thought of Jamal, Serge and Warrick. Probably not.

22

Gerald's reaction was her new favorite memory. When he saw Jaclyn sitting between Albert Tipton and Violet Ebanks O'Neal at Bonner & Taylor's large conference table Thursday afternoon, he looked confused, angry and scared. Mortimer Gandy and his younger brother, Sanford, sat opposite them.

On the surface, Gerald appeared confident and successful in his dark brown suit, tan shirt and bold pink tie. But there was uncertainty in his gaze as it moved from Violet to Jaclyn and then to Albert.

He looked to the firm's senior partner, Gregory Bonner, seated at the head of the table. "What's going on? I thought I was coming to review the Empire Arena contract with its new owners."

Sanford raised his right arm and waved his hand in greeting. "Hi, Gere. C'mon in and sit down. We're all friends here, aren't we?" The twinkle in the elderly man's gray eyes meant he knew they were not.

Gerald took the chair at the foot of the large conference table. "It's good to see you again, Sandy."

Mortimer hissed at his younger brother. "Control yourself, Sanford. This isn't a barbecue."

Sanford rolled his eyes. "I know that, Morty. I'm just trying to make everyone comfortable."

Jaclyn swallowed a chuckle over the brothers' antics. But she remained attentive to Gerald and his every move.

Gerald looked to the senior law partner and repeated his question. "What's going on, Greg?"

Gregory gestured toward Jaclyn and her friends. "I'd like to introduce the new arena owners. I believe you've met all of them before—Albert Tipton, Violet Ebanks O'Neal and, of course, Jaclyn Jones."

Gerald's jaw dropped. "Are you serious?"

Jaclyn smiled. She was shaking, but this time with excitement. "Yes, we are. Vi, Bert and I are partners."

Albert folded his hands on the table and leaned forward. "Jackie is the majority share owner with forty percent. Vi and I each have thirty percent."

Gerald shifted his attention between the two Gandy brothers. "You sold the arena to them? I thought you wanted to make as much money as possible on the sale."

Gerald's manner switched between disbelief and anger. Jaclyn watched him with intense satisfaction. Disbelief and anger were the emotions she'd felt when she'd realized Gerald had convinced Albert to help him destroy her team. She'd also had those reactions when she'd learned Gerald had entered into negotiations with Abbottson Investments to build an arena in Nevada for the Monarchs. She could well imagine he'd feel disbelief and anger. Even betrayal and desperation. She'd felt all of those and more because of him.

Mortimer pursed his lips. "Without seeming indelicate, they did offer a significant amount of liquid capital for the Empire."

Sanford shrugged. "Besides, how much money do we really need? We're pretty darn old. It's not like we're going to live that much longer."

Mortimer nodded. "In the end, we just wanted to get out of the arena business. Too many hassles, too much stress."

Gerald inclined his head in Jaclyn's direction. "It's fine for her to keep the Monarchs in the arena. But what about your legacy? The Monarchs are falling apart. Do you really want them to take your arena down with them?"

Mortimer's gaze met Jaclyn's. "Jackie reminded us of the special history the Brooklyn Monarchs share with the Empire Arena. It's fitting that the team continues to play there. And, when you think about it, it's fitting that the children of the franchise founders also take over the arena. Very fitting."

Sanford smiled at Gerald. "I wouldn't worry about Jackie letting the team fall into the crapper, Gere. Jackie accomplishes whatever she sets her mind to. Like today. She was determined to keep the team in the Empire, and she figured out a way to make that happen. We appreciate your concern, but you don't need to worry about our legacy. It's in good hands."

Gerald's gaze narrowed on Sanford with suspicion. "I'm just afraid that you may have made a mistake."

"We don't think so. Besides, it's a done deal." Sanford tapped the stack of papers in front of him.

"Signed, sealed and delivered." He winked at Gerald. "I've always loved that song."

Gerald turned his contempt on Albert. "And you're a part of this? What about all that cock and bull you fed us about wanting to focus on your clothing store?"

Sanford rocked back in his seat. "Hey, now. There's no need to be unpleasant, Gere."

Albert spread his hands. "That's the beauty of this partnership. I'm going to be very hands off."

Jaclyn smiled. "Vi and I will deal with the operations and management of the Empire, including our relationship with the Monarchs."

Violet nodded. "We're even considering opening the arena to the NCAA women's basketball tournament. But the Monarchs will be our priority client."

Heat rose under Gerald's fair skin. He again addressed Albert. "You're not even going to be an active partner? Then why are you doing this?"

Albert kept his eyes on Gerald. "A very wise young woman reminded me that the franchise isn't just about money. It's about community. I may have been a little late in remembering that. But I did remember. Buying a few shares in the Empire to help keep the Monarchs in Brooklyn is my way of making amends for at least some of the damage you and I have caused."

Jaclyn recalled Albert telling her the arena was the key. He did remember the motivation behind founding the franchise a little late. But late was definitely better than never. She blinked back tears. She couldn't appear weak in front of Gerald, especially not now.

Gerald shifted his gaze between Gregory Bonner and Dennis Taylor. "You couldn't have warned me that I'd be facing this farce? I came all the way to downtown Brooklyn for this?"

Gregory nodded toward Mortimer and Sanford. "Our clients believed that, as part owner of the Monarchs, you should be aware of the terms of the new contract. We were fulfilling our clients' request. We don't owe you anything."

"This is a joke." Gerald stood to leave.

"Wait, Gerry." Jaclyn couldn't mask the pleasure in her voice. "Don't you want to hear the terms of the new arena contract?"

Gerald glowered at her. "I'm sure I can guess what it says."

Jaclyn held up the document. "You've come all this way. You should at least hear the terms."

Gerald's lips tightened. He shifted his gaze to the other people in the room before settling his attention on Jaclyn. "All right. What are they?"

Jaclyn grinned. "The Monarchs have a contract term without restrictions for the life of the team to stay in the Empire. Isn't that great?"

Gerald glared at the lawyers. "Don't bother to see me out." Without another word, he stalked from the room.

Violet broke the comfortable silence. "Well, that was fun." She turned to Jaclyn. "Who're we going to piss off next?"

Jaclyn grinned as she stood. "I don't want to dilute the pleasure of this moment."

Albert rose from his chair. "Enjoy your triumph, Jackie. You've earned it."

Jaclyn wrapped her arms around her arena partner's shoulders. "With a lot of help from my friends. Thank you so, so much."

Albert gave her a hard hug before stepping back. "No, thank you. I've exorcised all of my guilt. Now, I can sleep more easily at night."

"I'm glad." Jaclyn squeezed his arm. "As soon as we're making a profit with the team and the arena again, Vi and I will buy you out of the Empire so you can go back to focusing full-time on Tipton's Fashionwear."

Jaclyn circled the conference table to shake hands with the lawyers and the Gandy brothers. "Gentlemen, thank you for agreeing to the contract. I know you had higher bids."

Sanford waved his signed contract from the Empire Arena sale. "No, thank *you*. Now I can live a little before I die."

Mortimer stood. "You were right. The Monarchs belong in Brooklyn, specifically in the Empire Arena."

Sanford scowled. "And when we read the article in the *New York Sports* about Gerry starting those horrible rumors about Marc Guinn, we knew there was no better bid than yours."

Jaclyn made a mental note to send Andrea Benson another thank-you card. Her article had been the catalyst that finalized the arena deal. "My grandfather would be very grateful for your support."

Sanford glanced at Mortimer. The older Gandy cleared his throat. "With all due respect, Jackie, this deal had nothing to do with your grandfather."

"Heck, no, kid." Sanford winked. "It was all about you. Good luck."

Jaclyn thanked the lawyers again before leading Violet and Albert from the conference room. Waiting for the elevator, she gave Violet a high five. "OK, partner. Let's see if we can put that business degree of yours back to work."

Violet laughed. "I'm so excited. I feel like I've got my game back."

"I'm . . . indescribably relieved." Jaclyn found Albert's gaze. "But then a part of me is afraid I've beat the play clock buzzer only to send the game into overtime."

Albert nodded. "That's a good analogy. You've kept the team in Brooklyn. Enjoy that. But remember Gerry will just try to find another way to destroy the team."

Violet frowned. "Why is he so determined to hurt the Monarchs? It's his family's legacy as much as it's yours."

Jaclyn looked at her former teammate and new arena partner. "He doesn't think so." She turned to Albert. "I guess I'll be looking over my shoulder a little while longer."

"Is this about the plays again?" Jamal lowered himself into the chair on the opposite side of DeMarcus's conversation table.

The rookie's Allen Iverson basketball jersey revealed the tattoos down his arms. He'd noticed Jamal's ink before, but he hadn't paid much attention to them. He'd been distracted by the shooting guard's apparent lack of interest in the Monarchs' playbook.

Most of the designs were team logos and numbers of some of the NBA's greatest players—the Los Angeles Lakers' Earvin "Magic" Johnson, the Chicago Bulls' Michael "Air" Jordan, and the Philadelphia 76ers' Allen "AI" Iverson.

DeMarcus sensed Jamal's defensiveness. He had to remember this kid was just out of college. He'd left after his freshman year. He was a lot younger—and somewhat less mature—than the rest of the team. "Let's approach it differently. What do you think you need to be more successful on the court?"

This bonding thing was a lot easier the second time. Or maybe it just seemed less awkward with Jamal. For all his aggressiveness on the court, the rookie wasn't as confrontational as Barron.

Jamal seemed baffled. "I am successful on the court."

DeMarcus narrowed his eyes. Maybe they needed to start with the basics. "How do you define success?"

Jamal braced his forearms on the table and leaned across its surface. "Every game, I strap the team to my back. Then, I go out there and give the fans everything I've got. To me, that's success."

"What about winning?"

Jamal pressed his back against the chair. A look of surprise settled on his face. "I can't do it all myself. Those other guys need to step it up."

DeMarcus frowned. It wasn't just him. Anyone would be confused. "Which one is it, Jamal? Do you put the team on your back and do it all yourself? Or do you play as part of a team?"

Jamal briefly dipped his gaze to the table. "Both?"

Was the rookie asking him or telling him? "Do you know how I define success?"

"How?"

"Winning." DeMarcus held the younger man's gaze and willed him to understand. "What do you need to be a more consistent winner?"

Jamal's eyes searched the office. DeMarcus followed the younger man's gaze to his MVP trophies, and his championship rings and Olympic gold medal set in cases on his bookshelf. He could guess at the player's thoughts, and he'd probably be right. How long would he have to wait before he could have one of those? Every rookie wanted to know that.

Jamal's dark brown eyes clouded. "I am a winner."

"No, you're not. Not yet." DeMarcus didn't want to crush the kid's ego, but tough love was kinder in the long run. "Winning comes with practice and with discipline. You have to prepare for the games. You can't just step onto the court."

"Are we talking about practice, man?"

DeMarcus scowled. Did Jamal realize he was parroting the tough and talented—but undisciplined—Allen Iverson's infamous quote? Was the rookie's identity crisis cause for concern?

"You're not Allen Iverson." DeMarcus glanced at the other tattoos on the rookie's arms. "You're not Michael Jordan or Kobe Bryant, either. You're Jamal Ward. Put in the practice time."

Jamal pushed away from the table and got to his full six-foot-five-inch height. "I was drafted my freshman year. I took my team to the NCAA championship."

DeMarcus lifted his eyes to meet Jamal's. "That's a great accomplishment. But you didn't do it by yourself. You were part of a team, just like you're part of a team now."

Jamal jabbed his chest with his right forefinger. "I'm a superstar."

DeMarcus stood. "Wearing Iverson's jersey, talking like him, that ink on your arms—those things don't make you a superstar. Your God-given talent and a whole lot of hard work is what will help you become a superstar. You're not there yet. Do you want to be?"

Jamal glared at him. DeMarcus held his gaze. He saw the struggle in the younger man's eyes. He understood the doubt in his mind. The rookie didn't know whether he should listen to his coach or continue believing he already was a winner in the NBA, even though he hadn't even played a full season.

Jamal broke eye contact. "Yes, I do. I want to be a superstar." He sat down. "I want to be a winner."

DeMarcus reclaimed his seat. "Good. First, drop the alternate personalities. Don't try to be someone else. Learn who Jamal Ward is and play to his strengths."

Jamal smoothed his hand over his brown, clean-shaven head. "OK."

"Second, I want a hundred and ten percent during practice." DeMarcus sensed Jamal's discomfort. "What is it?"

"The other players don't like me."

This was the NBA. Why did he suddenly feel as though he were coaching a Pee-Wee team? "The other players don't know you. You've been pretending to be other people. I bet you don't even know you. Once you show them you're committed to winning, they'll come around."

"OK."

Another problem solved? "And third, learn the plays. The offense and the defense. If you don't, I'll fine you."

Jamal's jaw dropped. "But—"

DeMarcus interrupted him. "OK?"

Jamal frowned. "OK."

"Good. I'll see you at the airport tonight." DeMarcus watched the rookie leave.

He had eleven more of these bonding sessions. Luckily, he'd spread them out over the next couple of weeks. But, if they were all like the first two, he'd lose his mind.

DeMarcus scrubbed his face with his hands. He was exhausted. He'd gotten to work at five o'clock this morning to better fit these player meetings in with the rest of his pregame preparations. DeMarcus stood and checked his watch. It was almost two o'clock. He logged back on to his computer to watch more game footage. He'd work for a couple of hours before heading to the airport.

The e-mail was waiting for him. It was addressed to all Monarch and Empire Arena employees from Jaclyn Jones. She'd bought the arena. The message went on to reassure everyone—staff, management, coaches and players—that the Monarchs were staying in Brooklyn. DeMarcus closed his eyes in relief. This must mean the Empire owners had accepted the bid from Jaclyn, Violet and Albert—without Jaclyn having to mortgage her house.

The good news reenergized him. He could only imagine the euphoria Jaclyn felt. DeMarcus locked his computer again and hurried toward his office door. There was a new arena owner he wanted to congratulate—and a woman with whom he wanted to celebrate.

Minutes later, DeMarcus stood in the threshold of Jaclyn's office. He was loathed to interrupt her intense concentration as she sat behind her desk reading the thick document before her. She held a pink highlighter in one hand and braced her head with the other. She was wearing her red skirt suit, the one he'd come to realize she saved for critical meetings.

He knocked on her door. Jaclyn looked up from her reading and went very still. DeMarcus recognized the distance in her and understood it. He still hadn't proven to her that she could trust him. That he respected her as his boss. He'd made a terrible mistake—a series of them. How was he going to make amends?

"Congratulations, Jack. You pulled it off. You bought the Empire, and without having to mortgage your house." DeMarcus crossed her office and sat in one of her visitor's chairs.

"That's definitely a bonus." Jaclyn seemed to relax by degrees.

DeMarcus laid his forearms on the chair's armrest. He was restless with this gulf between them, the awkward conversations that feared hidden meanings in every word. "I wish I could have seen Gerry's face when the lawyers told him you, Bert and Vi were the new arena owners."

Jaclyn's chuckle had a mischievous tone. "I should have brought a camera. It was a moment to remember."

DeMarcus took in her wide smile and twinkling eyes. Her cheeks were flushed with victory. Her joy was contagious. "You look so happy."

"I am happy. And I'm going to enjoy this feeling for as long as I can. It won't last."

That quickly, the light in her expression dimmed. DeMarcus felt her disappointment as his own. "You think Gerry hasn't given up?"

Jaclyn's full red lips twisted. She dropped her gaze to the papers in front of her. Contracts? "Not by a long shot. Bert said Gerry's nurtured his resentment for decades."

"But you've beaten him."

Jaclyn capped her marker and bounced it against the document. "Gerry's like the Terminator. He won't give up. I just wish I had some idea of what he'll try next."

So did he. Was he wrong to feel so protective? He

had to find the line between their personal and professional relationships. That line was his only hope of making his way back to her. "What can Gerry do? He can't move the team out of Brooklyn. You won't let him out of the Empire contract."

"There are other ways to destroy a team."

DeMarcus's hands tightened around the armrests. "Like planting damaging stories in the media." Gerald's use of the media was a sore subject with him, and it always would be.

Jaclyn nodded. "That's one way. He could delay managerial decisions—contracts, hirings, firings. When he and Bert outvoted me to hire you, I thought that was the end of the Monarchs' season."

DeMarcus's lips curved. "I remember that day vividly."

Jaclyn's gaze wavered. "He could also stir disgruntlement among the staff. That's why I sent the e-mail about the Empire. I wanted to make the announcement before Gerry could revise history."

DeMarcus nodded. "He'd have taken the opportunity if you'd given it to him."

"I know." Jaclyn fisted her hands on the table. "I wish I could buy him out. But he won't sell his shares."

"That's part of his revenge."

"His plan is to drive me insane."

"We'll just have to make sure we don't give him any openings to hurt the team."

Jaclyn looked at him. "He can still get to us through the media. He could use them to sow dissension among the players and distract us from the season."

DeMarcus felt Jaclyn's fear for her team. He was concerned as well. "We have the best media executive in the league."

Jaclyn's expression eased slightly. "We can't take Troy's talents for granted. The players haven't been playing like a team." She dragged her fingers through her hair. "How are your meetings with them going?"

DeMarcus relaxed. She'd been cautious when he'd told her he was meeting one-on-one with the players. He'd had the sense she didn't think he'd take these sessions seriously. "I've met with Barron and Jamal. I think you were right. These talks are giving me insight into the players."

A curious smile curved her full lips. "But you're not convinced they'll make a difference, are you?"

DeMarcus shifted in his seat. "Let's just say my mind is much more open for now. Barron thinks the game's all about him. I told him I'm making him responsible for his teammates' performance, starting with Jamal."

Jaclyn looked surprised. "I like that."

DeMarcus warmed with her words and reaction. "Jamal has multiple personalities."

Jaclyn blinked. "Are any of them going to learn the playbook?"

DeMarcus chuckled. "I told him I'd fine him if he didn't. That was Barron's idea."

Jaclyn arched a brow. "I'm impressed—by both of you."

DeMarcus lowered his voice. "I'm trying, Jack."

Jaclyn's eyes dimmed. "On behalf of the team, I appreciate it, Marc."

DeMarcus's words barely carried on a breath. "You're ready to trust me again with your team, but you won't trust me with your heart?"

Jaclyn looked away. "It's much more fragile."

23

Warrick Evans strolled into DeMarcus's office. The shooting guard's loose-limbed gait conveyed a confidence he hadn't shown on the court all season. His baggy, silver and black Brooklyn Monarchs warm-up jacket and pants concealed the strength and agility the twelve-year veteran could reveal on a dime—if he tried.

Why wasn't he trying?

DeMarcus gestured the player to the seat across from him at his conversation table. "Thanks for coming."

"No problem, Coach." Warrick sat and lifted his right ankle to his left knee.

DeMarcus arched a brow at Warrick's response. "The other players were either angry or anxious about meeting with me. You seem calm. Why?"

Warrick spread his arms. "What are you going to do? Release me? It's a little late in the season for that."

"Is that why you're not playing harder for the team? Because you don't think I'll cut you from the roster?"

Warrick's expression tightened. "You benched me, Coach."

"You don't seem upset about that. Other players would be hounding me twenty-four seven, stalking me night and day trying to get their spot back. You're coaching your replacement." Why was he trying to get a rise out of the other man? Was it for the good of the team? Or was he still jealous of Warrick's friendship with Jaclyn? He didn't want to face that answer.

Warrick gripped his fingers together on his left thigh. "*Are* you releasing me?"

DeMarcus noticed the player's knuckles showed white. He looked away. "No, I was just . . . Forget it."

"I love this team. I've been a Monarch since the day I was drafted out of college. I love Brooklyn, and Jackie's like a sister to me." Warrick rubbed the back of his neck. "But, if you decided the team should move in another direction then, hopefully, my agent could find a spot for me somewhere else."

DeMarcus eyed the veteran. Where was his ego to argue against being released? Where was his fight to reclaim his starting position? Instead of cataloging all the mistakes Jamal makes, Warrick coaches Jamal from the sidelines. Jamal didn't even appreciate Warrick's efforts. Instead, the rookie took every opportunity to undermine the veteran.

He knew what Warrick needed to succeed on the court. The shooting guard needed passion, fire, a competitive drive. He needed Jamal's spirit. And Jamal needed Warrick's mastery of the game. If he could combine the two players, the Monarchs would bounce into the play-offs.

DeMarcus sat back in his seat. "I'm meeting with all of the players. I'm not singling you out."

"I know that, Coach."

DeMarcus narrowed his gaze. "Then you probably also know that I've been asking everyone what they need to be more successful on the court."

The light dimmed in Warrick's brown eyes. "I'm not on the court."

"Then what do you need to get *back* on it?"

"I don't see it that way." Warrick sat straighter in his chair. "Sure, I want to play. But it's more important to me that the team wins."

DeMarcus nodded. "And if that means you sit on the bench, you're fine with that."

"I think, when I was playing, I made some positive contributions before I started to struggle. But I think I've proven that I can also contribute from the bench."

"As long as the team is winning."

Warrick nodded again. "That's right."

DeMarcus shrugged. "Because, either way—whether you're on the bench or on the court—you win, too."

Warrick's smile looked forced. "Right."

"That's bullshit."

Warrick's fake smile vanished. "Excuse me?"

DeMarcus leaned forward into the table. "Why were you struggling?"

Warrick shrugged. "I'm pretty banged up, Coach. I'm thirty-four. I've been in the league for twelve years."

DeMarcus frowned. "Your knees and back don't bother you during practice. You've got the fastest hustle and the most accurate shot of any of the players during practice. You only tank during games. Why?"

"My teammates don't hit as hard as our opponents."

"Jamal's been hitting you pretty hard, Rick." DeMarcus paused. When Warrick didn't respond, he continued. "I'll tell you what I think."

"What's that, Coach?"

"I think you're afraid of losing."

Warrick's brows came together. "What?"

DeMarcus sat back. "I think you play so well during practice because there's nothing to lose. But you run out of steam during regular games because you crumble under pressure."

Warrick held up both hands. "I can handle pressure."

DeMarcus shook his head. "No, you can't. All this bull you've been feeding me about contributing from the bench and winning is all that matters is a cover. You're afraid."

"Of what?" Warrick was exasperated.

DeMarcus relaxed. He'd broken through the guard's thick exterior. "Losing. Or winning. You tell me."

"I don't know what you're talking about."

DeMarcus held Warrick's angry gaze. "Figure it out because we'll need you on that court when we make it to the play-offs."

DeMarcus forced himself to cross his home court Friday night. "Congratulations, Coach." He offered Phil Jackson his hand. The veteran head coach's Los Angeles Lakers had destroyed his Monarchs, 101 to

76, during this mid-March game. "Good luck in the play-offs."

DeMarcus turned to make his way to Vom One, the tunnel to the Monarchs' locker room. Craig Sager, TNT's sideline reporter, stopped him for a postgame comment. If it weren't NBA policy to grant interviews, DeMarcus would have shoved the smaller man aside and continued on his way. But Sager was just doing his job. DeMarcus ignored the reporter's sherbet orange suit and responded to his question. "The Lakers outplayed us. We couldn't get our offense going and we couldn't defend their shots. They just outplayed us."

Sager thanked him for his time and wished him luck with the remaining games. He'd need more than luck. At this stage, he needed a miracle to get into the play-offs.

DeMarcus walked on to Vom One. He ignored the flashing cameras and waving groupies. But he couldn't ignore the boos of the few fans who'd stayed until the bitter end. He'd never been booed before. But he understood their disappointment. He felt like joining them.

Winding his way through the tunnel, DeMarcus pulled up short when he saw Gerald waiting outside the team's locker room. The franchise co-partner didn't approach him. He never spoke. He just stood there in his green pinstripe designer suit, braced against the opposite wall staring at him. His features were expressionless. Was this some sort of intimidation tactic? Was Gerald trying to get inside his head? DeMarcus wouldn't give him the satisfaction. He clenched his teeth and walked past the other man to the locker room.

He closed the door behind him and strode to the center of the cramped room. "What the hell happened out there? With the other losses, at least we'd been in the game. Tonight, the Lakers crushed us by twenty-five points. What happened?"

Barron rubbed his hands over his thick, black cornrows. "We were outplayed."

"Why?" DeMarcus shoved his fists into the pockets of his slate gray suit pants. "Jamal, Bryant only has one inch on you. You played him like he towered over you."

Sweat ran from the rookie's head and shoulders over the tattoo of Kobe Bryant's number inked onto his upper arm. "He's too good. He's a legend."

Anthony settled his hands on his hips. "Luke fourteen, 'He who humbles himself will be exalted,' didn't pertain to this game. When you humbled yourself for the Black Mamba, you allowed him to kill us. He was raining threes like manna from heaven."

Serge grunted his agreement. "Grow a pair."

Barron shifted closer to the rookie. "We talked about this last week, man. You can't let that crap mess with your head."

Jamal's misery was visible. "I can't help it."

DeMarcus put an end to the bashing. "It's easy for us to blame Jamal. He wants the ball but he doesn't know the plays. He doesn't give one hundred percent. But what about you, Barron? Did you feel like a superstar out there tonight?"

Barron went back to his locker. His brown features were drawn with anger.

DeMarcus found Warrick. "Rick, I gave you eighteen minutes. I'm still waiting for you to produce."

The shooting guard met his gaze. "I'm sorry, Coach."

"Sorry won't get us into the play-offs." DeMarcus studied the other players. "We're thirty-two and thirty-nine. Tenth in the conference. The last I looked, teams with losing records don't make it into the play-offs. What are we going to do?"

Serge shrugged. "We need to win."

DeMarcus nodded. "What's your plan? I'm open to ideas." He waited through a beat of silence. "Anyone? We're not leaving this room without a plan."

The players, including the backups, grumbled. DeMarcus didn't waver.

Anthony pulled a wide-tooth comb through his throwback natural. "Come on, Coach. We want to get out of here."

Barron arched a brow. "What are you in such a hurry for? It's not like you have a shorty waiting for you."

Anthony glared at the point guard. "Shut up."

Vincent looked up at DeMarcus from his seat in front of his locker. "You had those one-on-ones with us. Why?"

DeMarcus frowned. "I told you, to figure out how to turn the team around."

Vincent spread his arms. "It's fear. Do you have a magic pill for that?"

DeMarcus stared at the center. "Fear of what?"

Vincent shrugged. "Stupid stuff."

DeMarcus still didn't understand what Vincent was talking about. "Like what?"

The center nodded toward Barron. "He's afraid of not shining on the court."

The team captain glared at him. "Mind your damn

business, man. You don't know what you're talking about."

"Yes, I do." Vincent shifted to look at Serge. "He's afraid he'll be stuck on a losing team for the rest of his career."

Serge grumbled. "Who wouldn't be?"

Vincent scanned the room. "Rick's afraid he doesn't measure up, and Jam-On-It's afraid he never will."

Jamal pushed out his chest. "That's bullshit. I'm as good as anyone in this room, anyone in the league."

"Except Kobe." Anthony pointed to himself. "What about me?"

Vincent chuckled. "You're afraid of eternal damnation because of those thoughts you don't want to admit are in your head."

Anthony scowled. "Bling's right. You don't know what you're talking about."

Vincent chuckled again. "Confession is good for the soul, St. Anthony."

Warrick crossed his arms and propped his shoulder against his locker. "What about you?"

Vincent turned to smile at the veteran. "I'm afraid that I can't tell you that."

Warrick shook his head, grinning.

DeMarcus narrowed his gaze. Was Vincent right? Was fear holding them back? It made sense. "What about me?"

Vincent rose from his chair. "You're a control freak. You're afraid of not being in control. You're afraid of not having all the answers. But we're seventy-one games into the season. There are only eleven games left, and you're losing control."

DeMarcus locked eyes with Vincent. The center was right. He was losing control, and that scared him.

He was losing Jaclyn, and that scared him even more. The silence was heavy in the room. Thirteen pairs of eyes waited for his reaction.

DeMarcus took a steadying breath. "You're right. I am afraid of losing control." He met the gaze of every man in the room. "But if that's what it takes to win, I'll give it up gladly. Now, what's the plan?"

"He told me he'd win games to prove he cares more about the team than Gerry's threats, to prove that my team means more to him than his image." Jaclyn set her glass of iced tea on the restaurant table. She looked across the white embroidered tablecloth to Violet. "We lost to the Wizards almost a month ago—February twenty-sixth to be exact—and haven't won a game since."

Violet gave a sympathetic wince. "I know. That's a twelve-game losing streak. Now you're back at the bottom of the division."

"We're almost at the bottom half of the conference. And this is how he shows me that the team matters more?"

"You mean that *you* matter more."

"What?" Jaclyn gave her friend a sharp look. They were sharing lunch at their favorite Chinese food restaurant. As upset as she was, they might as well have gone to a fast-food drive-through.

"Sweetie, this isn't about Marc and the team. It's about Marc and you. You're not being disloyal to your grandfather if you put your needs above the team's once in a while."

"Vi, that's absurd. Of course it's about Marc and

the team. He's the head coach." Jaclyn drank more iced tea.

"Yeah. And for three months, he was your lover. And, judging by the looks of that man, those were three glorious months."

Jaclyn flushed. "That relationship is over."

Violet leaned forward into the restaurant's table. She lowered her voice to a conspiratorial whisper. "Why is that again?"

Jaclyn scowled at her former teammate. "Are you trying to annoy me?"

"You're being ridiculous. You broke up with Marc because he didn't tell you what Gerry was up to?"

Jaclyn shook her head. "It's more complicated than that." She released a sigh. She'd had two weeks of sleepless nights since making her decision to break off their relationship. It probably seemed a lot easier to DeMarcus and Violet than it had been in fact.

"Then explain it to me." Violet's tone was somber. Her violet blue eyes were sad. "Explain why, if this was a good decision for you, you're so miserable."

Jaclyn dropped her forehead into her palms. "Vi, it was hard keeping our personal and professional lives separate. I was afraid to hurt his ego by questioning his player decisions."

"You'd have to tiptoe around any head coach's ego."

"What about my ego?" Jaclyn sat straighter. "After the reporter left his office, he should have called me immediately. Instead he went to see Gerry."

"Yeah. Well, how eager would you have been to tell your boss that your other boss has accused you of doing drugs?"

Jaclyn gave the other woman a baleful look. "Whose side are you on?"

"Yours."

"It doesn't sound like it."

"Well, you're a little deaf right now, sweetie. But that's understandable." Violet leaned forward again. "Listen. Marc should have told you Gerry was blackmailing him. No doubt."

Jaclyn interrupted. "Exactly. If Andrea hadn't come to us, it would have been a horrible situation for the team."

"No. It would have been a *hard* situation for the team. But everything would have worked out in the end. On the other hand, it would have been a *horrible* situation for the team if your head coach really had been doing drugs." Violet nodded. "Right? That would have been bad."

Jaclyn opened her mouth, then closed it again.

Violet nodded again. "Yeah, you hadn't thought of that, had you? And, yeah, he went on a bit of a losing spree since promising to take you to the play-offs. But, you know what, Jackie? These aren't the dark ages when women stayed home wearing corsets while men went on quests for us. He shouldn't have to take you to the play-offs for you to let him love you."

Jaclyn's body warmed with that visual. Still, she fought against her friend's very valid points. "We'd finally started to win. Now we're losing again."

"Listening to you, no one would think you'd ever played on a professional sports team much less that you'd been the MVP of the WNBA. Teams get into slumps. You and Marc just need to figure out why the Monarchs are in a slump and how to get them back out. The season's not lost yet."

Jaclyn stared at her sweating iced tea glass. "What

about our relationships? Can we really work together and be together?"

Violet shrugged. "You're the boss. You can do whatever you like. What do you want?"

Jaclyn moved her steamed vegetables and rice around the gold-trimmed, white china plate. What did she want? She'd already ensured the team would stay in Brooklyn. "I want to make my grandfather proud. I want to restore the Monarchs to its winning tradition. I want someone to offer Gerry a well-paying, prestigious job in another country."

Violet chuckled. "What about Marc?"

That one wasn't as easy. She wanted their shared passion for basketball during the day and their passion for each other all night. But she couldn't go back to the way they had been, because he'd only embraced one part of her. "I want to know whether he can accept all of me, his boss and his lover."

Violet shrugged again. "So ask him."

Jaclyn shoved the fingers of her right hand through her hair. "I don't think he knows. I don't think he understands there's more to me than the woman he wants to sleep with."

"You said he told you he'd take the Monarchs to the play-offs to prove that *you* matter to him and *your team* matters more to him than his image."

"That's what he said." Jaclyn drank more iced tea.

"Then, sweetie, he does understand. Apparently, better than you understand yourself."

DeMarcus heard his father's footsteps behind him before Julian spoke. "You need to get some sleep. Tomorrow will come soon enough."

"It's already here, Pop."

Brooklyn Monarchs versus New York Knicks. Win or go home. DeMarcus crossed his arms over his black Monarchs jersey and considered the early-morning scene outside their sitting room's bay window. It was after one o'clock Wednesday morning. Still, there were lights on in other houses and cars cruising down the street.

Brooklynites had welcomed spring and turned their clocks ahead almost a month ago. Blossoms replaced the ice that had imprisoned tree limbs at the beginning of the season.

His father came to stand beside him. "You've done everything you could to prepare for the game tonight except sleep."

DeMarcus glanced at his father. The older man wore his blue and red flannel robe over his pajamas. Black slippers covered his feet. "Why are you up?"

Julian slipped his hands into the pockets of his robe. "I was thinking about the game, too. When I heard you come downstairs, I figured we could think about it together."

DeMarcus smiled and returned his attention to the view of his neighborhood. "A win tonight will move us into eighth place in the Eastern Conference and guarantee us a play-off berth."

"Thanks to your ten-and-three run, you're in control of your destiny."

"We're playing in Madison Square Garden." DeMarcus brought an image of the venue to mind. "The Knicks will have home court advantage."

"They've already clinched a play-off spot. This game doesn't mean as much to them as it means to the Monarchs."

DeMarcus shook his head. "This is a cross-borough rivalry. We can't fool ourselves that they won't bring the heat." He turned to meet his father's eyes. "I wish Mom were here. Win or lose, I'd want her to see this game."

Julian put his hand on DeMarcus's shoulder. "So would I."

He couldn't put off any longer the question Jaclyn had urged him to ask his father months ago. "Did she know how much I appreciated all the sacrifices you both made for me?"

"Your mother knew everything." The older man managed a smile. "She said you always called early in the day when you were lonely and later in the evening when you just wanted to talk."

DeMarcus chuckled. "I'd talk about nothing just to hear her voice or to make her laugh."

Julian dropped his hand from DeMarcus's shoulder. "This house had a lot more laughter when your mother was alive. And then when Jackie came into the picture."

DeMarcus stared out the window again. "I came back to Brooklyn because I wanted to be with you. I agreed to coach the Monarchs to honor Mom. But this win tonight against the Knicks will be for Jack."

"What are you doing for yourself?"

DeMarcus grinned. "Beating the Knicks. That way I get the win and the woman."

"But what if you lose?"

The question scared him more than he wanted to admit. "It's win or go home. If we lose, I'll come home."

"What about your relationship with Jackie?"

"I don't know, Pop." DeMarcus paced away from

the window toward his mother's chair. His bare feet sank into the Oriental rug.

"If you want her back, you'll have to do something more than get into the play-offs."

That was one of the worries that had driven DeMarcus from his bed. He ran his hand over his hair. "Like what?"

"You said she wants you to remember she's your boss."

"That's right."

"And she said she's in love with you?"

DeMarcus swallowed. His voice was husky. "Yes, she did."

Julian shrugged. "It seems simple enough to me."

DeMarcus watched his father settle into his armchair. "Care to share your wisdom?"

Julian smiled. "Jackie is rich and beautiful. She can have any man she wants."

DeMarcus took his mother's armchair. "No news flash there, Pop."

Julian held up a hand. "She's also an independent woman. She doesn't *need* any man, but she *wants* you."

"I still don't understand your point."

Julian shifted in his seat to face DeMarcus. "You fell in love with an independent woman. You're trying to change her and you don't understand why she's upset about that."

DeMarcus scowled. "I'm not trying to change her."

"She asked you to take her team to the play-offs. That's all. You were upset when she wouldn't let you buy the arena for her. Then you tried to handle Gerry's blackmail attempts without talking to her."

DeMarcus stood to prowl the room. "When I love someone, I want to take care of them. That's who I am."

"I understand, son. I'm the same way. And Jackie reminds me of your mother. We had to learn to make decisions together and not for one another."

Tension drained from DeMarcus's neck and shoulders. "I can work on that."

"Yes, you can. Now you just have to convince Jackie."

Some of his tension returned. "That will be harder."

24

Jaclyn stood in the visiting owner's box, watching the Knicks and Monarchs warm up before the game. Madison Square Garden's sound system played Jay-Z and Alicia Keys's "Empire State of Mind." Jaclyn thought of the record as a love song to the city.

Her heart was racing. Her palms were sweating. Every muscle in her body was a knot on top of a knot. If she didn't distract herself, by game time, she'd pass out.

"Thanks again for letting me join you in the box." Marylin Evans's tone was distant.

Jaclyn looked at Warrick's wife. "I appreciate your coming."

Marylin was similar in height to Jaclyn, although Jaclyn's four-inch black stilettos gave her a boost. The other woman looked pretty and serious in one-inch black pumps and a brown pants suit. The cream shell peeked from beneath the three-button jacket and complimented her cocoa skin. Her straight, dark brown hair was pulled back into a ponytail that fell to the nape of her neck.

The shooting guard's wife sipped her diet ginger ale as she studied the court. "Where are the other wives?"

"Over there." Jaclyn pointed toward the seats behind the Monarchs' bench where the players' and coaches' wives and girlfriends sat. "They tend to talk during the game. I was afraid, if that happened tonight, I'd take someone's head off. But you don't talk much during the game." And no one spoke to Marylin, which was something else Jaclyn had noticed.

Marylin's lips curved in the slightest smile. "I don't make it to many of them. It's amazing how many women go into labor during basketball games."

Jaclyn laughed. "Rick mentioned you and a friend were opening an obstetrics/gynecological practice. Good luck."

Even the slight smile disappeared. "Rick tells you a lot of things."

Marylin may prove more of a distraction than Jaclyn had anticipated. "Was it a secret?" She faced the other woman. "Listen, Mary, Rick has been a good friend to me over the years. I want us to be friends, too."

Marylin's smile didn't reach her chocolate eyes. "Of course."

Jaclyn turned away, disappointed. Where had the other woman's animosity come from? She hoped Julian arrived soon. She needed a friendly face during the game. Jaclyn had a feeling that wouldn't be Marylin's.

* * *

Gerald was waiting for him at the entrance to Vom Two when DeMarcus emerged from the visitors' locker room. "This is your last chance, Marc. Are you sure you're going for the win?"

DeMarcus planted his feet. "Positive."

Gerald shook his head. "That's not the smartest decision you've ever made."

"You've lost, Gerry. Jack owns the arena. The Monarchs aren't going anywhere. The community hates you. Sell your shares to Jack. She'll give you fair market price."

"That's what she wants." Gerald's dark eyes glowed with animosity. "For decades the Jones family has gotten what they wanted. Now I'm going to destroy what they care about the most. And if you won't help me, I'll destroy you, too."

DeMarcus stepped around the other man. "Get over yourself, Gerry. You sound like a bad nineteen fifties movie villain."

DeMarcus walked onto the court to watch the Monarchs warm up and do a final pregame check of the Knicks. Their opponents looked confident and relaxed. The Monarchs looked tentative and tight. That was their season in a nutshell.

He raised his gaze to the visiting owner's box. Jaclyn and his father stood with their faces almost pressed to the glass. The other woman in the box looked like Marylin Evans, Warrick's wife. Although he couldn't see Jaclyn's expression clearly, DeMarcus could sense her tension. Or was it his? The next four quarters would determine whether the franchise would end the season with a financial boost or start yet another year with a shoestring budget.

* * *

DeMarcus waited until Anthony Chambers took possession of the ball after the New York Knicks had added another three-point shot to their now thirteen-point lead. One minute and nine seconds remained in the third quarter.

Win or go home.

"Time-out." He would not lose this game. He could not.

DeMarcus pinned Barron with a look. "Pass the ball to Jamal."

The point guard hooked his hands on his hips. "For what? He doesn't know the plays."

"He's been wide open. He can take the shots." De-Marcus struggled with his temper. The television cameras could pick up their exchange. He didn't want his confrontation with the Monarchs' team captain to lead TNT's *Inside the NBA.*

"I can take the shots."

"You're forcing them."

Anthony put his hand on Barron's shoulder. "Bling, man, we're down by thirteen. Trust the rookie."

Barron shrugged off Anthony's hand. "He's a ball hog."

Vincent swallowed a gulp of water and recapped his bottle. "You afraid he'll shine brighter than you out there?"

Barron glared at the center. "Watch your mouth, Vinny."

DeMarcus clenched his teeth. "Are you going to pass to Jamal?"

Barron raised his chin. "No."

DeMarcus jerked his head over his shoulder. "Take a seat."

Barron's lips parted. "What?"

DeMarcus looked around. "Rick, you're in."

Barron's eyes widened. "You're replacing me with Rick? You should replace Jamal."

DeMarcus spared the team captain a glance. "This isn't a democracy." He spoke quickly to Warrick. "I don't know what kind of mental block you're working through. I don't care. You've brought the heat in practice. This is just like practice, but a zillion times more important."

Fear flashed in Warrick's eyes. "Coach, you need to keep Bling in the game."

Barron interjected. "That's right."

From the corner of DeMarcus's eye, he saw Oscar pull the angry point guard to the bench. "This is a time-out. Not halftime. I don't have all day. You get the looks, take the shot. No hesitations. Be aggressive. But, for the love of God, don't foul out. Jamal's already carrying four fouls." He grabbed the veteran's arm. "Do you have this?"

Warrick's shoulders straightened. His eyes focused. "I've got this."

DeMarcus commanded the other man's gaze. "Don't be afraid to lose."

The buzzer sounded. The starters hustled back on court.

Anthony inbounded the ball to Vincent. The Monarchs' center took the ball to the paint, gesturing his teammates into position. The Knicks' Timofey Mosgov shadowed him. Warrick and Serge had the perimeter, defended by Amare Stoudemire and Danilo Gallinari, respectively. Anthony stood at post with New York's Wilson Chandler. Jamal covered Bill Walker in the paint.

Vincent passed the ball to Warrick. The shooting guard pick-and-rolled to the post with a blind pass to Anthony. The Monarchs' forward grabbed the ball and slammed it into the net for two points. DeMarcus pumped a fist. Monarchs closed in on the lead, 86 to 75. Forty-nine seconds remained in the third quarter. Shot clock reset to twenty-four seconds.

New York's Chandler grabbed the ball, passing it to his teammate Mosgov. Mosgov hustled back down the court. The Monarchs set up their triangle defense. Mosgov flung the ball to Stoudemire. Warrick smacked it away. Jamal caught the loose ball and charged unchallenged back up the court. Monarchs fans went wild.

Jamal's feet left the ground. The guard soared toward the basket. He slammed the ball through the net: 86, 77, Knicks. The Garden rocked as Monarchs faithful thundered their approval. Thirty-eight seconds to go in the third quarter.

DeMarcus clapped his players on as they raced to defend their basket. "Keep up the pressure. Get on your man. Talk to each other."

The Knicks' Chandler took possession of the ball, passing it to Mosgov. Knicks looked to slow the pace. Monarchs circled like vultures waiting to feed. Thirty seconds in the third quarter, seventeen seconds on the shot clock.

Mosgov passed the ball to the Knicks' Stoudemire. Warrick leaped into the passing lane and grabbed the ball from the air. He sprinted to the Monarchs' basket, pulling up at the perimeter for an uncontested three-point shot: 86, 80, Knicks. Another basket from Serge and a three-point shot from Anthony brought the Monarchs to within one, 86 to 85.

DeMarcus remained tense. The Monarchs had taken the Knicks for twelve unanswered points. Could they keep up the pace?

Twenty-two seconds remained in the third quarter. With the Knicks' lead draining, their head coach called for a twenty-second time-out. The Monarchs walked off the court.

DeMarcus met them at the sideline. "Keep up the pace. You can't slow down. Stay strong on the defense." DeMarcus claimed Warrick's attention. "Good start. Now turn up the heat."

DeMarcus saw the fire in Warrick's eyes. The shooting guard was winning the mental game.

They'd barely begun to discuss their defense when the buzzer sounded.

The Knicks' Walker inbounded the ball to Mosgov. The Knicks' center snaked his way to the basket. When he came up against Jamal near the post, the rookie gave him a hard hit with his right shoulder. The whistle sounded. Jamal earned his fifth foul with twelve seconds left to the third quarter. One more foul and he'd be out of the game.

Mosgov made both free throws, lifting the score to 88 to 85. DeMarcus paced the sideline.

Serge grabbed the ball. He bounced it to Vincent. Vincent drove the ball past midcourt. Warrick signaled for the pass. The center flung it to him. Warrick danced back as the Knicks' defense charged forward. Shooting redemption from his fingertips, Warrick scored a three-point basket. The Monarchs tied the score with the Knicks at 88. The buzzer sounded, heralding the fourth and final quarter.

Win or go home.

With fire in his eyes and salvation in his hands, Warrick dragged his team through the back-and-forth brawl to redeem their season. The lead changed five times in fourteen minutes. DeMarcus watched the veteran transform before him. Warrick played like an athlete possessed. He grabbed rebounds, hurled passes and shot three-pointers like fire from his fingers.

The game clock wound down to sixteen seconds. Stoudemire's shot punched the Knicks to the lead, 100 to 98.

Warrick jumped for the ball. The Knicks' Stoudemire deflected his pass to Vincent. DeMarcus felt his Monarchs' thirst for victory as Warrick leaped forward, clawing for the ball. Stoudemire chased him down. Both players fell to the court in a tangle of arms and legs. The referees blew the whistle.

Jump ball.

Eight seconds remained on the game clock. The Knicks lined up on the left, Monarchs on the right. DeMarcus bent his legs, willing Warrick to win the battle of ascensions. The ref blew the whistle, tossed the basketball into the air and stepped back. Warrick leaped, body stretching, arm straining. His large hand smacked the ball just out of Stoudemire's reach. Anthony and the Knicks' Chandler tussled for position. Chandler ripped the ball from Anthony's hands.

Vincent joined Anthony in pursuit of the ball from behind. Jamal intercepted Chandler from the front. With a flick of his wrist, the rookie stole the ball and hustled up the court.

Four seconds to the buzzer.

Jamal landed on the perimeter line. DeMarcus held his breath. The rookie pulled up. He tossed the ball to Warrick far beyond the perimeter.

One second to the buzzer.

The veteran saved the ball in one hand—and sent a rainbow to the net. The arena went silent. DeMarcus didn't breathe. He tracked the ball from Warrick's hand. It sailed a high arc to the Knicks' basket.

Three points.

The arena exploded. The Monarchs had stolen the win, 101 to 100.

DeMarcus raised both fists in the air and threw his head back. He looked up at the visiting owner's box, at Jaclyn and his father. They were hugging and jumping like little kids at Christmas. As he watched, they separated to look at the court. His father waved. He waved back. He couldn't see Jaclyn's features clearly, but he could see her grin. He thought she'd blown a kiss. Then she turned and grabbed his father in another bear hug.

DeMarcus met Mike D'Antoni, the Knicks' head coach, in the middle of the court. "Good game, Coach. You gave us a scare." Then he savored the words, "We'll see you in the play-offs."

Althea raced into her office. The sight of her painfully professional administrative assistant engaged in such undignified behavior stopped Jaclyn midsentence.

"Jackie, get off the phone. Now." Althea leaned over her desk to issue the order. Her hair was mussed. Her eyes were wild. Her cheeks were flushed.

Jaclyn could feel the other woman's breath puffing against her face. "Vi, I've got to call you back." Jaclyn stood as she recradled the phone. Her pulse was beating in her throat. "What's happened?"

"Elia's been trying to reach you. Marc's agent's in his office talking to him right now about an opening with the Knicks' coaching staff."

Jaclyn had already circled her desk and was racing to her door. She cursed her stilettos for slowing her down. Then she cursed the elevators for doing the same. Minutes later, she tried to run past Elia's desk. The diminutive woman threw herself in front of Jaclyn and held a finger to her lips.

DeMarcus's executive assistant motioned Jaclyn to the door. Surprisingly, it had been left open a few inches. Was that by chance or did Elia have a habit of eavesdropping? Jaclyn tiptoed closer and strained to hear the conversation inside.

DeMarcus chuckled. "You won't change my mind, Chris."

Another man's voice, presumably Chris, responded. "The Monarchs are paying you peanuts. I told you when they first came knocking on your door, you should walk away from their offer. You deserve more money."

"And I told you, it wasn't about the money."

"It should always be about the money." *Chris is annoyingly persistent.*

"I'm happy with what I'm making now." Jaclyn knew that wasn't true. She remembered his comment about being paid minimum wage. Obviously, the Mighty Guinn didn't know what minimum wage was. But why would he lie to his agent?

"I can get you at least five percent more with the

Knicks—and that's for an *assistant* coaching spot. More money, less stress. Who wouldn't want that?"

Jaclyn held her breath.

"My contract is up in July. You can renegotiate for more money then."

She exhaled.

"Marc, be realistic. The Monarchs aren't going to be able to offer you five percent more than what you're making now. They're cash strapped and watching every penny." Chris made the Monarchs sound like the church mice of the NBA. She disliked him intensely.

"I'm not going to change my mind. Tell the Knicks thanks, but no thanks. Then renegotiate my Monarchs contract for more money. I don't care how much more, even if it's only half of a percent."

"Half of a percent?" Chris sounded like he was having a stroke. "What's the point of that?"

"The point is I like it here. I like the organization. I like the players, and I like the promise. I'm not interested in leaving."

Jaclyn lost her breath. Those words made her so happy. She felt as though she'd already won the finals and was holding the trophy. She blinked away tears.

Chris spoke again after a beat of silence. The guy was working Jaclyn's last nerve. "This is about Jackie Jones, isn't it? She's a beautiful woman and I understand you don't want to lose her. But it's not as though you'd be leaving the city. You'd just be a couple of subway stops apart. It wouldn't hurt your relationship if you worked for the Knicks. In fact, it could help your relationship if you didn't work together."

"If this were just about Jack, I would leave. But, as I said, I like the team. I'm staying here."

Jaclyn had heard enough. She pushed open De-Marcus's door and confronted the startled men. DeMarcus stood.

She nodded at the pudgy middle-aged man in the visitor's seat before DeMarcus's desk. "Chris Carl? I'm Jaclyn Jones." The agent's face flamed red as he got to his feet and shook Jaclyn's hand. "Please stop trying to pilfer my head coach. He's made it clear that he likes peanuts."

Chris's face glowed even brighter. "I think that's my cue to leave. It's nice to meet you, Ms. Jones."

"Jackie." She folded her hands in front of her.

Chris nodded. "Jackie." He glanced at DeMarcus. "See you later, Marc."

Jaclyn watched the flustered man stride from De-Marcus's office.

DeMarcus put his hands in the front pockets of his mustard Dockers. He studied the back of Jaclyn's head and the riot of black curls swinging around her shoulders. "Were you listening at the door?"

She turned to face him. Her grin was unrepentant. "Of course."

DeMarcus ran his hand over his hair. What did this mean? "I was going to tell you about the Knicks' offer."

"I think you need new representation." She folded her arms across her chest. "What kind of an agent brings you an offer of a new job while you're sitting in your office? That's not very bright."

DeMarcus searched her eyes. She didn't seem angry. "Chris isn't a bad guy. He wants what's best for me and realizes my current salary doesn't accurately reflect my worth."

"No, it doesn't. You put what matters most to you—your reputation and your family's name—at risk to bring the Monarchs a winning season. You got us to the play-offs." Jaclyn smiled that special smile that touched his heart.

DeMarcus swallowed. He'd waited a long time for that smile. Too long. "Does that mean you're open for negotiation?"

She stepped closer, circling his desk. "That depends."

"On what?"

"You said you like the organization and you like the players. How do you feel about the owners?" She stopped in front of him.

DeMarcus arched a brow. "I can't stand Gerry."

"What about me?" Jaclyn's words were breathy and unsure.

"I'm in love with you." DeMarcus's voice was husky with restrained emotions.

Jaclyn closed her eyes briefly. She gripped his elbows as she swayed on her sexy stilettos. When she opened her eyes, they were damp. "I'm in love with you, too."

DeMarcus removed his hands from his pockets and settled them on her slender waist. He wished that it was as simple as "I love you," but it hadn't been before. "What about separating our personal and professional lives?" He held his hands up. "I know I can sometimes be a control freak, but I don't mean to undermine your independence. I can learn to make decisions with you instead of for you. Just give me a chance."

Jaclyn smiled. "I know you're only overbearing because you love me."

DeMarcus frowned. "Is there a compliment in there?"

Her cool hand cupped his jaw. "You're a strong, courageous man who's willing to sacrifice a lot for the people he cares about, but never his integrity. What's not to love?"

"Did my winning that final game prove how much I love you?"

Jaclyn laughed and punched his arm. "Don't be stupid. Your choosing to stay with the Monarchs and work for me rather than going to the Knicks proved you love me—all of me. In and out of the arena."

Her words and the love in her eyes meant more to him than all of the trophies, honors and awards he'd ever earned. DeMarcus cleared his throat. "I can survive losing a lot of things, but I can't lose you."

Jaclyn lowered her hand to his shoulder. "We're going to continue to butt heads over decisions with the team and with the franchise."

"For a very long time."

Jaclyn nodded. "But it'll be worth it. And we'll make it work. We're both too stubborn to fail."

"That's because we're both champions, and champions never give up." DeMarcus lowered his mouth to Jaclyn's soft lips. Victory had never tasted so sweet.